Dervishes

DERVISHES

This book is a work of fiction. The characters, places, incidents, and dialogue are the product of the author's imagination and are not to be construed as real, or if real, are used fictitiously. Any resemblance to actual events, locales, or persons, either living or dead, is purely coincidental.

Copyright © 2014 by Neal Starkman

All rights reserved. No part of this book may be used or reproduced in any manner whatsoever without the prior written permission of the publisher, except in the case of brief quotations embodied in critical articles and reviews.

For more information, to inquire about rights to this or other works, or to purchase copies for special educational, business, or sales promotional uses, please write to:

The Zharmae Publishing Press, L.L.C.
1827 West Shannon Avenue
Spokane, Washington 99205
www.zharmae.com

FIRST EDITION

Printed in the United States of America

Zharmae Publishing, logo, and the TZPP logo are trademarks of The Zharmae Publishing Press, L.L.C.

ISBN: 978-1-937365-26-4 (pbk.)

10 9 8 7 6 5 4 3 2 1

Dervishes

Neal Starkman

Spokane, Washington

Dervishes

1. THE MASTURBATION CAMPAIGN

Masturbation turned me into a New Yorker. Or talking about it did. So my career is being sacrificed on the altar of departmental tightwadness. Okay. A slash to my academic innards, a cut to my prime. Five, six years ago, I would have been anxious. Today, I don't have anxiety. I have angst. Just like all those existentially morose New Yorkers you read about. It's like the flu or measles, with raging introspection instead of fever and tics instead of spots. My God, I write this, and my pen skips along the page as if eluding some phantom pen-rapist. Why is this so difficult?

All right, Carolyn, it's time to control these notes. Diarizing is the closest good Minnesota girls are supposed to come to therapy, after all, and while self-examination still isn't acceptable by family standards, Diary, it will have to do.

Hm. Is the diary an entity to be addressed, or rather my own private vehicle to inner peace and oneness? Vaguely philosophical, Carolyn. If I'd majored in philosophy—or maybe English literature—instead of physics, then I could say that thought was, oh, Descartesian. Or is it Cartesian? Maybe it's Descartesian only before sundown.

Neal Starkman

Okay, cut the bad jokes; this is serious stuff. My lover watches the Seattle something-or-others play—yes, it must be football, they're wearing helmets. The helmets let Stephanie enjoy the game without receiving continual visual reminders that only men play football on TV. It would never work with basketball or baseball. It's mystifying how she can appreciate what to me is an interminable series of time-rationed melees, but, Diary, Steph would probably find you mystifying as well. We're such compatible lovers that way. Tolerating our incompatibilities, that is. Ah, a maxim: "Compatibility is the toleration of incompatibilities." This diarizing is powerful stuff. *Reader's Digest* power.

I'm glad Philip's crazy uncle bought him that subscription to *Reader's Digest*; it made me nostalgic for the good old days when reading an approved magazine was not leisure but a highlight of the afternoon. "Carolyn, the *Good Housekeeping* is here." Hot shit, Mom! Another two hours of reading and wondering why I wasn't as satisfied with it as much as I thought I should be.

Back to angst. There we were, Philip and I, St. Paul, Minnesota, the fall of 1975. I was finishing my dissertation, but not in any hurry. In fact, I seem to recall some trepidation about Life After Phd. Of course, then I had a man to shelter me, and so the trepidation couldn't have been all that debilitating. Philip had already gotten his doctorate; he was part-timing at Planned Parenthood and full-timing with me. Days of such sociopolitical torpor that I can't even remember what my attitudes were about anything important, possibly because I didn't have any.

Nonetheless, I must have been ready. For what followed. Everything upstairs must have been clicking into place, waiting only for the proper stimulus to send me on my way. But that's hindsight. If we hadn't endured the campaign, and I hadn't chrysalized into a socialist, and Philip hadn't become disgusted enough to move to the West Coast, well gosh, I might still be a sweet young thing out of St. Cloud, Minnesota, drinking milk, getting in some good-natured joshing with the folks, going out with boys— God in heaven, Diary, one thing's for certain, and that's my ability before the campaign to end a sentence in under fifty words. My brain wiring must look as frantically peripatetic as those football plays Stephanie once tried to explain to me. (Stephanie cheers, almost spilling beer; how *can* she identify?)

History. There we were again, one evening in our nouveau crap St. Paul apartment, lying placidly on the Bed of a Thousand Dreams, so named because of an errant spring or two that made sleeping subtly uncomfortable. We had just finished doing the deed, and Philip served up the idea of running for mayor.

Well, Carolyn, damn it all. You're writing like a woman who's just been told she'll have to change her career—which, of course, has prompted this spate of literary self-abuse. But shape up, girl. You were miserable even before the I'm-sorry-Carolyn-but-would-you-mind-conducting-research-in-some-other-area-for-the-rest-of-your-life talk. If this is going to be a halfway successful probe into your innermost anxieties, frustrations, conflicts, and things repressed, then you had better compulsivate yourself into setting this down in an orderly manner. Ground rules. I will recapitulate events as best as I can recall them and then examine them for relevance to my current feelings. I will allow myself dramatic latitude, but I won't lie—no, not to you, Diary, to you I shall expose my raw impressions.

Which means backtracking. To before the masturbation campaign. Almost a year before. No one with most of her wits would believe your man is serious when he says he's running for mayor. Then again, no one with most of her wits would be reading your diary. A stalemate.

But let us state at least that it was tough to discern when Philip was serious. Certainly it was at the beginning, when I hadn't yet learned the cues—the tone of his voice, the minute flexing of the muscles of his neck, the slightly upturned corners of his mouth, not quite a smile—that indicated he was performing, often for himself.

I first met Philip Lester at an other-life lecture. He and I and about seventy-five other students from various academic disciplines—disciplines might not be the right word—were huddling in a cold University of Minnesota lecture hall to listen to a thirty-something professor-type with spectacles, springy black hair, and—God—a white turtleneck. Really, you could see the neckline of his undershirt beneath the turtle. A white turtleneck and a blue blazer. In 1974. No wonder I had my initial dubiosities about him. Only a chain and beads could have been worse. Professor Other-Life was running the lecture circuit, much as a carnival runs the small-town circuit or a comedian books into ski lodges.

Philip was sitting next to me, doodling. It must have been freezing that day; I have an image of accessory clothing draped on seats, hanging up on hooks in the back of the room, haystacked in the middle of aisles. I don't know what I was even doing there. Maybe I came in out of the cold. During Minnesota winters you sometimes have to run from building to building, letting a limb thaw here, tying a shoelace there. Maybe it was the cold that made my studies of superfluid helium seem so appropriate.

In any case, this professor-type was telling a rapt group of students—mostly undergrads, I suspect—about how he'd spent several previous lives as—oh God, I don't know—a peasant in England, a soldier with Napoleon, a Chinese princess, some damn thing. I'd like to think that even then I was a little skeptical. Snap! Snap! Carolyn's synapses refuse to process the information! Buzz! Hold off, they say, you're a smarty graduate student; you don't have to buy this just because everyone else is taking it in with a ladle. I make my head a beacon and see maybe 150 eyes entranced by the words of this hip-hip-hippie-dippie academician. Got the same feeling in a university church where the minister played the guitar.

The other-life lecturer is describing some battle in the Middle Ages from the first-person point of view—natch—and I am doing what I usually do when I get bored in class: scanning my surroundings and hoping to find something of interest to focus on—an animated conversation between a man and woman in the outside hall, teasingly out of earshot; a light fixture with a bulb out; different-colored chalk on the edge of the blackboard; someone's scarf, frayed at the edges; a map of Africa on the far wall—what building am I in, anyway? And of course I scrutinize surreptitiously the students sitting around me.

I look next to me—or maybe just glance, one can't stare—and here is this wool-sweatered, blue-jeaned, black-bearded young fellow writing on a pad the names of people from A to Z. They must be psychologists—I can see Freud for F and Jung for J. The rest are unfamiliar to Carolyn's unsocial-scientific mind. At least he's not taking notes on the battle of Agincourt.

I've resigned myself to a choice of listening to the lecture in earnest or leaving, when the man-to-be-Philip raises his hand. He continues attending to the list, almost complete except for maybe a Q and an X, and his left hand seems to rise autonomously, or else to be drawn up by an invisible puppeteer. I have the strange sense that he's not going to ask a question.

The speaker stops midsentence as he espies the arm-peak amid a plateau of heads. He and the class have apparently been approaching some sort of intellectual orgasm, judging from the intensity of the silence as he points to Philip. Lecturus interruptus.

"Sir? A question?" The class, slightly perturbed at the break in the transcendental flow of the other-life experience, turns to Philip.

"A comment," Philip replies serenely, and gazes up to meet the lecturer.

Pause. Lecturer is patient. "Yes?"

"I had another life." Oh, and then a tantalizing pause while the class further shifts its attention to him. The lecturer raises his eyebrows above his spectacles.

"You have—have you always recalled it?"

"Not always. Even now I can remember only pieces of it."

I'm looking at him from the side and I wonder, is he Flakey Jake? I can't tell. He speaks without inflection.

The lecturer is magnanimous. "Well, as I have been saying, it's relatively rare to recall a previous existence in as much detail and overall comprehensiveness as I have been privileged to experience. Perhaps when you develop more as a trans-biological being, you will find more and richer memories from your distant past."

"I remember stifling heat and much noise."

Another pause. Some of the class titter. I think, if this person is playing with us, he's got really good timing.

The lecturer nods. "Do you have any recollection of where this occurred?"

Philip is straight-faced. He is the only one in the room who knows how the tension he has so artfully built up will be released. He replies, "Under a hood."

And I know that at this point a warning light flashes in the brain of Dr. Other-Life, and alarms go off, too, and a little voice says, "Watch out, you're about to look like a fool." But the other reaction is too quick, and he says, "Under a hood?"

"Yes." And this time Philip responds quickly, but no less soberly, "I was a connecting rod in a 1953 Chevrolet."

Several students laugh, and most everyone smiles, including me, but definitely excluding Philip and the lecturer.

The lecturer evidently can't be 100 percent sure that Philip, still stone, isn't sincere. When you're a dilettante in parapsychology, it's hard to recognize your own. He repeats, "A connecting rod."

"Yes."

The lecturer smiles patronizingly at his class, ostensibly at Philip's expense, and says, "Let's talk about it afterwards, shall we," and continues his story.

But the damage is done! I am in awe. My neighbor recommences his doodling, but many in the class are still smiling, a few looking over at Philip, others whispering to friends. They now gaze distractedly at the lecturer.

Even if I'm sitting next to a crazy man, I am impressed. In those days of leg-shaving and man-adoring—both activities that involved abridgment of inexorable tendencies—I was more curious than assertive. I gently press a finger to his shoulder. He turns to me, eyebrows innocently arched, and I try to communicate "Were you serious?" with a frown. He blanks me with his face, but then, relief, Diary! The corners of his mouth crease, his eyes— I swear—his eyes twinkle, and I know.

God, the rest is so romantic, in a Philip sort of way. Dr. Other-Life drones on—much like a TV no one attends to—Philip returns to his list, and I have found something of interest to focus on. Luckily, Philip is somewhat in my line of vision to the lecturer, so I can eye him without making a complete jerk of myself.

His wristwatch is a cheap Timex, his knuckles are hairy, and his nails are slightly bitten. His hands are anyone's hands, undistinguished by calluses, scars, warts, or excessive smoothness or beauty. I find myself trying to attach exceptional qualities to his hands, and then look at my own hands. They're not so exceptional, either; one's hands must not be valid indicators of one's worth.

I feign interest in his list and daringly move closer to him; I cannot smell aftershave. There is a psychologist by A and a psychologist by B, and C— what is by C is the name of a psychologist, followed by "Coffee after the lecture?" I stare at it for a full minute before I realize I'm reading a message to myself. I hope he takes my hesitation for deep thought rather than a petit mal, and I lean over and write, "Love to," beside the L person. Thus we met.

Oh, I'd like to be able to sort out my feelings like valences, put them on different-powered orbits, and deal with them accordingly. I can see why Rutherford's idea of a simple atom mirroring the solar system had such appeal. Everything in its place. Not me, though. I'm more of a Thomson's currant pudding—everything a-jumble. Carolyn Behind-the-Times.

Professor Stanley Mankiewicz, chairman of the University of Washington's Department of Physics and all-round sage, suggested I write down my thoughts. "You're methodical, Carolyn," he said. "Pretend it's a condensed-matter problem."

Indeed. All physicists, but especially the theoretical physicists, think they could be psychologists—or economist or state senators, for that matter—if they had time to spare from more important work. Get the data out before you, Carolyn. Expel it from your innards. Not half-forgotten parental resentments or primordial urges of self-abasement, either: We want to see the *real* stuff, matrices and interaction ratios, formulae with at least seven Greek letters, not counting capital sigma. Then, when the calculations are ready to be calculated and the transpositions ready to be transposed, give it all to a grad assistant, wait two days—three, if the computer's down—and voila! another elegant, experimentally provable theory to explain Why Carolyn Has Been so Morbidly Self-Possessed Lately.

Of course the talk with my beloved chairman set me off. Yes, Carolyn, we do appreciate the work you've done with superfluid helium, and it is certainly important work. But, you see, there have been budget cutbacks, serious cutbacks, and, well, you're one of the places we're cutting back.

I don't have much to argue with. He's right about the cutbacks. And a committee rules on the specific curtailments. Actually, I think Dr. Stan (he's too much my senior for "Stan," but the relationship is too informal for "Dr. Mankiewicz") is sympathetic. Stephanie said I should sue him, and then maybe kill him, but I'm sure he's an ally. Besides, Stephanie doesn't realize that I would have to move if I sued him. Or killed him.

Saying good-bye to helium isn't all of it, though, and I need to keep that in mind. I have been miserable for weeks, and the talk with Dr. Stan was merely the capper. I even expected it, sort of; I tried to avoid him in the halls.

It starts with the masturbation campaign. I am perceptibly different now than I was then, five metamorphosogenic years ago. Why, look at me, Diary, I'm still five-foot-two, eyes of blue, but, my goodness, I'm ensconced in an easy chair by an easy book-shelved fireplace across the room from my easy lover, and she's *still* watching the game, cussing out someone or other at sporadic intervals. It's all so damn unbecoming. I've got a job, I've got a house, and I've got you, Diary. What did I have then? Philip, an almost-finished dissertation, and black holes where my knowledge of women ought to have been. So naïve. More naïveté than anyone should be forced to carry around inside them, Diary. Enough surplus naïveté to box up and send to world-wise children in Korea.

It should be said in my defense that only a small fringe of people in those days had a conviction that women really could do what men do. Oh, there was all the talk about equality and respect and feminism, but the actions rarely matched the words. Most people were in states of "Everything's fine." The sad part is that some of those people were women—uh, even women with advanced degrees.

As I said some time ago, Philip and I had just done "coupling," to paraphrase my mother ("They're a couple now."), and I was dropping off to a well-deserved Slumberland, when Philip, bless him, not rapturous over how wonderful Carolyn was and to what heights of ecstasy she'd brought him, instead says out of the vacuum, "Maybe I should run for mayor."

I was such a good little girl in those days; I'm sure I turned over and said something really bright, like, "Of what?"

A minor flashback, Diary; bear with me. When I was in junior high school, I went with a group of girls to Fort Lauderdale, Florida, for a church conference. Yes, I know it's an odd place for a church conference, but sometimes the truth itself is odd.

I remember only one incident the whole time I was there. The evening before we were to leave, we had a beach party. Very tame. But sometime around nine o'clock, I happened to glance out at the ocean—a novelty for me—and received one of those frights that last only a few seconds but command the participation of every organ, muscle, and nerve in your body.

On the horizon, an orange disk was rising from the sea. It was dawn, a slow, ineluctable dawn at nine o'clock on a warm Florida evening in July. All manner of apocalyptic thoughts rushed into my consciousness, no doubt nurtured by the gospel I'd been saturated with the previous few days. I recall thinking, wait, I'm not ready to die, not yet. But within about ten seconds the shock wore off and I tried to understand what was happening; in another ten I figured it out.

It had never crossed my mind that the moon rose. I thought it was just "there," in the sky. When it got dark enough to see it, you saw it. Period. But rising like the sun? Incredible! I motioned to several of my friends, who were not the least bit excited at my discovery. I, however, was transfixed and spent much of the evening watching Luna ascend to the firmament, lighten in shade, and take on her familiar appearance.

That, Diary, is how Carolyn first became interested in astronomy, and later physics. Anything that affected me so strongly, I wanted to know about. And that, too, in case you're perplexed about the relevance of this digression, Diary, is how Carolyn viewed public officials.

I thought they were just "there," like the moon. Well, I knew that many were elected and others appointed, but I couldn't tell you which were which. The process never interested me, and no one encouraged me, being female, to take an active part in it. I didn't vote until the year I moved to Seattle.

So when I said, "Of what?" in response to Philip's saying, "Maybe I should run for mayor," I was barely half-kidding. In my pre-campaign days I bought into the role of being proud of your ignorance.

But Philip wasn't ignorant—not about elections nor about primaries nor polls nor precincts nor politics in general. He wasn't ignorant, but he ignored my "Of what?" and responded by kissing me on the cheek and falling asleep.

The following evening, I was probably trying to balance an equation while Philip was probably reading a new Edward Gorey or an old S.J. Perelman, when he looked up at nothing, smiled, and said, "Masturbation."

"Come again?" I'm so damned cute. What a wit.

Philip nodded, as if punctuating a conclusion, and addressed himself again. "Masturbation—it's a natural."

I had another role. It was called "playing along with Philip, no matter what you've been doing." So I deliberately broke my pencil point on an irrational number and asked, "Dearest, whatever are you talking about?"

Philip recognized me and emerged from his reverie. "I'm talking about the Democratic primary for the mayoralty of St. Paul, Minnesota. I think I should run on a masturbation platform. What do you think?"

Now, you must see, Diary, that when Philip asked me, "What do you think?," he really wanted to know. Honest, Di—Di! That's it, I'll call you Lady Di! It's so much more dignified, yet retains a sort of personal charm to it. I'll feel like I'm confiding in my sister. My first sister, at thirty-one.

As I was saying—Lady Di—Philip did seek my advice on a variety of subjects. I will be brutally honest: I rose to the occasion less frequently than would be expected by a woman of my erudition and raw intelligence. In defense, I only plead that I was not accustomed to hold opinions on weighty matters outside my narrow field, much less to offer those opinions for others' consideration. When Philip wanted to know what I thought about a campaign for mayor on a masturbation platform, I replied with something like, "I think you're crazy, love of my life." And then I patiently listened while Philip explained what he had in mind. Carolyn the Sycophant.

"Tell me," he said, "what you think of this idea. First, I suggest to you that while elections are expedient ways to select those who govern us, election campaigns are insufferably fraudulent. Candidates lie about issues, they impart useless information, and they misrepresent themselves whenever it's feasible to do so."

"If you say so. I never pay attention."

"Second, I suggest to you that the only sincere candidates in an election campaign are the single-issue candidates, those for or against abortion, gun control, leash laws, prayer in schools—"

"Higher stipends for graduate students."

"Exactly. They're sincere, but they're also usually strident and limited in appeal, except to those overburdened with emotions."

"Present company excluded."

"In fact, they often detract from the proper focus of the campaign. Finally, I suggest this to you: Campaigns are dull and humorless. It's the same old thing year after year. You can almost predict what will happen—the speeches, the promises, even the personalities. Most of all, the personalities."

The moon began to ascend from the ocean of Carolyn's mind.

"Carolyn, I think St. Paul needs a fresh new candidate, someone who'll talk straight to the people."

The moon was full, and stark, and boded ill. "Philip, wait a minute. You're going to run for mayor by telling everyone to go masturbate?"

"Well, we have to decide if I should run for or against masturbation. That'll be one of the first important decisions."

I moved away from the table on which I'd been trying to make helium do on paper what it wouldn't do in the lab, and sat down on the arm of the chair in which Philip was now resuming his nodding. "Maybe you should get another part-time job," I suggested. "Once I finish up the dissertation, we can do more things together. It's really not necessary to run for mayor. Maybe you can take up sewing. Or bowling. Or hockey."

"You don't think it's a good idea?"

"Running for mayor? Or running for mayor on a masturbation platform? Oh, Philip, I never know when you're serious."

"Do you think either is a good idea?"

"No." Pause.

"Well?"

"Well what?"

"Well, why don't you think it's a good idea?"

Philip was carrying this further than I thought appropriate. I didn't know whether joining in the discussion would be tantamount to being upended with a gag or shackled with the responsibility of protecting the free world.

"Philip, it's not a good idea or a bad idea. It's a dumb idea. D-u-m, dumb. You're bored, and you want to shake up your life. But running for mayor of this city by advocating—or condemning—masturbation is gross, ludicrous, and totally unrealistic."

We had the first campaign meeting on a Thursday evening. I remember the day because it was my volleyball night, and for some reason the game had been canceled, one of those little detours on the road of life that send you careering off into unexpected territory. I was on a woman's team called the Generics. We all wore white T-shirts with black lettering. On the front the letters spelled "TEAM," and on the back "NAME," and below that "#." So clever. I miss that team.

We planned the meeting, which meant that I spent the entire day cleaning and making dips. Philip was on the phone a lot and seemed to be constantly chuckling. "Don't worry," he said, as I groomed the house for public show (the house-as-vagina), "there'll only be about a dozen people here, and they're all laid-back."

There were about twenty laid-back people at the meeting, laying back in our cramped living room, sitting on understuffed chairs, falling into our overstuffed couch, and folding their legs under their chins on the rattily carpeted floor that camouflaged every bit of food, every paper clip, every coin, and every pill of whatever size or color or shape that was dropped onto it. My friend David perched himself on the giant stuffed turtle Philip purchased at a garage sale "for a song," said turtle now gracing my living room, but in the corner. Stephanie doesn't know Philip bought it.

I was glad David was there, as well as his lover, Sally, both professional Planned Parenthooders. I recognized a few of Philip's former psychology cronies, all men, and one or two people from the neighborhood where Philip used to live before he moved in with me. They seemed to be intense as a group but not as individuals, just the opposite of what I'd expected. When I was introduced to someone, for example, he'd likely smile and say something innocuous, rather than force wisecracks or intellectual observations on me. All except one man, that is—Vince. Vince was not an impressive fellow to look at: unkempt hair and clothes, short and balding, glasses that kept sliding down his nose, and an irritatingly nasal voice. But everyone deferred to Vince, even Philip, and I found out later that he was a veteran of radical politics in the Twin Cities, an aging hippie who had practical information to offer the group and who forced his perspectives on you as if he were present at your creation.

I filled everyone's glasses with cider—we had decided the meeting should be nonalcoholic, lest its gravity diminish—and filled everyone's paper plates with chips, popcorn, celery and carrot sticks, and pretzels. A hint from Carolyn, Lady Di: apple cider does not complement potato chips.

I had fully intended to stay in the background, hostessing, while everyone else discussed the campaign—not the feasibility of it, mind you, but the strategy. My intentions seemed justified when Philip started the meeting by proposing that the group decide whether he should come out for masturbation, against masturbation, or both. His initial inclination, he admitted, was to alternate speeches, one praising it and the next condemning it. But someone argued that alternating viewpoints might be seen as too inconsistent. Someone else said that it might require too much energy to respond to questions.

Thus began what was surely the most absurd political discussion ever held, at least in any place *I've* lived. Picture, Lady Di, twenty adult men and women, many of us with advanced degrees, munching on cider-and-chips in a rather low-class St. Paul apartment, fall 1975, responsible job-holders in the community, family members, deep thinkers and espousers of complex value systems, engaging in a serious debate over whether the candidate for mayor should speak for or against masturbation.

Now, Lady Di, Carolyn Anderson at the time was twenty-six years old and no longer a ruralite viewing the world though Shirley Temple-colored glasses; but let it be noted that she was a preppy undergraduate before she ever heard the word "masturbation" uttered in public, and then only preceded by "mental." Furthermore, while she had certainly made some sociocultural gains in her eight-year tenure in the institutions of higher learning known as Macalester College and the University of Minnesota, to say nothing of the linguistic gains in her relationship with Philip, nonetheless she found herself frequently in a state of nonplusicity. The meeting was a quantum leap in the Politicization of Carolyn.

Incredible, Lady Di. I had thought that the evening would first be a huge bore and then degenerate into a Marx Brothers movie; I'd planned to be Jane Wyatt or Marjorie Lord or some wifey thing like that until the movie came on.

But everyone was so damned serious! I recall being afraid to make a joke, hesitant to trivialize such a profound discussion with my meager observations. So I sat and listened, and totally forgot about replenishing the refreshments. David scooted over to me at the beginning of the meeting; if it was tense for me, then it must have been excruciating for him.

David was a long-time friend from St. Cloud. Another naif from the small town—blond like me, short like me, but, oh, so much more even-tempered, good-natured, content. He wasn't always like that; in high school, David typified the existentially tormented male student. It's a credit to his innate non-competitiveness, however, that he wasn't intellectually intimidated by me, as opposed to every other boy I'd met until almost my senior year in college.

Only once, Lady Di, did David and I grope toward a more carnal relationship, back in eleventh grade. The grope was both literal and figurative, but, alas, quite inconclusive. The buttons on my blouse gave him trouble because his fingers were cold because we were in the car parking because if our parents even considered what filth might be germinating in our minds, we each of us would have been grounded until my menopause, which both my parents believed cured the desire for sex.

But we *were* in the car, and it *was* cold, and by the second button down I stopped him and said something terribly original like, "David, maybe this isn't such a good idea." And I'd like to report that he seemed relieved not to have to live up to some male aggressor role, but I don't think he was relieved. I sneaked a peek downward, pretending to tie my shoe, and he did not seem relieved at all.

We said nothing about that night, pushed it back into the womb, divided the zygote. We graduated; I went to college, and David went to pot. And then speed. And then acid.

When I saw him a year later, he'd been to California and back, fallen in lust with a fellow hitchhiker and ended up living with her for three months until she got tired of hitchhiking and left him to return to her rich family in Cleveland, done a stint as a rodeo clown, learned how to surf, picked berries in Oregon, been thrown in a Butte, Montana, jail for two days because he couldn't pay his motel bill, and gotten his buttocks tattooed. He was a different man upon his return to God's country—unrufflable, self-amused, and notably goalless.

This was the David who got his degree from a community college, moved to St. Paul, and eventually secured a job at Planned Parenthood, where he worked his way up to a mid-management position, met and moved in with Sally Copavic, and helped Philip find part-time work.

This was the David who sat next to me at the beginning of the campaign meeting and proceeded during the course of the discussions to spread every spreadable substance in my kitchen on his celery sticks.

And this was the David who confided in me weeks later in a drugged stupor that Philip was a bear who cowed him. More on that later, Lady Di.

The meeting progressed. Philip took charge at first and then relented when others began to contribute. It was decided that Philip should advocate masturbation. That done with, and this first issue providing a forum for everyone to get a feel for everyone else, the real planning got underway.

Astonishments, Di! There was this petite, eager-to-please, St. Cloud girl/woman at the meeting, Carolyn Anderson by name, who began to take an active part in the discussions: Philip should do it this way, the canvassing should occur here, we should get an endorsement from this person. They couldn't shut me up. Suddenly I was fascinated by publicity, scheduling, staffing, fund-raising, registering, the stuff of campaigns. I got pulled into the main group, leaving David and his celery all alone in the corner. I asked key questions, commented cogently on a wide range of matters, challenged several of the other participants, argued for my positions. Some of the men there patronized me, laughed me off, but either I didn't recognize it or I didn't care. It was so simple. I knew the city, I had an orderly mind, and I was conservative enough to consider contingencies. I was invaluable.

Thank the Lord for the opportunity, even that late in life. One of those black holes in my mind started backing up and letting out a little light, and I was aware that as I became more active, Vince became more passive. I hadn't dominated the group by any means, but once or twice I differed with him, and he obviously didn't like it. The Old Guard Left, their penises mightier than their pens.

We plotted until almost midnight, and in retrospect it seemed as if the seriousness had been necessary to get the meeting off in the right direction. By the time we'd finished, though, people were laughing and joking. The staff, as we now called ourselves, left on a remark that at the time provoked considerable mirth. One of the women from Planned Parenthood said to

Philip as she put on her coat, "Well, Philip, I sure hope the public doesn't take you too seriously. I'd hate to see you lynched."

"And you know where they'd lynch me, too," Philip replied, and we all laughed.

But later in bed, Philip turned to me. "Car," he said, "they wouldn't really take me seriously, would they?"

And good old reliable Carolyn, with her unerring accuracy for reading the situation, gently grabbed Philip's penis and said, "How could anyone take you seriously?"

It was fortunate, Lady Di, that I was in the middle of post-hoc library research, trying to find cryogenicists who would support the results of my experiments. That kept me from flinging myself headlong into the campaign. As it was, it probably added two or three weeks to my work. The campaign geared up, and I remained in the background. But how I wanted to be in the forefront—writing the brochures, assigning blocks for canvassing, lining up speaking engagements. Philip sought my advice regularly, but more than once he locked me out of a planning session so I'd be forced to work on the dissertation. "Carolyn," he said, "finish the helium first. For someone who thought this was a dumb—d-u-m—idea, you're pretty eager to participate."

Once I asked him if he, like Vince, was upset because I argued during meetings.

"No," he said, frowning, "why should I be upset? Why even is Vince upset?"

"Because women, I guess, aren't supposed to argue like men."

Philip laughed. "How do men argue?"

"No, I mean I don't think men like women to argue at all. Women are supposed to listen."

Philip nodded and put his arm around me. "I like you when you're doing what you want to be doing. It sounds like Vince has a problem, not you."

"Well, if he gets real upset, it's not Vince so much who has the problem, but the campaign."

"Oh, arguing with me, huh?"

We continued to amass recruits from local colleges, many from Minneapolis, since St. Paul is much stodgier. Our recruits were mostly bored students who were titillated at what we were doing and didn't mind signing up to spend a few evenings handing out leaflets. It was fun; everyone was having a fine time. Philip's work at Planned Parenthood was not demanding, and he devoted all his spare time to the campaign—making contacts, studying maps, preparing speeches, screening staff. Every once in a while he'd stop to grin.

The staff made two important decisions. One was to hold off the leafletting and other publicity until Philip's first major speech. More dramatic that way, we thought. The second decision was to give that speech at the local Jaycees' convention the following week. Captive audience, media coverage; it was made to order, we thought.

All right, Lady Di, you say that's a tad cocky, Jaycees not generally known for their liberal views. But the fervor of the planning sessions had overtaken us. What could we lose? The worst that could happen was that Philip would be laughed off the podium. He hadn't the slightest ambition to be mayor, anyway; he didn't even like St. Paul. At best, people would begin to think more seriously about elections and candidates, and possibly about masturbation. Which was all secondary, of course, to everyone enjoying themselves.

We were careful, we thought. We checked local obscenity laws to make sure Philip wouldn't be hauled away for obscenitizing in public. We even edited slang and vulgar idiomatics out of his speech. We sincerely hoped that the Jaycees would allow room on the agenda for Philip to speak.

Neal Starkman

I don't know why they did. Maybe they had a mix-up somewhere; maybe they couldn't find another speaker to talk about God and country; maybe it was another of those life-road detours.

He was in excellent spirit that night—eyes ashine, conversation abubble. "Carolyn," he said, as I fixed his tie—a concession he made to the staff— "it's a natural. Everyone has either masturbated or contemplated masturbating. No one escapes my constituency."

As it turned out, Philip himself barely escaped his constituency. Sally and David came by to drive him to the auditorium. I pleaded work to do, but, Lady Di, I won't hide anything from you: It was one thing to sit in the security of your own home and talk about masturbation. But it was quite another to do the same in front of maybe five hundred strangers. I was not made so audaciously then. Then, I was still St. Clouded.

So I didn't go, and instead stood there in my flannel shirt, blue jeans, and tennies, while Philip, blue suit and tie; David, Madras shirt and bell-bottom pants; and Sally, probably a frumpy dress—Sally never could get the hang of wearing clothes—all smiled and preened as if they were going to a wedding. Philip fantasized a rabid reception by the Jaycees. I'm sure he used that word, too—rabid.

"They'll carry me aloft," he said. "They'll cheer and make oblations and pronounce me the only fit candidate for the job. Car, you'll be First Lady."

"The first lady to abdicate because her lover was excessively gross."

Whereupon Philip scratched at his crotch and said, "Whaddya mean, gross?"

I kissed him for luck, while David stood by in his usual haze and Sally checked her watch. "Time to go," she said, and I closed the door on my three optimistic friends. That was the last I saw of the old Philip.

If we'd had any sense at all, we'd have done things differently. You just get involved in your little world with your little values and your friends with the same little values, and all of a sudden somebody knocks on your door and says, pardon me, but did you know there's another world out there, and it's a lot bigger and a lot different than yours? And you peek out and say, oh my, I don't much care for that, but it certainly is big, isn't it, thank you for making me aware of that.

Philip's door was really knocked that night. And the world came storming in.

I guess it was about nine. I was brewing some Red Zinger tea when I heard sirens; but we lived in a part of town where sirens and their attendant misfortunes were not uncommon, so I thought nothing of it. Even when the sirens became louder and therefore closer, I thought nothing of it and removed the little Chinese tea basket from the clear red liquid. I began to think something of it when the key sounded in the door and Philip staggered in, forehead bloody, tie awry, and shoes scuffed, followed closely by three of St. Paul's uniformed Finest. They pushed him over to the couch, sneered at me, and left without a grunt.

There are occasions when time freezes for us, as when we're confronted by an imminent disaster. There are other occasions when it speeds up to a frantic pace, as when we're under a deadline or enjoying the last of the pre-work morning in a warm and comfortable bed. And then there are occasions, as when Philip hit the couch, when time puts on its wet suit and dives underwater. I remember everything as if I were submerged: people moving deliberately, appearing before me intermittently and receding into the dimness, sound muted, senses dulled. Certain vignettes return to me, without beginning or end: my hand freezing from daubing the cut on Philip's head with an ice pack; Sally and David rushing in, disheveled; my noticing and then forgetting my pants zipper, open from, ironically, a whimsical masturbation just before I decided to brew the tea; the room seeming too dark for such momentous events to be occurring; and, most of all, Philip's dazed, perseverant monotone—"those fucking hicks, those fucking hicks, those fucking hicks…"

Neal Starkman

When Philip's blood-tide was finally stemmed and he managed to hold the ice pack himself—thanks, Mom, for teaching me how to make ice packs, it really came in handy—I turned to Sally. I don't remember where David was, but I think he was drinking my tea.

I would probably have turned to Sally in any case. Sally was of the Chicago working class, and her blunt demeanor was beautifully balanced by an easy, precise control of the language. Stocky and strong, she attracted me in much the same way, I suppose, she attracted David: She could be depended on.

I remember thinking that all I had to do was ask Sally what had happened, and she'd explain. She'd explain the police and Philip's bruised forehead and the speech and everything. When she'd finish explaining to me, then I would understand. I'm certain it was Sally's responsible presence that sustained me those first few hectic minutes. Sally was the rock amid swirling water.

So here's Sally and Carolyn, sitting on the couch next to Philip, who's holding the ice pack to his head, disregarding my protective hand on his knee, staring slit-eyed through our brown-eggshell curtains at the world outside our apartment, and embellishing his previous commentary with the addition of "goddam," thus: "those goddam fucking hicks, those goddam fucking hicks..." And I say something very simple, like "Sally, what happened?" And cool, articulate Sally, who was going to set everything straight for me, Sally who was going to restore order out of chaos, Sally the Rock, frowns, opens her mouth, closes her mouth, shakes her head, blinks rapidly, looks at me as if she knows what to say a dozen times but then censors it because it's insufficient, gives a fair impression of an aphasic and eventually utters, to my chagrin, "those hicks, those goddam fucking hicks..."

It must have been David who told me. Maybe the Red Zinger pulled him together. Either that or he was stoned and didn't get sucked into the mental maelstrom with Philip and Sally. He must have enjoyed the position of being sole authority and relating the sequence of events: Philip's mingling with various upper-echelon Jaycees; Philip's introduction to the audience after two or three other speakers had talked about local events and universal sentiments; the beginning of Philip's speech; the first boos; the hurling of programs to the dais; the stomping of feet; his, Sally's, and the moderator's efforts to persuade Philip to cut the speech short; Philip's increasing hostility toward the audience; Philip's departure from the speech to deliver some comments expressing that hostility; the crowd surging onto the dais; the security police begrudgingly encircling Philip; the cordon around Philip, Sally, and himself moving outside to "getaway cars"; the rock striking Philip on the head just as he was shoved into the back seat of the squad car; Sally and he becoming separated from each other and from Philip; their eventual high-speed ride back here in another squad car; and my zipper being open.

The blood from Philip's wound had caked in his hair, lending it a rather attractive auburn tinge, but I washed it out, anyway, and put him to bed—he went directly from rage to exhaustion and was asleep within minutes. Sally mustered enough vocabulary to articulate a desire for decaf. David sat back in our only semi-comfortable chair, reflective. I think Sally was embarrassed by her lapse into normalcy; and of course my insensitive recounting of the incident several days later in the form of an amusing anecdote to the staff did not assuage her embarrassment. After about two hours, I drove them back to their car. The convention was still going on, but there were no signs of the earlier disturbance.

I saved a box of campaign memorabilia, and I have before me the front page of the next morning's *Pioneer-Press*. Lower left-hand corner, three columns' worth: "Candidate Hurt in Jaycee Fracas." The article describes how Philip Lester, who worked for Planned Parenthood, "a sex-counseling and abortion-referral agency," incited the crowd by his use of "obscene language and sexual innuendos" during the campaign speech. No one called us until later that morning, when a few local journalists asked for comments. Philip said he would hold a press conference at four. When four o'clock came around, however, and he was still angry, I persuaded him to wait.

Neal Starkman

But the article is right here, Lady Di, in black and brittle yellow—The Turning Point for Philip, for me, and certainly for Philip and me.

We jumped today, Stephanie and I. Third time for me, fourth for her, but I feel I'll soon tire of it.

"It'll get rid of your tension," says Stephanie. "Plus, it's aerobic."

Plus, it's exhausting. Plus, I feel silly jumping up and down for five minutes ("We'll work our way up to thirty by next week." "Wonderful; we can celebrate with double coronaries.") in my underwear (can't stain my work clothes; carpenter Stephanie doesn't have that problem).

So we jumped for five minutes, and my anxiety disappeared for five minutes, ten seconds. "Don't you feel better now?" asks Stephanie. "(Puff) (gasp)," retorts Carolyn.

Stephanie has chided me for writing this. There is teasing to her tone; the rancor is levels down, in the sub-basement. My mother had that tone when she'd talk to me about my rare dates in high school. She evinced one level of friendly curiosity, but beneath that was a level of disapproval, and beneath that a level of concern, and possibly beneath that a level of envy. Now she feigns disinterest if I mention a man and hopes beyond hope I've found Mr. Right, or even Mr. Will Do. My mother is a professional dissembler, trained, as are we all, from infancy; she's a better student than I am.

I guess Stephanie thinks I'm being maudlin. I have to guess because she hasn't yet reached the point to tell me about it. What do you think, Di? Philip is obviously behind me, but is it maudlin to reflect on a lover of the past in order to figure out what you're up to in the present? I must remember to reflect and not to wallow.

The Jaycees convention should have been the end of the campaign. We should have said, all right, it was a lark, but let's all go back now to dissertations and abortion referrals and psychology classes and five years from now look back on this and enjoy a hearty chuckle.

The staff met, this time at Sally and David's, to reconsider strategy, such as maybe having no strategy at all except hanging up our maps. Someone actually called it a learning experience.

Oh, how did we line up then: Sally, now recovered and back to common sense, suggested strongly that we quit. She saw no purpose in continuing, since it was evident that we miscalculated the appeal of our message. Others, including me, agreed. Vince felt that we should continue; the publicity we got from the riot, he said (the size of the disturbance grew with each telling), couldn't have been better if we'd paid for it.

David was silent. I don't know what was going on inside that chemically altered St. Cloud head. I'm not even sure David knew. Sometimes I almost got the feeling that he was competing with Philip, though David's sense of competition was probably more metaphysical than most of us could comprehend. Still, there was our past to consider, and I found myself hoping that his occasional stares at me were not those of desire but merely the result of millions of tiny cannabis molecules bouncing around his nervous system.

Philip was adamant about continuing the campaign. Since I felt as if he held all the power in our relationship—which of course gave him de facto power—I hadn't tried more than halfheartedly to change his mind; but I had hoped the group could.

It was no contest. He was still seething from the insult he'd suffered at the convention. He was stunned, he was hurt, and he'd been challenged. "An error in judgment," he dismissed the incident. Nothing had changed. He would press on regardless of the decision of the group. If they all quit, then he would just go out and find more sympathetic staff as well as audiences.

Neal Starkman

Sally and David stuck by us in the end, as did a few others. Over the weeks we lost some workers, including Vince, who found another community project he was more interested in. But we picked up students, too. Di, it was unbelievable how many Twin Citians volunteered to work on our campaign. Given our literature.

We couldn't afford to print much, but what we did print was choice. Very subtle, if you can be subtle about masturbation. Such as:

PHILIP LESTER FOR MAYOR

Vote for Philip Lester in the Democratic primary for mayor. Philip's approach to government is like his approach to life. He believes it should be open, fair, and benefit the people. But first the people have to benefit themselves. Philip believes that all people have the right to help themselves—to educate themselves by attending schools, to feed themselves by working an honest wage, to ennoble themselves by praying to the deity of their choice, and to pleasure themselves by masturbating as often as they like. **Vote for Philip Lester, Tuesday, October 7.** The vote is in your hands like never before.

The campaign wore on, and so did we. Doorbells were rung, handouts were distributed, funds were raised—much at university beer fests—and the city was divided into categories of friendly, neutral, and hostile. We later downgraded them a notch, to neutral (enter at risk), fairly hostile (don't enter), and extremely hostile (don't even think about entering). We did draw some media coverage away from an anti-abortion woman. Every time she got publicity, Philip did, too, although our "publicity" was invariably a story about the audience reaction to one of Philip's speeches. None of the major papers or radio or TV stations covered his speeches substantively, and as a result Philip was either unknown or known as a kook.

They were odd speeches, to be sure. For one thing, they were hardly ever completed, because, no matter where Philip was, the audience would turn on him. Staff would place bets on how far into his speech he could get before the boos and hisses and other manner of directed cacophony drowned him out. For another thing, the speeches were mostly off-the-cuff. The first few were written, but it soon became apparent that it was wasteful to compose and write out a twenty-minute speech when you'd only get to deliver about four-and-a-half minutes of it.

My contributions to the campaign were intellectual rather than physical. I was one of the generals who moved toy soldiers on table maps and then sent out my forces to be slaughtered. I'd get news from the front either in the form of a frantic phone call from a raw recruit or, more typically, by looking into the battle-scarred eyes of the veterans as they trudged home after a rout.

I went to a speech early in the campaign; it was right outside an outer-city shopping mall (yes, Lady Di, another poor choice). I came along because it was a clear, crisp Saturday afternoon; because I was tired of reading about helium's lambda points and second sound and angular momentum and concentric cylinder viscometers; because Sally said I should come to get a better idea of what the campaign really looked like; and because I decided I hadn't been giving Philip the support I hoped he needed from me. This was, oh, probably Philip's fourth speech, and he'd already honed his style to approach the three-minute mark before being shouted away by hordes of outraged St. Paulites.

We picked up Sally and David in our Volvo and drove out to the mall. Everybody was dressed casually except for Philip, who'd inexplicably taken to wearing ties and laced shoes. He was in a combative mood, as usual; David was mellow, as usual; and Sally did a lot of head-shaking.

We arrived at the mall and set up our little stand—Vince had donated it. Our sign proclaimed "PHILIP LESTER FOR MAYOR" in red paint. We had a side table with literature, plus a few bricks to keep the handouts from blowing away. We had a step stool upon which Philip orated, and we played a tape of the "Washington Post March" to get the crowd's attention. Old-fashioned politics, Di.

For a mall, it wasn't that bad. It had been built circa 1970 and still looked modern. There were sixty stores under one polygonal roof, and the entire structure was situated adjacent to a ten-acre park. The green of the grass and the trees—now fading to brown—contrasted quite nicely with the shiny white concrete and red brick of the structure. I mean, it wasn't the Taj Mahal, Di, but it could have been worse. We set up our display on the park side of the mall, with the parking lot about a hundred yards to the rear. There was a walkway to the parking lot, and people had to pass us to get to and from their cars.

Now, Di, you have to understand our audience. It was a nice day, and Middle America zombies were on their way to the mall: a gaggle of teenaged girls, some with braces, who walk back and forth and around the big department stores trolling for boys; a young couple separated by their little boy, eating an oversized lollipop; two elderly women carrying sacks of yarn; a husband, wife, and parents, the men walking in front and discussing hardware; a woman in curlers and her daughter, suppressing embarrassment by looking in every direction except toward her mother; and so on. Almost everyone is white and Germanic, so that the few blacks and Mediterraneans are noticeable. Almost everyone is dressed without style, and, more significantly, without pretension to style. Almost everyone is receptive. Or, better put, unprepared.

Into this middle-class fiefdom came Philip Lester and his masturbation campaign. St. Paul was middle-class not like Portland or Seattle or even Minneapolis. St. Paul is middle-class like Peoria or Spokane or Sacramento. Like Velveeta and Charlie's Angels and Happy Faces. St. Paulites buy American, they look down upon outsiders, and they are probably proud of their namesake, that scourge of womanhood and all-round nasty. They undoubtedly have sex with the lights off, if at all. They didn't like the fact that we left Vietnam dangling from a helicopter, they didn't think Watergate was scandalous, they weren't aware that the United Nations declared 1975 "International Women's Year," and their sense of satire was limited since it was still a few days before the debut of Saturday Night Live.

David handed out literature, while Sally and I flanked Philip's other side. We watched the people go by, perhaps ten or fifteen a minute. I felt like a bodyguard rather than an aide, and I wondered why my fingers sweat, since it was about fifty degrees out. Philip started his speech.

"My name is Philip Lester, and I am running for mayor of this city of St. Paul." We had no microphone, and Philip had to project without sounding desperate. Out of the corner of my eye, I saw an old man take a leaflet and carry it with him to his car without reading it.

"You may have heard about me from the newspapers, or perhaps radio or TV. Then again, maybe you haven't. It's very difficult for a candidate to get publicity when he doesn't have a big bankroll or he's not already famous. How much publicity do you think *you* would get if *you* ran for mayor?"

So far, so good. Philip was just your everyday Joe, trying to exercise his American liberties. The listeners were lulled into security, as a group—an actual audience—began to form. Some were eating ice cream cones, some transferred packages to a stronger arm. I tried to keep from grinning. It was perverse. I knew what was coming and they did not. I gazed at David and couldn't read his face. Sally looked grim.

Philip made some mention of the mall, the weather, a news item, a joke. This is known as adaptation, he told me. More trusting faces, larger crowd. A crowd of people whose idea of controversy is television commercials that mention competitors' brand names.

"I suppose you're asking yourself, what does this guy stand for?" intoned Philip, getting to the crux of the speech. "Why should I vote for him as opposed to anyone else? Well, I'll tell you what I stand for, and then I'm confident you'll see that no one else in this race for mayor of St. Paul can offer you anything better.

Neal Starkman

"I stand for something as American as Mom's apple pie. I stand for giving the people of St. Paul the opportunity—the permission!—to take care of themselves for a change, instead of always looking to other resources to help them out. I stand for speaking forthrightly about something that's as natural and as wholesome as a rainbow."

What can he mean? they wondered. Free speech? Ecology? Public prayer? Now I was grinning widely—it's all nervousness—but it was okay to smile; people think we're friendly. Next to me Sally's eyes ping-ponged between the car and Philip, as if she were measuring emergency exit routes. The crowd was at ease, secure, homogeneous, like so many slices of white bread. They got up this morning with nothing on their minds except shopping with the family, enjoying the Minnesota autumn, saying hello to neighbors, planning dinner, fixing a leaky faucet, visiting boyfriends/girlfriends/relatives, considering what type of insulation to buy for the approaching winter, taking the car in for a brake job. I recognized the type of people I grew up with in this crowd, yet I felt distant from them, even as they remind me of myself.

"We continually find ourselves in emotional morasses," Philip was saying, "mired in anger and despondency. Inflation, unemployment, taxes, war, family pressures, we all have them, all of us—rich and poor, black and white, man and woman, young and old. I want to talk to you about a way out of that morass—a solution to headaches, heartaches, and even politics aches." Laughter now; the tension was unbearable. Sally took a deep breath. I noticed her eyes were closed.

"I don't promise a panacea." Those in the crowd who knew what a panacea was were with him now; he's a realist. "I don't promise that I can solve all your problems." Philip redundantized for those who didn't know what a panacea was. "Only fools and my opponents promise you that." Even now I laugh—but I realized something was pounding in my chest, and David had stopped handing out leaflets.

"I'll tell you this, citizens of St. Paul: If I am elected mayor, and my policies are put into action, and you follow the recommendations I'm about to put to you, then all your lives will be far more satisfying and fulfilling than they are now. I stand up here and tell that to you, not because I have to, but because I believe it. What am I talking about? I think you know." What, what, their eager, sparkling eyes asked, faces uplifted in gestures of hope. Tell us, oh please, tell us.

"I'm talking about masturbation."

Freeze. It was a 3.5-second freeze. We timed it. The chins were up, the eyebrows arched, the foreheads barely creased, the mouths smiling amusedly, the limbs relaxed, the bodies slightly slouched. The minds were clear and like a freckle-faced boy gone fishing on a summer afternoon, orange curls peeking out of a country hat, hand in pocket, rod on shoulder, barefooted on a dirt road, whistling a ditty, not a care in the world.

And now the word *masturbation* was in the air. The syllables insidiously converted to waves of pressure and, at 1100 feet a second, struck the eardrums of every individual within a 75-foot radius. The waves were passed on through three little bones in the ear, then to ligaments. Membranes reverberate and send signals further into the ear. The organ of Corti slides against the tectorial membrane, which stimulates hair cells, sending electrical impulses against 27,000 nerve fibers, give or take a few. The impulses make special contacts in the upper temporal lobe of the cerebrum, a myriad infinitesimal brain cells establish discrete associations with one another in complex patters and sequences, and at 3.5 seconds you can see it in the eyes.

The eyes went first; they glazed and watered. "Masturbation." Then the body tensed: Fists clenched, legs stiffened, twitches began to grasshopper over the crowd. "Masturbation." The eyebrows collapsed as the eyes dilate, forehead corrugating, and the jaw slowly lowers, the amused smile a casualty. "Masturbation." There was a second or two of disbelief, denial. He didn't say *that*, did he? No one says *that*. What did he say? Maturation? Matriculation? Education? Did somebody hear what he said?

There were gasps, and several people, mostly the older ones, reeled backward as if struck with a giant fist. Philip continued to speak, and the denial cedes to acceptance, which was the basis for the range of emotions—all of which we label "negative"—now evolving in the crowd. Philip was reciting a litany of the benefits of masturbation when the heckles started ("Get outa here, ya Commie bum!" "Shut your mouth, hippie!"). Much of the crowd began to dissipate, stunned and disgusted, trying to fend off their children's guileless queries ("What's masturbation, Mommy?" "Never mind, eat your candy.").

But the remainder of the crowd had turned ugly. By the time Philip reached the point of suggesting opportune times for members of the household to follow his policies, he could scarcely be heard. He stopped before relating anything about technique or something else liable to get us killed. The crowd was as one, homogeneous again in their wrath. Mild, passive citizens had been transformed into demons of ferocity, intent on preserving their memory of what was decent and acceptable.

We were soon rapidly taking down our props, while Philip engaged in a more personal discussion with a burly-armed gentleman who was offering to exchange Philip's teeth for his silence. We headed for the car, Philip lagging behind, cursing, the crowd behind us still yelling. I expected to see torches any second. Sally and David helped me get Philip back in the Volvo; he wanted to return to the mall. Sally was shaking her head again.

Lady Di, it didn't matter where we went. They showed Philip nothing but contempt. It got so bad that we deemed indignation a favorable response. He thought they would laugh, and they turned on him. "Fucking goddam hypocrites" slowly nosed out "goddam fucking hicks" as Philip's choice epithet. And he was all-embracing in its use, if only because he was continually decried by males and females of all races, creeds, ages, and philosophical dispositions.

We toned down the literature. When one of the staff produced a handout that didn't even mention masturbation, we knew that things had gotten out of hand, so to speak. Meanwhile, Philip had personalized the campaign: You could see two battles raging, one between Philip and the public, and the other between Philip and Philip.

When there wasn't violence or a threat of violence, there were "questions from the floor," most of which, despite Philip's best efforts, he couldn't answer.

"What gives you the right to stand up there and pour out that scum?"

"Why don't you go back to Planned Parenthood and kill some fetuses?"

"Do you believe in the sanctimony of the Almighty God?"

That last question came during a community meeting, not from the audience, but from a young, long-haired technician who had been helping out with the lights and sound. The boy had asked that of Philip as he left the stage amid catcalls. Philip told me afterwards that, although it was one of the few questions he could easily, if tersely, answer, nonetheless he decided to sacrifice a vote and politely suggested to the youth that he devour feces.

The staff began to work overtime, whatever that was, when it became obvious that not only was Philip not getting his point across, but he was also in continuous danger of flying eggs, rocks, and worse. We scheduled him in front of "friendly groups"—students, artists, civil libertarians, for God's sake. But either because the groups weren't as friendly as we had anticipated, or because the anti-masturbation forces—by now organized—infiltrated our audiences, he made no headway. Students were our most enthusiastic and least receptive audience; they cheered Philip as they would a touchdown or a rock star, deriving a rather vacuous enjoyment from his show. Philip even got angry at that. "Little shitheads aren't even thinking about what I'm saying," he protested. Near the end of the campaign, the anti-abortion woman switched her speechifying from against abortion to against Philip, presumably an easier target.

"Carolyn," Sally confided to me one evening as Philip was being chased out of a supermarket, "they hate him."

"I know. I feel so sorry for him."

Neal Starkman

"Sorry? The man's an idiot for provoking them."

Oh, Lady Di, I tried to be supportive, just like I was always taught women should be for their men. Unfortunately, Philip was always taught not to show any need of such support. None of us could talk to him. He would rant about the deadness of the minds in St. Paul, the hypocrisy of the people who plotted against his campaign. He rejected all conciliatory gestures and lived in an eternal snit.

"Goddam hypocrites," he would usually use for a reliable harangue-starter, no matter who was listening. "They masturbate, but they won't talk about it. They fuck, but they won't look at it. They swear, but they won't listen to it. How can you fight something like that? Goddam assholes. They hide behind things like the church, too. That really fries me. Why don't they take some responsibility for themselves? Shit-asses are dumbstruck if they see a joint; then they go drink themselves into a goddam blotto. And *then* they drive around and run over some old lady trying to cross the street. What kind of person doesn't fuck because a priest or minister says not to? What goes on in that person's head? It's just unbelievable."

And the world did not cooperate. We changed our phone number three times because of the obscene calls. Then Planned Parenthood laid him off. David had alerted him, in vain. The higher-ups couldn't afford to keep him on; the organization was getting too much adverse publicity. Philip said he understood; it was the same reason, he said, that Planned Parenthood changed its name from the Birth Control League years ago. Chickenshit, he said.

I got scared. I couldn't deal with the hostility. This was supposed to be fun, but it wasn't fun at all. I thought any day someone was going to assassinate us—a hail of bullets as we entered the Volvo, a bomb through the living room window (we lived on the second floor, but one's fears are not always logical), a bludgeon in a dark alley, black widow spiders via United Parcel. We were marked, I knew it (I was reading about Trotsky and remember thinking, he was killed with an ice pick, how clever; then the ice melts and there aren't any fingerprints). There was the Syndicate out there, financed by the anti-abortion lady and legislators of rural Minnesota, and none of them masturbated. They all wore black gloves. The Syndicate, the Mob, would get us, I was sure. My mother would never understand. The *Pioneer-Press* would headline, "Local Couple Killed in Freak Machine-Gun Accident."

And David smoked dope with me one afternoon and told me Philip had always intimidated him.

"He's a big bear, Carolyn, a great big bear who always looks to smother me or tear my arms from their sockets or bite my head off."

I didn't respond for a few minutes while I tried to picture Philip as any kind of bear but a teddy. Recognize, Di, that with only a bit of the weed, my spatial aptitude is enhanced tremendously. So there I was, Mary Janing, trying bear paws on Philip, who had become sort of a scruffy Ken doll. I tried on different bear heads, and then all four paws, and when I was done—well, David had been right; he *did* look like a bear.

"You're right," I said to David after what seemed like a week, "he is a big bear. What'll I do? He'll crush me." And I began to worry that the next time Philip hugged me, he would continue to squeeze and squeeze until my head popped open like a pimple.

"I don't know, Carolyn. What can you do? What will you do? What won't you do? What must you do?" This last David shouted at me, holding my head with both his hands but looking directly at my breasts. On that equivocal note we ended the conversation.

I recall this and I see David protecting me like a brother with incest on his subconscious. What kind of person was I, to be overpowered by Philip, protected by David, and probably patronized by others of whom I wasn't even aware? I was rearranging my insides, Di, but no one noticed. That fall, I was on the verge of becoming a physicist, and my assertiveness was budding even as the Minnesota flora was fading.

Neal Starkman

I became fascinated with politics, ravenous for the literature. Instead of reading Feynman and Landau for physics, I consumed Marx, then Engels, then Ricardo and Proudhon, my God, even Fourier and some of the lesser known syndicalists. I gravitated to socialism: I had a feel for the order, the logic of it. I attacked the subject as if it were a school assignment. When do different economic systems mesh? When do they conflict? How do microeconomic decisions influence the whole? The mosaic was compelling, and I couldn't learn enough. When I wasn't tucking in the corners of my dissertation, I was reflecting on the applicability of Frantz Fanon to Minnesota society.

Philip was busy. He devoted part of his time—now extended due to his jettisoning by Planned Parenthood—to strategizing and part of his time to just plain brooding. He worked increasingly alone, although, no matter how poorly the campaign seemed to be going, we somehow always had a surfeit of volunteers.

One afternoon, near the end of the campaign, when the frost was beginning to overwhelm the pumpkin, I persuaded Philip to go on a picnic with me. It will be a tonic, I said. You deserve it. It will help you think more clearly.

Unaccountably, he agreed. We took a bus to Lake Calhoun. Then we walked by the lake, hand-in-hand past young bored mothers pushing their children in strollers, male joggers exhibiting their ripples, old gray men in ill-fitting suits, and lonely-looking people being walked by their dogs. We found a delightful bench off the path that looked toward the lake and beyond, and ate chicken sandwiches and drank hot chocolate from thermoses.

Oh, Lady Di, he was so attractive that day, casually stuffing food in his mouth like a little boy, bundled up in his Penney's winter coat, red wine stain on the fur collar, forlorn buttonhole at the bottom. Heaven help me from surrogate maternalism. Even his beard and moustache couldn't alter the picture.

Talking altered the picture.

"Philip, I want you to stop."

"Sandwiches are good."

"Philip."

He swallowed. "No." He stared straight ahead and blew out his breath in a small circle. I remember thinking, if I try to reason with him, he'll clobber me. I'll bring it to him on an emotional level. Carolyn, the Anti-Feminist.

"Philip, I'm proud of you, I really am. I'm glad you're sticking up for what you believe in, but, Philip, I'm scared shitless you're going to get really hurt. There's a lot of crazy people out there, and you make them angry. I don't want a martyr for a lover. Can't we call it quits now, before it's too late?"

He followed the food with a few sips of hot chocolate and took my mittened hand in his. And he fastened on to my eyes for the only time in days as he spoke, measured as always, but also weary.

"Carolyn, I truly love you. And I'm sorry you're afraid. But I have to finish the campaign. Okay, I admit it, I was surprised at the reaction of the crowds. But it's different now. I'm not continuing the campaign to get laughs, or to expose the folly of one-issue candidates or multi-issue candidates or anybody. I'm continuing because I have a right to speak. I'm not going to let them shout me down."

"They *are* shouting you down! They hate you! You can see that!" God, Di, I wanted to pound the thermos over the bald spot of his head until he said, oh yes, Carolyn, you're absolutely right, what a fool I was not to see it sooner. Instead, he looked back out at the water. When he turned to me again, his eyes moved more, didn't capture me as they had, and I also became aware that we were no longer holding hands.

"Look," he said, "it's not all that bad. Lately, there's even been a small following, and that's a welcome change. I really don't think the crowds are violent, not since the Jaycees."

Neal Starkman

"Why press your luck?"

"Car, I'm almost done with the campaign. Next week is the radio program, and that's it. The audience won't be able to touch me. Then we'll all go out and vote, and it'll be over. I'm not on a 'free speech for all' kick. If anything, I'm on a 'free speech for me' kick. There's a big difference. I'm too selfish to be a martyr. I merely want to be heard."

"I think you're being selfish, all right. Selfish and stubborn, and I don't know why, either."

Conversations like that became more typical. Maybe I should have given more, Di. Maybe I should have demanded more. At the time I thought, I can't reach him. Now I think, he wouldn't let me reach him.

I met with Sally to discuss my relationship with Philip. Well, more accurately, Sally met with me. We'd been recruiting at the university, and Sally suggested hamburgers for lunch.

I think Sally's food went to her brain, though a good portion of it was deposited also on her thighs, arms, and elsewhere. The only unintelligent thing she did was smoke, and I ascribe that to her Chicago background, where I imagine rough-looking peers ostracize you if you don't excel in a vice. Sally got an RN in Chicago and moved to the Twin Cities, where, she said, she thought it would be cleaner. She returned to school, got a master's in some sort of administration, and eventually became what amounts to clinical director of Planned Parenthood, where she met David.

The Sally–David relationship was something to behold, particularly because it seemed to work. Sally was the purposeful, stable, energetic force in David's life. Sally wanted to help people, another female role that keeps our supply of nurses, social workers, and teachers brimming over into the unemployment saucer. Had she been less practical, she could have been a social worker. But Sally realized that she'd need a degree in administration to be able to accomplish anything on a large scale, because she was far from politic. Her manner was like her appearance—not given to ornamentation.

David was the poet in Sally's life. He fit in—everywhere. Nothing fazed David. He was just what Sally needed to pull back from her hectic selfless pace. David, with his stuporous eyes, easy manner, and uncomplaining lifestyle, relaxed her. A healthy symbiosis.

I know all this, Lady Di, not because I'm such an acute observer, but because both Sally and David had long discussions with me that fall, and I listened more than spoke.

When I asked David if he'd ever tried to get Sally to quit smoking, he smiled and said, "It reminds her she's tough."

And once Sally had this to say about David: "He never worries. I'm trying to decide if I want to help people or if I want to feel good about helping people. Important. Makes me think a lot. David—he's at peace. It's not that nothing is important to him; it's that everything is equally important."

So Sally, who didn't care about her size fourteen figure, and Carolyn, who worried about her size eight, sat down to a lunch of hamburgers and fries and milk shakes and other poisons gleefully dished out at the local Chez McDonald. And Sally, between bites, mentioned something to the effect that Philip and I seemed kind of strained lately.

Carolyn, reverting to dumb innocence, said, "Strained? What do you mean?"

Sally was so used to cutting to the quick that she could do it nonchalantly. "You two are missing each other," she said with french fries in her mouth. "Not picking up cues. David noticed it, too."

"Clues?"

"Cues"—hamburger in mouth, chomp, chomp. "Philip makes a comment that should get a response from you, but you ignore it. You do something that Philip should recognize but doesn't. I talk with you"—milk shake straw in mouth, slurp—"about the campaign, about birth control, about physics sometimes, about socialism, about life, and then I talk with Philip. I don't see any connection between you two, no shared life-views. What do you two talk about?"

"Oh, the campaign, mostly. The past few weeks have been awfully stressful."

"What about before the campaign?"

"What about what before the campaign?"

"What did you talk about? Politics? Religion? Sports? Crime and punishment?"

And I was stopped. I put down an onion half-ring and swallowed a chunk of hurt. The upsetting part wasn't that we hadn't talked about a lot of things; the upsetting part was that I'd always imagined we had.

I asked myself—per indoctrination—where did I go wrong? How have I not made this relationship work? I immediately assumed all the responsibility. It had been my duty to provide a decent relationship, and I had failed. My mind wandered into abysses of gloom, and my face must have reflected that, because Sally reached over and squeezed my shoulder.

"Carolyn, I'm only saying that the lack of communication is more obvious now. It's not the end of the world. Carolyn?"

"Oh, I know; I'm fine." But I couldn't possibly have looked fine, and Sally let it go.

"Steph," I say over Sunday breakfast—she likes to make pancakes with fresh-ground nutmeg on Sunday, a perfectly incongruous quirk that delights me—"how mature would you say I am, say, from one to ten?"

"Ten. Until now. Now eight."

"How did I lose two?"

"You asked me about it. If you were really mature, you wouldn't ask me about it."

"What made me rank so high to begin with?"

Stephanie puts down her fork and stirs her tea out of a cup with a hand-painted rose on it, a gift from a former lover I've never asked her to identify.

"You don't fly off the handle. You've always got everything all planned, all the angles covered. Like with your research, you know? You'll come up with something, I know you. I've been thinking about it more, and now I think you should do whatever they want you to do."

"That's quite a change from suing and then killing the chairman of the department."

Stephanie sips some tea and shrugs. "That's just me. I'd do something stupid, lose my job. Then what? I'd have to move away, look for another job. That'd be pretty hard on my lover." She shrugs again. Steph is a terrible actress. "I don't know, I can't picture you out of control, babe. I'd like to see you out of control. Make me feel better when I get that way."

I smile and realize that it pleases me to have the reputation of being in control.

"Don't let it go to your head now," says my brown-eyed lover, resuming eating her pancakes. "I only told you that so you'll help me clean the house today."

"Oh no, not today."

"You promised, Carolyn. Besides, you're a good cleaner."

I am a good cleaner, but I'd rather write to you, Di. I try to change the subject. "Rate yourself from one to ten."

"On maturity?"

41

Neal Starkman

"Yes."

She sleeves her mouth and sits back, crosses her legs at the knees, sips tea, and considers.

"Shit, I'm a five, I guess. Except when drunk. Then maybe a two."

"Pretty hard on yourself."

"Do you want the bathroom or the kitchen?"

"If you're a five and I'm an eight, why do we get along so well?"

Stephanie picks up her empty plate and goes to the sink, pausing to bend down and roll her tongue around my ear, which makes me giggle. She knows I hate to giggle.

"Because you like my pancakes."

I taped Philip's last speech. I thought it would be one of the few bright memories of the whole campaign.

The week before had been horrendous. The crowds seemed particularly inimical, there was a dispute between two of the staff members, we didn't get something printed in time for an important brochure, a check bounced, and Planned Parenthood issued a statement of dissociation from Philip, which tensed up his relationship with Sally and David, though neither of them could have prevented it.

Philip had slept badly all week, and he was so jittery that I tried to keep out of his way while managing to be around in case he needed me. Cute trick. What would you like today, sir: solace or space? I figured, one more week, I'll sacrifice. My dissertation was winding down, too. I had a few more diagrams to draw and a few more non sequiturs to reconcile, and then I'd send the whole thing to the typist.

We all were looking forward to the radio speech. Philip considered it a major opportunity to air his views without interruption. I just wanted it to be over. Some of the student staff thought that the speech could "put him over the top"—the top of what, they didn't say. All our publicity that week focused on the radio show.

Tom Froehlich was the host and producer of "Speak Out." I think it was David who arranged the spot. Froehlich had had on the anti-abortion/anti-Philip lady two weeks before, and David argued for equal time.

Froehlich was a typical conservative radio talk-show host. He bullied his phone-ins, waxed platitudinous, and displayed his ignorance of issues in a variety of ways. But he always let his guests speak, and that was what convinced us that Philip would do well. We felt that if Philip could avoid responding to hecklers and instead stick to a prepared statement, he would impress a lot of people. It was when he was baited that he got into trouble. So a few of the staff role-played telephone callers, just in case. We badgered him mercilessly—it was quite fun—but he maintained his cool. We were confident.

I went with him that evening. I wanted to be there when the campaign ended. I wanted to hold him when he went off the air and say, "Welcome back," and return to our old quiet life. But driving over there and realizing that I hadn't seen Philip smile in weeks gave me pause to wonder if he'd readjust so quickly.

We walked through the station to the taping room, and as we received glances from radio personnel, including the receptionist who ushered us into the studio, I became acutely aware of the physical differences between Philip and me. He had a foot in height over me and probably eighty pounds. But it was much more than that. It was his dark hair and beard, compared to my Norwegian "dirty blonde" (that's what Philip called it—an apparently non-pejorative Eastern expression for light brown); his set jaw and scowling eyes, compared to my eager-to-please half-smile and baby-blue innocence; his purposeful gait, compared to my nervous shuffle. The impression, I'm sure, was that this brute had captured me for unspeakable depravities. I wondered if Philip ever felt he was *bête* to my *belle*.

Tom Froehlich needed a shave and smelled of cigarettes; I disliked him on sight and smell. He was about fifty, with a glad hand, a glad smile, and a rapid way of walking that made you think he didn't really care how, when, or even if you reacted to him. He looked like your least favorite uncle, the one who scared you when you were little.

We entered the studio, and Philip and I were shown to seats at one end of a table with a small bouquet of dried flowers and a pitcher—but no glasses—of ice water. Froehlich sat at the other end and put on his earphones and set up his microphone. Philip must have had a microphone, too, but I don't remember it.

We waited a few minutes for the program to start—we were going out live—while Philip reviewed his speech. He had worked on it all week; it was reasoned and moderate. Typing it out further legitimized it. Froehlich conferred with some other men in the studio and then briefly with Philip; I made sure my tape was in the right place. The show began, I kissed Philip on the cheek, and I started my recorder as Froehlich was cued after a commercial, made a few opening statements, and turned to Philip.

"Welcome to 'Speak Out,' Mr. Lester."

"Thank you."

"Mr. Lester, why are you running for mayor of St. Paul?"

"I'm running for several reasons, Mr. Froehlich. First of all, I want to bring people's attention to the reality of a sincere candidate and to a one-issue candidate."

"'Sincere'—that's interesting, Mr. Lester. I wouldn't have associated that quality with your campaign. Let's get right down to it. Your one issue, your single issue, Mr. Lester, and I'll read from one of your own leaflets so the audience at home won't think I'm off my rocker—and please, ladies and gentlemen, if you are offended by coarse language, I urge you either to turn off your radios or to bear with me, but I'm going to quote now—your one issue, Mr. Lester, is, quote, the self-satisfying, positive act of masturbation. End quote. Mr. Lester, when I first heard of you, I found you hard to believe. Now you're here, your leaflet is directly in front of me. Frankly, I think you're nuts, and probably dangerous, too. Is this what you're advocating, sir—the self-satisfying, positive act of masturbation?"

"Yes."

"Mr. Lester, do you honestly believe that you can win this campaign for mayor?"

"Of course not."

"Do you *want* to be mayor of St. Paul, Mr. Lester?"

"Not particularly. I'm not running to win, as I was about to explain."

"So you don't think you can win the election, and you don't particularly want to be mayor, anyway. That's very informative."

"I'd l—"

"Do you have a job, Mr. Lester? I mean a regular job outside of campaigning for mayor."

"Until recently, I worked for Planned Parenthood."

"What happened?"

"They let me go because the campaign was bringing them bad publicity."

"They fired you."

"Mr. Froehlich, it was my understanding that I would be allowed time to speak on your program. So far, I feel as if I'm being interrogated. I don't mind answering questions, but I would like a chance to talk about what has happened to me during this campaign and why it's important for your listeners to hear about it."

"I'm only providing some background for our audience, Mr. Lester. I'm sorry if you feel you're unable to answer my questions. I've interviewed hundreds of other political candidates over the years, Mr. Lester, from the left and the right, serious contenders and fruitcakes like you. Some of them acquitted themselves well, Mr. Lester. Others came off like raving idiots, which they were, and I'm proud that this program helped to expose them to the American public. Let me ask you this, Mr. Lester. Straightforward. Do you believe in God?"

"What?"

"Do you believe in God? That's an easy question to answer, isn't it?"

"Mr. Froehlich, how often do you masturbate?"

"Mr. Lester—"

"How often do you masturbate? That's an easy question to answer, isn't it?"

"Mr. Lester, is there any way you can salvage an iota of self-respect from this campaign? You've been labeled—and I'm quoting from various sources now—a disgrace to the elective process, a purveyor of smut, a dangerous psychopath, and an impotent liberal with nothing better to do than make speeches about matters that belong, if anywhere, in the privacy of one's own mind. That quote was from the St. Paul *Guardian*. How do you respond to these accusations, Mr. Lester? Can so many people be wrong? What do you label yourself?"

"I don't intend to respond to any of those accusations, Mr. Froehlich; I merely consider the sources. And I label myself extremely impatient, and prepared to leave this studio unless I can be afforded the opportunity to speak, as I was promised."

"Mr. Lester, this is a great country we live in, despite the efforts of people like yourself to besmirch it. You may have three minutes, and then we'll take calls. I caution you, Mr. Lester, against obscenity."

"Thank you. The caution is unnecessary.

"When I first began this campaign, I had hoped to accomplish several goals. I wanted people to compare my sincerity with the sincerity of more legitimate candidates running for mayor. I wanted people to see that one could speak cogently and without stridency about a single issue. I thought also that people might be amused by what I was saying. I wanted to infuse this primary election with a certain spirit that is otherwise virtually nonexistent. My goals were to make this campaign useful, informative, and fun.

"In all these goals, these hopes, I was wrong. I naïvely miscalculated the public. I have met not understanding, but intolerance; not awareness, but ignorance; not enlightenment, but superstition; and not amusement, but hostility.

"The audiences I have tried to speak to have not opened their minds; they have not thought about what I've been saying. They have been listening instead to voices of their past— fearful voices, voices without reason. These voices, not I, have caused the anger. There is no conceivable justification to oppose what I've been saying these past few weeks. There's no reason for it. No reason.

"The issue of whether and to what extent one masturbates was chosen precisely because it is so harmless. And so universal. What possible negative…You know, I just didn't…

"I'm very tired. I'm disgusted myself. Things have built up…I have this statement here, and as I read it, I'm thinking, why bother? Am I really going to change your minds, influence you in even the slightest? Will I weave some magic message to snare each of you in my delusion that there is logic and tolerance in this world? You're so damned comfortable out there, listening to this, aren't you. So damned smug and comfortable.

Neal Starkman

"This is really all my dream, a fantasy. I'm in this radio station and I'm talking to you, and it doesn't even matter. I'm not getting through to you, I never have. Not from the beginning of this campaign. Never! I tried to reach you, and you'd have none of it. Who are you people, anyway? You listen to this hypocritical, troglodytic talk show. God, I'm talking to the people who have no minds. You don't think. You walk and talk but you have no minds. No critical faculties, no judgment, no taste. You lionize Mr. Thomas Froehlich, the paragon of sleaze, who, by the way, is masturbating at this very moment—

"All right, fuckers in radioland, listen to me out there! I'm talking to you straight and for your own good, you pansy-assed, people-fearing, Bible-licking, Tupperware dildos! It's time to make St. Paul the city of self-love! Make people proud to shake each other's hands! Jesus fucking shit, own up to it out there! Come right out and come! Bring masturbation out from under the sheets!

"Come on, Froehlich, start the ball rolling by starting your balls rolling! Let them hear you on the air! Americans will follow you. They love you, you egregious, smegma-faced twit! Come on, Froehlich, get that pubescent tumescence out on the table! Want some help?"

At this point, Philip lunged toward his aghast host, who tore himself away from his radio gear and fled, yelling, "Kill him, he's crazy!" There was minor pandemonium, and I did my best to calm Philip down and get him out of there before the police came. When I got him into the car, he was still breathing hard. And smiling. And then we both laughed hysterically.

That was Philip's masturbation speech, Lady Di. As he put it, he shot his wad right out on the air. That's only partially true, since the station operated on a three-second delay, and cut off the speech right after the "All right, fuckers" part, and that got out only because of an incompetent and, it was later revealed, doped-up technician. Sally and David were entertained even by that much, and they and many others called that night to find out what had happened. In fact, I think we unplugged the phone and wound down by watching dull movies on TV.

Dervishes

We gave a party the night of the election. Philip got 2278 votes, which was enigmatic in itself, because we realized that no one had considered how many votes he would, should, or might bring in.

The party was raucous. Everyone seemed frantic in their desire to have fun. We played the Froehlich tape a few times, and I have a dim recollection of our calling up people we didn't like—the list, Lady Di, was extensive—and playing the tape over the phone. Incidents that, during the campaign threatened to dislodge Philip's veins from his neck, now were reclassified to diverting little stories. Even Vince showed up, though no one remembered inviting him. He gave me a big hug and smile when he saw me, and I, remembering his earlier behaviors, patted him on his head and walked away. Philip drank Zinfandel, Sally quaffed endless cans of Grain Belt, David kept stoned on God-knows-what, and I had a little of everything, including the food that our friends potlucked. The party broke up in the mid-morning.

Somehow, with Zinfandel-and-guacamole clouds fuzzing out my brain, I made love with Philip that morning, and equally somehow, it was good. In fact, it was very good. Our relationship-in-the-nude had become erratic, symptomatic of the pressures of the primary. But that night/morning, the pressures were off, we were eager for each other, and we knew it. Di, there's just no better sex than when each of you is hungry for it, and each of you knows you're hungry for it. It was erotic, sensual, hard, gentle, powerful, protective, reassuring, lazy, wild. It was the radio speech, the campaign, the other-life lecture. It was our entire shared history compressed and reshaped into caresses and kisses and words of love and belonging. It was the messiness of hair in our mouths and the neatness of fitting our bodies to each other. It was sweating and gasping and moving together and holding tightly. It was losing ourselves in a bath of complete physical, emotional, and religious energy. Jesus, I can remember it today, Di, the fuck-as-communion.

The next day, as we rose late, showered together, and reluctantly cleaned up our apartment, a task commensurate with any of the labors of Hercules, I recall having some notion of "starting over." And as I picked my way through the living room in the eerie stillness, garbage bag in hand, I brought myself up and thought, hm, maybe I've finally admitted to myself that something has gone dreadfully wrong with this relationship.

I returned full-time to socialism and my dissertation, while Philip, refusing to ask for his old job back, despite Sally's assurance that she could "get him something," found work in a grocery store. During the next few months, he withdrew, never mentioning the campaign, but mumbling a lot, daydreaming, somewhere between pensive and comatose. We resumed a more normal pace, but our interactions with each other seemed superficial, as if there were nothing to fill the space where the campaign had been, and the lovemaking the night of the party had been with two different people.

The dissertation kept me mildly busy until December, mostly with administrative details. Then that too was over, and so were my orals, and the whole event was anticlimactic. I was a PhD, but I'd planned for it so long that when it finally came, I didn't feel anything but a minor closing of circuits. I was bored and post-partuming.

I sent out a few feelers for physics jobs, and one evening Philip and I talked about what we could do with our lives and where we'd like to do it. Given the possibilities of employment, given Philip's disgust with St. Paul, given our need for a change, and given our desires for a fairly progressive political atmosphere, we narrowed the choices down to San Francisco and Seattle, neither of which we'd even visited before. We thought that the San Francisco Bay Area might have more jobs, but the Pacific Northwest sounded more exotic, and living there would be cheaper. So Seattle won.

It was delicious being impulsive, Lady Di, and for once taking active control of our lives. Each of us had spent over twenty years in school, with everything planned—sixth grade after fifth, college after high school, graduate school after college. We'd gone where the education was. Now we were going where we wanted to go, an unknown city far away in the upper left-hand corner of the map. What accents did they have there? we wondered. What strange customs would we have to adapt to? Philip figured that we'd probably have to exchange our currency for dried bear dung.

I wasn't totally impulsive, of course. I did my homework, visiting both the library and a travel agency, and getting all the information I could about Seattle. I even wrote to the Chamber of Commerce, signed the letter Dr. Carolyn Anderson, and was deluged with brochures, real estate offers, and coupons for discounts at restaurants. "They're suspiciously eager," commented Philip. "Maybe we should send them some campaign literature and see if they still want us."

We were rejuvenated—for a while. But then we had to settle our bank accounts, utilities, and rent, and say good-bye to family and friends.

My folks put up a token struggle: "Seattle is so far away"; "We'll never get to see you"; "Are you sure about Philip?" and even, "Remember, there's always a place here for you," that being a time-bomb ploy, meant to take effect when things got rough on the West Coast. But, in general, they took the decision well and were stoic when we visited them in St. Cloud before returning to St. Paul and packing.

It felt odd to be leaving my Minnesota home, as odd as it felt when I first went to the big city as an undergraduate. I remember my parents dropping me off in the dorm, sticking around to make sure my roommate was a woman, and then leaving, my mother apprehensively. I remember the first taste of freedom, too, the first time I realized that I was on my own. There was a vending machine in the basement of the dorm, candy and such. I thought, I can use this machine any time I want. I could get five candy bars a day, if I desired. It was such a little thing, but it meant that no one was monitoring me.

"Take care of her, Philip," said my father, as we prepared to leave. "I hope she'll take care of me," said Philip as he got in the car, and the last thing I remember as I turned to wave good-bye was a typical American Gothic scene with the sole flaw in the picture being the puzzled frown on my father's face.

We drove back to St. Paul and paid our last visits to our friends. Sally and David helped us pack, and there was the usual nervous banter among friends who avoid saying what they really feel about each other.

Neal Starkman

Sally took me aside in the afternoon and gave me the oddest feeling, as if she thought she knew me better than *I* knew me. She cautioned me, counseled me, checked me out to make sure I was in a good frame of mind, did everything but take my pulse and temperature. David and I didn't talk. I promised that we'd be back to visit next Christmas.

The following morning, the Volvo bursting like an ass in tight jeans, we set out for the great Northwest. In addition to our necessities—clothes, kitchen utensils, books—I brought some campaign mementos—newspaper clippings, tapes, literature, a "Phil Can't Be Beat" button we attempted to distribute in a bowling alley, and a placard I couldn't resist buying for three dollars from an old man, which proclaimed "God Doesn't Abuse Himself." I was excited about our future and exhausted from our recent past. I dozed fitfully while Philip drove west and ruminated about dervishes. I tried to forget about the difficulties in our relationship and hoped that Philip, like me, would leave them behind us in Minnesota.

I just didn't read the signs.

2. THE THREE REASONS

I feel pressure, Lady Di, but it's so subtle, so vague, that I can't determine its source. I look to the obvious places—work; home, that is, Stephanie; family; health—and I see only the ordinary nettlesome forces acting upon me. Nothing powerful enough to cause this malaise, yet it's there. And, I fear, growing.

Steph obliquely suggests that you, Lady Di, are the cause. Yes, it's true. I know you'd rather hear it from me directly than find out by some embarrassing slip of the pen. She claims that I'm spending too much time in my heterosexual past and that I feel guilty about how I used to behave.

I should have suspected Stephanie was upset about my diarizing. Usually she gives me defined signals—when she's upset with me, when she's upset about something else, when she wants to talk, when she wants to fight. This time, though, I provoked a confrontation before she was ready for it.

I'd turned on an FM easy-listening station while making a pasta sauce for dinner. Steph's been working on a hotel ten minutes outside Seattle and gets home about six. This day, though, she bounded through the door an hour early, yelling, "Hooray for rain, hooray for rain"; depending on the job, finish carpenters sometimes bow to inclement weather. She glided into the kitchen, immediately took me in her arms, work jacket grimy-wet, and started to dance to the music. The next piece was slower, and she took off her jacket and we danced some more, holding each other close. Half an hour and six or seven dances later, onion and garlic still awaiting incisions, we parted with a long kiss. And spontaneous Carolyn, caught up in the act and not the person, blurted, "I'd never have done that with Philip." Stephanie visibly stiffened, even as I tried to leap forward and inhale the air containing the words. She said, "Carolyn, I don't care what you used to do with Philip. And you'd be a lot better off if you didn't, either."

God, what an idiot I am. There have been times in my academic career when I've been face-to-print with a long and complicated equation that I know is wrong, and I've tried to fix it by changing a number here, a function there. More often than not, though, the equation would become more convoluted, until I've had to discard it and begin anew. That's what I should have done with Stephanie, left her alone and begun anew another day. But I tried to correct the situation.

"No, Stephanie, I liked what we just did. It was beautiful."

"Compared to Philip."

"No, by itself. I wasn't even thinking of Philip."

"You just mentioned him."

"Yes, well, I did, but only in contrast. I mean, that's why I'm so comfortable with you. We can do things like this."

"But if you hadn't been treated like shit with Philip, you couldn't appreciate me, is that it?"

"No, Steph, please." I tried to hold her, but she retrieved her jacket.

"I've got to clean up."

Loose lips sink relationships.

Dervishes

I took a ponder walk to campus this morning. There won't be many days left to walk this year before it gets too cold. I'm spoiled; forty-eight degrees would be mild in Minnesota. Still, an hour's walk to the physics building—I walk slow—is just about right for these out-of-shape bones. Maybe Stephanie is right about my feeling guilty. But if that's true, then I still must examine those behaviors that cause the guilt. Exorcise those demons, girl!

I am one of four women professors out of forty-five professors in UW's Department of Physics. There's Dorothy Wu, who's a nuclear physicist, been there since 1960. There's Cynthia Wald, another nuclear physicist, but not as much a theoretician as Dorothy. And there's Mary Ann Simons.

Either despite or because of the fact she was born in China, Dorothy Wu has *overmastered* the English language: No one approaches her without brushing up on the dictionary the night before, and not a pocket version, either. Her head may look like it's connected to her body, but I'm sure that's an illusion. Dorothy is an extremely self-absorbed old lady, and someone told me once that she liked progressive jazz. Dr. Stan confided in me that she was an incurable paronomasiac, and I didn't even know what that meant, until one afternoon when I ran into her in the bathroom. She was running a comb through wisps of white, and it was obvious that the comb was not going to make anything stylish out of her hair; she just didn't have enough of it. She looked in the mirror, shook her head, and put her comb back in her purse. Chuckling at me, she said as she left, "Gilding the silly."

I don't get along with Cynthia Wald too well, though I've tried; she appears quite humorless, and I think she's crazy, too. She's rumored to drink a gallon of coffee and smoke two packs of cigarettes a day, non-filters. Cynthia looks like a hawk, walks like a reptile, and sometimes you can hear her muttering down the hall.

And then there's Mary Ann Simons. Mary Ann joined the department in condensed matter. She's like a kid sitting at the dinner table with the grown-ups for the first time. I do enjoy her. She brings a freshness, an innocence, to an otherwise jaded company. I talk to her often, and I can easily imagine her chewing gum and rocking to Dick Clark's American Bandstand.

I think I derive some power-pleasure from my relationship with Mary Ann. Got to think about that more, Lady Di. I seem to be able to affect her with very little effort. The first time I met her, I found myself feeding off the enthusiasm I had originally generated and fed to her. Enthusiasm warmed over.

She had visited me in my office, introduced herself, and asked what I "did here." I described some of my experiments with the helium, and she listened so attentively, so damn earnestly, that I began to get excited myself. Soon I found myself speechifying.

"It's miraculous, Mary Ann. You're alone in your laboratory, just you and the secrets of the substances you work with. Only *you* can unravel the mysteries, only *you* can find the patterns, it's as if you were battling with nature itself. Nothing else matters, Mary Ann. Politics, relationships, money—this is *basic*. Regardless of who's president, regardless of who your friends and lovers are, regardless of your bank account, this is the *basic stuff of life*. When I examine the matrices from a run, I stretch my mind as far as it will go. I ask myself, what am I seeing here? How can I decode the language? It's between the universe and me, a fight for truth and understanding. I can't explain that to you; you'll either find it out for yourself or you won't. I hope you do, because that's what makes this career so fulfilling."

Her eyes gleamed; God, I wasn't even embarrassed until hours later.

My office is somewhat larger than my kitchen at home, and the physics building itself is a four-floored variegated brick edifice, dark and hoary. From the outside, it's almost pristine, sitting among proud firs and shedding pines. There's a dancing fountain surrounded by hundreds of rosebushes that will make the spring and summer seem like a Crayola festival, and squirrels in their tree-condos playing hide-and-seek with oblivious passers-by, sometimes the lazy drone of a plane drowning in the gray sky, and always students—huddling over textbooks, dotting the lawns like giant mushrooms.

Inside the building, though, it is all business. The corridors are long and gloomy, the floors are hard. They combine with the stark walls and high ceiling to make common voices somber and authoritative ones absolutely magisterial. The bulletin boards are lifeless: Notices are doubtless screened to remove any hints of imagination or verve. Signs on closed doors attest to how seriously the building takes itself: "High Radiation," "Authorized Personnel," "Nuclear Reactor Room." I'm surprised the women's room isn't labeled "Caution: Female Lavatory Only." There is no laughter in the physics building; laughter would seem as out of place as ferns or children's finger paintings. From my tiny office window, I can see neither Mt. Rainier nor the Cascades nor the Olympics nor the fountain. I can see part of the walkway on the side of the building and about two hundred square feet of grass—my view of the passing parade. This is a sterile, bleak, definitely male building; if it were taller, it would be an ivory tower. As it is, it's an ivory tower without an erection.

But I am Dr. Carolyn Anderson, and, as such, certain perquisites fall to me. I am due prestige and respect and, given a comfortable niche in the hierarchy, power to influence and command. That's the trade-off, Lady Di, and for a woman it ain't bad. God help me, Di, I enjoy it. I don't revel in it, but I can understand how others do. My colleague Joe Bennett revels in it, as does Dr. Stan, each in his own way. Dr. Patricelli and his assholic buddies from Minnesota wallow in it, hogs in customized troughs.

The hierarchy hasn't helped me lately, though. I've worked with superfluid helium since I was a graduate student. Maybe I *should* look elsewhere for a job. Stephanie could find carpentry work elsewhere, though it's obvious from her change of attitude that she's not excited about either of us leaving Seattle. But at what price comes stability?

I took tea in the Union this morning—the walk was colder than I thought it would be, and I'd neglected to wear gloves. I considered the demons of the past and watched all the UW Husky students mill about, as once, years ago, I sat in the Minnesota Union and watched the UM Gopher students mill about. That time, I forced myself to drink coffee; that time, I tilted the academic seesaw and found that some power could slide to me. And a few months before I drank coffee in the Union, I had tea with Philip for the first time.

I was in my fourth year of graduate school at the time of the other-life lecture and was realizing that what I wanted to do for my dissertation would not wash with my adviser, Dr. Charles "Chuck" Patricelli. Had I been more foresighted, I would have attempted to develop a reputation as a maverick early on. But I'd been content to play cute and passive with my profs; they starved for a feminist education, and I fed them stereotypes. Even when I did assert myself with Patricelli, it was because my career was being compromised, not my womanhood.

When I first met Philip, I was discomfited only by what I saw as a purely academic conflict: I wanted to do one thing, and Patricelli wanted me to do another. I certainly had experienced sexism and certainly didn't like it, but so far it had hit me only in the head, not the vitals.

I think we had pizza, Philip and I, in Dinkytown, that little square of shops right off the UM campus. That's right, we had pizza, because on the way over, after we'd introduced ourselves, Philip told me about East Coast pizza. He said the best pizza in the world was in a place called Al Capone's in Boston. Funny what you remember. He tried to articulate what it was precisely about the pizza that made it so much better than any other kind. Something about the crust, the sauce, I don't know. Pizza is pizza to me.

Anyway, we were eating pizza and I was drinking tea, when we got into a discussion of my physics situation and all the professors in my department I didn't trust. I'm sure Patricelli was the primary focus of my ill-feeling, but there was also Borenson, and Scalwhi, and Kent, and others I've mercifully forgotten.

"Why do they lower their standards for you?" he asked, as I tried to eat the pizza non-slobbily. "I'd think they'd raise them if they didn't want you to succeed."

"Oh no, if they raised the standards and I failed, then I'd have cause for complaint. Besides, they don't lower the standards, really; they just make it seem like they're going out of their way for me. If I succeed, then it's because of their help. If I fail, then it's despite their help. They can say they did everything they could for me. I can't win."

"Why do you suppose they're doing that to you? What do they have to gain?"

"I don't know. Maybe they don't want women to be physicists."

"Why not?"

"I don't know. Tradition?"

"Hm. What kinds of things have they been doing to you?"

"Well—I can't even think of specific things. It's more of an attitude. You know, like I can't handle hard work. It's like—well, sure, they don't want me to do certain things I want to do, like for my dissertation—"

"Give me an example."

"Okay, except I'm not sure I can explain it non-technically."

"Try."

"All right. For the past six months, I've been working in cryogenics—freezing. Very low temperatures. I got a research assistantship with a professor who's working with liquid helium."

"Wait. It's liquid?"

"Yes, liquid helium. It's pretty exciting work. When helium is brought down to a really low temperature, called the lambda point—forget that, it's unimportant—when it gets really cold, like almost absolute zero, it does some things that no other substance does. It separates into regular helium and superfluid helium. I push the helium mixture through some plastic templates, and it turns out that the superfluid has very interesting properties. That's what I've been working with. Not many people have the skills to do what I'm doing."

"You should be proud."

"Well, the problem is that I'm not going to be able to do that work for my dissertation."

"Why not?"

"My adviser wants me to do the kinds of research he's been doing."

"Wait a minute. Your adviser is not the guy with the helium?"

"My adviser is the guy that wants me to run some electrospectroscopic analyses of semiconductors. Band structures, things like that. Very boring."

"I don't understand. Why don't you just tell your adviser that you'd prefer to work with the helium, like you're already doing?"

"Because you can't just up and tell your major adviser that you think his work is crap and you'd prefer doing something else. I've known him for years, and I'm sure his attitude is that I'm this cute little girl who gets good grades but will do as she's told."

"Sounds like you're in a bind."

"You know, I only have this year and maybe a little of next to finish. I'd really like to get out of this place without a major confrontation."

"But with a doctorate."

"Yes. And with references, too. But I don't know about that."

"You would think they'd want a woman to get a PhD; seems like it'd make the school look good. There can't be that many woman physicists."

"At this point I'm more concerned about me than the University of Minnesota."

Dervishes

"Understandable. I guess I have trouble internalizing the 'woman' thing, why they'd treat you differently from, say, me, if I were a physics student. But it seems to me that if you're getting shortchanged, then you should do something about it."

"I'm not used to complaining. I've never really done it much—it makes me too self-conscious. Why are you smiling?"

"Well, I'm doing *my* dissertation on complaining—why people do, why they don't. So when you talk about it, it sounds familiar."

"Tell me why people don't complain."

"Because they're too self-conscious. It came to me this instant, like an epiphany."

"Well, I expect to be mentioned prominently in the acknowledgments, if not the data."

"Data? Oh, that's right, you're a natural scientist. We psychologists rely more on what's known in the trade as 'gut instincts.'"

"I'll bet. Well, if you won't tell me why people don't complain, tell my why they do."

"I'll tell you why I used to think they complain. I used to think it was to achieve an objective, some goal; but the results haven't been bearing that out. Seems like even when people expect to fail, they'll still complain, if they feel that they should. They'll take a lot of shit if they think they're right. Believe it or not."

"Of course I believe it. You're the psychologist. What kind of psychologist are you, by the way? Or are you going to be."

"I'm in social psychology. You take away the clinicals—and you really should, they're all crazy—and the kid psych people and the animal psych people and the computer-memory psych people and the school- and loony-testing psych people, and what's left is the garbage area—social psychology."

"You look like a complainer. Are you?"

"Oh, sure. I wish people would complain more than they do. I get more pissed off at the person who doesn't complain about some injustice than I do at the perpetrator of the injustice. It's merely a matter of exercising independent judgment and then being sufficiently assertive to follow through on it."

"Easy for you to say. I guess you think I should complain to my adviser."

"Look, number one, you should complain because you're clearly miserable not complaining. Number two, you should complain so you can get to do the dissertation you want to do. And number three, you should complain just to get the hang of it. It's a useful skill."

"I don't even like to talk about it. Makes my stomach hurt."

"Maybe it's the pizza. Or the tea. Or the combination."

"It's probably the combination. You're not going to believe this, but I've never had pizza and tea together before."

"I don't believe that."

"Stop teasing me. Really, it's just that I wanted pizza, and I also like tea—I've never drunk coffee—so it seemed logical to have both. I mean, there's no reason why your beer should be more appropriate than my tea. Beer is grain, tea is herb. Not much difference."

"Convince your stomach, not me."

"Why did you do that back there?"

"Because he was bullshitting us."

"Do you know what I'm asking you?"

"Sure, you want to know why I told that monkey I was a connecting rod in a 1953 Chevy."

"That's right. I'd forgotten the car part."

"It's the only car part I know, other than the motor, and I'm not even positive about that. Listen, the guy was a fraud. One of my rules of life: 'Thou shalt not tolerate bullshit, but shall promulgate it when necessary.'"

"How do you know he was bullshitting us?"

"It takes one to know one, I guess."

"You're pretty sure of yourself. I wish I were that sure of myself."

"I'm only sure of myself in some areas. I'm shy around women."

"You don't—well, maybe you are."

"I haven't 'put the moves' on you, have I?"

"You asked me out for coffee, which ended up pizza."

"That's hardly a seduction. Besides, I did it for your sake. I knew your curiosity had to be allayed about why I disrupted the class."

"Oh, thank you, kind sir. What a gallant gesture."

"And you also looked like the kind of person who didn't know about East Coast pizza. When you come right down to it, I really had little choice."

"I guess not; I guess you were just forced into it."

"I agree with your professor about one thing, though."

"What's that?"

"You are cute."

Yeah, real cute. I think that's a reasonable copy of the actual conversation, Di, and I see myself talking and talking, and Philip answering questions and giving advice. I'm deferent and self-revealing and, dammit all, cute. Philip, meanwhile, controls the conversation like an interview and allows himself to be charming.

And what can I say? It worked. I was charmed. Philip was bright, energetic, self-assured, and, to top it all off, attracted to me, which meant he was discerning as well. And he was so moral that he'd developed his own formal Rules of Life:

1. Thou shalt not be intimated by anyone.

2. Thou shalt not tolerate bullshit, but shall promulgate it when necessary.

3. Thou shalt not hold anything sacred.

4. Thou shalt not be stupid.

I learned more about Philip Lester those first few months we went out: he was raised in Boston and got his BA at the University of Massachusetts in Amherst; his father was a big-city type, but Philip tried to "mellow out" like his small-town mother, hence his decision to go to graduate school in the blasé Midwest; he'd debated as an undergraduate; he fancied impressionist art and had even painted for a few years before he gave it up as "too self-indulgent"; his political leanings were leftist (he didn't trust people enough, he said, to be an anarchist), and he'd been depressed that the marches didn't have any effect on the Vietnam War; he was raised Jewish, but considered himself a "devout agnostic"; he had an eccentric sense of humor that often alienated people; he had few friends and no current lovers; he wore sweaters and vests to hide his paunch; and he was shy around women, until he was in bed with them.

Philip in bed was a study in what might be called quantum psychology. I think that with most people you become sexual with, you can see a gradual, fairly smooth increase in their energy, their interest, their physical expressions of that interest. You develop a relationship with them in bed like you would out of bed. First a little of this, then a little of that, some tentative intimacy here, more there, until you reach the level at which you're the most comfortable. It may be fast or slow, but you ascend a ramp together.

Not so with Philip. We'd be at one level, and then all of a sudden we were quite a bit higher, or at least he was. It was as if he were ascending the ramp in his mind, but only let me in on the progression at discrete, unpredicted intervals. So, for example, we might be in bed kissing lightly, and the next thing I knew he would be holding on to me like a tongue to an icicle. That would last for an indeterminate amount of time, and soon he would be near the bottom of the ramp again. I needed a course in intimacy.

Who knows what draws one to another? That an emotional insecurity belied his arrogance I found touching; like a mother, I cared for him, soothed his soul, crap like that. Or maybe it was his power; I was able to break through his intellectual hymen, touch his vulnerability. Or maybe it was my own insecurity: Philip had qualities I'd always been taught were admirable in men and consequently had never fostered in myself—confidence, articulateness, forcefulness. But Carolyn, you say, that's no reason to love someone; that's reason, perhaps, to need someone. I should bronze my insights.

Stephanie and I went to a ballet last night. I love ballet. Stephanie hates it. She traded the ballet for a country-western singer—I don't even know who she is—who'll be at the Women's Coffeehouse next month. I dread it. I am amazed that tickets for the singer cost nearly twice as much as tickets for the ballet. However, Stephanie says that the singer's performance is a benefit for a women's group in Chile.

After a year and a half, I'm really quite comfortable with Stephanie, excepting those times she coerces me into jumping with her. Sometimes I forget that I do feel pressure. Oh, she's been giving me reproving looks when I go into the bedroom or curl into a corner with you, Lady Di, but that's only minor jealousy. It's kind of sweet, actually. You're the other woman. But since I've been more discreet about it, our life is smoother, and I'm careful not to mention Philip. Why is it, then, that I feel pushed, squeezed? My professors back in Minnesota would have assumed it was my period. "Oh, Carolyn, of course you're upset. I understand perfectly. Don't worry about a thing." Assholes. I still flame up when I think of them.

Charles "Chuck" Patricelli. I could never bring myself to call him "Chuck," though he told me often enough, "Carolyn, I don't go in for this 'Dr.' title. Let's consider ourselves friends, partners. 'Chuck.' Okay?"

Sure. Good old "Chuck." I couldn't call him "Dr. Patricelli" after that; it would have been considered a rebuke. So I never called him anything at all. You know, you can do that; you can avoid addressing a person by his name. The only problem was when he was walking away from me down the hall and I needed to get his attention. I had to run up to him and start the conversation as nonchalantly as I could, between hyperventilations. I did that for years. Mostly, though, I avoided seeing him at all.

I do feel some guilt about initially knuckling under. But I really wasn't different from any other graduate student. We all lived in perpetual fear that the Big Bad Major Adviser would one day say, "No, I don't think you should do this for your dissertation." Or, worse: "Yes, those three years of research are commendable, and this fifteen-hundred-page report with all the analyses and charts and graphs seems to indicate a knowledge of the subject, but unfortunately I can't accept it. Let's start over, shall we?"

We were of different species, Charles Patricelli and I. Maybe the sperm hit the egg backwards or something. He was a willing participant in the system, a bulwark of the status quo. He saw the right people, went to the right parties, toed the right lines, and kissed the right asses. I first met him as an undergraduate, when he gave a lecture at Macalester, and he eventually helped me get accepted at the U of M. Naturally, I felt obligated to him.

It was that obligation, that loyalty, that bound me to him the first three years. I taught his labs, graded his students' papers, ran his experiments, and brainstormed with him on various condensed-matter problems. In return, I received teaching assistantships, second-author mention on two articles, and a certain measure, I suppose, of prestige and respectability. I wasn't just any graduate student.

The summer before my fourth year, I broke away. It was purely financial. Dr. Kent had a research assistantship open, and Patricelli had nothing for the summer. Kent was a nervous, older professor who didn't like people or sloppiness, and he'd been working in the cryogenics lab by himself for years; only lately had he admitted to himself that he needed an aide for some of the more delicate work—adjusting temperature levels, lowering the helium Dewar into a liquid-nitrogen bath to initiate the temperature plunge, even detecting malfunctions in diffusion pumps. His mind was still sharp, but he could no longer handle the lab work. That's where I came in.

It was interesting work. I became fascinated with all the strange equipment, the extreme of temperature, the theoretical structure upon which the behavior of the helium was based. It was a lot more engrossing than altering silicon five hundred ways to see what effect each new combination had on its electronic band structure, which was what Patricelli had in mind for me.

The problem, Lady Di, was that I never told Patricelli what I wanted. It's not easy to tell someone to whom you feel indebted that you don't want to work with him anymore, that you find his work dull, and that you don't want him to sponsor you for your doctoral dissertation. It's like studying for years under one piano teacher, then bringing on another one to prepare you for your concert at Carnegie Hall.

Tense times, Di. I'd meet with Patricelli, try to guide the conversation into helium, and helplessly listen to it veer back into semiconductors. I'd refer to what I was doing, he'd refer to what he assumed I would be doing the following year, and I'd leave, hoping he would be swallowed up by some terrestrial disturbance and never be heard from again.

I was nearing the time when I'd have to commit myself and order materials, let Kent know that I wanted to continue working with him—that was no obstacle—and face up to this man who intimidated me so much I couldn't even call him by his first name. So one frigid white day in late winter, I steeled myself with a bowl of Quaker's Oats in the morning and a vagina of Philip's semen the night before, and marched up to Patricelli's office. I had committed to memory seventeen different speeches, any of which would mesmerize my adviser into complete acquiescence to whatever I requested. Unfortunately, I forgot all but two of them on the bus ride over to campus and discarded those as I walked to the physics building. Even so, I felt confident when I reached Patricelli's office. I'd prepared my courage boosters, too: I had every right to switch research topics, as well as advisers; people in the department changed their minds all the time; Patricelli probably didn't care what I did, anyway. I didn't believe any of these, of course, but they were something to fall back on.

I stood by Patricelli's closed door five minutes before our appointment, supremely poised. But the crudball was ten minutes late, and that was just enough time to fall apart and feel nauseated. By the time he finally waltzed in, even the butterflies in my stomach were puking their tiny guts out.

"Hi, Carolyn, how are you this morning? Come on in, hang your coat up. What's on your mind?"

He sat behind the professor's desk, in a tilt-back easy chair; I positioned myself on the only alternative, a straight-back in front and to the side of the desk, where I could be reminded of his eminence by facing the shelves burgeoning with books and journals. Patricelli was festooned in a tan polyester suit and a tie emblazoned with purple letters that spelled out "PHYSICS" from northwest to southeast; I wore a high-necked black sweater (and the requisite bra for official appointments – female profs, rare and old-schooled, sneered at you, and male profs leered at you, as if by staring at your breasts they could will the nipples to rise) and blue jeans. His hair was short, greased, silver-streaked, and fashionably sideburned, for a forty-five-year-old man; mine was medium length, medium-combed, brown-streaked, and not fashionable for any age. He wore smiles as some people wear hats—no matter what kind they wear or how often they wear them, they never look quite natural in them; my upper lip kept faithful time with the quiver in my voice. Patricelli clasped his hands behind his head as he tilted back and crossed his legs; I clasped my hands around my left knee, then around my right knee, later around one of my ankles, behind my head, around parts of the chair. If I'd had other limbs, I would have clasped my hands around them. I think "Chuck" sensed my anxiety; he smirked.

"I wanted to talk to you about my dissertation," I said, and then added for no reason at all, "the weather's ready for it."

Patricelli must have been used to nervous students saying dumb things, for he picked up on the comment as if it weren't inane in the slightest.

"Yes, bundle-up weather. I was telling my wife just this morning that I think she should shovel the snow in the front of the house while I stay by the warm oven and cook dinner."

"Sounds like a good deal," I joked along with him.

"When I was in the army, I used to cook," he continued, while I fought off the urge to nod. "God, it was awful stuff. But you eat anything in the army. You don't always hold it down, but you eat it."

Pause. Silence. Smiles. Was it my turn to speak now? I didn't have any army stories.

"So, Carolyn, what *about* your dissertation? You haven't had any trouble obtaining silicon, have you?"

Deep breath. "Sir, I don't want to seem ungrateful or anything, but what I wanted to talk to you about was not doing the spectroscopic analyses for my dissertation. I've thought about it a lot these few m—"

"Do you have another analysis in mind, Carolyn?" He faded his smile into a condescending grimace as smoothly as if he'd exchanged his derby for a homburg.

"No, what I mean is, I'm not sure I want to do that at all. Any of the, uh, semiconductors."

"Is there something wrong? Something I can help you with? You do still want to write a dissertation and get your degree, don't you?"

"Oh, yes, of course!"

"Good. Because you're capable of doing it, Carolyn. You're a diligent student and a competent writer. You'll be able to make it through."

"Oh, I know I can make it through, I mean, I feel confident about that, it's just that I don't want to work with semiconductors anymore. I like it, I mean, it's all right, but I feel I, I think I'd rather work with what I've been doing since the summer, you know, with Dr. Kent and the helium—"

Patricelli shook his head and folded his arms across his chest.

"Carolyn, I really think that Wilbur's work is not for you. Don't be misled by a little summer assignment. You really don't have the background for cryogenic research. It's a whole other area from which you've been trained in. People spend years and years just learning the basics. Dr. Kent is what—sixty? Sixty-five? You'll spend the rest of your life watching chemicals freeze into blocks of ice."

"No, it d—"

"Carolyn, it doesn't lead anywhere. Come on"—back came the derby—"we've discussed the industrial implications of the spectroscopy. You'll write your own ticket after you get out of here."

"Sir, I appreciate that. But I'm not—this liquid helium behaves in a really fascinating way. I can show you some of the printouts—"

"Carolyn." I should have known better than to try to infect him with my enthusiasm. He was immune, and now he leaned forward for the lecture. He was shaking his head again, too. "It's one thing to be interested in your work. That's very important, and I can see you feel that way about your helium experiments for Dr. Kent. But, Carolyn, interest doesn't last. It's like being infatuated. You know how you feel when you first meet a good-looking guy. You overlook a lot of crucial details."

"Details?"

"About the work. You've been trained for years to do the type of work we've been doing. You've gotten published twice already because of your work under me." Stab. "And I think your dissertation would have an exceptionally fine chance of being published, especially under my aegis."

"But, sir, if I'm not interested in it, it seems silly for me even to write my dissertation, much less try to get it published." Bad move. He pulled me off center.

"Well, wait, Carolyn—" laughing like his dog farted—"I don't guarantee a publication. I haven't got *that* much pull. But I'll tell you—" Lady Di, at that point, he actually waved a finger at me—"I've been around long enough to see a lot of graduate students come and go. There have been others, there have been some who've come to me while writing their dissertation and said, 'This is boring, I can't do it anymore.' Or 'This is getting too hard, I can't do it.' I had a young man a few years ago who dropped out, with only about three months' work left. He couldn't take it.

"But what I'm saying, Carolyn, is that they've changed their minds. They've been good students, like you. Except for that man, who had other problems—personal problems—they've come back. I talked to them just as I'm talking to you.

"The key is seriousness. Are you really serious about becoming a physicist? If you're not, if you're not prepared for the hard work and the daily grind—because I won't kid you, Carolyn, it'll be hard work—then I advise you to pull out now and save yourself a lot of disappointment. It's no shame to drop out of a doctoral program, you know. A lot of women even decide that what they really want is to raise a family, you know, and—"

"But I want to do the dissertation; that's not the question. I've worked with Dr. Kent for almost eight months now. I'm not being...flighty. I probably should have talked to you sooner, but—"

Neal Starkman

"Well, I think you should have talked to me sooner for your own sake; you wouldn't have been so upset." I hadn't realized I *was* upset. "But look, Carolyn, both the department and I know what kind of work you're capable of doing. Your work reflects on the entire department, all of us. Don't let us down." Bringing in the big guns.

Lady Di, I hate to think of this next part, but I suppose exorcisms are never easy. Oh God, I'll never be able to let Steph read this now. He rose from his chair, came around his desk to my side, knelt so that he was approximately eye level with me, and put his arm—Christ—around my shoulders. I couldn't meet his gaze; I kept looking toward his desk, as if he were still sitting there. I was petrified; he was close enough to kiss me.

"Carolyn," he said, oh so sincerely, "you and I have always had a good working relationship. I'm asking you to trust me—based on my experience, my knowledge—trust me that you'll be doing work in an area that you may not be particularly fond of now, but that I'm certain you'll eventually realize was the best choice. I bet that within three months you'll be bouncing in here thrilled to the marrow about an analysis and I'll have to kick you out. How about it?" And he gave me a squeeze on the shoulder.

"Well, I don't know. Maybe I could see Dr. K—"

"Look"—business again, rising, returning to his desk to show me he was a friend to a point and that point had been reached—"I don't know what more I can say as your adviser. It's your decision, Carolyn, but I think you'll have to agree with me after you've seriously considered the alternatives." He glanced demonstratively at his watch. "I've got another appointment soon. Why don't you think about our discussion (!), and if you're still unhappy, we can talk about it sometime later in the week. But really, Carolyn, I don't think there's that much more to say, except that I'll put in an order for materials for you, if you can get me a list. By the way, I think you look very pretty with your hair like that. Did you do something to it?"

I had a cup of coffee. I remember that, Lady Di. I went to the Union and bought a cup of black coffee, sat down at a table, and forced myself to drink. I hate coffee, and I thought if I drank something I hated, my physical feelings would come into line with my mental feelings; it seemed important at the time.

It was a foul brew, and I tried to associate its taste with my experience in Patricelli's office. What had I done? More appropriately, what *hadn't* I done?

I reran the conversation, rationalizing. Patricelli was probably right; in the long run, I *would* tire of the cryogenics research. And there *was* a more secure future for me in semiconductors. I could work for any number of companies. I'd have a doctorate, a comfortable salary, a job as long as I'd want it.

More coffee. God, how can anyone drink that? The advantages of heeding Patricelli's advice were considerable. Then why did I feel so awful? I had lost an argument, true; but I wasn't so petty that I would begrudge someone besting me in an argument. Besides, I didn't have the perspective Patricelli did, with dozens of graduate students over the years seeking his counsel.

I sat and mulled and sipped, while around me students ate, laughed, studied, talked. Several joined me at the table. In a few minutes I got up and returned with another cup of coffee. I realized I was trying to convince myself that everything was okay, when it clearly wasn't. Why did I need convincing? What wasn't okay?

Well, I hadn't been respected. No, too general. What made me feel not respected? Patricelli hadn't listened to me. He hadn't considered me. He'd already made up his mind.

Well, what's wrong with that? He's decisive. Coffee. He's only doing his job. He's my adviser and he's looking out for me. He's advising me; he's giving me the benefit of his experience. That's what advisers are for.

Was there any case, I thought, in which I ought to get my own way? What was a situation in which he should say, "All right, Carolyn, do it your way"?

Neal Starkman

Suppose I decided to marry Philip. He'd have no influence over that. Of course not. Why should he? That's not in the purview of his job. More coffee. There was something I was overlooking, even though it was right there. Just like Heisenberg: Every time you focus on something, you alter it; it's not there anymore. What was wrong with me? Why couldn't I think?

And that was it, Lady Di. That was precisely it. There was nothing wrong with me, and I *could* think. But Patricelli wasn't letting me think. That's what was wrong—Patricelli was denying me my judgment; he was thinking for me. I knew me better than he did. Why should he tell me what to do with my future? He shouldn't!

I took a large, triumphant, eureka! swig of coffee, forgetting it was coffee, and yelled, "Aaaughh!" so loudly that the students at my table looked up from their sandwiches and books to see if I was all right. I shuddered the memory of the taste out of my system and continued to reason out my unsettledness, which was slowly changing into something else: anger.

Patricelli had said, in effect, "Carolyn, I am better than you are. Not only do I know what's good for me, but I also know what's good for you. I'm taking responsibility for you, Carolyn. I'm not even going to credit your arguments. I don't have to." I confirmed every bit of his perceptions of me as a silly little girl who needed an older man to tell her what to do with her life.

I steamed back to the physics building. I hadn't even planned what to do when I got there, but I recognized I was angry, and I wanted to keep myself that way. I should have brought a container of coffee with me. I retraced my steps to Patricelli's door and pounded on it. The secretary in the main office told me he was meeting with Dr. Owens, and asked if I would like to leave a message.

Owens's office was around the corner, so around the corner I went. I'd lost the lovely effect of seeing my breath in front of me outside but maintained enough fury to pound on Owens's door.

"Yes?"

I flung open the door and hoped my glare was insufficiently menacing. Owens was behind his desk, and Patricelli was in a straight back chair. The sense of private kingdoms was gripping.

"I'd like to speak to Dr. Patricelli."

"Carolyn, I'm in a meeting right now. Could you wait until tomorrow, or maybe later today?"

"It's important." Oh, Di, it's hard for a woman my size to project strength, but I iced up my blues and tried to freeze Patricelli where he sat. At that moment I wanted more than a dissertation choice; I wanted revenge.

"Do you need me to sign something?" he asked, his indifference provoking me even further.

"I want to speak to you. I believe you have treated me poorly, and I want to talk to you about it—here or in your office."

I must have given the impression I wasn't kidding. Patricelli gave one of those "Women!" shrugs to Owens, who in turn commiserated with a shrug of his own. Why is it that women never shrug? Maybe they don't get the opportunity to be patronizing. Or matronizing. Patricelli excused us and escorted me by the arm—rather roughly, I thought—back to his office and shut the door behind us.

"Carolyn, I assume this is important." And he sat down in his easy chair. This time, though, I was smart. I remained standing, directly over his desk, where I paused for a second to recall the humiliation, the demeaning position he had put me in not an hour earlier. I was shaking and pointed down at him like a grand inquisitor.

"You have treated me like shit!" The profanity surprised both of us. I half expected the "PHYSICS" letters on his tie to jump off and hide under the desk.

"You have treated me like a little girl without a brain in her head. I am not a little girl, Dr. Patricelli. I'm an intelligent, competent woman who is capable of making her own decisions about her own future. And that includes choosing a topic for my dissertation. I cannot believe that I sat in here and let you run my mind for me."

"C—"

"Let me finish. I honestly appreciate all the support you've given me since I've been here, but I am not a dummy. I am not your stereotypical 'girl' who is capable of only the most mundane research and needs to lean on older, more 'experienced' men to achieve any amount of success. I intend to ask Dr. Kent to sponsor my dissertation, and I am quite certain he will agree. And maybe I'll even get a publication out of it, but it won't be under anyone's 'aegis.'

"You know, at first I tried to accept what you said to me. I thought, Dr. Patricelli's only doing his job; I must be overreacting. But I'm not overreacting. Maybe I led you on to think you could get away with making decisions for me, and if I did, I regret that more than you can possibly imagine. But that's it. I'm sorry, Dr. Patricelli, really sorry, but I have taken all the horseshit I'm going to take!"

I must have been close to tears by that time, which was unfortunate, but also close to foam, because Patricelli was visibly upset himself, and I noticed with satisfaction that he had begun to clasp and unclasp *his* hands in various positions. He started to rise from his chair, reevaluated, and played with a paper clip instead.

"Are you finished?"

"Yes."

"First, let me say that there's no need to get upset. Why don't you sit down?"

I remained where I was.

"All right. Look, I don't know what's caused all this, Carolyn. This outburst has certainly taken me by surprise. An hour ago I thought everything was fine between us. Apparently, something happened during the past hour to cause you to react this way, or else you've been keeping things from me. Maybe you've got some other concern on your mind that you don't want me to know about. That's fine, that's fine. Let me suggest, right off the bat, that you consider taking a break, a short leave of absence—"

"I don't need a leave of absence."

"All right then. There's no call to be rude. I have no wish to see you hurt, academically or otherwise. And I'm willing to forget this scene because we go back so far. Maybe when you cool down you'll think differently about this." He tried to lean back in his chair, but he jerked backward and then brought himself to the original position.

"Now, about your dissertation. I would suggest, of course, that you come back in a week and we'll discuss this again, but you don't seem to be in the mood to accept that. Tell you what I'll do, Carolyn. The decision is yours, as I thought I made clear this morning. Evidently, our communication has been off. But tomorrow I'll call Dr. Kent, and we'll—"

"No. I'll speak to Dr. Kent myself. Today. I'm not asking you for permission, Dr. Patricelli. I'm expressing my anger."

"So I see. Is there anything further you would like me to do? Do you want me on your committee at all?"

He was trying to sweet-talk me, and I had to get out of there before my anger evanesced into mere petulance.

"Look, Dr. Patricelli, obviously I'm upset now. I'm sure, as you say, I'll feel a little differently later, and later we can discuss other stuff. But right now I'm telling you that I resent your patronizing me and that I'm going to work with Dr. Kent on the superfluid helium. Thank you for listening to me."

Neal Starkman

And I huffed away, leaving the door and Patricelli's mouth open. I went home and called Dr. Kent, and he agreed to be my dissertation adviser. Of course he turned out to be almost as much of a bastard as Patricelli. But at least I *chose* this bastard, and he never asked me to call him by his first name, which is lucky for me, because Wilbur is a silly name, and I would have smiled too much saying it.

This must all seem rather melodramatic to you, Lady Di, but it was one of the few times your faithful inscriber has ever lost her sense of propriety. I retreated to my safe apartment and collapsed into a bubble bath, rare for me, but I needed to be immobile. Philip, who by that time was living more at my rundown apartment than at his rundown apartment, came in while I was soaking. Always taking a keen interest in my assertive behaviors, he asked me what happened. I was never certain to what extent he was interested in me and to what extent he was gleaning information for his dissertation, but I traded the story for a sponge on the back, dramatizing it, I'm sure, Lady Di, as I have for you.

When I was robed and we were sitting in the living room with hot chocolate and popcorn, Philip played counselor.

"How'd you feel after you told him off?"

"Um, relieved, justified, oh, uplifted. I don't know, not as angry. Philip, are you going to use me for your dissertation?"

"No, I'm just interested in what happened between the time you let him run over you and the time you ran over him. What changed? What made you do it?"

"I told you, I got really angry. It wasn't only the dissertation, it was personal. It started out being academic, but then it was much more. I just couldn't stand the idea of that crumb thinking he could take responsibility for me. And I'd been so damned frustrated! Every time I'd try to say something, he'd interrupt. He'd do my thinking *and* my talking for me. I felt as if I'd let myself down, and the only way to make up for it was to go back."

That's what I told Philip back in 1975. If he were here now, more than five years later, I would tell him how difficult it is to challenge an authority figure when you're taught your whole life to accept authority figures unquestioningly. I would tell him how powerless you feel when you're physically smaller and weaker than most other adults and many adolescents. I would tell him how, no matter how brave and confident you are intellectually, there's still an underlying fear that characterizes any confrontations you have with men. And it's not fear; it's Fear—made up of smaller fears: fears of your father, your friends, your teachers, your employers, strangers on the street, students in class, colleagues in the department, even your lovers, all the fears of what they could do to you with their hands, their penises, all the violence that you know is potentially in all of us but that could hurt you and kill you if you happened to incite it in them. And I would have told him about a few fears you have as a youth, the fear of the White-Bearded One and His Holy Son, so just in case the tangible fears of men were insufficient, there was that metaphysical fear of a Great Man in the sky who always controlled you and who could always punish you. And the worst part of it was, you would deserve it.

But I didn't tell Philip any of that then, because I didn't understand myself how any of those things affected my interactions with men like Patricelli and like Philip. Instead, I told him what he wanted to hear about complaining and exercising my independent judgment. He seemed genuinely pleased with my assertiveness; in those days, it wasn't a threat.

"Have I ever told you about Lester's Law?" he asked.

"Is it like your rules?"

"No, the rules are behavioral norms. Lester's Law has to do with a universal phenomenon. I was thinking of it because of your difficulty today in arguing your case—the first time."

"This is an arguing law?"

"Yeah, I guess it is. Lester's Law is simply this: There are always three reasons for everything. At least three. They're out there somewhere, and all you have to do is find them."

Well, Lady Di, I must admit that I have attempted to use Philip's technique on occasion, though I'm much more successful with it when I write than when I speak. Lester's Law does have a certain elegance and utility. You don't really need to know much about what you're arguing. You use three arbitrary but pertinent reasons for what you want to do until you can think of a really decent one.

I could have said, "Look, 'Chuck,' there are three reasons I should write my dissertation on superfluid helium. First, I'm interested in it, and I'll do a better job on something I'm interested in than on something that bores me. Second, I have new ideas about the subject, and my work will contribute to the literature. And third, since Dr. Kent is old and I am the only other one in the university working in this area, my work will increase the breadth and enhance the reputation of the department, making you, as my former major adviser, look good."

The fact that the reasons are ordered conveys the notion of validity, you see. Philip also maintained that, should you come up with only two reasons and find yourself struggling with the third, you should say, "Third and most important," and that will motivate you in a hurry to think of the third reason. That part's a little scary for me, and I do it only with undergraduates, who'll believe anything I say, anyway.

Philip wanted to be sure I understood.

"Tell me why baby-killing is good."

"What?"

"Tell me why baby-killing is good. It's a test; give me three reasons it's good to kill babies."

"Philip, that's awful. Choose something else."

"Oh, it's okay, a little macabre, maybe, but it'll be a good test. Go ahead."

"Do I have to?" Wimpy Carolyn, reverting so soon after her triumph at the Chuck roast.

"No, of course not. You don't have to do anything."

"Oh, all right. Let's see. Okay, first of all, it keeps the population down. That's the first reason."

"Good, that's plausible."

"Uh, second of all, it, uh, it feels good."

"No, I won't accept that."

"Why not? That's legitimate. It feels good for me to go around killing babies."

"No, that's tautological. You're saying, 'It's good because it feels good.' Come on, you can do better than that."

"This is ridiculous. All right, all right, second of all. Ah! Second of all, there are plenty of unwanted babies, and this would eliminate many of them. I assume we're not getting rid of all the babies."

"Right, only one out of three. Excellent, one more to go, the most important."

"Do you know what it is?"

"No, but it's bound to be the most important."

"I don't know if I can think of any more. I've had a pretty rough day, you know."

"Try."

"Make it worth my while."

"Well, I'm working from two until five. I can take you out tonight."

"How about you're my sexual slave for a week?"

"How about I'm your sexual slave for half an hour?"

"All right, half an hour."

"Half an hour."

"Okay, the third and most important reason for killing babies, for killing one out of three babies is…uh, is this a regular policy, like by the government, or is it just me going around with a machete or something?"

"It's a regular policy. It came down from the feds. And they don't use machetes. You just throw the kids out with the garbage. The truck compactor does the rest."

"Oh, stop it, that's disgusting!"

"And a machete isn't?"

"Okay, how about this? If certain babies are killed, then the ones remaining will be loved more by their parents, and they'll grow up with a feeling of destiny and self-worth, knowing they were spared in infancy."

"Fantastic! See how easy that was? If you can come up with three quasi-plausible reasons for killing babies, just imagine what you can do with more, uh, grounded issues."

I'm a little embarrassed to tell you what I had Philip do as my slave, Di, but I won't hold anything back from you. I read aloud an article about superfluid helium while Philip, uh, administered, uh, oral favors. I thought the combination would be provocative, but I think it was more bizarre than provocative. Anyway, Philip didn't mind.

Back then, Philip and I really did get on well together, which was fortunate, since not many people got along with us. I emphasize the "us." A few of Philip's friends, I know, thought I was immature. And for many of my friends, Philip was much too unconventional. We lost a lot of friends when we began *us-ing*.

But we didn't need a lot of friends then. We complemented each other nicely. Both of us had analytical minds, but mine was more ordered, while Philip's was more creative. Both of us grew up without siblings, but my parents strove to impress me with the value of playing with other children; Philip said his parents taught him to rely on himself for fun. The lessons stayed with each of us: I learned to live with people, and Philip learned to live despite them.

My parents' feelings about Philip were truly obscure. First of all, they only experienced a watered-down version of my lover, since I threatened to leave him if he embarrassed me in front of them. Second of all, the communication between my parents and me has never been—shall we say—optimum, so I'm not really sure what they thought of him. And third of all, and the most important—how's that, Di—I'm not sure *they* were even sure what they thought of him.

My mother's eyes full-mooned when she first glimpsed Philip. We drove out the forty miles to St. Cloud for Thanksgiving, 1974. She had no doubt been standing by the front window for the worst part of a day waiting for us to arrive. Philip's Volvo sputtered into the driveway behind the Anderson Impala, we walked from the car to the open door where my mother was trying to smile, and I could almost hear her swallow.

I had brought boyfriends home before, but they just did not look like Philip. They weren't bearded, nor Semitic, nor large. My mother, at five-foot-one, took it well. "You're tall," she said, bravely offering her hand as if she'd never get it back. My father—you should know, Lady Di—is six feet, but then my father doesn't date me.

Being good, stolid Norwegian, and good, decorum-conscious German respectively, my father and mother exchanged pleasantries with Philip and thought they were making him feel right at home. They welcomed him, asked him how the trip was, commented about the weather, and my father asked him if he wanted a drink, the initial test of his masculinity.

Neal Starkman

Meanwhile, I sweated and ground my pearlies and wished I were on another planet.

Lady Di, I didn't know when Philip would begin playing outrageous. This was almost a year before the masturbation campaign, but I knew Philip well enough to be extremely nervous. After all, my father is a minister, susceptible to fits of sermonizing. The parameters of his understanding do not leave one breathless. Philip promised me that he'd be on his best behavior, and that satisfied me until I realized too late that I didn't know what Philip's best behavior *was*. And when I realized that, suddenly the universe was wide open.

My parents have lived in the same two-bedroom house for twenty-two years; they lived in another one about five miles away for twelve years before that. Pop has had the same congregation for eleven years. So you see, they're not dynamic folks. My father and mother are happy in their little community, and they've made a nice, warm, middle-class home there. Our house has a nice warm fireplace, a nice warm Sears couch and loveseat set, a nice warm leather recline chair in which my father reads the newspaper, and a nice warm kitchen in which my mother toils. If *Reader's Digest* ever held a contest for the "Home of the Year," I'd send in photographs of my folks' place in St. Cloud.

A few of my cousins were due to arrive, and Mom, Pop, Philip, and I were drinking Tom and Jerry's in the living room. Dad kept talking about the Minnesota Vikings, and Mom subtly tried to pump Philip for information.

"Did you say you came from New York, Philip?" she asked, even though she had already extracted that information from me on the phone. Philip and I hadn't moved in yet, but it was obvious to both of my parents that he was someone special.

"No, I'm from Boston. Ever been out there?"

"Do you go to Celtics games?" asked my father. "Boy, that team is fun to watch, isn't it?"

At this point, my father and Philip entered into a technical discussion about the merits and demerits of various basketball teams, leaving my mother and me sipping our Tom and Jerry's—mine with rum and my mother's without, but with extra cinnamon. I don't remember any of their conversation because I didn't ingest any of it in the first place. I was startled that Philip knew as much as he seemed to know about basketball—unless he was bullshitting.

My mother put up with this man talk for a few minutes, then, undaunted, burst in where she left off.

"I've never been out to the East, I'm afraid. Minnesota-born and -bred. Are your parents from out there originally, Philip?"

"My father's from Boston, and my mother is from Clarion, Pennsylvania. It's a small town near Pittsburgh."

"They must like it in Boston."

"I guess they do. New England is real pretty, especially in the fall. Boston turns all different kinds of colors. You should see it."

"Oh, I don't think you could ever get me to go out there."

"Why not?" I asked my mother, trying to get her to express herself more, a well-intentioned mistake.

"Oh, I'm too old to travel. Besides, Boston." She made a face. "All the trouble they're having out there with the colored…"

Oh God, I thought, don't let it happen. Not so soon. Let's at least wait until my cousins arrive.

"Trouble?" asked Philip.

Please, God, I thought, I won't swear for a year.

"Oh, you know," said my mother, "all the violence that you see on the news. The busing and looting by the black people. I'd be deathly afraid to live there. Though," she added hastily, "I'm sure your parents live in a nice neighborhood." What a tactician my mother is. She covers her tracks and runs a data search all in the same sentence.

"Oh, it's nice enough where they live," said Philip. "Except for the Monacans."

Oh, shit, I thought, he's offering her a ride on the merry-go-round as punishment for that remark about the "colored." Mom, let it go.

There was a long pause while my mother considered whether or not to admit her ignorance of the Monacans. Normally, Philip would have held out his hand and helped her on to the carousel by adding something like, "They're the ones you really have to watch out for." But, after all, he was on his best behavior.

My mother looked to my father, who had been absorbed by the newspaper since the conversation had drifted away from sports. I noticed my father's glass was almost empty and saw a chance to save the situation.

"Anybody for a refill?" I asked, and Pop said, "I'll have another, Carrie." My hope was to enable my mother to forget the thread of the conversation, and where were my cousins, anyway? "Anybody else?" I asked, while I tried to hypnotize Philip into shutting up.

I couldn't have been in the kitchen more than two minutes, but when I returned with the drinks, mine extra-rummed, Philip was telling my parents "…only see the rich ones on TV—Princess Grace and her friends. They exile the poor Monacans—actually, they call the rich ones Monegasques and the poor ones Monacans—they exile the Monacans to cities on the East Coast like Boston and New York. That way Monaco stays rich."

"What an interesting idea," opined my mother, who was obviously missing whatever point there was to be gained.

"Except the neighborhoods are really suffering," continued Philip sadly. "You wouldn't believe the way they live. And eat." He shook his head, and

I gulped at my Tom and Jerry. "Do you know they eat aluminum foil?" I closed my eyes and finished half the drink.

"Aluminum foil?" asked my mother, horrified, while my father frowned.

"Right off the roll," said Philip, as if to exclaim, what is this world coming to.

"What is this world coming to!" exclaimed my mother, and now all three of them were shaking their heads, though not, thank God, in time with each other. "Of course," said my mother, "we don't have much trouble like that around here, except, you know—"

"I'm hungry," I interjected, and Philip gave a "who, me?" look in response to my glare. "Can't we eat yet?"

My cousins, Bob and Ruth, and their respective spouses, Marie and Hank, arrived almost at the same time. Bob and Marie live in St. Cloud; Bob's a car dealer and Marie's a housewife. They have two kids. Ruth and Hank live in Minneapolis, where Hank works on an assembly line, assembling I-forget-what, and Ruth was taking night classes for her BA, having dropped out of college when she married Hank. (They got divorced two years after that Thanksgiving. Ruth remarried, this time to a high-school English teacher. She got her degree, and they both moved to Wisconsin. I just heard that Ruth was pregnant.)

We said grace; rather, we listened to my father say grace. I peeked to see what Philip was doing, and of course he crossed his eyes and stuck his tongue out at me.

The food was tasty. My mother must have worked her little buns off preparing the meal. Bob and Marie brought two bottles of wine, and Ruth and Hank brought a coffee cake. But it was my mother who took care of everything else. My mother is an intelligent woman, but not intelligent enough either to recognize or to avoid being used. I have no doubt that she enjoyed spending a day and night in the kitchen, roasting the turkey, creaming the onions, preparing the salads and stuffing, baking the cranberry bread and pumpkin pie ("But I thought you said Ruth made a coffee cake." "I know, dear, but cranberry bread and pumpkin pie are traditional. Besides, what if someone doesn't like coffee cake? This way, they have a choice. And your father likes my pumpkin pie."), polishing the good silver, setting the table, and all the rest good housewives do. I have no doubt that she enjoyed it, because I remember asking her, and she said so.

The dinner conversation was doubly tense for me. When it didn't include Philip, it was insipid or sexist, and I couldn't appreciate my food. When it did include Philip, it became dangerously fabulous, and I couldn't even eat my food. A sample:

Bob: So how's school, Carolyn?

Carolyn: Oh, coming along. I'm just getting into the background research for my dissertation.

Bob: Is that for a PhD?

Carolyn: Yes.

Hank: Ruth's thinking of getting a PhD, aren't you, honey?

Ruth: Oh, stop. He always kids me about that. I can get my BA in another year if I take six credits a quarter. Two classes. But I don't know if I can keep up the pace.

Hank: Pretty soon she'll be too smart for me.

Pop: When do you finish up, honey? June?

Carolyn: No, I think winter's more likely, Pop.

Mom: How about you, Philip? You're getting your PhD, too, aren't you? Here, take some turkey.

Philip: Thank you. I should finish this spring, Mrs. Anderson.

Hank: Two PhDs at the table! Watch out your kids aren't eggheads!

Bob: Are you in physics, too, Phil?"

Philip: Philip. No, I'm in psychology. Social psychology.

Hank: Uh-oh. Watch what you say. I knew he was looking at me funny. Maybe you can talk to my wife, Phil, figure out why she likes night school so much.

Ruth: Hank, you know why. It's cheaper than the day classes.

Mom: It shows good sense, Ruth.

Philip: I'm not a clinical psychologist. I'm in social psychology.

Bob: What's social psychology? Like how people act at parties? (laughter, most of it Bob's)

Philip: Actually, I've been studying men's relationships with women they perceive as stronger than they themselves are.

Pop: Does that have anything to do with the complaining study you were telling us about before?

Philip: It's in addition to that.

Mom: It sounds very interesting. I'd like to read it when it's done, if you think I could understand it.

Carolyn: These onions are really good, Mom.

Mom: Here, take more.

Marie: Do you mean like, when men marry women bigger than they are?

Philip: Oh, no. I mean men who are relatively weak-willed, marrying women who have a greater sense of themselves, more determination to act on their beliefs.

Ruth: Have you found out anything yet, Philip?

Philip: Yes, as a matter of fact.

Carolyn: Do you want any more wine, Philip, or have you had enough?

Philip: No, thanks, I'm fine. It seems that men who associate with strong women do so because they're insecure about their masculinity. That's not to say that all strong women have insecure husbands. But a great many insecure men apparently marry strong women. They often compensate for their feelings of insecurity, and sometimes their sexual confusion, by putting down their wives, embarrassing them, and so on. Mr. Anderson could probably verify that with the experiences of his congregation over the years. Haven't you found that men with sexual or emotional problems often keep their wives in positions where they can't exercise any power? It's almost as if the men can recognize the power in their wives before the wives can.

Pop: Well, I don't know. There might be something in that. Jesus preaches humility, and there's been many a man deaf to that precept. It's a common thing, of course, too common, to hear unkind words between man and wife. Sometimes we speak in anger when we shouldn't be speaking at all.

Hank: But that doesn't prove that a guy's sexually confused. Maybe the wife likes it that way.

Pop: We often use others' backs as our own step stool, Hank.

Philip: I was studying one man who kept his wife on drugs all the time so she couldn't think straight. When he was finally arrested, he cracked up completely, and they put him into an institution for psychotics, for the insane. They found he'd been eating raw meat for years because he believed it would cure his impotence.

Carolyn: (to herself) Jesus.

Marie: What happened to the wife?

Philip: She divorced him, went back to school, and eventually won the Nobel Prize in economics. This was some years ago.

Hank: What happened to the guy who was eating raw meat?

Philip: Well, it's not really dinner talk. I'll tell you later.

Bob: Has anyone seen how ridiculous those new Hondas are?

Mom: Who's for dessert? We have a choice.

Later, I found out that Philip had told Hank that the raw-meat man who dominated his wife had castrated himself and lived out the rest of his life in the institution washing bedpans.

The rest of the day was uneventful. In the evening, Ruth and Hank went home with Bob and Marie rather than drive back to Minneapolis; Hank had put away more beer than his coordination could handle, and Ruth couldn't drive a stick shift. I slept in my old bedroom, and Philip was assigned the couch in the living room. I'm sure he made me promise something to him in return for his not making a fuss over the separate rooms.

By the time we left after breakfast, Philip had completely charmed my mother. I must say, he gave the appearance of having an absolutely wonderful time—joking with her, laughing. At one point he even kidded her about the wrinkles on her neck, and I haven't even heard my father dare to do that. Philip and my mom, flirting away unabashedly, were fast becoming chums.

My father was typically more inscrutable. I'm certain he didn't believe the story about the Monacans ruining Boston, and I suspect that both he and Mom figured out what Philip was doing to Hank, but they didn't like Hank, anyway. My father enjoyed being inscrutable, keeping people guessing—more control that way.

Oh, Di, it was so complicated when Philip was there. I felt as if I were stretched from St. Cloud to the Twin Cities. I even had a dream that night—caused, no doubt, by the Tom and Jerry's battling it out with the turkey, creamed onions, and, yes, two different desserts, in a sea of gastric juice. In the dream I was walking through a valley. Far off to the left was a little house with a garden and a white picket fence around it. I think there were different-colored lollipops growing in the garden, standing erect on their white stems and reflecting sunlight off their shiny red and yellow and orange and green faces, like sunflowers without petals. I knew my parents lived in that house. There was a sense of peace about it; smoke issued from the chimney, birds flew over it. I looked in the window and there was a TV, but I couldn't see anybody watching it.

Then I was away from the house again, back in the valley. Way over to the right was the university, only it looked like a fortress, like Camelot. There were castles and drawbridges, and forbidding walls of stone, and parapets from which sentries and archers could detect approaching strangers. And then Philip was walking with me to the big gate that opened in to the university. He was saying, "You have to go in because you can't go in. You have to go in because you can't go in." It didn't make any sense. In my dream I started to cry and then became enraged because I was crying. I remember the tears continuing to pour out of me, making a pool of water around me, rising higher and higher, and then, just when I thought I would drown in my own tears, I woke up, shivered, and wished Philip were next to me.

I think my parents perceived me as more "grown-up" that Thanksgiving, Di. I "belonged" to Philip more than I did to them. Perhaps because we didn't fawn over each other like adolescents but rather related to one another like mature lovers, they recognized some sort of bond. Again, all speculation; my parents don't talk.

They've been good parents, though. They encouraged me just enough, disciplined me just enough, taught me just enough, and loved me just enough. And it helped, I suppose, that I didn't get chronic acne, I didn't need braces, I didn't have allergies, and, while I occasionally verged on thin, never worried much about my body. I always did well in school, and I went to church, uh, religiously.

In high school, boys avoided me, but I was only slightly interested, anyway. They were just so dumb; none of my male friends except David talked about anything remotely of consequence, and even David strayed into conversations about hunting. I enjoyed going on infrequent dates but never particularly pined for a husband, so I didn't make myself fall in love with everyone who asked me out. It would have been difficult: since I frightened off the jocks and the middle-achievers by being able to speak with some intelligence—something girls weren't supposed to do, especially around boys—most of my dates were the clinically academic. If it weren't for the church, I would have had very few friends indeed.

I was such a scientist about everything. I had sex in order to satisfy my curiosity, not to experience rapture nor to rebel nor to fulfill my passionate destiny with the love of my life, nor even to be accepted. I was a junior at the university when I first opened "my house" to visitors. Naturally, I was a little scared, a little clumsy, and, despite voracious reading and indirect interrogation of my more knowledgeable friends, a little naïve. It hurt more than I'd anticipated, and it was less pleasant than I'd hoped. All in all, hardly worth the effort. But in time I warmed to it.

The only thing I recall feeling really foolish about in those days was fondling my boyfriend's penis. For some unearthly reason, instead of stroking it up and down like any normal person, I would rub my palms against it as if I were trying to start a fire. And me, a sophisticated upperclass woman. You know what, Lady Di? I think I know why I did that. When I was a kid, I used to play with Play-Doh, you know, clay-in-a-can. When you wanted to make a long shape with your Play-Doh, you'd rub it just like that, between your palms, and of course the steady pressure would cause the clay to elongate. So I unconsciously made the transfer from Play-Doh to penises, clay to cocks. Jesus, Di, Play-Doh taught me the wrong way to jerk off a boy. There should be a warning on the package.

What's really funny is how many of my partners put up with what must have been terribly uncomfortable, if not painful, rather than show me a more appropriate, efficient way to bring them to erection or orgasm. How just: men don't communicate their desires, and their punishment is chafed penises. Needless to say, I was terribly chagrined when someone finally showed me "how it was done," saying sweetly that he'd never had a twirl job before. St. Cloud girl makes good.

I was isolated even within the isolation of St. Cloud. No heavy drugs, no heavy drinking, no sex beyond the innuendo stage, and certainly no mention of non-heterosexual sex. That was literally unthinkable. A blessing, maybe—for what is not thought cannot be repressed. It saddens me to think of my parents still in St. Cloud, not learning, not changing.

I honestly don't know how I "escaped" my parents' feudal upbringing. Maybe I just didn't think much about what I did, didn't communicate it to my parents, was probably thankful they didn't ask. I don't recall ever wondering, "Is this what Jesus would do?" and certainly not "Is this what Mom would do?" I guess I was born with the independent gene; sometimes I took advantage of it, and sometimes I didn't. Let's say it was benign neglect on Mom and Dad's part and benign obfuscation on mine.

Well. Some of us are lucky to have risen above the superstitions of human interaction. And some of us, I suppose, have had the opportunities for perspective and decided to ignore them. Steph, for example, cares only in certain ways. She identifies with women's struggles and is moved to action when sexism affects her or someone close to her. But with Steph, it's definitely restricted to women. It doesn't bother her whether people in general act a certain way. Philip, on the other hand, considered the human race a personal insult. He maintained that there were certain ways people ought to behave and other ways they most definitely ought not to behave. As a result, he was continually appalled.

And me, Lady Di—I guess I'm between both of them. I should change my name to Carolyn In-Between. In between St. Cloud and the Twin Cities, in between Stephanie and Philip, in between physicist and, yes, dear Di, journalist. Hyphenated names are so chic.

Dervishes

I sit in the back of the bus and look at the heads of the other riders. They look like a poppy field, or like the lollipop garden by my parents' house in my Thanksgiving dream.

The bus is almost full; it stops for about six riders. One person is a well-groomed, goateed student carrying a rolled-up poster. The second person is an elderly lady, umbrella in reserve, hair net, smiling apologetically to everyone for being slow. The third person is a "suit": maybe an insurance man, tight, dull, attaché-cased. The fourth person is a teenaged girl, pretty, a little blush, too-tight jeans, and a brand-name blouse. The fifth person is another student, a young woman who throws her cigarette into the grass before boarding the bus and who is clearly nervous about a future appointment or past misfortune.

Any of these five could easily sit next to me. But it never happens. The sixth person always sits next to me. He's about twenty-eight. His head is shaved along the top, as in a reverse Mohawk, and the rest of his hair is dyed purple. He has a safety pin in either his ear or nose—someplace it doesn't belong—he's making a god-awful noise with his sinuses, he's wearing a motorcycle jacket with something obscene sewn on the back, he's carrying a book of obscure ravings by some cult figure, he's grinning as if planning to bomb the bus, and he smells. I shudder and try to portray a mannequin.

I rode the bus downtown to shop for a present for Stephanie's birthday—her thirty-fifth is next week—but I ended up thinking more about me. And you, too, Lady Di. I've had the urge to call Sally lately; I haven't spoken to her for years. The last time I was in St. Cloud, last Christmas, David called and said that they were "temporarily separated." No news since then. I'd like to see her, though she might react badly if I came out to her. I think it would muddy the equations of our relationship. And we can't have muddy equations.

I may buy Stephanie some ben wa balls. Or a book, or a record. She doesn't really need anything. A loofa? That would be good for me, too, because I love to sponge her back. Stephanie's skin is smooth and, oh, like that color in the paint-by-number sets, burnt sienna, I think—a light tan. Burnt sienna and long black hair, marriage of the Philippines and the Old Sod. Great stuff.

My mind wanders when it's preoccupied with muddy equations. Probably avoidance. It's so trite, you know, thinking about yourself, your place in the world. And Philip explained to me all the defense mechanisms I use, so now I can name my moods. Oh, Di, I changed a lot in the year following the masturbation campaign, and I feel I'm in a transition again. But then I had a reasonable idea of where I was going. Now, I'm being blindfolded and taken for a ride.

I'm a late bloomer. Sometimes I think Stephanie was born knowing who she is. There's no doubting her: She's a clean vector, sharp, pointing in a consistent direction, forceful. I'm a damned scattergraph. I'm so fettered by all this education and training, I have to look at something eighteen different ways before I judge. Always the scientist.

I was home alone, after most of the day in the lab, when I decided that I loved Philip. I must have asked myself a dozen questions that would indicate whether I loved him, then answered them all affirmatively. Then I probably double-checked by asking myself, well, if I didn't love him, could I still answer these questions affirmatively? Fallacy-testing.

He had moved in about a month before. He was heavy into his dissertation and spent a lot of time at the university and in the "field," conducting interviews. I remember sitting on the floor and grinning like I'd just discovered a new element. That was how he found me when he came home from the U.

"What did *you* swallow?" he asked, hanging up his coat.

I said nothing, but skipped over to him and gave him a passionate, slobbery kiss. The kiss finally caught on, and he meted out some of his own carefully allotted passion. Two shakes of Carolyn's tail and we were in the bedroom making love—those were the last of my spontaneous Pill days. When we had exhaled and separated sweatily, I goggle-eyed him. I couldn't keep from looking at him, every minute part of his body, from the errant gray hairs invading his temples to the ingrown nail on one of his toes.

Philip was a suspicious sort, given normal circumstances. Making love in the afternoon was not a normal circumstance for us, so he was quite curious about my behavior.

"Uh, Carolyn, is there any reason why you're looking at me so strangely? And is it perchance connected with this unprecedented burst of passion?"

"Do you think I'm looking at you strangely?"

"Do *you* think you're looking at me strangely?"

"Yes." By now I had resumed my stupid grin. I seemed to have lost control of my facial muscles.

"Then why are we still having this discussion? *I* perceive you're looking at me strangely, *you* perceive you're looking at me strangely, and I was kind of wondering why. *I* don't know, and I thought *you* might know."

I kissed him again, pecking away on his mouth, his neck, his chest, then back again, quickly and repeatedly. Then I stopped, saw his exasperated expression, and laughed. I couldn't stop laughing at him. The Great Philip, always so much in control, couldn't figure out what was going on. But then I lay my head alongside his on the pillow and stroked his cheek.

"Philip?" I said quietly.

"That's me."

"Philip, I love you."

The effect was dramatic, for Philip. The half-smile disappeared, and his eyes grew large for just a second. I could feel a sudden tightening of muscles in his face.

"Um—"

"I love you. I love you. I decided today that I loved you. I really love you."

The moment of vulnerability was passing even with the bob of his Adam's apple. He swallowed all his feelings in one gulp and returned to Philip Normal by asking me, "How do you know?"

It was like that a lot. There'd be chinks in the armor, as Senator Jackson once unwittingly described the vulnerability of the US defense system to a threat from China. Philip would open the door, let a little of himself show through, then close it again. I'd have to time my own vulnerability with the open door.

I decide to get Stephanie the ben wa balls after all; then I can call her "Jingles." They don't jingle, but it'll be cute, anyway. Maybe she'll forgive me for lagging behind in my jumping. Steph says my mind's not into it, but I tell her it's my legs and lungs that aren't into it.

I also told Stanley Mankiewicz, Dr. Stan, that so far I haven't had the time to come up with a substitute area of study because I've been at a critical phase in my helium experiments. I know I'm postponing the inevitable, but maybe Dr. Stan thinks I'm giving the matter serious consideration. I won't tell him that I'm enjoying his suggestion of journaling; he's one of those people who give themselves so much credit, you hate to compliment them. They always beat you to it.

But I do enjoy talking to you, Lady Di. I can write all over the place, jump from Philip to Stephanie to my parents, back to Stephanie, and it doesn't make any difference to you. I can present arguments haphazardly, and you'll understand. I don't have to be logical if I don't want to.

With Philip, everything had to be logical. He and his damned three reasons. Talks with him were like seminars. We'd bandy words, and he'd intellectualize whenever he felt he needed to defend himself. We'd quibble over a definition, get sidetracked on irrelevant issues. He could never be wrong, not with logic on his side. It wasn't that I didn't trust his opinions; it was that sometimes they were meaningless.

It's only been recently that I've thought about him very much. I'm not even sure why I kept all the memorabilia from the campaign. Maybe I knew that one day I would need to sort through it and isolate the emotions.

There's a tape here. Not the radio speech, another tape. Philip made it on our trip west. When we left St. Paul, he told me that he wanted to talk to me about dervishes. Whirling dervishes. When Philip was an undergrad back in Massachusetts, one of his roommates was a dervish, I guess. It sounds rather odd, but that's Philip. He'd mentioned him to me once, but only offhandedly, and I didn't think to follow up on it.

Philip was quite taciturn in the months following the masturbation campaign. If he wanted to talk, then I wanted to encourage him. We had the tape recorder in the car from the campaign and a blank cassette.

"You're going to talk?" I said sarcastically. "Let's get this down on tape."

"Oh, no," he said. "I don't want to talk into a tape recorder."

"Oh, come on," I said. "You did fine on the radio. You won't even know it's on."

"Sure I will. I can see it, and I'll be able to hear it, too."

"No, I'll make sure you don't look at it. You're supposed to keep your eyes on the road, anyway."

"Why do you want to tape me? I won't be able to be spontaneous. Can't you merely listen, and tape it in your mind?"

"It'll be fun," I said. "We can record it for posterity."

"Posterity? What do you think I'm going to talk about?"

"Philip, you never know. Look, first, you should humor me because I'm your best girl. Second, it's good practice for you to choose your words carefully, knowing they're being recorded. And third, and most important, uh, it'll provide a pleasant history of our trip to the great West."

So he agreed, and I taped his conversation. But you know, Di, we started out through Minnesota and North Dakota, and it was such a boring ride. I was tense from leaving the state I grew up in and exhausted from the tension. Lady Di, I fell asleep. I stayed up long enough to turn over the cassette, but I fell asleep soon after. I didn't wake up until we got to Fargo. When I awoke, Philip said nothing to me. I never asked him to repeat the story; I heard the first part but didn't know how much I'd missed. And he never mentioned it again. It's been quite awhile since I heard his voice, so this might get...nostalgic.

3. THE DERVISH

"Okay, relax. I'll tell you a story. Shit, I hate talking into this tape. Look at that sign, only fifty-two miles to Fargo. Maybe we should settle in Fargo. Raise, I don't know, wheat or something. Alfalfa. Rocks. We could raise rocks and sell them to parts of the country that have too much soil, how's that? Philip and Carolyn's Rock Emporium.

"Well, okay, the story. I told you I once had a roommate who was a dervish, right? Well, I did. I know I mentioned him. Anyway, I've been thinking about him more since the campaign ended. Not steady. Just on and off the past few months. So I'm going to tell you more about him now. Get comfortable.

"Gordon Havilland was his name, at least during fall quarter. Gordon Havilland was my roommate during my junior year at UMass, late 1969 and early 1970. Big year, 1969. Woodstock, Nixon, man on the moon…the Amazin' Mets, too, though I don't suppose you keyed in on that.

"I was—let's see, what did they call us—a rad lib in those days. The National Guard had yet to shoot the bums at Kent State, and I still thought we could end the war by yelling, 'Ho, Ho, Ho Chi Minh, the NLF is sure to win,' very, very loudly. It probably would have been as effective to yell, 'Yummy, Yummy, Yummy, I Got Love in my Tummy,' which was a big song that year. But I went marching because I believed.

"I was also studying my fucking brain cells out. I'd taken all the intro psych courses already; those were behind me, all the textbooks that warn you, 'Remember, yours is a great power. Never abuse this power by interpreting your friends' behaviors or dreams.' And so naturally, we all went around doing exactly that. I made a woman cry once. I told her that she'd never get married until she admitted that her father was jealous of her boyfriends because he wanted to screw her himself. Hey, we were young and foolish.

"But I digress. At the time of Gordon's first whirl, I was mired in physiological psychology, cognitive psychology, probably a few other psychologies, and some communication courses. I was a real academic then, Car; you wouldn't have recognized me.

"Gordon was from Worcester, Massachusetts, a very pedestrian, working-class kind of town. His father was French ex-Catholic, his mother English. I forget what his father did, but he worked his way up from lower class to middle class. The family evidently had enough to send Gordon through college, and he was the third of five boys. Maybe they had enough money to be upper-middle class, now that I think of it, but Gordon would never rise out of the multitude.

"It wasn't that he was unintelligent; he was—oh, shit, I don't know—uninspired, I guess. Just your average guy: no particular belief system, no particular idiosyncrasies, no strong will to do this or that. He even looked average: about five foot ten, medium build, brown eyes and hair, brown glasses. If he was a color, it was definitely brown. A real dull-o was Gordon.

"He was a philosophy major, and our discussions were maddeningly abstruse. It was ridiculous. I tried to be respectful. I'd read a little about the well-known philosophies, you know, enough. But what was homework to him was bullshit to me. Each new guy he read about—Spinoza, Kant, Aristotle, for Christ's sake—was the man of the hour. His new hero. You just knew Gordon had the groupies. But I tolerated it, no big deal. So my roommate was a philosopher. Could've been worse. He might've been a drummer. Or an anthropologist.

"We lived in a dorm, and the room was one of many in a long corridor. There were two beds, two desks, two chairs, an overhead lamp, and whatever appurtenances we cared to add to the room—tensor lamps, tiny refrigerators for beer and pickles, wastebaskets, and posters. We weren't allowed to tape posters to the walls, but everyone did, anyway. I had one depicting a Vietnamese horseman galloping into town, yelling, 'The Americans are coming! The Americans are coming!' Sort of a Paul Revere takeoff. Gordon put up a calendar from a local health food restaurant. The calendar was loaded with notations of obscure Eastern holidays and profound sayings, like 'When the Spirit is revealed, all else will be invisible.' Stuff like that.

"Gordon had gotten a job in the restaurant about a month before the evening I'm going to tell you about. I guess there was a group there that he fell in with immediately, and, I don't know exactly how this all happened, but suddenly he wouldn't refer to them by name anymore, but rather as 'The Brothers.' I found out about them later. To tell you the truth, I wasn't that hot to know about it. I was always busy studying.

"Well, one evening, oh, in November, I guess, I *was* studying, in bed, the best place to study as far as I'm concerned, and Gordon was in his bed, too. He'd come in an hour before, all puffing from the cold—I thought it was from the cold. You know how you have this suffusion of energy when you come in from the cold? How it just spreads out from you, so you charge up the whole room, make everyone aware of your presence? Well, that's how it was. Shit, it *is* cold in November in Amherst. I figured it was the cold.

"So I was studying—cranial nerves, some garbage—and there's the usual dorm noise in the background—a radio of revolting songs, some sophomoric sophomores down the hall, a girlfriend's giggles. You get used to it.

"Well, I hear Gordon breathing, and I think, subconsciously, now that's odd, why suddenly am I hearing Gordon breathing? But, you know, it's all I can do to concentrate on my book, and I keep the thought down below.

"After awhile—it couldn't have been more than a minute—I hear the breathing again, and this time I consider it consciously, and I decide, that's *really* loud. I look over to Gordon, and he's sitting up in bed, book tossed to the side, eyes closed, and he's definitely doing the inhale-exhale bit.

"'Gordon,' I say. I'm caught a little off-guard. But even as I wonder what to say or do next, Gordon's activities on the bed take on kind of an alarming intensity. I mean, his whole body is participating in this. The breathing becomes deeper, more rapid, kind of raspy, and his fingers start to twitch and tremble all over. Then it's like gangrene: the trembling climbs up his fingers, his hands, his arms. I see his feet start moving, and the rasping becomes a groan, and I'm thinking, this is not in a normal person's repertoire of behaviors. Perhaps, I think, I'd better seek some assistance.

"'Gordon,' I say again. 'Gordon, are you cool?' And I start to get out of bed, either to him or to the door, I'm not sure which, but by this time, Gordon has been transported elsewhere. He just sort of quivers out of bed and onto the floor, standing, but like he is being shot through with electricity, you know? So I'm watching him, trying to decide what to do. I figure I can dash for the door or stay and observe. I end up compromising: I stay and observe from the corner of my bed closest to the door.

"Now Gordon's movements become more regular. If he was being shot through with electricity before, now at least the jolts are paced. The groans become more of a chant, his feet adopt a certain rhythm, and his convulsions resolve into something more fluid, less jerky. His eyelids are blinking real fast, head bobbing with the chant; his arms seem to kind of grab his fingers, keep them from flying off, and he folds his arms together over his chest, and his bare feet rise so he's on his toes.

"Gordon begins to whirl.

"Now let me explain why this part was reassuring. You might not think so from listening to it. Up to this point, I was somewhat, oh, 'frightened' is too strong, let's say 'anxious.' Who knew what was happening to my roommate? Had a mysterious dorm disease overtaken him in the prime of student-hood? Or maybe an insidious brain disorder rooted in his family tree from the pillaging and raping of the Thirty Years' War? The unknown, Car; it's terrible to behold. But the whirling told me something: Gordon was in control. Sort of. And while I still might have to call the loony tunes doctor to come take him away—I hadn't progressed far enough in my coursework for a reliable diagnosis—still, I felt I could deal with him, for a little while, anyway.

"Well, Gordon starts to spin in as large a circle as the room will permit, several feet in diameter, and I give him a few more inches by pushing my desk chair in. The chanting monotones out. It's not too loud, really, but the pace of his exertions quickens, and he spins around and around, the circle tightening, not all that smoothly as, say, an ice skater, but pretty fast. It's like he started revolving, then ended up rotating, arms still folded, like a Russian dancer. Faster and faster. All his energy—and it's a considerable amount—is pouring into the whirl. I'd never noticed how agile he was; he could have killed me in tennis, if I'd played tennis. All I can hear is his gasping, and all I can see is his blurry body whirling and whirling, like he's going to corkscrew into the floor. The whirl climaxes after about a minute, I guess, though it seemed more like a century. In mid-spin, Gordon gives a little orgasmic shout, flings himself face down onto the bed—I'm glad he was on target—and finally in a dramatic, sweaty coda to this strange symphony, wheezes down from manic-land.

"Now, understand, Car, I am not the absolute picture of calm. My otherwise level-headed, middle-of-every-road roommate has just frenzied out in front of me. No stimulus, no perceivable reinforcement, one minute he's normal and the next he's a pecan log. I remember being surprised that no one next door bothered to see if everything was okay, but I guess whatever ruckus Gordon was causing was within one or two standard deviations of dorm norm. It was, however, outside my standard deviations of acceptable roommate behavior, and I went for the door and the hall phone. I guess I was thinking of calling the infirmary, or maybe one of my profs.

"As it happens, though, just as I open the door, I hear a faraway voice say, 'Philip (breath), things (breath, breath), things are cool.'

"I yell at him: 'Things are cool? Things are *cool*?' I think perhaps I might have been a bit tense. 'You go flippo on me with no warning at all, right in the middle of my damn physiological psychology book, and you say things are cool? Do you realize what the fuck you've been doing the past five minutes?'

"'Whirling, man,' he says, and I'm sure he's smiling into his pillow.

"So I wait, oh, maybe half an hour, until Gordon returns to the real world—I didn't go back to my psych book—and then I repeat my 'Things are cool?' speech, and he tells me about whirling, but not until I give him feedback about his whirl. You know, like he wasn't there to see it himself. What do they say, the Sufis, something about the rest of you being absent when you're with God? Anyway, I give him his damned feedback. Do you know how hard it is to assess a fucking whirl, for Christ's sake? It isn't as if I had a catalog of all the whirls I'd ever experienced. I gave him a B. He seemed satisfied.

"Gordon told me about whirling. He said he'd joined a group called the Brothers of Light, which was a chapter of a much larger group of Sufis. The Brothers apparently called themselves something else, too, but I've forgotten—Mawlawis, I think. It means 'dancing dervishes' or 'whirling dervishes.' You get the picture.

"It's hard for me to explain this, Car. First, I didn't understand it all then. Second, I'm not certain how much Gordon told me was true, and unexpurgated. And third, I've forgotten a lot.

"The gist of what they believed was that everything was controlled by God. I mean, everything. And you didn't question it. It wasn't even the case that good acts were rewarded and bad ones punished. You know the old

Dervishes

'God works in mysterious ways'? That was it. God could do any damn thing, and that's the way it was. A real Walter Cronkite religion. God could fuck you up, down, and sideways, and you accepted it. Whirling, or dancing, brought you closer to God, though why anyone would want to be closer to that kind of a god is beyond me, unless it was to take a good potshot at him. This god, of course, was a nonphysical, totally ineffable entity. They always are. Shit, I guess I'd stay out of sight, too.

"I was curious at first, because it was so different from what I believed, and the whirling was a nice touch. But soon Gordon gave me the traditional response of all religions, namely, that intellect was not the way to knowledge. Gordon himself was a *murid*, an initiate, and he had to be holy for a thousand and one days before he'd be accepted as a full-fledged dervish. If he had even a one-day lapse, he'd have to start the thousand and one all over. Pretty strict, those Mawlawis.

"Well, I bought that; why not? It certainly seemed to help Gordon. Whereas before he was rather a lifeless soul, you know, a blender—not a kitchen appliance, but one who blends into his environment. Now he was always animated, his eyes shone, he smiled more, and he just, I don't know, enjoyed life more. He was a dervish, a goddam dervish. My fucking roommate.

"So. During the next few weeks, Gordon got more and more into whirling. We had this deal. He wouldn't whirl while I was trying to sleep, and I wouldn't call the cops or his folks. We got along fine, mainly because he was trying so hard to be so goddamned holy. First thing, he changed his name. 'Parananda.' He wanted to be called 'Parananda' from then on. It had come to him in a dream. Okay by me. Then he started to wear Indian clothes, you know, flowing robes, with his winter coat on top, of course. Evidently the people at the health food store had some kind of connection to all the accoutrements good dervishes need—robes, sandals, prayer candles, incense, and all manner of books and pamphlets.

"I glanced at a few of the books once while he was taking a holy dump. They seemed pretty legitimate, steeped in history. Maybe eight centuries back. The pamphlets were something else again. Locally produced, very crude. It reminded me of some of the SDS stuff circulating in those days—uh, Students for a Democratic Society, you know them.

"So, anyway, there's a split here. If you're whirling because you can get closer to inner knowledge or spiritual peace or, I don't know, some religious epiphany that I don't care to examine, hey, go crazy—literally, if need be. Whatever helps, right? But I couldn't help but think that *this* type of whirling wasn't quite that; it was more, I don't know, like the latest hairstyle or rock band or glib expression. It was a *fad*.

"Well, then Parananda changed his diet. No booze, and a lot of vegetarian-type foods to start—vegetables, of course, and kefir and tofu and yogurt and wheat germ and sprouts. Okay, that was fine. Standard far-out one-with-the-universe food. But then he got weirder. Supposedly there was some proscription about eating anything dark. The idea was that the lighter the food, the holier it was, if you can believe that. Parananda believed it. I couldn't even believe *he* believed it. White rice was holier than brown rice? Parananda said there were exceptions. Okay. Milk was holier than tomato juice? Yeah. Bananas holier than peanut butter? Maybe. Potato chips holier than broccoli? He'd get back to me.

"Parananda improved his whirling. He'd whirl maybe two or three times a week, depending on whether anything good was on the TV downstairs or he had a date or he was too weary from his spiritual discussions with the Brothers of Light. He was a pragmatist, you see. He said there was no need to renounce all material things, as some religious orders did. He said material things weren't so much as 'the wing of a gnat' in God's eye, so why bother renouncing them? I didn't respond as cynically as I could have, because, well, he *was* still learning.

"And he *had* become a more interesting person, I'll give him that. I was satisfied. I didn't care what he ate or wore, and his whirls were becoming things of grace and beauty. He didn't try to convert me, so, hell. 'Course, people in the dorm started calling us 'Spin and Marty,' but other than that kind of shit, I didn't care. It broke the monotony.

Dervishes

"I settled back into my groove as an earnest student. I tell you, Car, I was a regular scholar, despite all the marches I went on and angry letters I wrote and imprecations I hurled—subvocal though they may have been—at establishment figures. Pre-Parananda, I lived out of books. That was the way I thought it had to be.

"Well, there was a mixer—in the gymnasium. Okay, you know what mixers were like—lights dim, that meant three-quarters of them were turned off, loud records reverberating from wall to wall to ceiling to floor to eardrums and back again, and party decorations trying to make the place look festive, but, you know, a gym is a gym is a gym. Everybody there is so goddam polite. 'Oh, what's your major, what's your major, you're from Schenectady, how fascinating, what's your major?' Everybody there wants to get laid. Every guy there wants to say, 'What's your major?' to some buxom Scandinavian goddess and have her reply, 'English lit.; by the way, I'd sure love to fuck.' It's true.

"I went with Parananda, looking for some buxom Scandinavian goddess. I calculated the odds at about one in eight billion against my finding one, but that was still better than zero in eight billion, which were the precise odds of a buxom Scandinavian goddess bursting into our dorm room and expressing a desire to do wonderful things to our bodies.

"Parananda and I didn't do much socially, mainly because I didn't do much socially. But it was a Friday night after midterms, I was in my usual quasi-depression, Parananda was in his usual quasi-euphoria, so we went. It was either that or reading for me, and if you read too much psychology at one time, hair grows on your palms. If you're a woman, your clit turns blue. Honest, it happened to a friend of mine. I mean, I only heard about it.

"Well, we got to the gym and milled, or mixed, or whatever it was we were supposed to do. There was beer and wine, and there was a lot of jostling and stuff like that. Mostly people stayed in groups, either for protection or aggression. There were some hustlers, and some homesteaders, and some wanderers, like me. I left Parananda with a paper cup of orange juice and began to search for my goddess, vaguely listening to the background stereo music and to fragments of conversations that I suspected were no less desultory than the whole conversations.

"It's a big place, the gym, and it was crowded, and I just let myself pinball from one person to another. I was asking women what their majors were and replying variously—pre-law, forestry, one time I went for broke with massage, but I don't think I convinced the woman. She laughed and walked away, shaking her head. Other women would counter with an astute remark about the weather or where the best skiing was that winter. Once or twice I glimpsed Parananda, seemingly mute and nodding in agreement with some inner discussion. He was easy to pick out; not many students wear white robes with parkas.

"It must have been about ten o'clock when I concluded that sex was something that happened only in books and movies. I was bored and horny, a really nasty combination of woes that has afflicted me much of my life. I think I was explaining to a wide-eyed redhead that I was combining my interest in gynecology with my skill in art by drawing all the female genitalia in medical texts, when I heard this faintly familiar sound. I thought, what *is* that? Where have I heard that sound before?

"It was an eerie sensation. The music had stopped, and the crowd wasn't making crowd noises any longer, you know, almost like they were letting me hear the sound. It was kind of like a machine, a rhythmic 'whoosh, whoosh' that reminded me of those movies where you hear the people breathe with their scuba tanks.

"And then I thought—breathing. Oh, shit. He wouldn't do it here. He wouldn't do it in front of all these people.

"I started making passageways between people until I got to Parananda, who was already in the first stages of what undoubtedly was going to be a monster whirl. He was starting his show, and a people-circle had formed around him, pulsating in and out, like no one could decide what to do.

"I yelled at him. 'Parananda! Gordon!' But it was too late, I guess. Somebody shouted, someone else went for him. Maybe they thought he was having a seizure. I don't know. The whole thing's foggy, but I remember thinking, I've got to keep people away from him or someone's going to get hurt. And I guess I took charge. Actually, it wasn't that difficult. Once Parananda started his whirl—and it was definitely one of his best; maybe the crowd turned him on—well, they just let him do his thing. Some started to clap, and others yelled, 'Go! Go!' It was like I told you before: once you knew what he was doing, it was fine; you let him alone.

"It was after he collapsed that I had to step into the limelight. First there was the crowd to disperse. Everyone was laughing, cheering, or frowning. I really would have preferred to disappear, but, shit, he *was* my roommate. And he was so goddam helpless after he whirled. So I had to ward off any curious onlookers, and there were plenty, until he came to. Then I had to offer some explanation of what he was doing, you know, like Leonard Bernstein does after concerts, or goddam Alistair Cooke. Cops arrived on the scene and wanted good reasons why they shouldn't put both me and Parananda in more constraining quarters. All this while Parananda was imitating Jell-O on my shoulder, acting like he had drunk the entire Italian Swiss Colony.

"Fortunately, I was sufficiently glib to escape with my histrionic roommate, though with Campus Cops, I don't suppose that's any achievement. I probably told them he had some disease, he was due to start vomiting in about five minutes, and I had the pills in our room.

"So I bundled us both up and weaved out of the crowd and out of the gym, all my goddesses I'm sure regretting their indifference since they'd seen what an action kind of guy I really was. And I was walking Parananda back to the dorm, all the while thinking, 'Why the fuck does he do this?' when he began laughing.

"'Boy,' he said through a guffaw, 'we sure broke up that party, didn't we?'

"At first, I was really pissed off at him. Using me, letting me make a fool of myself in front of all those people. I think I even said, 'Give him air!

Give him air!' at one point. Shit, I should have hollered, 'Close in! Close in! Suffocate the bastard!'

"But then I reconsidered and, well, it wasn't all *that* humiliating. If I stretched it, I could even say it was a little fun. You know, it was an experience, a different experience for me. I mean, the protest marches were fun, but I wasn't center stage in those. I was anonymous. This was different. I guess I liked it. It was one of the ingredients missing from my life. I hadn't been having any fun; I had been content to be part of the masses.

"That was the decisive break between me and academics. Oh, I still went to school another five, six years, but I studied differently after that. I studied globally, didn't worry so much about names and dates as I did about ideas, reasons, paradigms. I used to think learning was antithetical to fun, that it was only a chore, though a necessary one. But I began to see that I didn't want the learning without the fun. Interesting how things like that turn out. That idea, of making school enjoyable, must have been inside me all the time, but Parananda was the catalyst that got the idea into the conscious and finally into my behavior.

"But to get back to Parananda: His life was becoming increasingly dominated by his role as a dervish. You couldn't talk to him about anything else. He'd interpret a newspaper article as an example of some Sufi principle or the ignorance of that principle. He'd judge people on a holiness continuum. Nothing else; just holiness. He surrounded himself—physically, psychologically, emotionally—with dervishism. We talked, we argued. Or I argued. He was too holy to argue. Every goddam thing that occurred in the universe was related in one way or another to the Brothers of Light Dancing Dervish Show. It wasn't a novelty anymore, and it started to wear on me. How much of that can you take? He wasn't human; he was an extension of a dogma. Maybe the tail wagging the dogma. Sorry.

"Our whole relationship changed. I wasn't good enough for him. No, I was irrelevant—that was it. Anybody or anything that didn't relate to the Mawlawis simply didn't matter. I mean, somewhere along the line he rationalized staying in school, but his whole damn life became one fucking whirl. No, different whirls, 'cause he had different whirls for different occasions. Jesus, some were slow, some went in different rotations, the chant was different in others. He probably had more whirls than Christians have sins.

"I remember one winter morning, we were in Northampton. I don't know what the hell we were doing there—maybe I knew someone at Smith—but there we were, walking down the main drag, me in my fur-lined winter coat, heavy cords, and some boots or something, because there was snow all over. But Parananda was wearing his whites, plus his parka, and sandals with heavy socks slit for the thong. Fucking nuts. By this time I didn't even notice others' reactions to us. I was telling Parananda about a UMass professor in the chemistry department I'd heard about.

"'He works day and night in his lab,' I said. 'Spends all his time mixing chemicals, boiling solutions, distilling gases and shit, writing up his results. Total immersion. Sleeps there.' I paused for effect. 'They say he doesn't know who the current president is.'

"Parananda didn't reply, either because he didn't get the connection or because he was 'meditating.' He'd taken to speaking aphoristically with others and tersely with me.

"'What's the difference between dervishism and this guy's chemistry research?' I said, eschewing subtlety. 'For that matter, how is what you're doing different from, say, Catholicism?' It was a low blow, but I wanted to get his attention.

"I thought I saw his holy eyes flicker, so I kept on. Shit, it was for his own good.

"'Everything is whirling to you, Parananda. Whirling is the magic elixir. If you're unhappy, you whirl. If you're angry, you whirl. If you're bored, you whirl. Catholics do the same thing. If you were into Catholicism as much as you're into whirling, all you'd think about would be Jesus. You'd be telling me that going to church was really important, and you'd play with your beads, and you'd go through a lot of dumb rituals, and twenty years ago you wouldn't have eaten fish on Fridays. What's the damn difference?'

"He looked at me with that beneficent Sunday-school face that he knew irked the hell out of me. 'You speak like an ass supporting a load of books,' he said.

"'All right, fuck it,' I said. 'So I'm an ass supporting a load of books. At least I'm not shivering my balls off because I have to wear a robe in the middle of the goddam winter!'

"He nodded, and I knew I was in for a condescending speech. 'Philip,' he said, 'I am nothing, less than nothing, before God. If I be like you say, dumb or preoccupied, then God has made me that way. You could discuss moral imperatives and logical positivism and all intelligences with Gordon Havilland. But I am not Gordon Havilland anymore. Please understand that. I have explained this to my parents and my friends, and they understand. Why do you alone persist in badgering me?'

"His parents, by the way, did not understand. They called me one night, asking me why it was that every time they spoke with their son he sounded like Charlie Chan, and I finally convinced them it was merely a phase he was going through. I didn't tell them he'd gone to court to have his name legally changed to Parananda. I think he would've had his foreskin sewn back if they gave it to you in a jar like they do your baby teeth.

"'Parananda,' I continued, 'don't you think you might be missing out on something? I mean, you're twenty years old, and you're shutting yourself out. Your women whirl with you before sex; you write all your assignments on some aspect of Sufism; God knows you don't talk about anything else. Don't you feel you might be losing a little perspective? Why not put this off until—you're retired? Then you can take trips to Bermuda and the Virgin Islands and whirl on the beach.'

"No dice. 'Philip,' he said, 'God in his grace has caused me to be this way. He has allowed me to tread the path from an unhappy, unfulfilled, pointless life to one of ecstasies unbound and an awareness I regret to say you will never possess. God is the rain to my dry valley. He is the architect to my ruined city.'

"It seemed to me that, if anything, God was the pie-in-the-face to Parananda's Soupy Sales. But, shit, I let it go. I tried, and that's all I could do. After all, he never tried to get me to be a dervish—they probably didn't want me—so why should I try to re-convert him?

"Again he catalyzed my thinking. I began to doubt everything, be more skeptical. Even of myself. Who was I to judge Parananda, anyway? Of course, later on I amended this philosophy. I figure now I can judge anyone I damn well please, but I'm still pretty skeptical of others', uh, life performances. But then I concluded that I did the best I could, and if Parananda was destined to be a dervish, then I sure as hell wasn't going to upset the cosmic order of things by persuading him to return to the mind-set of Gordon Havilland, non vivant from Worcester, Massachusetts.

"I met a few of the Brothers of Light once, when we bumped into them in the library. They looked exactly like anyone else: no shaved heads, no wild stares, no weird mannerisms. Except for the white robes and the peaceful smiles that made someone like me want to go wallow in some sludge, they could have all been raised in Worcester. Or Springfield. Hell, everyone's got to come from somewhere.

"I never saw Parananda again. Just one of those dervishes that pass in the night, I guess. Maybe he opened a health food store and got capitalized back into society. On the other hand, maybe he started an Academy for Dancing Dervishes somewhere, or a correspondence course for novice Sufis. Sufi Helper, maybe.

"But he was important. Parananda was important to me. Not only because he got my head out of the books and into the world, but also because he showed me what can happen when you decide to whirl instead of think.

"I saw that again with the campaign. It really brought Parananda back to mind. There are so many goddam whirlers out there. The damn Christians and the damn Democrats and that anti-abortion lady. Everybody's got a thing, and they make the reality fit the thing. They whirl, and they say: hey, this is me, I'm more acceptable, more defined now.

"Well, I don't want to do that, goddamit. I don't want any sweeteners or preservatives in me. I want to be aware of what I'm doing all the time. Not sell out to some group or standards. The only standards I want are those that keep me thinking, like not being intimidated, or not tolerating any bullshit.

"You know, Car, I think it's okay to join a group for, oh, affiliation, you know, having a good time and all. No problem. Even for approval, if that's where you have to get your strokes, although I'm not so crazy about that idea. But joining a group for identity really rubs me wrong. It doesn't seem like it ought to work. When all the glitter's blown away, sooner or later you have to say, who am I? And you're not going to be a Catholic or a Republican or a Macho or a Suffering Victim or even a Tormented Individualist. You'll be a lot of those things, and none of them, too.

"People don't think, goddamit; they don't think. All those audiences in the campaign—they didn't think. They didn't listen. They used words they didn't understand to describe ideas they hadn't thought through.

"Damn, all it takes is a little logic! What could be harmful about masturbation? Why does everyone have all these notions about this and that, when they don't make any goddam sense? Can't they break away from what they've been taught?

"Oh, Carolyn, you do look pretty when you're asleep. Innocent. All you'd need is a thumb in your mouth, and I could be arrested for conveying you across the state line. Well, why should I expect you to be interested in this? Maybe I didn't make the connection between Parananda and me quick enough. Or maybe you're just not interested in *me*. I don't know. I'm not sure it matters. Well, the tape will listen to me, and years from now your great-grandchild will find it buried under some of your old diaphragms.

"I'm feeling apart these days, pumpkin. I lost something in the campaign, that sense of community I used to have—flimsy though it was—with the human race. You know when you're black you can tell nigger jokes, and when you're Jewish you can tell Jew jokes? Well, I'm finding it pretty tough to tell people jokes anymore.

"I've thought a lot about the campaign these past few months. You don't understand; you weren't up there. You couldn't see all this venom directed at you. No, that's not right, either. It wasn't the hostility. The hostility I could handle. It was a surprise, but I adjusted to it. It wasn't the hostility that changed me.

"It was something else: a deadness, like you'd see in those films of Nazi rallies. Oh, not nearly as extreme as that, but I think it's the same basic concept. Yeah, a deadness, where you just know people aren't thinking, they've cast in with the crowd, the groupthink. Nothing new about that; I don't even know why it bothers me that much. But seeing it, up close, seeing that vacuousness. Jesus!

"I really want the world to be a certain way, Car. I want people to meet certain standards. And they don't, goddamit.

"You couldn't understand why I wanted—why I needed—to continue the campaign. You thought it was because of some principle: I was being moralistic or something. But it was pure, unadulterated selfishness. Just like I said on our picnic, I did it for me. I couldn't—I just couldn't believe that people were reacting that way, that I could be so wrong. I thought I knew people. I mean, I've never trusted the 'capital-p' people, but I've, you know, I've been fairly positive about 'small-p' people, individuals.

"But, shit, when I stood up there, I saw 'little-p' people behaving like 'big-p' people. Of course. It makes perfect sense. I shouldn't have expected otherwise. But each time I gave a speech, I kept hoping I'd find the right audience, a thinking audience. I mean, I was so close to them, standing up there, and I could see them as individuals—it wasn't like I was in a stadium—I could see each of them, and they still acted as a mass, an unthinking mass. That's why I continued the campaign. I needed to find people that...that didn't whirl.

"Shit, I'm sounding so damned insipid. It's this tape; I feel like I'm confessing. Only there's no one here to give me absolution.

"We're really growing apart, Car. I can feel it. I think it's probably me, but I'm not sure. I don't know what I can do about it, either. I don't even know if I *should* do something about it.

"Hm. I remember we talked about love once, right after you first told me you loved me. I couldn't believe it, I really couldn't. I still can't. Talk about insecurity. It's as if someone said, 'Philip Lester, what would you want most to happen to you?' And I would reply, 'Well, I'd like for me and Carolyn Anderson to be in love.' And there it was. Like winning top prize on the Rod Serling Quiz Show. I mean, I feel that, even if I do deserve you, I don't usually get what I deserve. So how can you love me? Well, who knows. Maybe you only think you love me. Maybe that's as good as the real thing.

"Jesus, I can't remember when I've talked so much. You should tape me and fall asleep more often. Except now I'm more self-conscious about it, because now I really am talking to the machine.

"I had a conversation last year that really sticks out now, though I didn't think much of it at the time. Just a minor irritation. I was eating lunch in the West Bank Automat when a man and a woman I only slightly knew bumped into me. I remember them from some radical group on campus. Anyway, we got to talking about my dissertation, since that was prominently on my mind then.

"You remember the interviews I did, trying to determine what made some people complain and other people not complain. Well. I told them— these two acquaintances—that one factor that seemed to influence women not complaining was when you were female and your parents brought you up to think your opinions were worthless. You know, you never get the opportunity to take responsibility for your independent judgment, so you end up never exercising independent judgment. A legitimate finding. Out of many.

"Well, they jumped all over me. They wanted to know why I didn't devote more discussion to that particular finding. I should have followed it up, they claimed. I should have spent at least an entire chapter on that one datum.

"I explained to them that my dissertation was about complaining, not about feminism. I could have added that I considered complaining a more basic issue than feminism, but I thought better of it. They didn't listen to me, anyway. I was sexist, apparently, because I didn't write a tome about how women are raised to be passive.

"It was so fucked. They were treating me like your average macho asshole who guzzles beer and thinks a woman's place is by his side refilling his glass. Shit, I don't deserve that. I mean, I try to be aware of sexism, and maybe I still have a ways to go, but what the hell, why don't they point their fingers at those who *really* oppress women? Shit, I didn't even have to *mention* that thing about women. Do I have to devote my life to battling sexism in order to prove myself a worthwhile human being? You choose your battles, you know?

"But they didn't care about that. I had to choose *their* battle, whichever one it happened to be at the moment. I mean, a year before that it was the war; a year after, it'll be something else, Chicanos or something. Damn dervishes. It's okay. No, it's more than okay. You *should* fight for what you believe in, but—shit—how about some perspective? Some people, you take away the issues, and there's no people left, just clothes and movement buttons.

"I sure do feel silly driving down this empty, flat road, talking to myself and listening to you snore.

"I do love you, though, pumpkin. There's this guileless something inside you, this goodness, like you couldn't ever deliberately hurt anyone. I really get off on that, maybe because it's so different from me. I'm so goddam jaded. Sometimes I feel like an ogre next to you, and I want to change into someone who looks and acts like David or somebody else from a Norman Rockwell town like St. Cloud. I feel as if I'm tainting you or something. Real healthy attitude.

"You know, I think I'd like to run a sex house when I grow up. No, a beginners sex house. People who've never had sex before, or who've never had good sex, can come there and we'd teach them all kinds of positive sexual behaviors: kissing, hugging, gentle caressing. What a great place that could be.

"'Course, where could we build it? What community would be so perverted to allow such an ungodly institution as a sex house within its boundaries? I mean, shit, we can't have folks running around enjoying themselves. What would happen to the moral standards?

"Yeah, I guess the sex house is out. Same with a masturbatorium. Hm, I kind of like to orate. Maybe I could be a minister. Nah, I'd probably have to join a church. That's out.

"I could be a stud. Or an apprentice stud. Less responsibility.

"Seattle should be nice, eh, my sleeping beauty? Lush gardens, parks, arbors, endless vistas, majestic Northwest mountains. We'll actually see mountains. And we won't have to worry about driving in the snow or wearing sixteen layers of clothing from November through March. I just hope there's an actual city there, not a bunch of St. Clouds sitting next to each other. All we need to do, I figure, is get a couple of jobs that will keep us comfortable for the rest of our lives. Then we can spend our off-hours eating and fucking.

"You know, Car, things will get tougher between us. I hope we can make it. If we can keep from whirling, we should be okay. But actually, neither of us is the whirling type. I'm too vigilant, and you're too innocent. We should be safe.

"Of course, if you resist the whirling, you're going to be lonely, too. Sometimes the pressure is just too great. Jesus, Carolyn, I don't want you to be lonely. I wish I were more confident about us. I'll miss you a lot."

"Fargo!"

4. THE POPE'S ASS

Last Christmas, Steph and I flew to St. Cloud for a week, hiding our relationship, of course. I was continually aware of saying the wrong thing, of Stephanie saying the wrong thing, of betraying the true nature of our relationship in any number of ways. Two things saved us: first, my parents don't think along the lines of their daughter being a lesbian, so they weren't looking for signals. We were thus able to inject into conversations double entendres that only we understood. And second, my parents kindly arranged for us both to sleep in my bedroom, which now has twin beds for guests. We settled for eye-hugs until bedtime.

Talk about deception. One of us would lie in the bed for a minute, twisting and turning, messing up the covers, and then jump into the other bed, where we slept together. Making love in my old bedroom was something I truly never believed could happen. If my parents had been more tolerant when I was younger, who knows, I might be married to David now.

But what was the alternative to deception? Sitting my mother and father down on the Sears couch and telling them that their only daughter is a lesbian and their houseguest is her lover?

"Pop, you know how you really like women?"

No, no. Too flippant.

"Mom, I'm gay."

Nope, too direct.

"Folks, I'm very attracted to Stephanie."

Too personal.

"Hey, guess what *we* did last night!"

Much too personal.

It doesn't matter. My father would have me committed to the St. Cloud Dungeon for Wayward Daughters, and my mother would become catatonic, emerging only to prepare meals and clean up afterwards. Maybe I'll come out to them when they're old and too senile to comprehend…

My parents like Stephanie, but I get a strange feeling that they don't trust her. Strange because there was no reason to suspect her of anything. Maybe they received some primeval vibration when the two of us stood close to one another. No doubt they were disappointed that I didn't bring home a male, i.e., a potential husband. My mother, her hints becoming less subtle as I grow older, dragged Steph and me with her to look at place settings, ostensibly for a neighbor of theirs getting married the following month. But my mother kept asking me, "Is this the kind of pattern you think *you'd* like, dear?" Stephanie cried that night, and I longed to return to Seattle.

Stephanie knew that she was seen as a displacement of the time and energy I was supposed to use for man-acquisition. Obviously, PhD or not, I may as well write off my life as an abject failure if I can't hook a man. So Steph tried hard to make an impression, even with my father. She found out that his feet had been hurting him and that once or twice he had had to curtail a sermon because the pain was so distracting. We went to a junkyard, found a few pieces of wood, bought some felt and cotton, and she whipped him up a little foot stand to relieve some of the pressure from his ankles. My father was surprised—he hadn't totally believed that Stephanie was a carpenter—and thanked her, but without any warmth. Shit, maybe he thought she was coming on to him. God, that would explain a few things, including my mother's coolness, which continues to this day over the phone. Ah, yes, my lover and my father. Ministers are so damned perceptive.

With Philip it was different. Philip lied through his teeth so often to my parents that I was surprised he didn't speak with an echo. He probably impressed them more as an alien than as a lover of their daughter. But they trusted him: through all his preposterous stories and bizarre statements, even through his bitterness the last couple of times we visited, they trusted him.

Incredibly, Pop made some attempts—feeble though they were—to find out more about Philip. In the fall, for example:

"Doesn't his beard scratch you?"

Not where you'd think, Pop. "Oh, sometimes, but I get used to it."

"When I was your age, a lot of my friends had beards. They were quite the rebels."

"Well, I don't think Philip wears a beard to be rebellious. I think he just hates to shave."

"Your mother thinks he might look better if he didn't have it."

In the spring:

"Honey, explain to me again why Philip isn't graduating. I think I was helping Mother with something when you told me before."

"He is graduating. Rather, he's getting his PhD; he's not going to be in the ceremony, that's all. He doesn't like ceremonies that much. First of all, crowds make him nervous. Second of all, he doesn't believe that a ceremony is necessary. Uh, he believes that the doctorate is honor enough. And third of all, uh, there is another reason, uh…"

"Won't his parents be disappointed?"

"His parents, that's the third reason, and the most important. His parents can't come out, you know, from Boston, and so there really isn't any point in participating in the ceremony."

"It's too bad they can't come out. Can't afford it?"

"Uh, I don't know. Mr. Lester teaches at a community college; he might not make that much money. Mrs. Lester paints."

"She's an artist?"

"No, uh, she paints houses. Not many, though. It doesn't pay much, I'm sure."

"Well, it's a shame we won't get to meet them."

"I've never met them, either. Philip says they're really nice."

"I'm sure they are, honey. Did you say they had accents?"

And in the summer:

"Philip's a nice boy. What does he do now? Teach psychology?"

No, Pop, he's into abortion referrals these days. "Oh, he does a lot of different things—some teaching, some counseling. He's keeping his options open."

"As long as he can support a family."

Jesus. You should know, Lady Di, that I was never interrogated about *my* plans after graduation, except that my parents knew that I would probably get a teaching job someplace. By that time, I was considered an adjunct to Philip. It's a wonderful society we live in, when a woman's parents relegate her life to a point below that of her lover's. Evidently, my destiny was to conceive and raise Philip's children.

I'd lived with someone once before, in my senior year of college. Each of us had needed a companion, and our relationship was convenient and short-lived. He was a geologist and went to work for Shell after graduation. They were supposed to train him to find oil and sent him to Colorado, but not before my parents had their way with us.

Oh, they wailed about how their daughter had soiled the family name and would burn in hell for eternity, and so on and so on. Fucking they might be able to tolerate, it seemed, but making a public declaration about it was going too far. My father sermonized at the pulpit about concupiscence for three months straight, not naming names, of course. I think he'd actually gotten it out of his system after two months, but church attendance was so high he was probably reluctant to give up a winner.

They passed through all the phases, Lady Di. They ranted; they threatened; they laid on guilt; they pleaded; they withdrew; they each coaxed me to change for the sake of the other; they gave up; they adapted. Finally, my lover left town, and the case was moot. They never met him, never called.

Fortunately, Philip didn't have to endure any of that. I'm not certain my father would have had the sense not to start an argument with him. It might have become a patriarchal duel, the prize being the right to take care of me. I would have viewed that battle with about as much enthusiasm as I view the jockfests Stephanie watches on TV.

Stephanie liked the ben wa balls; she inserted them pretty easily, though she's going to have to practice using them. We had a lovely birthday. I cooked her up some chicken adobo, a recipe from her Filipino father, who'd dictated it to her Irish mother years ago; her father would never cook. We drank Steph's favorite wine, which lamentably is Mateus Rose, and we ate by candlelight. Then I gave her the ben wa balls, and we made love while the dishes remained in the sink. That was another present. I never leave dishes waiting to be cleaned. Something to do with order, or maybe aesthetics.

Later in the evening, a few friends came over with a birthday cake and more presents. Ann got her an X-rated coloring book, Jo a beautiful yellow blouse, Marcie a sexy nightgown (I told her what to get), and Debbie and Pam got her a set of red suspenders and a gift certificate to an Ace hardware store. At eleven thirty we all squeezed into Marcie's Dodge Dart (yclept Monica) and went to see *The Rocky Horror Picture Show*. Finally we had a quick drink, including a toast to Steph's next thirty-five years, and then back home.

Alone, Stephanie and I sat over a bottle of sherry—Harvey's Bristol Creme from her work crew—and talked quietly.

"Big day," I said.

"Yeah. Nice day. Nice birthday. Thanks."

"I had a good time. That's a great-looking nightgown Marcie bought you."

She smiled. "Marcie told me you suggested it."

"Actually, I picked it out."

"How did you get Marcie to agree to that? She doesn't like that kind of thing, you know."

"What, being sexy?"

"Dressing sexy. Women as objects."

"Jesus, Steph, she never said a thing."

"Well, I guess she figured this was an exception. You're lucky. I've seen her tear somebody apart for admitting she liked low-cut dresses."

"Well, that's a little different, don't you think?"

"Yeah, I guess so." Stephanie's fingers drummed on the stem of the glass. I waited.

"Carolyn?"

"Hmm."

"Carolyn, you're going to stay at UW, aren't you? I mean, you've come up with another field of study?"

I took her hand, the drumming one. "I'm not leaving, Steph."

It was a peaceful house. Stephanie looked beautiful, despite having drunk too much wine. Her face epitomizes the contrasts in her personality: the Irish in her strong cheeks and jaw, resolute, daunting; the dark Filipina eyes and hair, mercurial, alluring; and a hint of freckles on her nose that don't seem to come from either side of the family, the playful Stephanie.

"How do you feel being thirty-five?" I asked. "And don't give me those slick 'older and wiser' answers, either. I've heard that too many times tonight."

"What should I say, I feel the same? I do. No different. Same job as last year, well, same crew. Different hotel. Same friends." She raised her glass to me, swallowed the remainder of the sherry, and smiled. "Same lover."

"I like *that*," I said. "I come after job and friends."

She shook her head and played with the empty glass, sticky-coated with a thin layer of sherry. "No, Carolyn. You come first. You're everything to me."

"Oh, come on," I said, "let's not be so serious. It's your birthday. I was only kidding. But thank you." I kept staring at her face. "I love you, Steph."

"You *are* everything to me," she whispered. Suddenly her eyes widened, and she exploded into a yelp and laughter. I tried to find out what was going on, since she'd been so sentimental only a moment before, but I couldn't get her to stop laughing.

She finally calmed down and wiped tears from her eyes. "I forgot," she said. "I put 'em in."

"What?"

"Your birthday gift. I put them in before we left for the movie, and I forgot about them. But I was thinking about you just now, and all of a sudden, whoop!"

What little I've told Stephanie about Philip rankles her. She tends to lump him—no, that's unfair—compare him with other men she's known, admittedly a small and skewed sample. But, Di, I'm in a dilemma. If I attempt to tell her more about him, she'll accuse me—quite rightly, I suppose—of belaboring the past. But if I tell her nothing more about him, she'll perceive him no differently than any other male victimizer. And maybe that's quite right, too. Maybe I need to see Philip more through Stephanie's eyes. The thing is, we were a twosome for only a few years, and yet…and yet, so many things happened to me that were so pivotal, either because of him or despite him, or…

I miss him. It's true. Damn! Damn!

Dr. Stan noticed a tic the other day. My left eyebrow refused to obey my commands to lie still. Dr. Stan speculated that I was nervous about the article I had to complete by the end of the month to submit to the *Journal of Low Temperature Physics*. Not so, but I let him think that.

The tic doesn't arise from my class: my students like me and may even be learning something from me. It's true that the helium involves some decisions now. I've rotated a cylinder of the superfluid in the manner of Vinen, and little eddies appear, vortices. But they appear only at certain temperatures, and then they disappear. Fascinating. If I lower the temperature directly to 1.3°K, nothing happens. But if I then heat the damn thing up to 1.6°K and cool it back down, I get my vortices. That implies that the normal helium/superfluid helium ratio is critical. It's as strange as scrambling eggs and suddenly finding the yolks reforming into little whirlpools.

So I have my article; I can write it up; but I don't know the "why" of it. Isn't that the reason I do this? I should dose the whole system with electrons, or at least set up a magnetic field around the rotor. I already use second sound to probe the vorticity field; magnetism wouldn't be that much bigger of a step. But it would mean another three months of data collection and analysis for uncertain results, and I'm not likely to get the extra equipment or money for a helium swan song. If research were my life rather than my job, I might sequester myself in the lab and throw caution to the ventilation system. But it isn't and I won't.

Still, I can't leave it alone. What causes those vortices? Can I really write the article with the standard "more research is needed" paragraph without intending to do the research? Is that hypocrisy or pragmatism?

I showed Mary Ann around the lab today. She's relegated to teaching duties this year, and I wanted to get her thinking about research. She was duly impressed. She seemed preoccupied, though. Boyfriend problems, Lady Di. I shared a little of my problem, but the best she could come up with was, "Carolyn, I think you should do what you feel is right." Maybe I'll ask Joe Bennett to look at the data, though he reveres publication more than life itself.

Oh, Di, I can live with the article as is. I've made those vortices do everything except get up and sing Dixie; I don't need to be greedy about it, even if it may be the very last work I do with superfluid helium. If I had tenure, then we'd be talking fight. But I'm only an assistant professor, and we're talking bend. In any case, the tic is not from work. Even though I'm switching fields, I feel competent, I feel respected, and I'm absolutely sure I'm not repressing anything. About work. All I have to do is tell Dr. Stan that I'll work on something else. He'll say okay, give me the materials I need, and that will be that.

And despite what Steph thinks, I'm not suffering from guilt over my heterosexual past, either. I do feel a little guilty about it, but I'm aware of the guilt. It's not that. It's something else that makes me suspect the Greeks were right, and your uterus really does break loose and travel around your body. I'll have Stephanie check it out with a flashlight.

Soon after the masturbation campaign, late 1975, Philip and I spent a weekend with the folks. It was my idea; I thought we should get out of town and relax. Needless to say, Di, we told my parents nothing about the campaign. I'm certain I offered at least one prayer a day to any god who would listen that the St. Cloud newspapers wouldn't pick up what Philip was doing in St. Paul. Lord, my father would have sent out a Lutheran hit squad after Philip.

Ruth and Hank were another source of worry. Living in Minneapolis, they had access to St. Paul political information. But I figured, even if the news did make it into Minneapolis, Ruth was too smart to say anything and Hank was too stupid to read the papers.

I decided to show Philip around St. Cloud. I'd never done that before; we usually stayed in the house or drove to a specific location and back. And I hadn't been out to see what changes, if any, had occurred in the years since I'd lived there.

I like St. Cloud. It's a nice, pleasant town of forty thousand, about an hour's drive from the Twin Cities. Just like my folks' home, "nice" is the best word to describe it. Nice people live there, who own nice stores, all of which do nice businesses. There are nice schools, a nice hospital, even a nice reformatory. Nobody gets very excited about anything, except maybe hockey, and there's the usual small-town gossip and corruption. St. Cloudians could be poster babies for "Middle-Class Disease."

Philip detested St. Cloud.

Dervishes

He reviled the small-town, small-time thinkers who lived there, the ones who were content to—God, how did he put it: "let their lives drain out into a cesspool of mediocrity" or something rosy like that. Life was a struggle to Philip, and he believed that those who didn't struggle were giving in and up, and pretending everything was fine when it obviously was far from fine. He couldn't understand "getting along," but that's exactly what St. Cloudians do.

Listening to his grumbly judgments, I drove Philip around St. Cloud; I wanted to show him what a pretty town it really was. I took him to my high school, to our church, to "downtown," to parks, to some of the outlying areas. An unstopped jug full of childhood memories overflowed at each place we went, evoking faces, sounds, events. I bounced around from age to age like a pogo stick over used calendars. Here I was at five with long blonde hair, going shopping with my mother. Here I was at fifteen, breasts developed and mascara applied, trying to eat with the salad fork on a "heavy" date in a fancy restaurant, chaperoned, of course, by two older church members. Here I was back at ten or eleven, playing in the snow with my friends and almost being buried when a snowdrift collapsed on me. And here was the drugstore where I bought my first box of tampons (that was well before I had resolved both the fear that I would lose my virginity by using them and the confusion over where in fact they were supposed to go. Oh, surely not there, I remember thinking). Here was my first kiss, here my first experience driving a car, here the house where my best friend, the one who got pregnant in high school, lived. Here was my first encounter with a crazy man who shouted at pedestrians. Here I actually slapped a boy because he told me that I acted like a snob, and that only dumb girls acted smarter than they really were. It took me awhile to figure that one out.

But Philip saw a different town. He pointed at the immense concrete monolith in front of St. Cloud's newest, most modern church, and carped that the money to build the church and especially the monolith should more appropriately have been spent on local needy families.

He illustrated how "insensitive" the town was by putting its elderly in a four-story rest home and its sick in a hospital right off a noisy highway.

Neal Starkman

He pointed out all the signs that deliberately misspelled words to describe various businesses: "E-Z," "Sav-Mor," "Kar-Kare," "Klippen Kurl," and "Shop Rite."

He showed me litter in the park, potholes in the street, graffiti on fences, and ugly billboards everywhere we drove.

He continued his observations in a department store by citing a list of items he maintained ought to be destroyed immediately: digital watches that you needed both hands to operate, personalized stationery, high heels, cocktail stirrers, orange-juice squeezers, hamburger presses, ties (no doubt a reaction left over from the campaign), stockings, bras (no argument there), purses, steering-wheel covers, makeup, hats, couch pillows, room deodorizers, indoor thermometers, lettuce spinners, popcorn poppers, plastic garbage bags, electric coffee makers, toasters, greeting cards, ironing boards, deep fryers, exercise equipment, cigarette lighters, spice racks, and teapots. Philip could be quite a downer.

Part of me was infuriated. It was my town! And he was spoiling it for me. He was spoiling not only my memories but any future experiences as well. Some things you just do not want to look at that closely.

But part of me understood, too. He was venting. The campaign was still seething inside him, and he was slowly letting out the steam like a gashed chestnut. More later about people-as-chestnuts. St. Cloud happened to be there when Philip needed it, just like it was there when as a child I needed it. In sum, I didn't take it personally, and my hometown seemed none the worse for his virulence.

My reaction wouldn't have been the same today. I no longer believe in trading my sense of well-being for someone else's. Times have changed. I was raised with the notion that my pleasure came last, if at all, and then it was incidental. I accepted it. Stephanie was raised with the same notion, only she fought it.

Stephanie's family was poor, her father a laborer, her mother burdened with pregnancy most of the time—five boys and two girls, good Catholics.

Steph had to fend for herself: if she didn't assert herself, if she didn't *aggress* herself, she simply didn't get. Her feminism grew out of that, a feminism based on equal parts of Simone de Beauvoir's *Off Our Backs* and Thomas Hobbes. Stephanie knew the feelings before she read the words, and I think only recently has she begun to read the important feminist literature. But she's been involved with women and women's groups over half her life, and she knows more about what it is to be a woman than anyone I've ever known.

My lover is not verbal, but when she talks about women, she rhapsodizes. It's like a pep talk—angry, reverent, inspiring. To Stephanie, a woman radiates beauty. She has the emotional capacity to empathize with sisters of all ages, races, and stations in life. She has resolve: she knows where she's going because she's aware of where she's been. She can give birth to a child, feed it from her own body, and care for it from a depthless supply of love. She is competent and heroic and compassionate. And her sexual apparatus is so sophisticated, so magnificently constructed, that she can have orgasm after orgasm without once getting the bed messy.

Oh, Lady Di, there are so many influences. Am I living first Philip's world, then Stephanie's, then my parents'? How do I know? Doesn't anyone else have this problem? I need a vacation.

There are so many biases that you overlook them. I know I'd feel awkward going to, say, Mexico or Club Med, with Stephanie. I'm still self-conscious going to the drive-in with her. It disgusts me to feel that way. I'd not think twice about going to a drive-in with a woman who was only a friend. I never felt this way when I went with male lovers. But when I'm with Stephanie, I feel like I have a "Scarlet L" for lesbian branded on my chest. It's not as if we cavort on the hood or climb in the back seat and get wet. It's just *lesbinoia*. Even today, in liberal 1980 Seattle.

Carolyn: "Some popcorn, please."

Sneering concessionaire: "Sure. Do you want one for your lover, too, or is she going to share?"

It would be the same on a vacation, or in St. Cloud. I should be able to bring Stephanie home as my lover, and my parents should accept and welcome her as they did Philip. But my father would never, ever understand. He's not made to understand. How can you change a man's mind when he's spent so much of his life not only believing in rigid doctrines but also preaching them to others?

Philip claimed my father was a sexist and a bigot, and I was put in the position of defending my father. Forget how insensitive it is to castigate your lover's father; the point is that it was difficult for me to disagree with him.

Waiting in the theater for *A Thousand Clowns* to begin, audience gathering, I spoke in muted tones, Philip in normal ones:

"Why don't you think my father's a good man? He cares for his family—"

"He *should* care for his family. Listen, Car, it's like Ford. What do they say about Ford? He's an honest man and an honest president. Honesty is one of his greatest assets. Bullshit, assets! (It's a middle-class theater; I look around apologetically.) Honesty should be a goddam requirement, not an asset! Why is Ford a good man? He's about as intelligent as a belch, he's impervious to the problems of the underprivileged, he's intolerant of any but the most traditional attitudes, let alone behaviors. Why is Ford so good? In comparison to what? In comparison to what he could be like? Terrific. What a standard!

"Why is your father so good? What does he do in order to so generously care for his family? He entertains people! He reinforces them for thanking Jesus Christ for all the wonderful things they have and blaming themselves anytime there's a shit shower! (I consider falling to the floor to search for an imaginary contact lens, but I know Philip will continue to perorate.) Great way to make a living! Makes me proud to know him!"

"Philip, I don't want you talking about my father like that. All right, you don't believe in Jesus Christ, but many people do. My father helps those people, and he's very giving. There's nothing wrong with devoting your life to something you believe in."

"What does your father believe in? I think he's in it for the power and the glory! He's a Christian! What does that mean?" (I receive glances from neighboring theater patrons; the glances are not friendly. I consult my watch; do movies ever begin early?) "Judging by the way he treats you and your mother, he obviously doesn't believe that all people are created equal. We all may have been made in God's image, but there sure seems to be a hierarchy of respect."

"That's a little simplistic, don't you think?" (It is so difficult to convey indignation when whispering.) "My father respects people. He gives of himself every day of his life. It's not a nine-to-five job being a minister, you know. And you can't pick and choose who will need spiritual care. All right, he's sexist in some ways. He can't help it. He was brought up to believe that women have a certain place, predominantly as raisers of families. Everyone in his life believes that, including my mother. Jefferson had slaves; it's the same thing. He's a product of the forces that act on him continuously, Philip, just as you are. You're a product of your upbringing. You've had different experiences. My father is not cruel."

"Your father's a hypocrite, Carolyn, and for that matter, so was Jefferson." (A fat middle-aged couple sits next to us, guarding in their laps what seems to be half the refreshment bar—popcorn, pop, candy, ice cream. Her hair is in rollers, his ought to be. They are studiously trying not to listen to us.) "I don't buy this upbringing shit! That may explain how the bigotry got there in the first place, but unless you're stupid, there's no good reason why you can't change. You either respect people or you don't. I can see showing disrespect for what people do or for what they make of themselves. But that's a hell of a lot different than disrespecting people for being born a particular way—female, or black, or whatever."

"You think my father doesn't respect me?"

"I think he doesn't respect you as a woman. He can lead a congregation, but you can't. He can support a family, but you can't. He can be aggressive, but you can't. Hell, he can make love with a woman, but you can't!" (Someone actually shushes us; Philip ignores the shusher. I sweat.) "Your father condemns you for being a woman. You didn't choose to be female; you had nothing to do with it. You should be neither praised nor condemned. But your father's a hypocrite if he claims to respect people. He makes invalid distinctions."

"Jesus, Philip, if you take that line, who *isn't* a hypocrite?"

"I don't know, Car. All I know is that some of us are more hypocritical than others. But the churchies, like your father" (and, I think, like half the people within earshot), "are the biggest hypocrites of all, 'cause they're the loudest in their pretensions. I'd bet a plate of brownies that the Pope's ass is covered with hickeys."

As you might have been able to guess, Di, that conversation was post-campaign, when Philip was bristling with resentment. I had hoped that after the radio speech things would return to normal, and I would have my old lover back, the funny one, the sarcastic but perversely life-affirming erstwhile psychologist who was as curious at the way people behave as I was at the way atoms behave.

Not so. Philip's conversations went from seminars to screeds. Hypocrisy was at the top of his hit parade, probably because, like me, he cherished order and logic, and hypocrisy is neither orderly nor logical. I just didn't like him to erupt in public. You would think that I'd have adjusted by that time; I was tempted to buy Groucho Marx glasses.

Steph and I talked last night. Debbie and Pam had come over for dinner, and I was not my usual gregarious self. It could be because Pam had had a fight with a friend, and we all jumped for about fifteen minutes to help her relax. Luckily, that was before the pasta and sausage.

Steph thinks I'm preoccupied with these reminiscences, which is true, and that I'm heading for a depression if I keep writing, which also may be true. I don't think she appreciated my response that I may need to be depressed to find out what's bothering me.

"I thought you were worried because you were so hyper," she said. "You're not hyper tonight. Maybe you're cured."

I'm not cured. If anything, I feel worse for making Stephanie anxious. She's thinking, but hasn't yet expressed, that I'm still being influenced by Philip. I really don't think that's true, but I'm aware that I might not realize it if it were true. I'm careful not to mention him around her, anyway.

Philip was important: he knew heterosexual Carolyn, socialist Carolyn, feminist Carolyn, bisexual Carolyn, and, I suppose, lesbian Carolyn. But there's a big difference between his being important and his holding sway over me. Lady Di, I'm telling it to you straight, I am noted for being an independent thinker, and I do things Philip would sneer at.

I remember giving an independence talk to women undergraduates last fall. I helped organize the women's caucus at the university, comprising women professors and administrators from all the departments. We watchdog the administration on salaries and personnel decisions, and we speak before incoming freshwomen.

I was telling this group about all the women's programs available in the university, about the Women's Information Center, about women's groups and organizations in the Seattle area, about their legal and ethical rights. I spoke about careers in the sciences, and about how few women were represented in, for example, physics and chemistry. But I didn't push them one way or another. I told them that they had to make up their own minds about what they wanted to do. I want to be only an indirect influence, you see.

But, you know, I was talking about all this, giving these two hundred young women the benefits of my knowledge, and I saw from my little podium maybe half a dozen women applying makeup. There were several others not paying attention. Don't get me wrong, Di, I am not the world's most captivating speaker—but they were applying makeup! While I'm talking to them about their rights, their opportunities!

"You! In the third row! With the eyeliner! Yes, you! Stand up!"

"Wh-What?"

"You heard me! Stand up! Now, what is your name?"

"Sandy Carson."

"Sandy Carson. How old are you, Sandy?"

"I'm eighteen."

"I see. Sandy, do you like eyeliner?"

"What? Y-Yes, sure, I guess so."

"Good. Eat it."

"What?"

"You heard me. Eat it, all of it!"

"B-But—"

"Hold her down, that's it, she'll learn…"

Well, Di, maybe I want to be more direct some times than others.

Philip was raised to be independent, always encouraged to do things on his own. I envy that upbringing, although I suppose there's a trade-off. Philip always felt alone, never had any ties—family, religion, not even me. I don't know what Philip's opiate was. Maybe it used to be humor, then the self-indulgence of depression.

Stephanie won her independence by ignoring her parents. Her father was a male supremacist who physically and mentally abused her mother; her mother passed on the authoritarianism to her children, especially her daughters. Mrs. Marillo was a strict Catholic, her faith apparently confirmed by the misery in which she continually found herself.

"Your mother never told you about sex, did she, Steph?"

"My mother? By the time my mother even got around to it, I knew more than she did and wasn't listening to her about anything, anyway. Shit, she told me something once about spiritual happiness, and what God expected of me, and what my obligations were to my husband, all that crap. The straight line."

"She believed it?"

"Doesn't your mother?"

Yes, of course my mom believes it. My mother doesn't even mention sex. It's one of those things like bad weather. She just puts up with it. She realizes that all the rain and snow are necessary, but it's still a nuisance. My folks probably stopped having sex after I was conceived, figuring they'd met their responsibility to spawn.

I have tried, Lady Di, to break through to my mother. I tried last Christmas. I've desperately wanted to meet the woman behind the facade. All these years I've been closer to Pop. Too late I see what a mistake I've made. I catered to him just like Mom has. He has all the control in the family. He is so persuasive that I began to identify with him rather than with my mother, which, in part, explains why I haven't ended up a mom-clone, ironing some man's shirts and watching soap operas.

Last year, though, I felt the need for, I don't know, the unity with my mother that I know exists. We're both women, both been raised as women. A strong bond: she's my sister as well as my mother.

I guess I felt that she was always in the background and needed someone to ask her the right questions. Then, Lady Di, she would be revealed as a clever, insightful woman with worthwhile ideas. That was the plan. I determined that once she recognized I was open to dealing with her woman-to-woman, she'd revert to the individual she was before committing herself to a lifetime role as Pop's housewife.

My father had gone to the store. Stephanie tagged along with him to curry favor and to leave my mom and me alone (Pop no doubt suspected that Stephanie was considering seducing him). Mom and I were tidying up the kitchen after lunch. It was a perfect setting. Her graying hair was in a bun, her apron was creased yet unstained, and she looked the epitome of traditional middle-aged womanhood. What a scene: daughter dutifully drying dishes; mother putting on water for tea, Lipton pekoe, of course; the house still, the wallpaper secretly peeling. We could have been on a calendar with the Lord's Prayer.

And now, here are the two women sitting over their Lipton, mother stirring it with honey, daughter impatiently waiting for the right time to bridge the gap. We've talked before, of course, but in generalities, abstractions. If I hadn't been nervous, I would have asked an appropriate question, like "Mom, how do you feel about not having a career all these years?" But I was a little nervous.

"Mom, do you love Pop?"

Tentative toleration. What's my college daughter up to? "What a question; of course I love your father. Why do you ask something like that? Dear, is something wrong?"

Ah, shifting to the offense. Best to ignore it. "Can I ask you something without your getting upset?"

She gets up to rummage for a napkin and brings back two, in addition to a bowl of fruit she quickly composes from individual items in the refrigerator. "Well, how do I know whether I'll be upset until I hear whatever it is you're asking me? I hope I won't be upset. Don't ask me, dear, if you think it's going to upset me. Your old-fashioned mother is used to her ways, you know."

Okay, laying the foundation for the guilt, just in case it's needed. "I just wonder, Mom, if you like sex. You know, if you like sex with Pop. You never talk about it."

Frantic stirring of tea. "Carolyn, I really don't think it's anything to talk about. Private matters should be left private. There's no reason to talk about it. Your father and I have a warm, beautiful, loving, Christian relationship. That's the important part, the only important part. The flesh should not be our concern."

Why did I begin with such a touchy subject? I'm such an idiot sometimes. But press on, it's too late to retreat. "But why shouldn't you talk about sex? I just wondered if you enjoyed it or not."

"And I suppose you enjoy it."

She tries to shift again, but she does it wrong. "Yes, I love sex. I think it's extremely pleasurable. What about you?"

"Carolyn, we have tried to raise you with certain Christian principles. Some of these principles you have stuck with, I'm glad to say—" God, which ones?—"and others you have chosen to disregard. Your father and I have borne you as the fruit of our marriage. I have done my part by providing your father and you with a home that respects the Lord, and your father has done his part by spreading the Word."

"Is that your only role: raising the family, taking care of the home?"

Gulps of tea; it must scald her. "Yes! And it's good enough for me! Even if it's not for you!"

A deep cut to my quick. She does it better than Sally. I persist, though; we Andersons are stubborn. "You never told me if you enjoyed sex."

"I just want to know how such ideas get into your head in the first place. Never mind, I know." Philip, but later she'll regret saying that. "Young lady, I *am* upset. I'm upset because you concern yourself so much with the physical side of life and ignore the spiritual side. It's not good for you, sweetheart. You need to find a good Christian man like your father. We love you, and we want to see you happy and settled down." End of tea. End of discussion. End of bridging the gap, until next time.

If I were there constantly, Di, I could get to her, I know I could. But I'm too far away, and she has Pop and all her friends and the church to feed her the wrong gospel, and that's besides the normal influences of TV shows, "women's" magazines, the economic and legal systems, and advertising.

I need to spirit her away and deprogram her: first break down her resistance by forcing her to eat without napkins; then surround her with ardent feminists; then get across some vital ideas in regard to women and their relationship with a male-oriented society. I'd start out with simple, nonthreatening ideas and work my way up to the big stuff.

I'm in an old farmhouse in the middle of a field. I'm sitting in an old, sparse room with Stephanie, Marcie, and a few other friends. I alternate between perching on the end of a tattered davenport and pacing the dusty floor. I'm chain-smoking. My friends take turns consoling me with kind words and gentle hands on my shoulder. The house is very quiet, except for two ominous sounds. One is the steady tick-tock of an old upright timepiece. The other is muffled shouts and occasional whimpers from the other end of the house. I stare at the clock when I'm not fidgeting or attempting to peer through the walls into the other room.

"Relax, Carolyn," says Stephanie.

"Relax? She's been in there almost four hours. How can I relax? We're talking about my mother."

Marcie comes over and holds my hand. "Birdie's the best in the business," she says. "You have to trust her."

Stephanie pours refills of some strong liquor, and we continue to wait. Sometimes there is a commotion, and I grimace; other times it is quiet, and I imagine what can be going on. It seems as if we have been here, in this lonely farmhouse, all our lives. We have always waited, always strained to hear telltale noises from the other room, always inhaled the musty remnants of people and things that occupied this room in another existence. There is no sense of time or space here; neither has beginning or end. I am glad my friends are with me.

We hear, faintly, a door open, and several moments later Birdie and my mother appear in the hallway. A few of us are standing. Both Birdie and my mother are disheveled, smudged, hair mussed. Birdie's forehead is bruised, her long gray hair in tangles. Her wise face is sallow, her body limp. Birdie's eyes are dull, her mouth set, but I can detect a grim smile buried underneath; it will take time to dig itself out. My mother looks hazy, as if she's just come back from a long journey to a place she never wanted to see.

"I think your mother wants to tell you something, Carolyn." Birdie's voice startles me; it is hoarse, like an emery board might sound. She reaches for the cigarettes on the table, lights one, and takes a long draw and looks at my mother.

"Mom?" I say, walking up to her.

My mom's lips quiver, and her eyes meet me briefly before jittering off. "Carolyn."

"Are you all right, Mom?" I want to hold her, but Birdie senses it and gestures me off.

"Carolyn," my mother says, looking through me and speaking as if someone just taught her how to use her larynx, "women are—are oppressed, and they m-must rid themselves of the tethers fastened by m-men intent on dom-domination. Women should be free to earn a fair wage, keep their names when married…"

Even in her robotic voice, she falters, but Birdie commands, "Go on."

My mother approaches tears, and I want to comfort her, tell her everything will be fine. But I know there's time for that later.

"W-women must be free to—to choose how to deal with—with pregnancies." My mother drops her head, and the tears fall, disappearing in the dust. She is the stranger here, little woman absurdly overdressed. No one moves.

Neal Starkman

"Continue!" shouts Birdie, and I look to her as if to plead, no more. But she is unyielding, and her eyes regain some fire.

"Please." My mother shakes her head. Then she looks at me, weeping still, but with a new resolve I have never seen before. Behind me, Stephanie sniffles.

"And," my mom says in a firm voice, "women must be free to love other women."

She falls into my arms, and now everyone is crying. Birdie joins the embrace, and then Stephanie comes over. It is done. I hope my eyes convey gratitude to Birdie. I know she has been through this dozens of times before.

Well, Di, we can only hope it doesn't come to that. Maybe it will be spontaneous. Maybe my mother will slip into an altered state of consciousness. I've gotten her subscriptions to *Ms.*, but I think she misses, or *Ms.es*, the point. She thinks that developing herself to her full capacity is just fine but doesn't see that as conflicting with kowtowing to Pop or frittering away her life washing dishes.

Philip was right about people being hypocrites, but they're not malicious. They're afraid. My mother is afraid to dance to another tune lest she stumble. My father is afraid to permit my mother to become his equal; he feels that the more she gets, the less he keeps. And probably the Pope is afraid of having sex and enjoying it. And of letting those hickeys on his ass show through his satin undies.

And Philip too was a hypocrite. I listened to the tape and felt his struggle and his conflicts. Maybe he couldn't show me the hickeys on his ass, or else then I'd see that he was afraid of my becoming his equal.

Oh Di, does that fit? Does it make sense? Am I changing the facts to fit the theory? I don't want this to be a revisionist history of me-and-Philip. When I stray from a certain order, I get in trouble. And I feel I need to tighten these reminiscences. I want to know what was real, what continues to be real.

I know Philip loved me. I know that after the masturbation campaign, he needed to love me more than ever, yet that's when he constricted himself into a little coil where I couldn't get to him. The biggest casualty of the campaign.

"He ripped you off!"

Oh Di, I definitely should have opened up sooner—and wider—to Steph. Evidently, I've not been paying as much attention to Ms. Marillo as is warranted by our commitments to each other. And of course I did something stupid again.

She'd had a bad day. Her boss refused to give her a three-day weekend that she'd wanted next week in order to take a little vacation with me. I knew she was upset when she came home and jumped for twenty minutes. Then, I'd been supposed to make dinner—no afternoon class—but instead spent my time walking in Ravenna Park and writing to you, Lady Di. Finally, I inexplicably volunteered the information that Philip had been a tolerably good cook. Smart move, PhD: Stephanie hit the roof.

"How can you say that he ripped me off?" I said. "You didn't even know him."

Stephanie's eyes blazed, incongruously sensual. "I know *you*, Carolyn! And Philip was a man. And he ripped you off, just like any other man would. Maybe he was smoother than a lot of others, all right? But sure as shit, woman, he did a job on you. He's still doing a job on you!"

"What do you mean?"

"What do I mean?" She shook her head like she was trying to teach me something that I should already have known. "Listen, Carolyn, how much of what you think now was fed into you by Philip?"

"Oh, I don't know. I suppose I hold a few attitudes that might originally have been nurtured—"

Neal Starkman

"A few? A few plus a ton. A few. Look, Carrie, I'm sure that Philip was good to you in some ways. You're not like those women who let themselves be battered and crawl back for more because they're 'lost in love.' You're smart, okay? But, sweetie, you've got to realize, he played 'Big Daddy' with you. He forced his attitudes on you. Carolyn, he was your counselor, father, and priest all rolled into one. He used you, Carolyn, until he didn't need you anymore. Is that a commitment? Is that a loving relationship? You and I have been together for over a year, and I guess I hoped that I was satisfying you in a way that he couldn't. Put him behind you already!"

"Stephanie, why are you so upset about this?"

"Why am I upset? Because for two weeks now you've been lost in the Wonderful World of Philip. How would Philip react to this, what would Philip say about that?"

"I've hardly mentioned Philip at all."

"You don't think you've mentioned him. You just mentioned him before, with the cooking, the damn cooking. Philip was such a good cook. Carolyn, he's always here! I didn't sign up to live with him, only you! You never used to be like this. Now, all of a sudden, you're thinking about him all the time!"

"Oh, so now you're a mind reader, Ms. Marillo. I hadn't realized the extent of your talents."

Oh yes, Lady Di, Carolyn reaches into her bag of defensive weapons and, what do we have here? Heavy sarcasm! Wonderful! And Carolyn uses it on her lover. But being heavy, it bespoke its origins, and I apologized. I apologized for everything, several times. I held her and we stood there for a little while and I apologized several more times.

"Carolyn—" she pushed me away to look at me—"I don't care about Philip. But I care lots about you. You're eating yourself up over him. I'd rather eat you up." She smiled. "I just want you to be careful, honey. Write in your diary, go ahead. But, dammit, Carrie, keep things clear, will you? You're my woman, not Philip's. Not anymore."

I nodded, a chastised child, and we kissed and held each other some more. I told her she was right and that I'd make sure I paid more attention to her, because I loved her.

"Friends?" I asked.

"Friends and lovers," she said, and gently squeezed my ass.

So I'm putting things into perspective now. I will remember that I have a life out there, and that diarizing must be secondary. Oh, Lady Di, you aren't hurt, are you? I love you as much as ever. We just can't do it as often, you know?

The person-as-chestnut, as I promised, Di, a few days ago. I was eating chestnuts with Darrel, a gay man I met last year at a local conference for sexual minorities. Darrel lives with his lover in a rather dilapidated house on Capitol Hill. But they've fixed it up quite a bit, bought expensive furniture, laid in some rugs, the predictable ferns, and attractive French posters. The house has a fireplace, too, something I wish our house had, but we took what we could get. Anyway, we were poking the chestnuts under the grating with forks, so they'd get cooked from all sides. Little by little they'd open, and we'd use the forks to roll them out, crack open gingerly, and eat even more gingerly.

"Have you ever done this without scoring them first?" asked Darrel, hot-potatoing one of them.

"Of course; hasn't everybody? Except this was in the oven."

"That's right," he said. "You don't have a fireplace, do you?"

"No, I wish we did."

Neal Starkman

"I love it."

"Yeah."

"What happened with the chestnuts?"

"Well, Stephanie had never had chestnuts before. Can you believe that? A Northwest native never having had chestnuts. I'm from Minnesota, I've had chestnuts—although I guess they're from Italy, anyway, aren't they? Well, I was going to surprise her, so I scored about half a dozen of them and put them in the oven. When she came home, I put the oven on—you know, about four hundred—and in a little while we had roasted chestnuts."

"Did she like them?"

"She hated the first one, but then she started to get into the texture."

"Oh, artichokes always do that to me."

"Yeah, me too. Artichokes and peeling hard-boiled eggs. I like that, too."

"You know, Carolyn, how you can steam them with a little butter and lemon, and then pick the petals off—"

"And eat the meat with your lower teeth, sort of scrape it off—"

"Oh, God, that's great. Next time try some tarragon with the butter and lemon."

"Well, it's the same thing with chestnuts. I guess she liked the graininess. I don't know, maybe at first she was expecting it to be like a walnut or something. Then when she got used to it, it was okay. Well, she really got into them and went back into the kitchen to put a bunch more into the oven."

"And you forgot to tell her to put the little gash in them."

"It just never dawned on me; it's so automatic. You knife a little x on the end; everybody knows that. So, Steph came back, and we continued eating the rest of the chestnuts. All of a sudden—"

"Boom!"

"It was actually pretty funny. Stephanie shouted, like 'Ah!,' and I started laughing at her. I knew what it was immediately. Pretty impressive, huh? A physicist not remembering about heated air escaping from a closed cylinder. If I did that in school, they'd can my ass and make me pay for the damage."

"Things explode when you make them hot," said Darrel, nodding. He looked so reflective; I can never tell when Darrel is double-enténdring.

"Anybody I know?" I asked.

"Steven's like that." He finally picked up on my smile and returned it. "I mean that non-sexually, dirty mind."

"I was going to say, sometimes you *want* people to explode when you make them hot."

"I mean in terms of anger. I can almost see him churning away inside when he's tense. And then he gets so angry. It's like, he works in a pet store, and he has all these bitchy ladies bringing in their little dogs to get cleaned. Oh, Carolyn, I tell you, these dogs would send you up the wall. They're just awful. He gets mad at them; you know, they yip and nip at him. I don't know how he puts up with it. One day I just know I'm going to find what's left of a Pekingese in our Cuisinart."

"Oh, Darrel!" I laughed at the image, and he did, too, shaking his head.

"No, no, I'm only kidding. Steven wouldn't do that. He's too responsible. All he does is smile. Like this." Darrel gave a shit-eating grin. "But when he comes home, he's ready to burst. I'm glad he's not an alcoholic."

"Do you cut a gash in him?"

"If there's time. Sometimes it's too late."

"It's harder when they don't talk," I said. Or, I thought, when they do nothing but talk.

"Yeah." Darrel was lost in visions of Steven.

"It's too bad," I said. "When you gash them, and they open up, the meat is so sweet inside. When they explode, all you've got is a mess to clean up."

One of the big problems Philip and I had was his recognition of me-as-woman. He'd have none of it. Philip insisted that I was simply Carolyn, with a tangle of characteristics, one of which was my sex.

I could not make him understand, or admit to understanding, that being a woman, as opposed to being a man, was not *a* difference, it was *the* difference. It was not the same as my being five-foot-two or my liking peach ice cream. But Philip, who could be so broad-minded about some things, was so—how should we say—porcine about this.

Between the times of the masturbation campaign and "My First Lesbian Experience"—you really do have to capitalize that, Di, like *Anno Domini*—some months after we arrived in Seattle, I became interested in women. I can't even plot the course. It seemed so natural that I remember recriminating myself because I hadn't pursued it before.

My interest in politics, my fascination with socialism, was the opening. The campaign showed me that I was both competent at playing politics and interested in learning about it. And it also showed me that I shouldn't count myself out of anything that I'd been conditioned not to be a part of. For some women it's natural sciences; for others, it's business; for me, it was politics. And for me, politics was not so dissimilar from physics. Substances interact in certain ways, and we can alter those interactions by modifying the variables. And political systems interact in certain ways, and we can alter those interactions by changing the environment. Inviolable laws govern the political world as well as the physical world. The order was there for me, Di; the challenge was finding it.

The more I studied and the more I observed how systems worked, the more I realized two things: first, the variable of women was never figured into the equations. Class differences accounted for something; racial and religious differences had an impact on history; certainly wars have been waged over nationalistic differences. But change because of sex differences has been systematically ignored, either because it hasn't happened or because all the historians have been men.

The second thing I realized was that the variable of women *could* make a vital difference. When you added in the extra variable—women voting in a bloc, women controlling money sources, women asserting their familial rights—then change was inevitable.

I read more, and I joined a feminist group, and I talked with people. Soon I found a theory of explanation, a structure upon which I could base many of my feelings, my observations, and my experiences over the years. Well, of course, I thought, this explains why boys in high school shied away from me, why I often saw my father get angry but never my mother, why some of my relatives laughed when I told them I intended to be a physicist. This was why I had a harder time getting information on birth control than I did on quantized vortices in superfluid helium. This was why I always felt either like a rock or a window when men looked at me. It all made sense, and it still makes sense. It's not me at all. It's not that I'm strange or ugly or stupid. It's that I'm female, and that others react to my femaleness in strange or ugly or stupid ways.

For the scientist in me, this was a revelation. Seldom do theories appear that are so elegant, so parsimonious, so entirely encompassing of the facts. But there it was; how could I have ignored it for so long? The politics of women pushed away the politics of socialism in my consciousness; the issue was paramount. The discussions I had those first few months in Seattle were extremely life-affirming, exhilarating.

The discussions I had with Philip, on the other hand, frustrated me beyond endurance. It's not as if I had to address his sexism, not quite. I'm not sure—I'm still not sure—if his attitude was sexist at all. In some respects, I was the one with the sexist attitude. I *wanted* him to discriminate because of sex.

"But I *am* a woman!"

"True enough. You're a woman, you're Caucasian, you have blue eyes—"

"Philip, you know what I'm talking about. You and I, we're different. And we're different principally because you've been treated as a man your entire life and I've been treated as a woman my entire life. That makes for some very large differences in our personalities—whether or not you approve."

"How would you wish me to treat you because you're a woman?"

"You don't have to treat me in any particular way! Just appreciate the fact that because I'm a woman, the world reacts to me in different ways than it does to you. Every day I feel it. I see it, Philip, whether it's intercepting a leer from a downtown construction worker or talking to women friends who've been denied promotions or being patronized by a clerk or reading about another rape in the park or watching a sexist ad on TV or reviewing a physics text with not a single goddam reference to any woman in the past thousand years. It really hurts, Philip, what's gone on, what continues to go on; and if you're going to remain an important part of my life, you've got to understand that."

"Carolyn, I don't dispute any of your claims. I sympathize. But we're talking about me and you, not about men and women. I have more in common with you than with—shit—Richard Nixon, though evidence indicates that he and I each have a penis and you don't. There are too many other factors involved: intelligence, wealth, humor, friendliness. Sex isn't that important to me, with the exception that I like having it with women and not with men."

"But it's important to me! Can't you see that? It has to be! If Richard Nixon were born a woman, what do you think her chances would have been of being elected president? Or even senator? Virginia Woolf wrote about the same thing: Shakespeare's sister would never have had a chance. Philip, my sexual identity is the most important thing I have. I'm proud of that, I'm proud that I'm a woman. Why are you closing your eyes?"

"Because you're whirling."

Useless, Lady Di, utterly useless. That was the gist of our "discussions." I couldn't talk *isms* with Philip, particularly feminism. I'd say something about men in general, and he'd defend himself. It'd be like saying, well the Jews killed Jesus, and Philip jumping up and shouting, hey, I wasn't even there that night.

And because he was defensive, he took the opposite line of whatever I brought up. If I mentioned economic inequities, he'd point out that I had a job and he didn't. If I remarked on the disproportionate number of women in the professions, he'd suggest that many women had the option to remain in school but instead chose to drop out and raise families. Philip, of course, was pure. Philip never contributed to any inequities.

The Seattle women's groups saved me. The women in my groups respected me for my accomplishments and also for my perspective. They reflected my observations back to me, made them stronger and more valid, like a special fun house mirror. Philip reflected my observations, too, only they came back all mangled and squashed, barely recognizable.

Oh, Di, it's still easy to be all caught up in this. And I don't have the time or energy for it. I have my undergraduate class and my graduate seminar to teach, and I have the article to write. And I have the women's caucus meetings, and different Lesbian Resource Center events, and my own advisees, and of course Stephanie and you, Di. And I'd like to do other things, too. I'd like to get on a volleyball team again; I don't get enough exercise, and I'll never be an Olympic jump-in-placer. I'd like to write a text. I'd like to spend more time with friends, even make some new friends, and go to more shows and plays and dinners and ballets and operas.

And next week I'm invited to a dinner party at Joe and Marge Bennett's. My closest colleague in the department, Joe, works much too hard; he's got his teeth into so many projects his toothbrush must be a mile long. And Marge is the kind of captured woman who'd *swallow* her teeth if she had an inkling of what I did with my social life.

Lately, though, it sounds as if Marge has been stretching a bit, looking around her for something more. It will be interesting to see if Joe's self-professed liberalism will stretch as far as Marge's needs.

Joe suspects I'm lesbian, but he's too devious to ask me about it, which is just as well, except he hints around at it with what he must think is slyness. I tolerate him. I have little choice, actually. He's a good scientist. He knows something about superfluids, and he's been careful lately not to mention anything about my research—aside from general data interpretations—because he knows it's ending. It's as if my studies have contracted a terminal illness. I suppose they have: *budgetitis*. Everyone tiptoes around, not mentioning the dreaded *budgetitis*. So Joe's sensitive enough not to talk about it. I respect that, even though I have to block out how much of a turd he is most of the time. Anyway, I enjoy watching him watch me.

An example from last week. Scene: my office. Time: about ten o'clock. My door is open, I'm grading student papers, and Joe comes smiling in. How he believes he has a trustworthy face is beyond me. He comforts himself in a chair and engages me in conversation without checking to see if I'm otherwise engaged.

"Carolyn, how'd you like a handsome man escorting you to lunch today?"

"Are you lining me up with someone?"

"Very funny. I'm referring to myself, and you know it."

"I'm sorry, Joe. Well, I think my ego can stand it. Are we celebrating because you have an insight about my data?"

Joe turns serious; academics is no joke. He advises me to concentrate on the angular momentum, to try a reverse rotation, to alternate rotations with rest periods—all things I've done.

"I've done all those things," I say. "I thought I mentioned that."

"Well," says Joe with Joe-candor, "I don't see your problem. You've done what any journal editor would expect. Go ahead with the article. I've read articles with a lot less work in them, Carolyn. Hell, I've written articles with a lot less work in them. You're just not used to the publishing business. You've got your article, Carolyn."

"How about eleven thirty for lunch, Joe? A nice salad someplace? I appreciate your feedback."

"Eleven thirty's fine with me." Joe returns to the imp. "You have no problems with a married man escorting you in public? I mean, people might talk. What would your friends think?"

"*My* friends? What about *your* friends? You're the one who's married."

"If you'd listen to Marge lately, you'd think that was a mistake."

"Trouble on the home front?"

"Oh, nothing much. I'm exaggerating. I think she's just bored. You know how you get into a rut. She needs some new activities in her life. She signed up for a mechanics course at North Seattle Community College."

"Sounds useful. Anyway, Joe, I don't think my friends would be worried. I'm sure you're a noble escort."

"Now I'm insulted. Are you telling me you can't be seduced?"

"I can be seduced if I wish. But my friends would have faith that I'd be in control of the situation."

"Oh, I see. Always in control, huh? Are you talking about your woman friends—like Stephanie—or your men friends? There might be a difference."

"There might. Actually, I don't have that many friends in Seattle to begin with. I should really join a group."

"What kind of group, Carolyn?"

"Oh, I don't know. Maybe overly pensive physicists who don't pense on physics."

"Not too many women in that category."

"Sometimes I feel it's only me. But you're right. It would be a little silly to join an all-men's group."

"Maybe not. Maybe Mr. Right's waiting."

"I somehow doubt that, Joe."

"You're not looking?"

"Let's say I'm passive when it comes to meeting prospective lovers. There are some traditions that are hard to break."

"Broken any lately?"

"Oh, I break them all the time. I even mark down for spelling errors these days, and physicists have never done that."

"I don't know, Carolyn. You're gettin' old. Kids, you know. Better happen soon."

"Why, Joe, I don't need kids. I've got my colleagues in the department."

I'll feel like a jerk at that party, Di. The physics pooh-bahs will be there, of course; why else would Joe have the party? And Marge will be at her hostessing best, straight out of a Denny's restaurant. She'll have the bouffant and the smile you can use on your pancakes and the empty conversation. The only thing missing will be the menus and her saying, "The waiter will be with you in a moment."

But I'll smile, too, and chitchat with the minds, and that part's exciting. Male or female, I enjoy intellect, father forgive me. I do feel a little funny talking shop at a party, though, and I'm not sure that these guys talk anything intellectual but shop. And what else do we have in common? They're older, richer, and far more conventional than I ever was, even as a St. Cloudian.

Their wives will be worse. They will seek me out as a comrade—except those who view my singleness as a threat to their hubbies. But then they will shun me, too, when they realize I know nothing about children, lawns, dishwashing soap, or TV soaps. By that time I'll have been expelled from the men's group, too. Shit. Maybe the food will be good.

Stephanie won't go; she went to a department party once and said people treated her like Karen Black in *Five Easy Pieces*—like she just arrived from Appalachia. Besides, it will be much too heterosexual for her.

Steph recognizes how politic I have to be in regard to our relationship. I don't hide it. I haven't lied to anyone, but I haven't stopped people on the street to tell them about it, either. The Pope wouldn't normally moon an audience, and I wouldn't normally say, "Oh, Dr. Stan, funny you should mention the weather. I really appreciate sunsets more since I became a lesbian."

Friends—Marcie, especially—think I should be more vocal. Marcie works as a caseworker for the Department of Social and Health Services. She's open about her lesbianism, and every day is another hassle for her. I respect her for it. She's not concerned about losing her job because she's planning to enter into a counseling partnership with two other women, anyway. Every day she passes out literature, fights with her bosses, tries to make changes in the superstructure of the organization, and walks around with the knowledge that she's known as The Lesbian. I don't know if I could do all that; there's just so much time in one day and so much energy in one person. Ah, defensiveness again.

Shit. The whole damn world whirls, you know, Di? That was Philip's problem; the whole damn world whirls. Say that ten times fast. Joe Bennett's whirling in a three-handed climb up the ladder of success: one hand to hold on to what he's got, the second to reach for the next rung, and the third to push away those he views as competitors. Smiling all the time. Marcie: she's probably whirling in lesbian politics. Me: who knows, Di, maybe I'm whirling in myself right now.

So, big deal. I understand some people's behaviors using a Philippic metaphor. Where does that leave me? Doesn't help a bit. I still feel pressure. I still feel the goddam pressure.

Damn him. It really hurt when he accused me of whirling because I insisted he recognize me as a woman, even when I didn't understand what whirling was. I shouldn't have had to insist, not of the person who ostensibly loved me. He should have been forthcoming with that empathy, with that support. I needed it, and he didn't give it to me. He never gave it to me.

I can picture Philip's world, from his eyes. He's in a room, and everyone except him is whirling. He tries to make contact, but is spun off each whirler he approaches. He can't stop the people from whirling, and he can't communicate with them because they're going too fast. The more he tries to make contact with them, the more battered and frustrated he gets. Finally, he settles for just avoiding the whirlers and bitterly criticizing them.

I'm not so pessimistic. Even if people are whirling, even if they are dervishes like his roommate, they're going slow enough so that I can share with them. People make the effort to communicate. It seems as if they do.

What time is it, boys and girls? It's crisis time. I gave Dr. Stan an outline of the work I'd do with semiconductors, silicon, the type of analyses I did with Patricelli before taking over Kent's helium studies. Di, that's the only other area I could feel even halfway comfortable in. Dr. Stan was gentle, if defensive. You know, he said to me, this is purely an economic matter, not an abridgment of your academic freedom. Yes, yes, I said; I understand. So tell me, Carolyn, he said, what is your experience in this field? What can I tell the committee?

"Are you doubting I can do the work?"

"Carolyn, it's just for the committee. They don't know you. Give me something I can put in print."

"Well, I'm sure I can dig up some papers. I'm only second author on them, though."

"Who's the principal author?"

"Charles Patricelli."

"Professor?"

"Yes. Uh, why are you writing down his name?"

"Carolyn," said Dr. Stan, upping his gentle quotient yet another few points, "I want you to know your job is in a certain amount of—peril. Once your helium studies are done, I have to persuade the committee to keep you on. It would be much cheaper, you know, to hire a new person than to maintain your current salary. I'll need all the help I can get. That's why I want to talk to this Charles Patricelli and secure an endorsement from him."

"Well, that sounds reasonable," I said. I thanked Dr. Stan and left his office coolly. A tip, Lady Di: always act cool when you're ready to throw up in front of your department chairman.

An endorsement from Charles Patricelli! Philip could have gotten an endorsement from the Jaycees more easily. I can see Chuck's letter now:

Neal Starkman

Dear Dr. Mankiewicz,

Carolyn Anderson is a slovenly bitch who doesn't know a semiconductor from a train conductor. It's my studied opinion that once she overcomes her tendency to plagiarize and to tamper with "inconvenient" results, she'll make some physicist a fine wife.

Sincerely,

Dr. Charles "Chuck" Patricelli

No, that's not his style. He'd more likely slime his way into a "forced" admission that "Carolyn's bright enough, but when she was with me, she really was adamant about her loathing of this type of research. Now, maybe she's changed her mind, but the work is highly complex and does demand a certain dedication…" Which, Di, is all too true. My career depends on kind words from the biggest asshole in the academic Midwest.

I sit here in Discovery Park, Di, enjoying the days I have left, speculating on taking a contract out on a middle-aged professor at the University of Minnesota. I couldn't afford it, even if Steph loaned me some money. But there is something else gnawing at me. With all the ramifications of this latest bombshell, I'm tense about something. It's not the news; I don't really concern myself with the Iraq–Iran War or the political campaigns—although I can't imagine anyone voting for Reagan—or even Mt. St. Helens erupting. Okay, I was in fact fascinated with St. Helens, but after a week, you know, that was that. I'm interested in stuff, but as for getting tense about it, well, it's 1980, but it could just as well be 1880.

Discovery Park is a magnificent park, very big, very quiet. There's a bluff here where you can sit, just over the protective rail, and look out over Puget Sound, the Olympic Mountains in the background. The mountains are clear today, snow-peaked, sharp. Blackbirds dot the sky like caraway seeds in rye bread. The water looks very still from this distance, except for the wakes from barges and freighters and fishing boats. It's a panorama—sea, mountains, sky. Few people pass by to disturb my thoughts. You'd think it would be easy to arrange my ideas out here, away from all the distractions of the university and home. You'd think I could isolate what's bothering me.

5. THE AFFIRMATIVE ACTION

Having slept through Philip's intimate revelations, I suppose I deserved the acerbic humor and taciturn conversation he supplied the rest of the way out to Seattle. At the time I attributed it to moodiness.

Oh God, Di, *mea magna culpa*. I was tired, I fell asleep. He was talking about some roommate back in Massachusetts. How could I know that he was going to take a crazy roommate and turn him into a philosophical treatise on social behavior? I thought I already knew his philosophy.

It's tempting to play "what if." What if I had discussed his damned dervishes with him back then? What if we had reached an understanding of each other before arriving in Seattle? What if I had played back the tape while we were still living together? It's senseless. There's not a thing I can do about it, not now, not ever. I intend to rationalize away every vestige of guilt.

Seattle welcomed us in its Februarily raw resplendence. All the mountains were out, the Cascades and the Olympics like ornate bookends to metropolitan Seattle's variegated sprawl. Even Philip perked up. At once I could understand why people never leave the West Coast. My homesickness vanished; St. Cloud and Minnesota seemed flat, without character, tame. There must be a correlation between the terrain and the personalities of the people who live there.

Seattle was definitely a *city*, too, allaying some of Philip's anxieties. There were enough tall buildings, automobiles, and freeways to protect him from the encroaching environment and to insure a modicum of sophistication. He'd been worried that Seattle was a one-horse city, if you can understand that, Di. But that day he admitted, "Well, it's Minneapolis-size, anyway." You couldn't ask for more.

Meanwhile, I was won over by the sheer amount of scenery—mountains, hills, houses, lakes, tunnels, bridges, parks, skyscrapers. The ubiquity of the water excited me. I vowed to buy a boat within five years. Philip vowed to ride in it with me. Later he remarked that, had it been a more typically cloudy day, we might have missed the city entirely and ended up on the seacoast.

We checked into a motel and reconnoitered for a place to live. I got out my maps, my phone directories, my brochures, my real estate information, and my listings of schools. I made a few phone calls to businesses, colleges, mental health agencies, and the library. I determined which factors might influence our choice of a location and assigned weights to each based on criteria I felt Philip and I would agree on. I summarized all the data and gave it to him, with recommendations.

He chose an apartment in Rainier Valley because it was cheap.

Now Seattle really doesn't have any slums, not like New York or Detroit or even San Francisco. Nothing that a cab driver would hesitate approaching. But Rainier Valley, despite its poetic name, is not your classiest neighborhood either. You don't take midnight strolls there.

We wanted to scrimp. We didn't know how long it would be before we found work. And Philip looked fairly countercultural with his scraggly beard, though in a white-liberal sort of way. And we found a place without a lease so we could always move out. The truth is, we were innocents abroad and figured nothing would happen to us.

We moved in during the day, and it didn't look appreciably more threatening than our old St. Paul neighborhood. It was a street of apartments and small houses, not quite a project, but definitely verging on turning into a ghetto. There was garbage about, a lot of beer bottles and cans, kids running around with torn clothes, and radios blasting disco music. We were tolerant liberals and realized that this was a particular cultural milieu to which we in time would adapt.

Everything we owned had been stowed in the Volvo. We unpacked in about ninety minutes. There wasn't much storage space in our apartment, so we didn't unpack everything. In any case, we were exhausted from lugging the stuff up two flights of narrow stairs and down a long hall.

I remember the hall more than the apartment, Di. It was long, as I said. The walls were losing their paint like snakes lose their skin. It was dark, odoriferous—let's take a guess at five parts cheap booze, three parts cheap booze after it's passed through a body one way or another, one part tobacco, and traces of items I'd rather not go into.

But we told ourselves we were right on the bus line, we'd be saving money, and it would be an adventure.

The first night we met our neighbor Will Jackson, who came over at two in the morning with beer and belches to welcome us to the milieu. The second night there was a fight—I don't mean a verbal dispute, I mean a fight—between people of indeterminate number, sex, and motivation. That was between 10:00 and 11:00 p.m., 1:00 and 1:30 a.m., and 5:00 and 6:30 a.m. We huddled in our bed and speculated on the sturdiness of our locks. We didn't call the cops because we hadn't yet ascertained the cultural norms and, anyway, our phone wasn't connected.

The second day we took the bus downtown. When we returned, our Volvo was gone. So was Will Jackson. We walked to a phone booth and called the police, who found the car in downtown Seattle, sans the battery and Will. That night our only window was shattered by a rock, which we tried to assume was a chance meteorite. The third day our electricity went. The following day we went. So much for roughing it.

We relocated to a more genteel part of town near the University of Washington and tried to salvage our liberalism by discussing the hard life Will Jackson must have led to feel compelled to do such a thing to us. That lasted until Philip said, "Fuck it, I hope they disembowel him when they catch him." So much for the salvage job.

The UW neighborhood was more civilized to our way of bourgeois thinking. The apartment was small, but we tried to consider it alternately cute and cozy. It was often noisy at night, and there were occasional drug and beer fests, but somehow the university populace seemed playful, while the Rainier Valley populace seemed menacing. Di, I guess I'm an old classist at heart.

Philip and I settled down to two major preoccupations. The first was securing telephone, electricity, water-and-garbage accounts, car insurance, medical insurance, mail service, voting privileges, newspaper delivery, library cards, and a bank account. It also took some time to figure out where everything was in Seattle and how to get there. Seattle's topography pleases aesthetes but vexes drivers: you can't go east or west without running into a freeway, a lake, a hill, a cul de sac, or railroad tracks. And who knew what "arterial" meant? Or that "city center" was downtown in disguise? We rode the bus a lot.

The other preoccupation was far more significant, but just as mundane: jobs. For me it wasn't much of a trial. I checked around at the community colleges, called Dr. Kent in Minneapolis, interviewed a few times, and in three months was hired to teach elementary physics and astronomy at Seattle University, starting summer quarter. The pay was only fair, but the job was a foothold, and Philip and I celebrated over steaks at the Space Needle.

For Philip, the situation was entirely different. He was more certain of what he didn't want to do than what he did. He was determined not to work for an organization whose policies he disagreed with, which automatically disqualified universities, sales agencies, corporations, factories, and the state legislature. Further, he'd done all sorts of manual labor during his student days and refused to do any more. He briefly considered several careers that on the surface appealed to him: clam digger, concessionaire at baseball games, restaurant critic, and governor. None looked very promising.

In the end, he wound up searching where we both knew he would: in the social-service agencies. That's one role reversal we were always cognizant of: Philip needed to help others; I didn't. It was a major rent in his cynical crust. No matter how vitriolic his diatribes against people became, he'd still go to work helping them. Maybe it was compensation, sugar with the bitters, or an ego-assuager to surround himself with the unfortunate and powerless. Whatever it was, it was strong, and neither of us professed to understand it.

I've never had a compunction to help others. My father takes care of that department. Perhaps Christianity filled me with such horrors that I ultimately became more concerned with what could happen to me than about what could happen to somebody else. Thus I am a physicist, not a nurse, social worker, waitress, flight attendant, dental hygienist, teacher, or housewife and mother. One servant in the family—rather, one paid servant and one unpaid servant—is more than enough.

So Philip followed his destiny and applied for social-service jobs, in addition to scores of other jobs. He had serious objections to many of them, and I wrote down some of the rules for him:

Rule 1: The job must not require a preponderance of manual labor.

Rule 2: The job must not require moral compromise or a relinquishment of personal dignity.

Rule 3: The employer must not be an institution that systematically develops useless or harmful information or products.

Neal Starkman

Rule 4: The job must not require selling anything that falls under the description of Rule 3.

I presented the list to him one evening about two months after we had become fixed in our routine.

"What do you think?" I asked. "You have your Rules of Life. Now you have your Rules of Employment."

He smiled as he read them. "Very good. You think I'm being stupid about this, don't you?" He continued to smile, and I felt a gulf.

"No, I don't think you're being stupid about it."

"It sounds like you're making fun of my philosophy. You think I'm being too idealistic."

I denied that, and he walked away.

During the next six months, Philip ran into all manner of obstacles, among them employers who thought he was "overqualified" for social-service work, jobs that were already wired for in-house workers, sexist attitudes that prevented him from landing clerical positions, and affirmative action. He scored 98 percent on a civil service test, but came in fifty-third out of 380 because he wasn't a veteran. He went to the State Employment Office, where he waited thirty minutes for an interviewer to give him a reference for a job that had closed. He scoured the want ads and checked out federal employment, state employment, county employment, municipal employment, school districts, community colleges, and even employment agencies.

"How was your day?" I asked him following an afternoon in which I'd gone to the downtown market and he'd gone to his first employment agency.

"Disturbing. How was yours?"

"Okay; I found mushrooms on sale. Plus something called a geoduck that looks like a cross between a clam and a horse's penis."

"Did you buy it?"

"I couldn't face the public. What happened at the employment agency?"

He was shaving. Even with a beard and moustache, he still had to shave his neck and cheeks. He made himself shave every afternoon, not because his hair grew like cancer and he wanted to look decent, nor even because his stubble irritated my face. I think Philip shaved to keep up his morale, like the British Prisoners of War did in World War II, or at least in World War II movies. After so many months of frustrating rejections and feelings of utter uselessness, he suspected that he was perilously close to clinical depression. Shaving gave him something to do, and it made him feel that he was still part of the respectable world. The fact that he was shaving *after* the employment interview attested to his disregard of its cosmetic importance.

There's something very touching about the way he shaved, white soap all over him like a street mime, wincing now and then when he'd nick himself. And when he'd towel off and gaze at himself in the mirror, I'd try to peer into his mind.

On this day, he led me into the living room, sank into one of the springs of our fifth-hand couch, and shook his head, looking at me as if he'd just decided not to run for mayor.

"Do you really want to hear about the employment agency? It's not a pretty story, Car."

I was curious and prepared to be sympathetic. "Sure."

He took a deep breath, and his eyes were lackluster. Philip's eyes were interesting in their blandness. He had such a forceful personality that you expected his eyes to be more piercing, or more limpid, or more something. But they weren't. If you saw anything in his eyes, it was woe. Even when he was joking, you got the impression that he'd witnessed great misfortune, either in his experiences or his imagination.

"Everyone was wearing suits," he said, without affect, "even the women, and the women were young, twenties and teens, I guess, a lot of eye makeup. Purple, green, blue." He shuddered.

"Eye shadow," I assisted.

"Whatever. Everything is very—controlled there. Muted. Carpeted. Big office. Nine-hundredth floor, views of the whole city. And the office is in sections, like work areas. I filled out all their forms—a lot of them—and handed them back to the receptionist. Everyone smiles there, too. No matter what you say or do, they smile at you. You could shit on their magazines, and I bet they'd still smile at you. And so I waited in this, like a big living room, you know, for my forms to be processed.

"So this woman comes over to the waiting area, late twenties, suit, makeup more subtle than the receptionist's, and calls my name. I get up, she gives me a big smile, outstretched hand. 'Hi,' she says, 'how are you? I'm Barbara Blake. Why don't we come into my office.'

"Well, she doesn't have an office. She has a cubicle, but what the hell—let her live in her delusions. She motions me to a chair by a big executive desk. Nothing on the desk but a blotter, some pencils in a pencil box—they're sticking up, the pencils, and they're all like pinprickly pointed, like they were never used. And the desk also has this stand-up thing on it with her name, and an ugly magenta telephone that clashes with the carpet. I remember that, because I thought it was weird she had a telephone that color, that they deliberately ordered it that way.

"So she smiles at me again and says, 'So, Mr. Lester, you're looking for a job.' Game-playing time, right? I mean, why else would I be there? I say, 'Yes, that's right.'

"She starts looking over my application, very professional-like. She's got it in this big folder she must use so people can't see what she's reading.

Now at first I think she's impressed with my application. I mean, I've done a lot of things, you know, twenty years of school, clerical skills, research, teaching. Don't you think she should have been impressed?"

"Yes, honey." I patted his knee.

"Well, she raises her eyebrows now and then, frowns, nods her head, all that, you know, like she's really fascinated by this application I've just filled out. She smiles, of course, though I don't remember writing anything funny on it, and I just wait. Well, she looks at me and asks me what a PhD is."

"What?"

"She asked me what a PhD was. She wanted to know if it was like a master's."

"Oh, no."

"It's true, I'm not lying to you. The person that's going to find me a job doesn't know the difference between a PhD and a fucking master's degree."

"Oh, Philip."

"So I explain the difference to her. I mean, what could I say, I told her that the PhD took a few more years to get than a master's, and she's nodding like she understands and that it wasn't the stupidest question she could have asked me, and I'm really getting that sinking feeling.

"Then she puts the folder down on the desk and crosses her hands over it, like you do in fourth grade when you're trying to look like you didn't just shoot the spitball. And she asks me what kind of a job I'm looking for, even though I've written it right on the damn sheet she was just holding in her damn hands with all the fingernails. Maybe it's a test. Maybe some people come in and write down that they want a job as a neurosurgeon, and then she trips them up when she asks them and they say, well, a bus driver. But she didn't catch me. I said I'd like a clerical job, because, you know, there always seem to be typing jobs open, and I can do about eighty words a minute.

"No way, Car. I couldn't have gotten a more skeptical expression from her if I'd told her I wanted two chrome-plate dildos. She smiles and says, 'Oh, Mr. Lester, I really don't think I could find you a typing job. Most of the employers who use our services want girls for those jobs. You know, they want somebody to be a receptionist, too, and girls are usually better at that sort of thing.' Well, you know, I guess I could have stayed to argue, but it would have been like arguing with a watermelon. I think all that—what was it, eye shadow?—all the eye shadow and shit blocked incoming stimuli."

"Honey, I'm sorry."

And I was, too. I wanted Philip to find a job. He hadn't had any meaningful work since Planned Parenthood laid him off during the campaign. Besides, he was becoming increasingly callous, more withdrawn, and developing a central attitude of how he fit in with the world. Or didn't.

I was sorry, too, because the issue of affirmative action and of women getting jobs he wanted were causing a rift between us. My own sense of myself as a woman was emerging at this time, and Philip was completely insensitive to that. There is no doubt, Lady Di, that Philip lost one or two jobs—maybe even more—because an employer needed to keep the feds happy by hiring a woman or a racial minority. But Philip could not see the big picture on this issue. He didn't *lose* perspective; he never had it to begin with.

He kept dealing with "shoulds." People "should" relate to one another as individuals. Employers "should" hire based only on qualifications specific to the job. He was stuck in his own idealistic fantasy world. It was the epitome of Philip's stubborn individualism to the exclusion of everything else.

Di, I don't even remember the arguments. We had maybe three blowups and then truced. I recall yelling at him for the first time and feeling angry for losing control and feeling sad for alienating him further and feeling angry all over again for feeling sad.

Dervishes

Marcie, Stephanie, and I went to a male strip club last night. A curious evening. We started by climbing into our sweats and having a nice jump, Stephanie fifteen minutes, Marcie seven, Carolyn Weak Knees three and a half. I was the timer. I've come to hate jumping. I don't mind the timing, but I hate the jumping.

I'm not really sure why I went to the strip club, and I'm even less sure why they went, because neither of them gets off very much on male bodies. Maybe they wanted to cheer me up about the impending disintegration of my career. In any case, at least two of the five men who stripped during the evening were not bad-looking. All of them had incredibly toned bodies, although most of them were too muscular for my tastes.

There's still some St. Cloud in me. All right, a lot. I blushed at the beginning, and I'm glad Steph and Marcie were too busy attending to "Cowboy Dan, the Struttin' Man" to notice. After an hour of watching the gyrations, melding with the virtually all-female crowd, and downing a few glasses of wine, I felt more comfortable, although it's not in my constitution to yell, "Take it off!" and "Let's see what you got!" as did the earthy women at the table next to us. Marcie and Steph clapped and whistled but did not contribute vocally, for which I was thankful.

In some ways, the atmosphere was invigorating. The idea of women being assertively sexual is an appealing one. And they were certainly assertive here. The dancers would play to them as much as to the brassy music, thrusting, rolling their eyes, snapping their jockstraps—or is it g-strings—simulating intercourse with the floor, each lewd gesture eliciting the appropriate squeals, yells, and comments from the crowd. Each dancer had a specialty: one was a cowboy, one a sheik of some kind, one seemed to be a pimp—great turn-on. Then there was the guy in the dinner suit that zipped up and down the sides, and finally the one that was supposed to be a college professor, complete with pipe and cardigan.

I appreciated the bodies from an aesthetic point of view, and I appreciated the acts from an entertainment point of view. But nothing was very erotic, with the possible exception of the dinner suit and when I thought Mr. Sheik was developing an erection. Mingling with my appreciation, though, was a feeling of discomfort, either that I shouldn't be there or that no one should be there.

"Come on, Carolyn," said Marcie from the back seat as I drove home. I'd offhandedly mentioned the possibility of the men being exploited. "It's about time women did some exploiting. Jesus, how many women strip shows are there in this county alone, not including topless waitress bars and cocktail waitresses who stick their butts in men's faces? Only one male strip joint; fuck, I think we need more of them. Let them show *their* stuff for a change."

Marcie was a little tipsy and less coherent than usual. Stephanie sidewaysed me from the passenger seat.

"Are you serious, Carrie?"

"I was only wondering if it was hypocritical, that's all. I mean, we deplore women taking off their clothes for men."

"Carrie, that's different. Women do that because they have no other income, or because they're being forced into it some other way. These guys tonight make more money than we do. Shit, they're not being exploited."

"And if they are," Marcie came back, "who cares? I mean, who really cares? I don't. Do you?"

I stopped for a red light and turned to Stephanie, who was looking at me with some concern. "I don't know," I said, "maybe I'm taking it too seriously. You're probably right."

I like coming to the lab in the evening. It's quiet, and if I don't think about it, I'm not frightened. Maybe I should carry something besides mace, which Marcie gave me for Christmas last year. Lovely gift. But I somehow feel that I'd be more vulnerable with a weapon. Isn't that strange? Maybe I think that if I carry a knife, then I'm fair game. Ridiculous, but, as enraged as I get about women being accosted and raped and beaten, I suppose it will have to affect me personally before I can take the step of carrying a weapon.

I got a creepy feeling today, too: a student winked at me. James Andrews—tall, well-dressed, collegiate-looking—is a B+ senior, and, as I handed a paper back, he unmistakably winked at me. No smile, just a wink. I ignored it, but he knew I saw it. I wish I knew what it meant.

Oh, hell, neither James Andrews nor anyone else could attack me here; the sign on the door says very plainly, "Authorized Personnel Only." And I'm the only authorized personnel.

I'm here in my little laboratory, forcing helium down in temperature, first by surrounding it with liquid nitrogen to bring it down to 77°K, then dropping it the rest of the way, this evening to 1.9°K. Mighty cold, Di. And then I start my rotors and set my transducers, check the Mylar strips, and watch that helium spin. It's so civilized here, so peaceful, so harmless. I could be the only one left in the world. It's difficult for me to accept that I may never see another lab like this again, not after Dr. Stan places that call—or writes that letter—to Dr. Patricelli, and Chuck responds. Maybe he'll send a dead fish wrapped in one of my old articles. What's the physics corollary of the kiss of death? What will I do with myself after being banished from *physicsdom*? Old physicists never die; they just, uh, lose energy.

These vortices in the helium, they're like little dervishes. And they appear only at certain levels. Why is that? I don't know what causes them or disrupts them. They've definitely taken a hold on me, as if they're challenging me to find out what they're about before I have to pack up my lab in a crate and send it aflame into the Pacific. Quantum physics is not so different from religion—you have to accept a lot on faith. The big difference is that, in quantum physics, you accept on faith as a last resort, not a first.

Just before I got hired at Seattle University, Philip and I suffered what you might call wryly a crisis in faith. We applied for teaching jobs at Seattle Pacific College. Understand, Lady Di, we'd been searching for almost three months and were beginning to feel a little financial pressure. We hadn't been employed under the right circumstances to get unemployment benefits, and our savings were running low. Also, Philip was tiring of fruitless interviews and form rejections. And, no kidding, Di, there was no way to tell from the outside that Seattle Pacific College was a religious school.

It's a cute campus, modern but not pretentious, very personal. I remember thinking, wouldn't it be nice if we both got jobs here? God, I was couply then, still polishing my old dream model, working in a career beside my man. Having your colleague and eating him, too.

So, here's Carolyn and Philip, trudging up to the main desk to get our names on a list of applicants. Philip was tense and somewhat irritable; he'd just been rejected for a job at an alternative school because he refused to shave his beard. Both of us were wearing our usual jeans-and-tennies outfits, since we hadn't planned on interviewing. I didn't notice it then, but all the students strolling through the lobby were pretty spiffy. Not suits, but not jeans and tennies, either. The men had short hair. Nothing dawned on us. You know, like my parents not thinking along the lines of "These people might be lesbians," we didn't think along the lines of "These people might be religious zealots."

The woman—girl, really—behind the high counter smiled continuously, as if her mouth were stitched open. When we told her we were looking for faculty positions, she gave us each a multi-page application she took from a pile in a box on the countertop. Then she gave us pens, smiled, and walked away. We stood at the counter and began to fill out the applications.

Well, the first page was personal information—you know, height, weight, age, place of birth, current residence. Perhaps because Philip didn't always answer questions he considered irrelevant or insulting, he completed page one a few seconds before me; I heard him turn the page. Page two was educational and work-related questions, and again I was a few seconds behind him, which proved to be unfortunate when we got to page three.

Page three was a Christian creed.

I didn't realize what it was at first, but when I did, my stomach fell to my toes. It was a list of twenty statements concerning the applicant's moral behavior both at the school and away from school, a pledge of fealty to Jesus, and a space for the applicant's signature. I flashed on Philip, who not six months before had conducted the masturbation campaign in the face of hysterical Bible-toting Midwesterners, who had shown little tolerance for religious people even before they had made his life a misery, and who by all accounts was not in a very good mood.

He had summoned the girl back before I had an opportunity to stop him. I had a feeling he was not going to sign page three nor, for that matter, continue on to pages four and five, the contents of which to this day I am unaware.

The girl came back, smiling, eager to help. She looked at Philip, who was frowning. He pointed to the page.

"What is this?" he asked, as if he'd never seen a Christian creed before.

The girl followed his finger and smiled. "You mean that question, or the whole page?"

"The whole page."

"Oh, that's our creed. It's a formality, really."

"I don't understand."

"Philip."

"No, honestly. What does a creed have to do with getting a job here? I assume you have to sign this in order to get a job here."

"Well, yes, sir, everyone who works or goes to school here signs the creed and lives by it. It's what we believe in. Is there something on it that bothers you?"

"Do you believe in love?"

"Love?" The smile was becoming worried. "Yes, we believe in love."

"Do you believe in making love?"

"Wh-um—"

"I'm merely curious. Are you all virgins?"

"Mr. Darrington," she called, without turning around.

"Are you permitted to masturbate? I'm merely curious."

"Mr. Darrington!" she called again, a little more shrilly. The girl whispered the gist of what Philip had been asking to her coworker, while I decided whether I should leave immediately or try to referee. Mr. Darrington appeared from an office behind the counter, and others in the lobby casually ambled within earshot. We were approaching the status of a hubbub.

Mr. Darrington was a Republican; you could tell by his stern exterior, the careful trimming of his moustache, and the way he said, "Yes, Janine?"

Janine pointed to Philip, who looked innocent enough, and Mr. Darrington said, "Yes, sir. How can I help you here?"

"I was curious about the epistemological ramifications of your creed," affected my lover. "That is, I was concerned about the duality necessarily posited by an undervalued ecclesiastical system *vis à vis* the behavioral machinations of its constituents. I hardly need mention the incidence of community institutions rendered inefficacious by such a schizophrenic acclimatization of formerly liturgical students. That is precisely why I sought to determine the extent of masturbatory activity engaged in by Janine over there."

Mr. Darrington frowned and looked at Janine, who was listening and frowning herself. Mr. Darrington sought my assistance.

"And you, miss? Are you with this gentleman?"

"I sup—"

"Do you smoke marijuana, Mr. Darrington?"

A little muscle in Mr. Darrington's neck flexed. "No, sir, I do not," he said with conviction.

"I see," said Philip. "I think you should, to expand your perspective. And your rectum. You appear to me to be quite tight-assed."

Janine choked, a few of the others giggled, and Mr. Darrington appeared not only quite tight-assed but quite angry as well. Being tight-assed, however, he controlled his anger.

"Sir, I'll ask you to please leave now. Both of you."

"I need to know," said Philip earnestly, "what makes you think the way you do? Why are you afraid of me? Why do you need this...this creed? What's inside you?"

Mr. Darrington declined to answer and, as an alternative, threatened to call the cops. We left.

I didn't see anything particularly humorous in this, Di. I'd assumed that Philip thought it comical, but when we made it back to the car, he wasn't laughing. He said to me, "Why is he like that, Car? Why are people like that?"

"When are you going to let me read your journal?" asks Stephanie as we're driving to see *My Brilliant Career*. She catches me off guard, and I play stumblebum.

"Um, my journal?"

"The one you've been writing in every time I turn around. Remember? The one with Philip in it?"

"I'm sorry, I know. Why, uh, why do you want to read it?"

"Carrie, if you don't want me to read it, that's okay. If it's too personal…"

"Well, it's pretty personal. I was wondering if you wanted to read it for a specific purpose."

"Oh, I thought I could learn more about the *real* Carrie Anderson. And who knows? Maybe there are some good sex scenes in it."

"Well…"

"Am I in it?"

"You? Yes, of course. But it's written so badly, I mean, like, a lot of it is fragments and not very well thought out."

"Okay."

"I mean, it *is* personal. And I guess I'd rather not show it to anyone. I'm speculating on a lot of things, and I think it would be easy to read out of context."

"Suit yourself."

"Are you upset?"

"Nope."

Like hell.

Philip lost out on more interviews and became more arrogant and reclusive. Meanwhile, I hooked up with Seattle University and did all the busy things people new on the job do: I became oriented to the school, I met my fellow teachers, I learned the administrative procedures, I began to develop a curriculum, and so on.

Once that was underway, I devoted time to my new group, which was rather free-floating in content though definite in design—purportedly an examination of five "left-wing" writers of the century, one of whom was Emma Goldman, who always interested me. The group met weekly as part of the University of Washington's Experimental College. Four women and seven men. We met in a house not too far from where Philip and I lived. One of the women was Shelly.

Philip saw some courses in the Experimental College that appealed to him, too, but I think he thought that I would think he was being dependent on my decisions. The usual third-guessing. So he opted for studying up on chess by reading library books. I would rather have seen him do something more social at that time, but at least he was doing *something*. Looking for jobs had taken a lot of energy out of him.

But Philip had other problems, for which he'd need a lot of energy. I became bisexual.

The Introduction of Carolyn Marie Anderson into the Forbidden World of Bisexuality, Being a Thrilling Account of Her Initial Dalliance

Though the class to which I had committed my Tuesday afternoons stimulated my intellect as well as those higher faculties that seem to be evoked when deliberating abstractions, nonetheless I was quite unprepared for the visceral effects I experienced when interacting verbally and particularly visually with one of the other female members of the group. I

Neal Starkman

say this with candor. The effects were pleasant, surprising, welcome, and in all honesty appeared to be mutual.

What do you think, Di? Is that too elegant for this episode? Maybe I should bring it down a little.

Wet Encounter

I could feel the moisture in both my mouth and my jeans as she looked my way and gave an enticing smile, a suggestive turn of the head, and a cross of the legs that spelled out only too clearly what it was she desired of me. I shuddered and tried not to imagine her writhing on top of me, wringing lathers of lust from every pore of my yearning body. But I couldn't keep the scene from my mind. I found that the class was her, the world was her. I ached with an exquisite passion that threatened to consume me.

Oh, I don't know, Di. Maybe I'd better not make it so dramatic. I don't remember ever expressing an attraction to women as a youth, probably because my parents would have buried any tendencies so far into my subconscious I'd have needed a derrick to get them out. My only memory of homoerotica is peering down the freckled cleavage of my sixth-grade teacher's blouse one day when she picked up the chalk she'd dropped on the floor. I remember enjoying that but not reflecting much on it.

I masturbated for the first time when I was fourteen. I woke up on Saturday morning with my hand between my legs. Well, that feels pretty okay, I thought. I glanced around my bedroom, met the gaze of my stuffed panda bear, and turned my body to the wall as my fingers dissociated themselves from the Anderson family and changed into decadent little pleasure-givers. It was quite a thrilling experience that morning. Di, I think it was the first time I felt truly competent and in control.

In high school, I know that when classmates or girlfriends happened to undress near me, I felt a little stimulated, but I didn't think anything untoward about that, either. I appreciated the female body. It was almost clinical: I'd be interested in nipples, for instance, and why they'd sometimes protrude when it got cold. It just didn't translate into eroticism for me.

Even in college—notice, Di, how I define my life by my educational attainment—when I figured out that a lot of people thought that homosexuality was perverse, even then I never applied it to myself. I was too busy for considerations like those. Rules didn't apply to me, except that I fell in with men because that's what I was trained to do.

The masturbation campaign, followed by the local and national campaigns all around the country, got me thinking about politics and how women fit into it. I was very open then, very secure. I had a job, I had a home, I even had a man, although I wasn't feeling too successful in *that* enterprise. Philip had been unemployed for seven months and was often depressed, despite my attempts to nurture him. The frequency of our sex had diminished, and I had been feeling as undesired as he must have felt.

Into this congeries of forces came Shelly. We'd spoken to one another a few times, in addition to our regular conversations in the study group. She was a student at Seattle Central Community College, twenty-one years old—she'd dropped out of school for a few years to live in Europe—and held down part-time jobs to get by. Gregarious and playful, Shelly was the kind of person who might be nicknamed "Sunshine," only without the cutesiness. She had short, curly brown hair, a pretty smile, light complexion, and a fetching body with large breasts, though barely an inch taller than me. I noticed her immediately—she attracted everyone, I'm sure—but I really didn't feel any excitement until she snuck up behind me one afternoon, pressed those breasts against my back, and "guess who'd" her hands over my eyes.

My initial Shelly fantasies weren't full-blown, linear ones. I never pictured her nude, for example. What I did was let myself feel good. It was amazingly emancipating; I had never let myself "feel good" at the sight or thought of another woman. It wasn't that I thought she was Ms. Right. Far from it. We were much too different from each other, and besides, I was living with Philip. It was just that I enjoyed Shelly, she was fun to be with, and fun was something I hadn't had in a relationship in a long time.

So I fantasized about Shelly without thinking about sex. It was a sexless eroticism, if you can understand that, Di. Until "That Afternoon" anyway. I remember "That Afternoon" as one remembers momentous events in one's life: fondly, and with a pride that one had the good sense to act in the way one acted.

I'd known her for several months, and once or twice we'd gone out for a drink or late lunch after the group. I never invited her back to my place, even though Philip and I lived only a mile away and I had the car. Shelly knew I lived with Philip, and I knew she lived alone in East Queen Anne. We'd always laughed a lot with each other, talked about the other people in the group, exchanged basic histories. She was surprised when I told her I was twenty-seven, and I grinned vainly at her surprise.

"That Afternoon," instead of drinks, she invited me over to her apartment for iced teas and Oreos. It sounded perfect. She gave me directions, and I drove over there, feeling very good about myself and life in general. It was a warm day, the group had been lively, I was making a good living, I was excited about my forays into feminist literature, and I was on my way to meet a friend for refreshments. I looked in the rearview mirror and smiled at myself.

"I got in trouble today," said Stephanie while I was giving her a back rub. I'd convinced her that having me rub her back was preferable to jumping in place until she fainted. Besides, I was working on some vortex equations and wanted a break.

"But I enjoyed it," she said. "Aren't you going to ask me what I did to get in trouble?"

"I'm almost afraid to."

"You'll love it. I burned Haggerty's *Playboy*."

I had to laugh; it was so Stephanie. "That must have made him pretty angry. Did he fire you?"

"No. But he was mighty riled. I told him that reading that rag was an insult to me and every other woman on the crew. Janet and Junior were in on it. They cheered when I did it."

"Where was he reading it?"

"On the job, during lunch break. That was what was so outrageous, like he was flaunting it."

"What did he do?"

"What could he do? He screamed a little, and we laughed at him. He couldn't fire all of us; he'd lose the contract. Oh, a little to the left. Up. There. Yeah, good."

"What about when the contract is done, Steph? You're going to lose this job, aren't you?"

"Yeah, guess I am, babe. But that's okay; finish carpenters are always in demand. And I think I can find an all-woman crew if I look hard enough. There was one in Tacoma, but they weren't taking anyone on. That was six months ago, though. Maybe they're looking now."

"Oh, Steph, did you have to set his magazine on fire? That's going to make things so unpleasant on this job. Couldn't you have just told him to read it someplace else?"

"He had no right to read it in front of me, Carolyn. It was obviously a challenge. He thinks he can do whatever he damn well pleases, especially

Neal Starkman

with the women. Well, now he knows he can't. Besides, it was more exciting this way."

"Taking a match to his *Playboy*?"

"Taking a match to his *Playboy* while he was reading it."

Shelly's apartment was in a basement, and it suited her, casual and eclectic: one big living room with a fireplace, a small kitchen off to the side, and a tiny bedroom and bathroom down the hall. The living room was the showcase, though. There were cushions and pillows strewn about, some paperbacks on Eastern religions, records ranging from Neil Diamond to Dory Previn, a fairly new sound system, a small TV, an expensive-looking couch and love seat, two or three chairs, a throw rug, a coffee table, unframed posters of assorted styles, several magazines—one a *Playgirl*—tossed haphazardly, a camera, a cowboy hat, a tennis racket, and schoolbooks. There was no theme to the apartment. Rather, it appeared as if she'd gone through a succession of phases and acquired material possessions during each phase. It wasn't hippie, or academic, or young professional, or even starving student. I liked it; there was something somewhere you could identify with.

She went to the bathroom, and when she returned she started to prepare the tea. We talked about nothing in particular; at least, I don't remember any heavy discussion. In a little while, the tea was ready and we were munching on Oreos, which turned out to be not Oreos at all but Sunshine Hydrox, my preference, anyway.

We drank our tea from strawed glasses and nibbled on too many cookies and laughed at how brown the crumbs made our teeth. Shelly told me about how when she was a kid she was allowed only two cookies at a time but would take six and hide the difference under her pillow. She slept in the same room as her older sister, so when she ate them at night, she had to suck them until they were soft enough to chew without making noise.

"It was a real problem," she said. "I liked the crunchy cookies the best, but I couldn't enjoy them as much, 'cause I had to suck them soft." She smiled. "You sure have nice hair, Carolyn."

You know, Di, it's good to write this down, because I can see the pattern of Shelly's conversation now. She'd reveal something of herself and then follow up with a compliment. She'd talk about how she was always afraid she wouldn't do well at school and then relate how her "mind boggled" when she found out I had a doctorate. She'd mention being nervous about joining the group, because she really didn't know that much about either socialism or feminism, and then say how my friendliness made her at ease.

Di, I didn't know I was being seduced. No, that's not accurate. I didn't care one way or the other. I was in a terrific mood, I was confident of myself, I was receptive, I felt close to Shelly, and when I looked at her breasts I felt a chill of anticipation. There wasn't any pressure. I didn't feel as if I had to take care of her, like I sometimes did with Philip. I didn't feel as if I would be coerced into an argument, as I sometimes did with Philip. I didn't feel as if I wasn't being told the whole story, as I sometimes did with Philip. I recall leaning back on the couch, crossing my bare feet at the ankles on the coffee table, stretching my hands on the back of the couch, and thinking, "What a lovely afternoon this is."

"What are you thinking, Carolyn?"

I didn't change my pose. "I'm thinking that I'm awfully comfortable, that you're a great hostess, and that I'm in danger of falling asleep."

"Well, we can't have that," she said. "How would you like a massage? That will keep you up, I promise."

I don't know, Di, it didn't sound sexual, or corny, or anything out of the ordinary. I think now, Jesus, a massage, what a classic. But so many things were going on then. Part of me was truly insouciant—yes, a massage would be rather pleasant, wouldn't it now. But another part of me was racing, spirited, like a hyperactive kid on Christmas Eve. So what if a massage is a ploy as old as the Pleistocene? She used it. And it worked, too.

"Mm, sounds perfect," I said. "What kind of massages do you give?"

"Oh, all kinds. What kind do you want?"

"One that will make me feel good all over, not enervated, but tingly, alive."

"Well, I don't know what 'enervated' is, but I can give you the tingly part. Why don't you relax and come on to the rug. You'll probably want to take your pants off."

I did take off my pants, and my top, and my bra, because that's how you get a massage, and I lay face down on the rug and decided, it's time to be passive. I won't resist, I won't push; I will let myself be taken wherever I'm to be taken. I wasn't giving Shelly control as much as I was relinquishing my control into the air for her to take or not. Instead of thinking, I felt; instead of planning, I experienced. I closed my eyes, stretched out my arms and legs, and knew that no matter what happened, it would be just fine.

"Is there any place in particular you'd like me to rub?" she asked.

"You're the masseuse."

She didn't use oil, but her fingers felt very soft and slid rather than pushed against me. They kneaded the backs of my calves, tickled the inside of my knees, and caressed the occasionally ego-worrying flesh on my thighs. Then she began to work on my back, a little harder, up and down my spine, on my shoulders and neck. I felt looser, ever more passive.

"That feels wonderful," I said, as she massaged my neck.

She stopped for a moment, and I heard the sounds clothes make when they're taken off in a hurry, and then she was back on me, but this time covering me, not kneeling between my legs. I could feel her breasts compress against my back.

I can't say how long any of this took. She began to touch her lips, cold from the iced tea, to different parts of my back, until it felt like I had twenty backs, each receiving a caress. She kissed my shoulders while brushing my hair to the side, and she licked at the tiny hairs on the back of my neck. She continued to kiss my neck, sometimes gently but increasingly with passion, and I reached behind me to touch her, to feel this woman that was lying on top of me and pressing her legs to mine as if she were trying to push me into the nap of the rug.

I was facing the side of the room near her magazines, and I will always retain the image of the *Playgirl* magazine, fixed directly in my vision, a hairy-chested man on the cover, muscular arms folded across his pecs, glinting eyes observing me, a tight and derisive smile at the sound of suctioned air being released as Shelly applied and withdrew her mouth from my skin, a smile at the odor of our bodies as they began to move together forcefully and with purpose, and most of all a smile at the sight of my clumsy gropings, my awkward reaches, my labored breathing, my ridiculous posture. I didn't want to see him looking at us, I didn't want to think of him looking at us. Shelly kissed my ear, my cheek, and then I turned over to embrace her.

I don't remember when I—or Shelly—took off my underwear, but I do remember thinking, fleetingly, there goes my heterosexual underwear. And that was the only time I thought of "what type of sex" I was having until much later. I didn't even think of sex. I held Shelly to me as close as I could and we kissed and pressed together and rolled together and touched each other and I wasn't having sex, I was making love. No pressure, no fear, all softness, all process, all togetherness. As trite as that sounds, Di, it was true. I was more of a participant than I ever was before. She knew my body astonishingly well for the first time. Then I thought, of course, she's a woman. Now I think, yes, there was that, but there was also her experience.

How can I explain how it was sexual and more than sexual? I hesitate to generalize, but, with very few exceptions, when I've made love with a man I've been conscious of one, his comparative strength; two, his penis; three, his climax; four, my climax; and five, a sense of "differentness." The man's body, his whole body is so different from mine that, however enjoyable the sex, it's never been as *comfortable* as with a woman. I have had bad sex with women as well as with men, but, for me, the bad's much worse with men.

We lay together for what seemed like a day, but I doubt it was more than an hour. I honestly can't recall what we said to each other. I know I had enough control of my verbal centers not to say anything extraordinarily out of character; I think our conversation was probably as banal and superficial as most lovers'.

Lovers. As I lay there, my intellect returned as with the slow summer tide. I thought, I'm lying here naked with a woman. This woman is my lover. But I didn't get much past that thought. I was too overwhelmed with pleasure to analyze "what it all meant." Later would come the confusion, the self-doubt, the paranoia, the uncertainty. But at the time the only thing I wanted to do was to feel Shelly's soft skin against mine and reflect on how very nice it was to have somebody desire you.

"Carolyn, I want you to meet a friend of mine. Harold Sellers, Carolyn Anderson. Harold is a writer, Carolyn; I've told him all about you."

"Hi, Harold. Don't believe Joe. He doesn't know all about me."

"Well, if half of what he says is true, you're a hell of a girl."

I should have known that the party was going to be trouble when I got the official invitation in the mail—you know, formal, inscribed, and pseudo-cute: "It's a Bennett wingding!" and so on. It might have been all right without the exclamation point. But the inscribed exclamation point was the clue.

I presumed, however, that it was going to be a career party—Joe's career, that is. But when I get to Marge and Joe's house—split-level, not quite suburbia, but with a backyard and a garden that seemed to be upholstered—I look around for department people and don't find any. The only people at the party are a few of Joe's friends and what must be everyone that Marge Bennett has ever gone to community college with. Have I misinterpreted Joe's invitation? No, I slowly realize as I nod my head intermittently at Harold Sellers, Joe wants me to be here. It's either a test to see if I'm a dyke or an attempt to save me from dykehood if I'm already committed. Or, I suppose, maybe everyone he invited from the department except me decided to do something else tonight.

Marge is braless, wearing a flannel shirt and a made-up face, as if she hasn't decided which way to go. Every time she moves rapidly, she glances down to check her sway. She's shown me where the punch bowl and decrusted sandwiches are, and I help myself to punch while she rattles on about something to do with a restaurant that makes decrusted sandwiches by the gross. I smile and say that I hope they save the crusts for all the ducks in Green Lake. Marge laughs uproariously in her best hostess fashion at that clever remark; I shrug and move into the crowd.

"...called it *My Dog Spot*."

"Excuse me, Harold, the name of your book is *My Dog Spot*?"

"No," he chuckles, "everyone thinks that when I say it. I knew I couldn't catch you, though. It's *My Dog's Pot*. The pot of my dog. I deliberately chose that title."

Pause. A pregnant pause that aborts when I say, "Why?"

"Why did I choose that title?"

I nod and have no interest in his answer. He's a good-looking man, tall, well-dressed in a velour-like shirt with a high neck, an expensive pair of pants, and sixty-dollar shoes. I wonder where he gets his money, because he impresses me as a boob. He can't possibly make his money writing.

"Well, it's about a dog, only this dog is not your ordinary dog. His owner regularly gets him high. And the idea is, when the dog smokes dope—pot— he switches brains with his owner, so the guy is totally blasted out of his mind and the dog acts like the guy, sort of. Then both of them do all kinds of crazy things."

I'm thinking of doing several myself. Behind Harold Sellers, Marge is talking animatedly with an older man. I find myself appreciating the vacuity of Harold Sellers, because it allows me to suspend part of myself and think about other things. This must be what most people do, leave their body to nod and smile and frown and make all the appropriate gestures and comments while their minds take little vacations, sometimes extended ones. The effect, however, is unsettling for me, and I try to focus in on what my writer acquaintance is saying.

"…in about three months." Harold is smiling; it must be my turn to talk.

"Three months," I reply. What can he be talking about? How long it will take him to finish his novel? How long it's been since he's been laid? I decide to say something relevant.

"I would have thought it would take longer," I say. I sip my punch and wish I were miles away.

"Well, I thought if I dragged it out any longer, people would think it's hokey," Harold replies. "But I don't know, I could add a few more incidents, I suppose. I mean, I could talk to my agent. How long do you think he ought to hang on?"

Hang on. His agent? Damn, I need more clues. "Oh, uh, maybe six or seven months. That should be enough time."

Maybe Marge will save me. The man she's talking to looks like he's doing what I'm doing. Maybe we should all sit in a circle so we can ignore each other face-to-face.

"Hm. Maybe. Well, do you know of any lingering dog diseases?"

"Uh, no, not offhand, Harold. Dog diseases?"

"People have to believe that he would last that long, though I guess I can make up something. I kind of wanted to finish this week, though. Get the book out by Christmas, you know. You're much prettier than I thought you'd be. I mean, Joe said you were good-looking, but I pictured, you know, a physicist and all…"

This is quite absurd. I do not belong here, not with Harold Sellers, not at this party. I belong back in my lab checking leaks in diffusion pumps or watching TV with Stephanie or talking about strippers with Marcie. I begin to feel that feeling again, the one that prompted me to write all this down in the first place. I feel as if I've walked on stage in the middle of someone else's play, and I don't even know the character, much less the lines.

"Can I get you another drink?" Harold asks.

"Oh, no, thank you; I actually have to leave soon. I have some work to do at the lab."

"What do you do as a physicist, Carolyn?" His eyes are homing in on me now, whereas before they merely were making reconnaissance flights.

"Well, I work with superfluid helium—"

"Sounds interesting. What do you do for fun?"

God, my head feels like the party's inside it. Can't this person disappear?

"My lover and I go to concerts. Hello again, Marge."

"Well, hi, Carolyn. Hi, Harold. How are you two getting along? I just knew you'd hit it off, like Joe said you would."

"Where *is* Joe?" I crane my neck, but just for effect; when you're five-foot-two, craning is pretty useless.

Marge looks around, while Harold continues staring at me through my sweater. "Oh, I saw him before," she says. "I think he was with his friend George. George is in orthopedics, you know, and Joe's leg has been bothering him lately. I told him to see our regular doctor, but you know Joe, has to do it his way. Has to do everything his way."

I have no interest in pursuing that skein of the conversation, but Marge returns to the main thread by saying, "Has Harold told you about his book, Carolyn? Isn't it outrageous? I can't wait to read it and then see the movie, right, Harold?" She winks at Harold like a pro.

"I think it's just as well Joe's not here with you, Carolyn," Marge continues solemnly. "Harold, when those two get together, it's nothing but shop talk. You might as well be listening to another language. I don't think I'll ever understand physics. Carolyn, can I get you another drink or something? A sandwich?"

"No, thank you, Marge." I've either got to leave here at once or set the house on fire.

"Carolyn was just telling me what she and her lover do for fun," Harold says with an edge. He stares at Marge and gives her a smile that hides a less friendly expression.

Marge reacts with aplomb. "Lover? Well, this is unexpected, Carolyn. Someone new? You devil, keeping him a secret from us."

Well, Lady Di, sometimes you think, and sometimes you speak.

"Not a him," I speak. "A her. Stephanie. I'm surprised Joe didn't tell you. I was sure he knew."

I left Shelly's apartment at about six o'clock. I hadn't even thought about Philip until after I'd gotten in the car to drive home. I was trying to think of how I felt and how I ought to be feeling. I decided I felt exhilarated and that I ought to be feeling exhilarated. Telling Philip, of course, was another matter.

Neither of us had been "unfaithful" before, to use an ambiguous and misleading word, but we didn't have any restrictions on each other. Philip was not the jealous-lover type. Jealousy would indicate need, perhaps even dependence, and that was not even to be considered. We'd never discussed gayness, either, not in relation to ourselves, but again, I was confident he'd be open-minded about it. One thing Philip didn't tolerate was people telling other people what to do with their sex lives (masturbation excepted). I remember stopping the car about two blocks away in an attempt to organize my thoughts. I concluded that I should assign top priority to how I was feeling about what I'd just done and continue the passive mode. Second priority was Philip; that would have to take care of itself.

"Hi, where've you been?"

"With Shelly. You know, the one from the group."

"Oh, yeah. Curly hair."

"Did I tell you she had curly hair?"

"Several times. Large breasts, too."

"Well, she does have large breasts, but nice ones. I didn't realize I told you that. How was your day?"

"About the usual. A rejection in the mail, from that counseling place in Bothell. Form letter. Nothing in the paper. I went down to Seattle Center, a few other places. Just your typical unemployed day."

"I know, Phils. Things will get better. I love you."

"Yep. Want to eat out tonight cheap? I didn't have the energy to cook. Or did you eat with Shelly?"

"Let's eat out."

I was dreamy during dinner, and, whether or not Philip picked up on it or on my sporadic and seemingly adventitious smiles, he didn't try to force the conversation. I resolved to tell him as soon as we got in bed.

"Philip, I need to talk with you."

"I figured."

He sat up in bed, switched the light back on. I sat up, too, though it was cold.

"Philip." I pulled up the covers; it was getting colder. "Philip, I made love with Shelly this afternoon."

I don't think he showed any reaction at all those first few instants. Eventually he frowned and nodded in a sort of shrug.

"How was it?"

"Oh, God, Philip, it was wonderful, totally wonderful. I—"

"Did she initiate?"

"Yes."

"Was it the first time for her, too?"

"Uh, no, I don't think so."

"Was this a surprise? I mean, did you plan it, like, 'What do you want to do after class?' 'Oh, I don't know, why don't we make love?'"

"It was a surprise. Well, I had the idea something was going to happen, but I didn't plan it. That was the wonderful thing; I didn't plan it. I decided to let it happen, just let my feelings take control, not think about anything. It, the moment, was just right, everything was perfect. The mood, everything."

"You'll be seeing her again?"

"Oh, yes."

"I mean sexually."

"I do, too. Philip? I can't seem to get any reaction from you. All you're doing is asking questions, which is fine, but I'm wondering what you're feeling."

"Well, I'm still assimilating, I guess. Let's see. I'm glad you had a good time; why wouldn't I be? And I'm assuming you weren't seduced, that you made the decision yourself."

"Yes, I made the decision myself."

"Hm. Well, do you, uh, do you feel any less toward me?"

"Oh, no, Philip, no. Why would I feel less toward you?"

"Well, you know, you had such a good time with Shelly, I thought maybe I would be passé now."

"Oh, no, of course not. Philip, one thing has nothing to do with the other. I love you, Philip." And I went to kiss him, but he pulled back.

"I'm not through thinking. Is this, uh, is this going to be the trend now? Women instead of men?"

Lady Di, until he asked me that, I hadn't even considered it. I'd been thinking about continuing to see Shelly, not continuing to see a woman. It was only after making love with Shelly that the impression came to me of making love with a woman. But when Philip intimated that women as a group might become a sexual *orientation*, I had to admit to myself that that indeed was an issue to consider.

"Well, I don't think so. I still like penises."

"How do *you* feel about all this? I mean, this is a pretty big step for you. Are you okay? Any feelings of regret, guilt, shame? Anything I can do to help?"

"Oh, Philip, I feel really good about it. I do. I don't know how I'll feel tomorrow or the next day, but right now, I feel as if it was completely the right thing for me to make love with Shelly. I feel terrific, I really do. I made love with a woman, and it felt good. I didn't care about society or convention or anything, I just went ahead and did it, and it was great!"

"I understand that. You've already mentioned that it was great and that you feel absolutely wonderful about the whole thing. I was merely trying to find out if there were some emotions other than glee and rapture that you were experiencing."

"I'm sorry, I guess not. I'll try to respond more accurately to your questions."

"It's just that you rarely get that excited about *our* lovemaking."

Whoops. "Are you jealous, Philip?"

"No. Was it better than our lovemaking?"

I was ready for that one. "You really can't compare the two. They're too different."

"Hm. Did you have an orgasm?"

"Yes, but I do with you, too."

"I know that. I was only curious."

"Philip, I do love you." I put a hand on his shoulder. He didn't move it away, but he didn't respond, either.

"I guess I have to think some more, see where this goes, Car'. I doubt I have any problems with a woman-woman thing. I really don't think it would make any difference if Shelly were a man. And I certainly don't mind your having sex with someone else. I do have some concerns about the extent to which this might affect our relationship. But I suppose we'll have to wait and see." He took my hand off his shoulder and held it—tightly, as I recall.

"Are you going to cut your hair short?" he asked. "Shall I call you 'Butch' from now on?"

"Oh, Philip, that's not funny," although I was laughing. It helped me to laugh, and it helped Philip to make me laugh.

"Tell you what," he said. "Maybe you can pick up some pointers and pass them along. You know, women knowing each other's bodies and all."

"I love you, Philip."

"Car'?"

"Yes?" And he looked at me very pensively. "Are you satisfied with our sex life?"

"Yes, of course I am. I really am, Philip. I love you." And I snuggled close to him.

I was all wound up that night, and I replayed the afternoon with Shelly a thousand times, from different angles, with high and low lighting, and my favorite parts in slow motion. When I finally fell asleep, I dreamed not of Shelly, though, but of Mom and Pop, vaguely. I woke up once about three o'clock to go to the bathroom, and when I returned, Philip was staring at the ceiling.

6. THE INDEPENDENT MAN AND THE OTHER WOMAN

Tex prepares to ride out of the town he has just cleaned up for the good folk.

"Don't go," begs Sam the storekeeper. "Why not stay and marry Bess, my beautiful daughter?"

"Thanks all the same," says Tex, and giddyaps his horse down the main street, as the townsfolk synchronically wave a grateful farewell.

You never see Tex's face after he rejects Sam's offer and Bess's company, but you know damn well he's smiling. Why is he smiling? Three reasons: one, he's pumped up by the adulation. Two, he's in control of the situation. And three—and most important—he knows there will be other towns and other Sams and Besses down a piece. He doesn't need them. He's the independent man.

Philip was the independent man, with one critical qualification: he didn't think there were any other towns. Leaving me involved sacrificing his needs for his ideals; he had to maintain that image of independence. The all-powerful male can't let his guard down and show weakness.

When I met Philip, I knew within a short time that he was a very special man. Not because of his humor, which attracted me; not because of his intelligence, which fascinated me. This was a man who asked nothing of people. Back in 1975, Philip *was* independent. Before the masturbation campaign, he was supremely confident of his own worth. Even if he made mistakes, even if he came across like a fool, it didn't matter. Philip was Philip, and he was satisfied with that. He was free of the insecurities that guide the behaviors of most of the rest of us. And he was so assured, so peaceful, that he was having fun.

That's what he eventually lost, Lady Di, the ability to have fun with himself as well as with others. His confidence changed to arrogance, his sense of singularity to alienation, and his playfulness to bitterness. Later, when I found out about how much he hated whirling, I was tempted to think that his "anti-whirling" was whirling because he got so caught up in it. I'm not sure about that, but it's possible. In any case, Di, I did nothing to halt the change. Helpless Carolyn.

After the other-life lecture, we had a pizza and talked. A week later we went to a movie and talked some more. We went to a play, walked around campus, talked, attended a few more lectures, and finally made love. Six months later, he moved in with me. And a month after that, Di, I was still being stimulated by him in more ways than I'd ever been before by anyone else, and I told Philip I loved him.

That afternoon my smile was my face, and we made love, and I was teasing him because he didn't know what was going on. I said, "Philip, I really love you," and he paused for an instant before replying, "How do you know?"

"It's physics. The atoms tell me."

"The atoms, huh? I see."

"I always trust the atoms, and they tell me that I, Carolyn Anderson, am in love with you, Philip Lester."

He looked at me, glanced down at my naked body, and shook his head with a wry smile.

"How can you love me?" he said. "You don't even know me."

"I know you."

"*I* barely know me."

"I don't believe that."

Again he looked at me, this time as if trying to plumb my eyes to determine the depth of my sincerity. When he spoke, his voice was like cracking eggshells.

"I, uh, I guess I'm not used to someone saying that to me. Not anyone like you."

"Like me?"

"I have strong feelings about love."

"So do I."

"What is love to you?"

I had anticipated his question. I told him that love was when you'd do anything for the other person, when his well-being was as important as yours, when you couldn't keep him out of your thoughts, and when his being with you made everything else seem insignificant.

"Hm."

"'Hm?'"

"Have you ever been in love before, Carolyn?"

"No."

"Were there times when you thought you were in love, only to find out later that it was something else?"

"Oh, maybe. Listen, what difference does it make? I love you. It would be nice if you reciprocated the feeling in some way, but if you can't, that's okay, too. I still love you, Philip, no matter what you feel. I'll get a notarized statement if you like. I know a stack of Bibles wouldn't impress you. You *could* just accept it, you know. It won't hurt. I promise."

He put his hand on my cheek, then took it back. I remember thinking, what an odd gesture. We finished making love only fifteen minutes ago, and now he's afraid of becoming too intimate with me?

"Car', I'm sorry. I'm just trying to figure it out. This is the way I do it. We have different conceptions of love."

"What's your conception?"

"Oh, brass bands, starbursts, firecrackers, skywriting in big capital letters L, O, V, E; like that."

"Come on."

"It's even more than that. I think, more than anything, love has to be based on understanding. It's very difficult for me to imagine that happening to me. I, uh, I never think about it much, I guess, because it doesn't seem that that will happen. It doesn't seem reasonable to me that anyone would take the time and energy to do that. I mean, I'm not rebuffing you, I'm only saying that, uh, that I'm not sure how to react, and I thought I'd tell you what, uh, what love meant to me."

He was looking down at our bodies again; it was becoming dark out, and the light filtered through the window shade to lend a dramatic shadow-land feel to the room. I took his chin in my hand, turned his head so I could look directly into his eyes, and said with as much force as I could muster, "Philip, I have taken the time and the energy to do what you said. And I'm telling you right now—and you ought to believe it, because you've never heard anything more true—I'm telling you that I understand you, and that I love you."

Lady Di, I'll always remember what he did next. The gesture itself wasn't so extraordinary; it was the way he did it, and the fact that it was Philip who did it. I was looking at him, to my left, and he was gazing downward, thinking, analyzing, reacting to what I'd said. And, except for that brief hand on my cheek, he hadn't touched me since we'd made love.

He ruminated for over a minute; it was silent except for the usual neighborhood noises—two buses Dopplering each other, kids retreating from school, a radio DJ. Philip didn't look at me, but affixed his gaze to my leg, as if it were the first object he'd seen after being blind his whole life. And he pushed his legs down the bed and pressed his lips against my thigh, very gently, but for a long time. Then he rested his head against my leg, while he caressed it as one might a kitten.

I was astounded at the position, for he never allowed himself to lean against me—and he never did after that. As he patted my leg, I ran my fingers through his hair. Soon I felt a drop on my thigh.

I don't think Mary Ann Simons really wants to be here. Mary Ann got her degree from Oregon, left her fiancé in Eugene to be a part of the University of Washington, and is having a tough time of it. She's twenty-six and seems twenty years younger than me.

"You know, Carolyn," she told me this afternoon over salads in the Union, "all my life, everything has been planned. I've been in school for twenty-one years. Now I think maybe I don't want to be in school anymore."

"I've had similar feelings," I said. Mary Ann often counted on me as her sounding board.

"My phone bills are enormous," she continued. "Ray's, too, for that matter. And I know the Seattle–Eugene plane, train, and bus schedules by heart."

"Maybe when he finishes this year's teaching, he'll come up."

She shook her head as if the issue were an old skirt she'd previously tried on and discarded as inappropriate. "He loves teaching there. The kids love him. He's in line for a part-teaching, part-administrative position, and he's getting certified. No, he's got too much invested in Eugene. He wants me to move down."

"Move down? You just got here."

There went the head again, on a permanent swivel. "I don't know, Carolyn. I don't know what kind of a future I'd have here. I'm never going to be the Queen of Physics, and I'm miserable without Ray. But, by the same token, physics is my field, and if I want to establish a record for my career, I can't quit."

"Do you think your relationship can survive the distance?"

"It can this year, but how long can I keep it up? I don't want to lose Ray. I've never met anyone quite like him. But I think I'd lose respect for myself if I gave up a career for a man. I feel like a fool even saying that in front of you. I mean, Carolyn, I can't imagine you even considering that."

"Listen, don't put me on a pedestal; I've sold out more times than I care to admit."

"I doubt that." She grinned like a schoolgirl with a crush on her sixth-grade teacher.

"It's true," I said. "My research may be coming to an end—lack of funds—and I think I'd sell my firstborn son in order to stay in superfluid helium."

Mary Ann's eyes glittered for a second. "Carolyn, I didn't even know you were married."

"Just a figure of speech."

"Oh." She seemed disappointed. "But they can't stop your research, can they? Just because of money? Isn't there some sort of protection, academic freedom or something?"

I chuckled and tried to finish my salad, but the lettuce was wilting even as I looked at it. Just like my career.

"I've tried, Mary Ann, believe me. I actually may be out altogether if I don't get a good reference from a former professor in Minnesota. I was sort of on the outs with him, and I can't count on him for a recommendation."

"Carolyn, you?"

I smiled. "It happens to the best of us. No recommendation, no money, no professor. Well, there's always community colleges."

"Carolyn, I'm worried about you."

"Don't be. Sometimes you just have to give in to the system."

"It doesn't seem fair."

"Anyway," I said, "what about *your* predicament? That doesn't seem fair, either. If you decided to move back to Eugene, I would hope it would be something *you* wanted to do, not Ray."

"But we both want to be together."

"But there's a difference between his saying, 'Stay with me, wherever I am,' on the one hand, and your saying, 'I've decided that being in this particular relationship is more important to me than being a physicist,' on the other. Do you see what I mean? *You* should make the decision, not him. It's *your* life. You wouldn't be giving up a physics career for him. You'd be substituting lifestyles, one relationship with the world for another. The point is that you make the decision. Frankly, I think it would be a lot tougher to get back into physics if you left here than to get back into a relationship if you stayed here, but you have to take into account, I suppose, how satisfied you are here and how satisfied you'll be in Eugene. It'd be nice if you could get hired into Oregon's physics department."

"Ray's already looked into that for me."

"Nothing?"

"Nothing. I've checked a few other places, too. Even Portland State would be manageable. Nothing yet. Meanwhile, my concentration is not where it should be. It's hard to get through a class without thinking of Ray, or Oregon, or moving."

I really wanted to tell her what to do, Di. She'd talked to me before about Ray, and I always thought about his kind of relationship with women like a person smoking a cigarette. You know, you inhale all the insides and leave just the paper, and then exhale smoke. There are men like that, consuming the pith and substance of women, giving nothing in return, and leaving only paper and smoke. Mary Ann had a lot of things to offer a man or a woman, and she was slowly being consumed by this guy in Eugene who placed his career above hers and had her convinced he was right.

"Mary Ann, have you discussed why, for example, Ray's career is more important than yours?"

"Well," she said, again shaking her head—that was her reaction to everything, perhaps her all-embracing way of expressing that the world was just too much for her—"it's not a question of whose career is the more important; he's made that clear. It's that he's got more invested down there, like I said. I've only been here a couple of months, and I didn't even expect *that*. I think Ray feels a little betrayed."

"Why?"

"Well, you know, I think he—we—both felt that I wouldn't be able to get a job and that we'd live together down there, get married and all. Now, things are a lot different."

"What do you think you'll do, Mary Ann?"

"I don't know, Carolyn. I'd like to make it through the year, get a sense of myself as a physics professor, before deciding anything major."

"That seems prudent."

"But it's tough."

"Well, maybe deciding that you'll stay the year will make it easier. There won't be the anxiety of indecision, anyway. You have a contract to consider as well. I assume you haven't mentioned this to Dr. St...Dr. Mankiewicz, or anybody else in the department."

"No, not yet."

"Is either Ray or you seeing anyone else?"

She shook her head. "No, I don't think either of us is interested in anyone else. Besides, we've been spending a lot of weekends together, either here or in Eugene, mostly Eugene."

"Can you see yourself without Ray sometime in the future?"

"No; are you saying I should plan for it?"

"I don't know, Mary Ann. It sounds like the two of you have mutually exclusive needs. We need good women physicists, women who can contribute to the field, get their names in textbooks for other women to read. I wish I could fold the map for you and make Eugene right next to Seattle. But these days I'm having trouble just keeping my own head above water."

"Well, Carolyn," she said, "maybe I'll think of a way out."

I ran some tests today. It was six o'clock when I discovered a slow leak somewhere in the system. Within half an hour, I'd localized the leak and developed a pounding headache. But it wasn't set off by the leak.

I'm still wondering about the paper. The vortices enthrall me. When I increase the rotation of the helium, the vortices become disordered; spectrum analyzers don't lie. But I need to see it happen more clearly, find out why and how the disruption takes place. I have to keep the key temperatures constant and examine the vortices and everything around them. The idea of putting out a "safe" paper on this is becoming more and more obnoxious. All it would be is a fancy restatement of things everybody already knows, wrapped up in some super math that I would get help on, anyway. If I have to end this research, I'd like to go out with a flourish. I should ask Dr. Stan for money to hook up an electromagnetic system that would really test the vortices. Maybe, considering Chuck Patricelli's impending reference, I should ask Dr. Stan for money to rent a U-Haul.

Life doesn't seem to have changed since I came out at the Bennetts' party. It probably shouldn't affect anyone in the department, but one never knows if there are closet bigots hanging around. Stephanie, of course, sniggered for an hour when I told her what I'd said and what Marge Bennett and Harold Sellers had looked like after I'd said it.

"I just know we can turn Marge's head around," said Stephanie.

"Oh, come on, she's happily married to a very nice jerk."

"I talked to her once. I know these things."

Well, maybe she does. Still, she wasn't there when Marge's face blanched, blushed, and finally settled on a rather unattractive blotchy pink for her official reaction. Too bad, she could be kind of cute.

Maybe I'm upset in general today. There was an article in the paper about male prostitutes in downtown Seattle, and how everyone is outraged because they're so young, you know, eleven, twelve, thirteen. But no one gets outraged at the female prostitutes; it's only when the pride of American male youth is in jeopardy that the public eye attends to sexual abuses.

I try to avoid reading the paper. Every day something else makes me angry. A sixty-eight-year-old man kills his wife and is judged insane. Fine, except he shot her once before, years ago; where were the courts then? The Sunday "Women's" section has a decent article about how women are becoming more aware of politics; but it's followed by a recipe for spinach-stuffed shells. A California congressional candidate says that unwed welfare mothers should give up every child after their first for adoption, because every child "needs two parents." And of course every woman now lives in even more fear than before that her tampons may cause toxic shock syndrome. It's unlikely that they would have discovered that about condoms. Finally, and possibly worst of all, there's a rapist loose in Fife, south of Seattle. No clues, nothing. Just a man running free, attacking women. Maybe Marcie was wise in giving me that mace. Oh, Di, it's tough being aware.

I saw Shelly about twice a week for five months, usually the night of our group—Tuesday—and either Friday or Saturday nights, which spilled over into mid-Saturday and -Sunday afternoons. We didn't do anything particularly exotic—visited friends, took in a movie, watched TV, basically just played with each other.

Shelly was so refreshing. She enjoyed being impulsive, whether it was deciding to go to the hot tubs instead of dinner on the way to a restaurant, or taking up ceramics after she saw an advertisement in the campus newspaper, or quitting her part-time job because she overslept one morning and realized she never wanted to see another doughnut again. I didn't have to be on guard with Shelly; I could be silly or secretive or intellectual or mushy. She didn't care. And I never tired of her. She was like a new playmate, a playmate with whom I always found new ways to bring myself pleasure.

Not once did Philip admit to being jealous. I know he wanted me to stay with him those nights I left for Shelly. I know he hurt every time I kissed him good-bye. He never showed it. I'd ask him if he had anything special he wanted to do on either a Friday or Saturday evening, but he never did. He always left it up to me. Fire on the inside, ice on the outside.

"But how do you feel when I go away?"

"I feel bad. Nothing against Shelly—she seems like a nice woman."

"Why am I reminded of my father telling me that you were a nice boy?"

"Carolyn, I won't pretend that I have no preference. I'd rather you be with me than with someone else. But it's certainly your prerogative to choose the person with whom you want to sleep. Besides, why should I feel bad because you're feeling good? That doesn't make sense."

"It can't be that simple, Philip. How can you be so calm and rational when your lover is seeing another woman?"

"That's what Art asked me today. Not in those words, precisely."

"Who's Art?"

"He's the guy at State Personnel. I told you about him. You see a guy weekly for six months, it's only natural you talk to him. I had lunch with him today, and he wanted to know about you. So I told him. I figured it'd be okay, since he doesn't really know you, and I don't think I've mentioned your last name."

"Who else have you told about me?"

"No one else. What, am I being indiscreet?"

"No, that's all right. So what did Art say?"

"He said I was crazy."

"Why?"

"Because, he said, if two people are committed to each other, then they ought to be faithful to each other. You shouldn't want to see anyone else, and if you did, then you shouldn't, anyway. He said that you were taking advantage of my good-heartedness and that I should be more assertive in the relationship. To sum up, he said I was a sap."

"Well?"

"Well what?"

"Well, what do you think?"

"About what he said? He doesn't understand. Look, Car', I've explained. I don't like it when you leave. I love you. I love your body. But because I love you, I want you to do what you want to do. I'd expect the same from you. Jesus, staying here with me because I requested it is about the worst reason I can think of."

"Would it be different if I were seeing a man?"

"I don't think so. Hard to say."

"How about an animal?"

"Male or female?"

Halftime on a Sunday afternoon, and Stephanie brings us beers from the kitchen. I always liked beer and pretzels and chips and popcorn but never could quite get into football, even in Minnesota, where the Vikings all but approach sainthood. Naturally, my father never encouraged me, even though he must have yearned for someone to watch the games with. My mother would knit while he cheered his heroes. I'd be more likely to read a book, as I did today. But a cold beer definitely makes Andronikashvili go down a little easier.

"Steph, why do you watch the games here with me when I haven't the faintest idea what's going on? I might as well not even be here." I'm curled up in the chair near the stuffed turtle, while Steph has been fastened to the TV like those spaceships in the movies that get pulled into hostile planets by super-magnetic beams.

She takes a swig of beer. "I like you being here. Sundays, you know, you feel like being home. It was like that when I was little. No matter what shit came down the rest of the week, Sunday was kind of peaceful. So I like it like this. Doesn't matter if you say anything to me or not."

"But wouldn't it be more fun for you in a bar? Or at least with people who can root with you? Why don't you invite some people over? I don't mind. I feel like such a drag, like I'm depriving you of fun or something."

She comes over to sit on the arm of the chair and kisses me on the cheek. "Hey, Carrie, I know you like to read. I'd rather be with you reading than with ten other people yelling and screaming."

That makes me smile. "Gee, you must like me a lot, huh."

"Guess so. What're you reading? No, never mind, don't tell me. Somebody last week asked me what you did, and I told them you were a physicist. Then she said, what kind of a physicist, what exactly did you do, was it nuclear physics? And I said, no, I didn't think so, I thought you did something with crygenics? Cryogenics?"

"Cryogenics."

"Cryogenics. I told her you took hydrogen and froze it to see what happened to it at four degrees. How'd I do?"

"Not bad. But it's helium, and I don't freeze it. I just get it really cold, but it's still liquid. I told you that."

"I forgot."

"That's why it's called superfluid helium. Incidentally, it's four degrees, but on the Kelvin scale, not the Fahrenheit scale. It'd be about minus 450 degrees on the Fahrenheit scale."

"No shit? Damn!"

I laugh, because that was exactly her reaction the first time I told her what I did.

"You can also say I work in condensed-matter physics," I continue. "That's what it's called. Or just say that I examine the properties of helium at extremely low temperatures. Or," I add, "that I used to."

"I think I'm just going to say you teach at the U, and if they want to know anything more, I'll give them your phone number."

"I shouldn't be surprised you don't remember any of what I do. I don't remember anything you've told me about carpentry."

"Yeah, but you're supposed to be the smart one."

"Who says?"

"Okay, you're right; we're even."

"Yes, neither of us knows a whit about the other's profession."

"How're you feeling today?"

"Fine."

"No more headaches?"

"A little one, that's all." It's true; I can't shake it, since I started observing the vortices.

"Let's take a vacation, Carrie."

"Can't now. I have classes to teach, and unless my cryostat blows up or I get more leaks or the computer goes down or the roughing pump decides to quit on me like last summer, I should be getting some final data to plug into my earthshaking article. Anyway, I told you about Patricelli. I may have lots of time for vacations pretty soon. No money, but lots of time."

"Carrie, they can't just kick you out. They wouldn't believe that prick over you."

"They can and they would. That prick is a tenured professor at a respected school. Steph, I refuse to worry about it. If they kick me out, I'll just look around at community colleges. I'll get employment. I'll sell my body."

"Shit, girl, we'll starve that way." She puts a cold, beery tongue on my neck. "Did you decide if you're coming to the party next Friday?" she asks, as I transfer her kiss from my neck to my fingers.

"What party?"

"Debbie and Pam's. Remember?"

"Oh, that's right. Sure, why not?"

Steph smiles, that white-tooth-against-tan-skin smile that used to dazzle me and now speaks a different language, a language that maybe husbands and wives silently speak on Sunday afternoons, when they look into each other's eyes and realize that they're really glad they chose each other. I know Stephanie is happy I'm coming to the party with her.

"I'm glad we're together, Steph," I say.

"Me, too, babe."

"Steph?"

"Yeah?"

"What would you do if I went out on you?" It isn't that abrupt a change of topic for me—my mind often hopscotches—but it evidently is for Stephanie, because her smile vanishes into her cheeks.

"Are you going out on me?"

"No," I reassure her quickly, "and I have no plans to."

"Phew! Good. I guess I'd ask you whose lap you wanted to sit in."

"What if I wanted to sit in both laps?"

She shakes her head. "Those things don't work out. I've been in too many of them where everybody comes out bad."

"You'd want to know about it, wouldn't you?"

"I'd probably know, anyway. Why are you asking me all this? Carolyn, are you seeing someone else? Tell me, I want to know."

"No, Steph, I told you. I was just thinking about fidelity and all that. Would it make any difference if it were a man?"

"You wouldn't fuck a man now."

"Oh, I wouldn't? And why not? I suppose Miss Hotsie Totsie here can satisfy me like no man can?"

"Damn straight, Cream Butt, and you know it. I've had men before; I know what it's like. It's damn uncomfortable. Sloppy, ugly, and over before you can get up a good head of steam. If you started fucking with a man, I'd think you went off the deep end for sure. But I know you won't. Anybody who can understand cryogenics or hydrogen, helium, whatever it is you're reading, ought to be smart enough to not go fucking some man."

I'd always speculated how Steph would take to monogamy. When I met her, she had three steady lovers, not trivial lovers, either, but good friends as well. One by one she ended her sexual relationships with them after we decided to live together. We never spoke about it; it was just understood. With us, it wouldn't have worked any other way.

I met Stephanie in a women's bar, Lady Di. I'd been frequenting bars for several months, usually alone. It was a place to select my pleasure. I could listen to the music, or dance, or talk with friends, or even get picked up, though that didn't happen often. One evening this striking, faintly Asian-looking woman came to my table and asked me to dance. I said no thanks; she attracted me, but for some reason I'd been more morose than usual, and I felt like being alone. She said how about if I promise not to rub against you. Her sheer bravado made me laugh, and I said, sure.

Well, three dances later, it was a slow dance, and she did rub against me a little, but it was okay. She impressed me with a sincerity that belied her outward show of brazenness. We went out for a cup of tea at about two in the morning and then said good-night. I actually expected to spend the night with her, but she made no move at all, and I found myself curiously disappointed. I asked Steph about it later, and she couldn't figure it out, either. "It's not my style," she said, "but I think I wanted you when we weren't drunk or tired."

A few weeks later, we weren't drunk or tired, and the lovemaking was so good that I wanted to turn myself inside out, so the rest of me could experience her, too. We became closer, and I knew she loved me when she made the commitment to monogamy. That was tough for her, and I was touched.

Philip got a job in a nursing home. He was something called an Activities Director, a liaison between the residents and the administrators of the home. It seemed like an adequate job, the meager pay notwithstanding. He got to *do* something, and after almost a year of doing nothing except applying for jobs and brooding, it was a welcome change for both of us. He took his friend Art out for a good-bye lunch, and I treated him to a fancy dinner. It was like an old-fashioned Christmas miracle, and the good fortune ameliorated his Christmas mood, which was Scrooge-like at best. "The Season of Hypocrisy," according to St. Philip. I was thankful for Shelly.

It was a day in March 1977. A gift subscription to *Reader's Digest* had come in the mail from Philip's crazy uncle. Philip's crazy uncle lived in

Canada somewhere, Toronto, I think. He taught Latin and, because Philip had taken a few Latin classes in high school and college, had assumed a strong bond between them. He always kept track of Philip's address, though he hadn't seen him since Philip had his bar mitzvah. Every March, Philip received a gift from his crazy uncle, not for his birthday, which was in July, but to commemorate the Ides of March. Some years Philip got the gift early, some years late, but he always got it.

The gifts were the last thing Philip needed to stave off alienation. One year it was a Western tie. Another year it was a game of Risk. The year before the *Reader's Digest* subscription, it was a potato baker, one of those pronged things that you can use to bake five potatoes at once. Philip was disappointed with the *Reader's Digest*. "I thought it might be something more useful," he said, "like an oar."

Philip's crazy uncle's gifts would have been amusing, except that Philip characteristically saw the dark side. He interpreted them as eminently reasonable for a good part of the population, and they only reminded him of how alienated he was from that good part of the population.

But that day we had other things on our minds, namely, a dinner guest. Philip had taken a liking to one of the women in the nursing home and had invited her to dinner. This being the first woman he'd brought home with him, I was in no position to argue. We were tizzying around the kitchen, opening and closing cupboard doors, trying to create a suitable menu out of the vagabond foodstuffs we kept around the house.

"Philip, what does she eat?"

"Uh, I don't know. I didn't know how to ask delicately. I thought of barging in on her during lunchtime, but it never worked out."

"Well, *can* she eat? I mean, does she have teeth?"

"I suppose so. Sure. At least false ones. She never mentioned, and I figured it was rude to ask."

"Well, you're right on that account. What about seasoning? Is salt okay? Sugar? Give me a hint."

"Car', Jesus, I don't know. I've only been working with their social and recreational needs. I don't know everyone's diet. They eat a lot of Jell-O, I think."

"Oh, fine, we'll have Jell-O for dinner. That's nutritious. And maybe chocolate pudding for dessert."

"Look, how about spaghetti?"

"Oh, I don't know, Philip."

"But it's soft. She wouldn't have to chew it. There's nothing bad in it. We could make a nice, bland sauce—"

"What if her coordination is off? I don't know if I can handle spaghetti draped all over an old lady's face."

"Her coordination is fine. But now that I think of it, her sight's not too keen, and I don't know how her depth perception might be with spaghetti. Didn't you have any old relatives in Minnesota? What did you feed *them*?"

I thought for a second, and the only one I remembered was my grandfather Sven, who ate weird things, like peanut butter and American cheese sandwiches, and who used to mash everything up on his plate with a spoon and then mix it all together until it resembled something that might eat *you*.

"There's no one relevant," I said. "Maybe there's someone we can call at the nursing home."

"No, I don't want to do that."

"Well, how about steak?"

"Too bulky."

"Chicken?"

"Too greasy."

"Veal?"

"Too expensive."

"Fish?"

"She could choke on a bone."

"Liver?"

"Carolyn, you can't invite someone to dinner and serve her liver. No one likes liver."

"How about a quiche?"

"Quiche! Sure! Well, there's cholesterol in it, but we can use skim-milk cheese. Great! Cheese, eggs, milk, maybe some mushrooms, a green vegetable. We shall have quiche!"

"What time are you supposed to pick her up?"

"Five-thirty. Plenty of time. It'll be a splendid meal."

Lucy Nardquist was the most wrinkled woman I'd ever met. She looked like someone had thrown her into the washer and dryer and left her rolled up in a ball too long. I recall hearing about my own grandmother; she owned a corner grocery called "Oma's," and they said she was a hale and blustery woman, sharp-tongued and robust from the pleasures and pressures of small business womanship. As a matter of fact, she divorced my grandfather when she was sixty-two and moved to Chicago. Lucy Nardquist wasn't frail, but she didn't look like she could run a grocery, either.

"Mrs. Nardquist," said Philip ceremoniously, "this is my *intimata*, Carolyn."

Neal Starkman

Philip and I had long ago discussed what word we would use to refer to each other in the presence of a new acquaintance. "Lover" seemed too trendy, and "roommate" indicated specifically that we were *not* lovers. Neither of us liked "boyfriend" and "girlfriend"—too juvenile. "Close friend" and "good friend" seemed euphemistic, as if we knew what we were but were too ashamed to say. We considered inventing a word—Philip liked "bodacizer"—but then we'd just have to explain what the word meant. Next came the flippant alternatives: "the receptacle of my manhood," along with "the piston of my ecstasy." Merely saying each other's names did not convey enough information. Philip was partial to "paramour," but I thought it sounded too illicit. I wasn't familiar with any Swedish phrases, but Philip dug into the Latin and found "intimata" for him to use and "intimatus" for me to use. Second best was "enamorata" and "enamoratus," but the connotation there is that we spend most of our time together in a mutual swoon. So we use the Latin for "intimate," and hardly anyone ever questions us on it, especially when we say it ceremoniously.

"Your what?" asked Mrs. Nardquist.

"The woman I live with," said Philip. "Carolyn, this is Lucy Nardquist."

"How do you do, Ms. Nardquist," I said. "Philip has told me how much he enjoys working with you."

"Has he told you that I prefer to be called *Mrs.* Nardquist?"

"Sorry," said Philip to me.

"Oh, I'm sorry, Mrs. Nardquist," I said. "I'll remember next time."

"I was married twenty-two years; just like to remind myself, that's all. Your Philip does a good job out there," she said, as Philip guided her to the couch. Now that I could get a better view of her, she didn't look all that weak, merely—well, impaired. She was still taller than I was, by at least an inch, and I noticed she wasn't wearing heels. Her body moved slowly, but with a certain smoothness that in past years might have been grace. Her arms were wrinkled but not varicosed, and she wore a simple dark dress and a moderate amount of jewelry for an older woman. Her face was very lined, but she used only enough eye shadow and rouge to give it some life. No lipstick, no nail polish.

"I hope you didn't make me old-fogey food for dinner, Miss Carolyn."

"Oh, no, Mrs. Nardquist. As a matter of fact, Philip made most of the meal. We were thinking you might like quiche. It's sort of a cheese pie with veg—"

"I know what quiche is," she snapped. "I watched—what's her name—that funny lady on TV cook it once." We talked about it later and decided she must have meant Julia Child.

Dinner went well. Mrs. Nardquist ate daintily, as I'd expected. Her coordination *was* off a little, and she compensated for it by slowing down her movements, so at least she'd give the appearance of fluidity, if not quickness. There was something noble and poignant in the way she accepted her limitations and pushed herself right to the edge. Her mind was certainly spry. In fact, she led the conversation into areas I would not have guessed common for her.

On some issues she talked like a progressive; for example, she had no problems at all with a man and woman living in unwedded bliss, or, in our case, unwedded strain. But on other issues she was strongly conservative, even reactionary. She was clearly racist, firmly against abortions, and didn't see why wives wanted to get jobs when they could stay home and raise children. She'd say something outrageous—"In my day, they wouldn't have thought of busing the colored, except to haul them out of the state"—and then we'd tiptoe into the fray, after which she'd mellow her stance. Her politics were undefinable, but she held no respect for politicians: "rapscallions and scoundrels." It was impossible to type her. What's more, I got the distinct feeling during the meal that she was trying to categorize *us*.

"Time for ice cream?" I asked.

"Pistachio?" said Mrs. Nardquist.

"Close," I said. "Vanilla. Tea, Mrs. Nardquist?"

"Coffee, if you have it, dear."

We moved back into the living room for ice cream with coffee for Philip and Mrs. Nardquist, and tea for me. Mrs. Nardquist asked if we might have any brandy, but we were all out. I looked at Philip. He shrugged.

Mrs. Nardquist smiled at us; she didn't smile often, and then it was a mannered rather than a genuine smile.

"You two seem like pretty modern people," she said. "I can see that, even if my eyes aren't so good."

"What makes us so modern?" asked Philip.

"Nothing special. I just get the feeling. I've been studying you, you know. I can read you like a book, Philip. And even Miss Carolyn here isn't too hard to figure out. Nobody is, if you set your mind to figuring. Everybody's the same, anyway, don't you think? Old and young, men and women. What do you think?"

It was hard to know what to think. She seemed to be asking us something, but at the time I didn't know what it was.

"Well," said Philip, "I think there are some important differences between us. But on some level you're right: we have the same tendencies, fears, superstitions."

"What about men and women?"

"Uh, what about them?"

"Well, do you think there's differences between them?"

My turn. "I think there are obvious differences, but the ones some people think are important aren't the ones that are really important."

"You two get along?" Mrs. Nardquist asked out of the blue, which is where many of her questions hailed from.

"Get along?" said Philip. "Sometimes we do, sometimes we don't."

"You know," she continued, "sometimes I think it's better that if one of you goes, the other one should walk down the same path. 'Specially if you've lived together a long time. There are some folks in the place I live, they're in pretty bad shape."

"It's too bad it has to be that way," I said.

"Oh, I'm lucky, in some ways," she said. "I know I'm lucky, and I'm thankful for what I've got. I'm still pretty sharp. I can usually outfox those big shots where I live."

She never used the word *home* to describe where she lived.

"But I'll tell you what I'm not thankful for."

There was an unexpected pause, and Philip said, "What?"

Mrs. Nardquist examined the two of us again, squinting through bifocals, slowly spooning ice cream into her mouth, deliberately sipping coffee from another spoon.

"You know the worst thing about the place I'm in?"

"Seeing your friends pass on," suggested Philip gently. But he was way off the track.

"Heck, no," she said. "Oh, that's sad, all right, but we all have to go when the Good Lord taps us on our shoulder. No sense carping about what you can't do a thing about. I'm talking about something that's just plain foolishness. They just don't let you mess around in that place."

Mrs. Nardquist spooned some ice cream delicately, while Philip let his melt in his spoon. I almost dropped my teacup.

"Now I can talk to you about this," she went on. "That's one reason I waited, Philip."

Philip recovered to say, "I don't understand, Mrs. Nardquist."

"We're not doing business now. We're doing friends. I can talk about things, some things, and it's okay now."

"Oh, sure," said Philip. "I'm not obligated to report what you tell me. But I wouldn't feel that way, anyway, Mrs. Nardquist, unless it was a matter of your health or safety."

"Miss Carolyn," she ignored him, "I was once pretty like you. Even had yellow hair, though you wouldn't think so. But I've lost a lot of pretty, have to use my charm more now. And that's fine, sometimes. Sometimes it's even hard to turn it off, know what I mean? Why, poor Mr. Remington, I believe, would give his uppers to go shillelaghing with me."

She laughed, the first time that evening, and Philip spilled his ice cream.

"I guess I was never aware of the problem before," he said apologetically.

"How would you like it?" she asked of him.

"Well, I wouldn't like it. I guess I'd try to do something about it."

"That's my boy!" She laughed again. "That's what I've been doing the past month."

"What have you been doing?" I asked.

"Something about it."

Philip and I looked at each other, and I'm sure we each had the same bewildered expression. I was almost afraid to ask the next question. "*What* have you been doing about it, Mrs. Nardquist?"

She turned to Philip as if it were clear what she'd been doing about it. "Philip Lester, I can't keep something like this away from you for very long. That's why I'd rather tell you straight up. You're not like the rest of them there; I know that. And Miss Carolyn, too."

"Mrs. Nardquist," said Philip, "if you're, uh, shillelaghing with Mr. Remington, or with anyone, I think it's commendable that you're doing it and unfortunate that you have to sneak it. In fact, it's deplorable. I'm glad you told me. I'll do everything I can to see that you're guaranteed as much privacy as you need to do what you, uh, need to do. And I want you to feel free to speak to me on the job without being afraid I'll betray your confidence."

Mrs. Nardquist sipped her coffee and nodded slowly, as if she were weighing all the data she'd been collecting about Philip the past few months and about me the past few hours.

"It's not so simple as all that, Philip. You know, I've always been a pretty free-spirited gal, all my life, especially since Mr. Nardquist left me. And I also figure, what I do is my business. Know what I mean?"

Philip nodded.

"You can make recommendations about room assignments, can't you, Philip? I've seen it happen a few times, folks next-door to each other not getting along and all."

"Sure. I've made two recommendations already. But you get along with your neighbors, don't you, Mrs. Nardquist?"

"I know I get along with my neighbors. I'm not senile. I never said I didn't get along with my neighbors. If I remember correctly, I started talking about messing around, having to sneak. Do you remember that, Miss Carolyn, or is this memory lapse of your intimate boyfriend here catching?"

"I remember, Mrs. Nardquist," I said, smiling at Philip. "And then you were saying that you always were free-spirited." I had an odd feeling that we were going to have a bombshell go off in our living room. I put down my tea.

"Thank you. Now, Philip, do you find in your memory the name of Wilma Ann Torrance?"

"Wilma Ann? Oh, sure, I know her. Third floor. Real nice. Is she a friend of yours?"

"Philip, I don't really want to have to spell this out for you."

She paused, Lady Di, and I knew what was coming. Philip was completely lost, but I knew what Mrs. Nardquist wanted. When your mind is fixed on something, then all your experiences confirm the validity of that fixation. But I still couldn't believe it until she said it.

"Philip," she sighed, "sometimes you frustrate me more than Wilma Ann does, but you're the only one who can do this. If you could fix it up so that she and I roomed next-door to each other, without one or the other of us either slinking down the stairs like a prowler or waking up half the wing by taking the elevator, why, you'd be making both our stays in that place a lot more bearable."

Stanley Mankiewicz called me into his office today. I told myself to remain calm, no matter what. Many people change careers, some even on purpose.

Dr. Stan looked up from his desk when I came in. "Good news, Dr. Anderson. You can keep your helium for the rest of the year."

I made an effort to take the statement without a visible reaction. "What about Dr. Patricelli's endorsement?" I asked.

"Didn't even need it. We found some money we didn't think we had, so there's no pressure to scrub your work. Just don't take longer than a year to relearn your semiconductors, because you'll have to switch over then. But you can work on the helium till June."

"Really?"

"Really. No more questions."

Dr. Stan is so kind-looking. He's got that cute little gray moustache and the chubby face to go with his indulgent waistline, and he always makes you feel comfortable. He wields his power differently than most men. Thank God.

We engaged in a ten-minute discussion about the weather, the women's caucus, and how my parents were doing. Dr. Stan takes an interest in my parents; he himself has family in Wisconsin, and I think he feels that asking about my family substitutes for keeping up-to-date with his own. There was a lull, I got up to go, and he said, "One other thing, Carolyn," and leaned forward in his chair. He started to fill a pipe, and I sat back down.

"Yes?"

"I hear through the grapevine that you startled quite a few people the other night."

"What? I...oh." Joe Bennett didn't waste any time. I suddenly felt vulnerable. "I guess I did."

Dr. Stan bobbed his gray head and started the interminable process of lighting his pipe and keeping it lit. He was beginning to look far more like Dr. Mankiewicz than like Dr. Stan.

"Well, Dr. Anderson," he said, puff, puff, "as chairman of this department and, of course," puff, puff—God, why wouldn't that thing light—"as your friend, I have at least one observation to make about this."

Neal Starkman

At last, the pipe caught, and he relaxed in his chair, though I was as stiff as a data card.

"Yes, sir?"

"I think it does Joe Bennett good to get startled now and then."

Oh, Lady Di, it's so nice to have friends in high places.

The tempestuosity of my relationship with Shelly affected Philip. Sex with her was something I anticipated, reveled in, and frequently called to mind. My intellect, initially shoved aside so that I could enjoy myself without restriction, now returned to support my feelings. I was giddy with the change in my life, with the physical pleasure I was experiencing, and with Shelly herself.

Philip couldn't help but notice my excitement before leaving to spend the night with her and the distracted conversations I kept having with him. Our sex diminished further; it stabilized only after I realized that I was not attending to what I still considered my primary relationship. But by then I could do nothing to allay Philip's insecurity.

Shelly suggested we leave the study group and join a group of bisexual men and women. In fact, I joined one group with her and another without her, the latter bisexual women only. The women in both groups helped validate what I was feeling, something Philip was unable to do. The issues I'd resigned to meeting alone were no longer so mysterious or so unique to me. The camaraderie was vitalizing, and I found myself less resistant to articulate my feelings, because I knew they would be received with respect.

Shelly and I went to the group in addition to our regular social engagements, and Philip grew less and less tolerant.

"Carolyn's home! Your Carolyn's home!" Picture: buoyant Carolyn arrives home at five-thirty or so, a little hyper, saunters into the kitchen, and kisses Philip on the cheek. Philip is slicing carrots for a dinner stew. He is, let us be generous, laconic.

"Hi."

"The group was great!" Carolyn now munches on a few carrots and strolls around the kitchen while relating the events of the afternoon. Philip continues to prepare dinner.

"Lorraine says the Mormons are really gearing up for a legislative offensive against bisexuals and gays. You just wouldn't believe the organization they have! God, they're awful! Oh, and Marilyn told us about coming out to her mother. That was awful, too. Her mother—she lives in Seattle, I think that's why she told her, she got divorced last year—her mother told her she never wanted to see her again and started crying and getting hysterical, and then she called up the hospital to see if they could do something, you know, like change her back or something. I can't imagine telling my folks. You know my father. Then we got a little into stereotypes...Are you listening to me?"

"I'm listening. I have to do the dinner, too. I can do both."

"We got to talking about the stereotypes straights have and how we can go about educating the public. There seems to be some sort of split between those who want to actively educate and those who don't care as much about education as they do about legislation, you know, protection laws and all. We're also planning something with the women's chemical dependency program, maybe do some school counseling. I've heard some real horror stories about what goes on in high school; there's just no sensitivity at all."

"Do you want broccoli in the stew?"

He could be such an asshole.

"You know, this is important to me."

"I'm listening. I merely asked you a question. It doesn't mean I'm ignoring you."

"Well, why don't you say something about what I've been telling you, instead of asking me if I want broccoli in the stew! You don't care about anything I'm doing."

"I care about *you*. There's only so much I can listen to about bisexuality."

"Would you rather I didn't say anything about it?"

"I don't mind listening to what you did during the day. But you can't expect me to be as excited about it as you are. Do you want broccoli?"

"I don't care about the damned broccoli! Do what you want with it. Shove it up your nose." I start to leave the room and either fume or drive over to Shelly's.

"Wait a minute!" he says and puts down the knife. "Why *should* I be so excited about your bisexual group? Except for you, it doesn't make any difference to me. Look, Carolyn, I think your becoming bisexual is fine. More than fine. I wish *I* could be bisexual. I wish I could relate sexually to people as opposed to only women. But sex doesn't make up that large a portion of a person's life, or it ought not. And it seems to me that the only difference between heterosexuals—excuse me, 'straights'—and non-heterosexuals is whom they make love with and whom they want to make love with."

"Philip, it's much more than that. You know, I honestly think you should examine your prejudices. When I first started seeing Shelly, you were pretty open-minded about it. But now that I go to gay bars and belong to bisexual groups, it's quite a different thing, isn't it?"

"You think I'm prejudiced against non-heterosexuals?"

"I think it's a distinct possibility. Look at how you call us by the opposite of what you are. That's like calling fish 'non-mammals.'"

"Oh, come on, Carolyn. How can you possibly think that, knowing me? How—"

"Philip, all I'm saying is, take a look at it."

He turns away from me, shaking his head.

The key, I think, was control. Everything was fine if he was in control. But as I learned more about myself, became stronger, and began to demand more from the relationship, he was threatened. He struck back not by fighting me but by withdrawing from me, while making it seem as if I were the one who was withdrawing.

One new spring day, I broke up with Shelly. She dropped me for a man she met in the mixed bisexual group, a divorced man with two children and a law practice. I never trusted him in the group, and I would certainly never have trusted him outside the group. Shelly had mentioned him only a few times in passing, and I was stunned when she told me what was going on and what *would* be going on.

"I don't understand this at all." She had chosen a bench on the UW campus to tell me, not a likely place for a scene. We had met for lunch and a "talk." I thought that she was going to ask me to move away from Philip and into her apartment. I'd been prepared to say no but to offer a compromise, because I didn't want to lose her. What prescience.

"Carolyn, I'm sorry about this. I don't want to hurt you."

"Forget about hurting me. Explain it to me."

"There's nothing much to explain. Rick and I have gotten to be close, and it's getting serious. I didn't know it was going to turn out this way. But we might want to make a go of it."

"Pretty quick work, wasn't it?"

"I've known him almost two months."

"Pretty quick work, wasn't it?"

"Carolyn, don't make it harder. I really think a lot of you. But I think it's best this way."

"What is this, the cliché corner? Why didn't I know anything about this? All the time you've been seeing both of us, and you don't say anything? You go to the group and you pretend he's just another guy? You sit next to me and hold my hand while you're playing flirty-eyes with him across the room? God!"

"I didn't want it to get messy."

"Messy? What do you think it is now? Neat and clean?"

"Carolyn—"

"Shel', I thought...I thought we meant something to each other."

"We do, Carolyn. You'll always mean a lot to me."

"It doesn't sound like it. It sounds like I'm being tossed overboard, and you're steaming to port with Rick the Prick."

"Carolyn, Rick and I have a chance to really be something beautiful, something lasting. It could never be that way with you. Not with Philip and everything."

"Why does being with Rick preclude being with me? I'm with Philip and with you."

"Carolyn, I don't like it that way. I don't like sharing my lover. I don't want to share either of my lovers anymore."

I remember trying to think calmly, trying to say the right words, the ones that would convince her that she was making a mistake. If only I had been warned, if only I could have prepared!

"Shelly, why can't...I don't want you to leave me. I just really like being with you. Please, can't we—why don't we go back to your place and talk about it. Maybe we can work something out."

"Carolyn." She glanced around us, failing to be casual. "It was what it was. We'll still be friends; we'll still see each other. I've thought about this a lot, because you mean so much to me, Carolyn. We've had some pretty good times together."

"Don't you think I know that? Why do you think I'm crying?"

Maybe it was because we were outside in public, but she didn't hold my hand, or take my head in her arms, or even pat my knee. She just looked straight ahead, as if she were in the midst of some unpleasant chore that would soon be completed.

Philip held me, though. When he came home, I was in bed, having canceled my class, and was still crying. It must have been an interesting mixture of emotions for him: concern for my sadness, relief at my return, and perhaps even curiosity over whether I'd be as upset if *he* left me. But he held me, he actually kissed away my tears, and he listened to me tell him all about Shelly. He held me all night.

Shelly and Rick got married within the year and divorced one year later. I heard from her a few more times, though she had quit the bisexual group. We had lunch once; she'd joined a Buddhist church and was planning a trip to the Far East.

Steph and I went to Seattle Center to celebrate my renewed career. I still can't figure out just how it happened that Dr. Stan "found" more money—the physics fairy—but I'm not complaining.

We ate junk food, played some dumb carnival games, hesitatingly tried one of the tamer rides, held hands—quite daring for me—and decided to have our pictures taken.

Neal Starkman

You know those booths where you go inside, close a curtain, and get a bunch of snapshots taken of you for about a dollar? Well, we thought that sounded like a good idea; we didn't have that many pictures of us together. And, if they came out decent, we could enlarge them and perhaps give them to friends. That's what we told ourselves, with the straightest faces this side of heartbreak. But as soon as we sat on the little stool and I closed the curtain behind us and Stephanie put the quarters in, we started giggling and kissing, squeezing each other on our breasts, posing with our hands on each other's crotches, and generally acting like a couple of libidinous teenagers. It was great fun, and I was still laughing when I stepped out of the booth in front of a very quiet, blank-faced Cub Scout troop. They stood there, not saying a word, while we cleared our throats, stifled our giggles, wiped our eyes, finally retrieved our pictures, and slunk away.

Oh, Di, I was so embarrassed, much more so, I'm sorry to say, than I would have been were Steph a man. It's not only that the public is belligerent toward a lesbian relationship. It's that I must be somewhat belligerent toward it myself.

It makes me angry again.

The computer's down, and I'm writing to you, Lady Di, from the Academic Computer Center. There has always seemed to me to be something *deus ex machina* about waiting for data to be disgorged from a large machine you never see. I wait for the truth here—the Great Solver of Problems and Answerer of Questions. The data will show me "What Really Is," nothing less—provided I've run a clean experiment and punched the cards accurately. But "What Really Is" really isn't until one, I've looked at it; two, I've published it; and three—and, of course, most important—it's accepted by the scientific community. So truth must be the public perception of truth. If helium spins in my lab, does it make a scientific sound? Not if I don't publish. Not if the academic powers deny it. Maybe that's why I can't kiss Steph in public yet.

I saw Joe Bennett earlier today, and he told me he was glad that I'd admitted I was gay, because now the sexual tension between us was off.

"What sexual tension?" I asked.

"Oh, come on, Carolyn. It's perfectly natural, perfectly obvious. I've been aware of it for a long time. You know, we've worked together for a while, and now we can relax. You've let me know where you're coming from, and I don't feel any pressure."

Men never cease to amaze me, Di. If Joe's ego were any bigger, it would swallow him. No doubt he's overcompensating. Latest word is that Marge is interested in a man from her mechanics course. I hope it's not Harold Sellers. That would be insulting even to Joe.

It's a minor wonder they don't boot me out of the physics department for having a low academic quotient. Sometimes it's obvious I really don't belong here, not even at their parties. Jesus, I came out at fucking Joe Bennett's party. What would I have done had they treated my lesbianism like a social disease? Or if they'd needed the endorsement from Chuck Patricelli, and he'd laid on the "Curse of the Purple Physics Tie"? I can't work on hotel windows like Stephanie. I can't wait on tables and smile when people are rude to me. Not anymore. Maybe I could be a bouncer at the male strip club. Ah, woman in search of niche, please notify if found.

Philip had no niche. He cried once. Tears, that is, snailed down his face. Unprecedented, it frightened me, and it came at an odd time and place.

I never saw the specific catalyst, whether it was a particular item in the store or some snatch of conversation he picked up while walking along the busy aisles. He was so unaffected normally, could confront the most emotionally laden situations without any loss of control. He raged during the masturbation campaign, of course, but that was a controlled rage. He *wanted* to be angry.

We were in a shopping mall. It might have been Christmastime, I'm not sure. But the mall was crowded, I was searching for a gift in a department store, and Philip tagged along. There was nothing extraordinary about the mall or the store. It was a 90-store, covered mall, not unlike the ones in St. Paul or St. Louis or even St. Cloud—Walden Bookstore, Penney's, Woolworth's, shoe stores, yarn shops, and men's and women's clothing stores. The usual items were on sale in the department store, with the usual displays, the usual clerks, and the usual ambience—plain old people looking to buy plain old things. It was a mall.

Philip rarely went into malls, much less big department stores. When we first entered, he looked at all the people and the vast quantity of products as if he were in a big store for the first time, and he moved close to me. He might've even taken my hand.

We were in there, oh, maybe half an hour, and I wasn't paying much attention to him. We'd taken the escalator up and down a few times to different floors, I'd sought the advice of a few saleswomen, and I'd browsed through several racks of clothing. We were being jostled by the crowd, normal for a heavy shopping area.

He hadn't spoken, or even responded to my small comments, but that wasn't alarming. All at once, I felt him grip my arm. I looked at him and saw tears in his eyes.

"I have to go," he said hoarsely, and hurried out of the store.

I was startled and rushed to catch up with him. I asked him what was wrong, I thought he might be hurt, but he just shook his head and walked faster, until we were out of the mall, through the parking lot, and back inside our car, where he sat in the driver's seat holding himself like his insides would explode. He just stared out the front window—no, he stared *at* the front window—and the tears continued to wet his face.

"Philip, tell me," I said, feeling his stomach. "What's wrong?"

He took a deep breath. I put my arm around him and started to breathe heavily myself. Finally he closed his eyes, fingered away the tears, sniffed, and turned to me. His voice was deliberate, taut.

"I can't explain it. I'm like an alien in there, a goddammed alien, like I'm not of the same, I don't know, I don't belong. There is nothing in that store that even remotely interests me. Nothing. I was in there all that time, and yet the people, all the people, are eager for…It's not even the products, it's them, the way they, I don't know, are so *immersed*…" He began to shake his head, and the tears came again.

"Hey, it's okay," I said, and held his hand. But it wasn't okay at all.

It was when I was seeing both him and Shelly that it became apparent how radical our lifestyle was. I didn't trumpet our situation, but those I did tell reacted negatively. Philip was a weak man, Philip didn't love me, Philip had an excuse to see other women, Philip was—as someone said—henpecked. As for me, I'm sure I was considered unfeeling, oversexed, degenerate, and unfaithful. "You can't possibly be all you can be to both of them," a friend told me.

I'd reply, well, of course I can. It's not as if I have only, say, two liters of affection in me, and if I give one liter to Shelly, that means I have only one liter left for Philip. One doesn't diminish the other in the slightest.

It was fortunate that Philip and Shelly were so different. Sex was quite different, of course, and it was about this time that both the frequency and quality of sex with Philip began to decline precipitously. It was only rarely exciting, too often perfunctory. I never tired of Shelly, though. It was a common wish of mine in those days for Philip to have Shelly's body and sexuality.

"Is there anything I can do," Philip asked me one night after we'd pecked each other on the mouth and rolled back-to-back, "to enhance our sex life, such as it is? Anything that Shelly does, for example, that you enjoy?"

I turned over and so did he. I liked his asking but hated to respond.

"I enjoy everything Shelly does."

"Anything in particular I could pick up?" He wasn't pleading, only asking, like he was on his way out to the store.

"Philip, I don't think so."

He sighed. "I didn't think so, either. Thought I might ask, though."

"Thanks for asking."

"Sure."

"I love you, Philip."

"Sure."

No one in my groups had simultaneous, serious relationships with men *or* women. Many slept around, some were in the midst of leaving primary relationships, and others were celibate, afraid to commit to one sex or the other. In fact, it wasn't a bisexuality issue at all; it was a monogamy issue. And no one seemed to understand it.

Shelly took the whole thing rather lightly: "What's the problem? You've got me, you've got Philip if you want him; just relax. If *he* doesn't care you're over here, why should *you* worry about it? Enjoy yourself, Carolyn. If you'd put that planning and controlling and analyzing energy into storage, you'd be a lot better off. Let Philip take care of himself."

Philip couldn't take care of himself. He rode out of town, fists clenched over the reins. He didn't see any other towns on the horizon, but it didn't matter. He just left. He withdrew inside himself until it got so crowded in there, no one else could get in.

I couldn't do a thing about it.

7. DAMNED

"When I was a little girl, my father ruled the house. He expected dinner on the table when he got home from work. It if wasn't hot and ready for him, he'd insult my mother, and she'd accept his insult without question. If he decided to stop off for a few drinks on the way home, the dinner my mother had cooked got cold, and she had to make him something else when he did come home, often drunk and swearing. Some nights he didn't come home at all, but he never offered an explanation. My mother knew better than to ask. If she even dared to question him about something he considered none of her business—and that decision was always arbitrary—he might slap her. He raped her more nights than not, but if she was assertive in the bedroom, he would call her a whore. One evening, he came home drunk and slapped my baby sister, breaking her jaw. That was the night my mother took me and my sister and left him, after twelve years of slavery called marriage. Even then, it took two years of court fights and finally a move out of the state to be rid of my father. No child support, no nothing, just leaving us alone was all my mother wanted from him. He tried to get me, he tried to get my sister, and he took fifteen years off my mother's life. But she was strong; she fought harder than he did. In the end, he didn't really care about any of us, didn't care what happened to us, and he found another woman to subjugate.

"My sisters, the only atypical part of my mother's marriage is that she ended it. There are millions of women today who continue to live under the yoke of men—at home, in the courts, in the marketplace, in the media, and in the schools.

"I say men have dominated us for too long. They tell us how to dress, how to speak, how to work, how to play, how to love, and how to think. I say, no more! No more will we let somebody else do our thinking for us! No more bullshit! Note, that's bullshit, not cowshit.

"It's time for every woman on this campus to take a look around her. Take a look at your own university, take a look at the city you live in, take a look at the world beyond this city, and you'll see. You'll see that it's not only your struggle, it's the struggle of every woman today and every woman who comes after us. It's the struggle of every woman who finds herself disenfranchised.

"We don't want any more than our rights, but we won't settle for any less. We demand the right to earn as much as men for comparable work. We demand the right to enter any profession we wish; we demand to be astronauts, plumbers, dentists, athletes, and presidents. We demand the right to choose our own lovers. We demand the right to do with our bodies what we see fit and proper without fear of being butchered. We demand the right to equal treatment under the law and equal respect from the language.

"My fellow sisters, there is work to be done, a great deal of work. It is more than making speeches, more than signing petitions, more than marching in parades. The work will take us to the legislature, it will take us to people's homes, it will take us to the courts, it will take us to our own husbands and mothers and fathers and daughters and sons and sisters and brothers. It will be hard work, and sometimes it will be painful work. But I am prepared to do it. Are you?"

Speeches like that inspired me during my Shelly days. Everything started fitting into place, all the inconsistencies I could never articulate, all the half-formed arguments I could never make without feeling half-ignorant. And, while I have never been as antipathetic to men as have many of my friends, I still believed that, because men are in power, they must change before conditions change.

Philip and I ride to West Seattle to take advantage of a two-for-one coupon at a restaurant neither of us has ever been to. Philip has had a rough day at the old-folks home, having been admonished for recommending Mrs. Nardquist's room change without providing sufficient documentation; the change, however, is approved. I have taught a class, collected a compliment from a Seattle University physics professor concerning my theoretical article recently accepted by the respectable *Journal of American Physics*, and am considering the prospects of being hired at the University of Washington the following year. I have also been duly inspired by a rallying speech given on the SU campus by a visiting feminist. As usual, Philip's energy and my energy flow in opposite directions.

"I heard a pretty good talk today."

"On campus?"

"Yep."

"What was it about?"

"The oppression of women. Beth Hargraves, from the Women's Collective at Berkeley, was the speaker. She's also written a couple of books, and I guess she's real active in the movement."

"The women's movement."

"Yes. What else?"

"Well, I don't know. It could have been the bisexual movement, the lesbian movement. There's a lot of movements these days."

"This was the women's movement, Philip. I told you she was from the Women's Collective."

"That could mean anything."

"Look, never mind. Let's talk about something else."

"No, go on. I'm interested."

I'd always try, Di. I'd tell myself to keep the communication open at all times.

"She talked," I gamely continue, "about men controlling women, having all the power. About a male-dominated society."

"Do I dominate you?"

"Philip, I'm not talking about you; I'm talking about men in general."

"I merely asked; I was curious. You said that men dominate women. I'm a man, and I wanted to know if you thought I dominated you."

"I didn't say that men dominated women. I said that *she* said the society is male-dominated."

"What's the difference?"

"Individual men may or may not dominate individual women. But the society as a whole is controlled by men. Women have to live by the rules made and enforced by men."

"Did she talk about women's roles in that?"

"What do you mean?"

"Well, don't women—some women—perpetuate some men being in power?"

"Yes, *some* women perpetuate men being in power. But most women, by far most women, have little or no power. Men are the obvious targets. They are the ones in control. That's what counts."

"Do any women oppose what the women's movement is doing?"

"Philip, why do you always come out against what I believe in? There are women who are against feminism, I'm sure. But mostly they don't know any better. They're still doing the bidding of their husbands, their fathers, boyfriends, bosses, ministers; they're still subjugated. It's not so easy to shake off years of tradition and an acculturated oppression."

"Well, it sounds to me as if you're selling women short."

The cost of keeping the communication open is becoming prohibitive. If I were driving, I know I would turn around and go back home. But I make a fist out of my jaw, gaze out the evening windshield, and say, "How am I selling women short?"

"Isn't it possible, isn't it just possible, that some women—many women—are not controlled by men, that they understand the issues you've presented to them, and that they've made the independent, rational judgment that they disagree with you?"

"Philip, what's the difference? You're looking at an infinitesimal sample. I'm talking about the average woman, the millions of average, typical, everyday women who haven't exercised any of your independent judgment, who don't even know how to make an important decision, because they haven't been permitted to do so. Philip, this was in your dissertation, if I'm not mistaken. You told me about this. I'm talking about the woman who's married to a sexist slob who ignores her during the day, treats her like shit in the evening, and rapes her at night. That's not an unusual situation. *Your* situation is the odd one. Your type of woman, who's completely aware of all the issues, who's completely free from any male influence, and who's still against upgrading the level of her sex—she's the one who's the rarity. You just have no idea what the average woman goes through, Philip. And every time I try to explain it to you, you get defensive."

"Of course I get defensive! You keep saying, 'men do this' and 'men do that.' Well, I'm a man, and I don't do this or that. You'd be defensive if I started accusing women of being dumb or manipulative or catty or any of the other stereotypes."

"Some stereotypes are rooted in facts, Philip. Facts. All you have to do is look at police blotters or income scales or court records or even attitude surveys. Look at the laws, look at the damn Constitution, look at the number of men who head corporations and banks and state houses. Look at the US Congress. Look at any statistic of any field of endeavor—look in the history and science books—you won't find many women there, Philip. Those aren't stereotypes."

I love being able to speak both knowledgeably and emotionally. Unfortunately, Philip was not one to give in to either knowledge *or* emotion.

"Carolyn, I'm not disagreeing on effect. What I am saying is that it's a big mistake to focus on men as the cause of female oppression. It takes slaves to make masters. I don't dispute for a second that laws are unfair, that women are treated miserably in many ways, and that most of the people who control our lives—yours *and* mine—are male. But women buy into the system. Whether you like it or not, a lot of women buy into the system. I refuse to accept your statement that the majority of women are going to see the light and throw off their shackles."

"I didn't say that."

"You implied it. You have to admit that there are millions of women who will cling to their feminine roles as long as they can walk through an opened door or ignore the bill for dinner, just as there are millions of men who would be only too happy to shed the macho role. Getting drafted, you know, is not a picnic."

"Philip, you don't understand. You're trying to compare two totally different things. There are masculine roles and there are feminine roles. But that doesn't mean that we're equally oppressed, not by a long shot. You're still in control."

"Me?"

"*Men* are still in control. Many men are still in control. And they established the roles. Women didn't have any choice. They still don't. Suppose a wife wants to break out of the stereotype? What can she do? Walk out on her husband? Where will she get a job? Where can she get trained for a job? And she has no say whatsoever about her children. Either she's got them and can't force the ex-husband to pay child support, or she can't get them because she was the one who walked out. Women are stuck in their roles, Philip. They haven't got the legal means, the educational access, or the economic power to escape. You can get a high-paying job a hell of a lot easier than I can, even though our degrees are identical."

"You make twice as much as I do."

"But you could make twice as much as *I* do, if you were willing to work for a corporation. What chance do I have to work in a corporation and move up the executive ladder?"

"With affirmative action, probably a hell of a lot better chance than I have."

"Philip...oh, forget it. Just forget it."

We arrive at the restaurant listening to radio music both of us hate but need. The restaurant turns out to be inside a bowling alley. Neither of us is *that* hungry, and we go home. Our kiss goodnight is even more mechanical than usual, as you might expect, Lady Di.

But, just so I can't have any unadulterated emotions about Philip, three days later I receive in the mail the following missive:

Neal Starkman

Dear Carolyn,

I've been very disappointed in you lately. You used to be such a wholesome girl, especially when you lived in Minnesota with that bright boy Philip.

But then you started messing with things you should leave alone. I'm referring, of course, to Shelly's genitalia. Carolyn, don't you know by now that anything that feels good is bad for you? Why do you think they call it dope?

You're on the road to more trouble, you can't hide it from Me. And I'm talking Trouble. Go back to Philip, Carolyn. He loves you, and besides, he's a good lay. I still have faith in you, My daughter, but there *are* limits.

Warmly,

God

P.S. Salvation is yours for the asking, but if you continue your decadent ways, I promise you, girl, you'll burn.

The discussion must have upset Philip, because his humor by that time was in short supply. He went to great pains to assure me he was only kidding about "going back" to him, and I went to great pains to assure him that it didn't matter. Then he got upset all over again and said that obviously I could do whatever I wanted; he didn't need to be reminded of that. He stomped off, and I was frustrated.

It wasn't simply that I was frustrated; that would be a great understatement. Near the end of our relationship, I asked Philip if he felt alone. He smiled like he'd just chugged a glass of vinegar. He said that at first, he'd felt alone; then, after a long, long time of feeling alone, he'd gotten tired of feeling alone; then, a long time after that, he'd gotten tired of being tired of feeling alone. I felt the same way with frustration—after countless aggravating, senseless arguments, I was tired of being tired of feeling frustrated.

An acquaintance of ours, a lesbian woman, is changing her sex. Susan is becoming a Stewart. Where do weird notions come from? Not Susan's, mine: my first thought upon hearing that was, gee, it's too bad her name wasn't Frances or Carla or Pat.

I don't know Susan very well. In fact, if she were to change her hairstyle or glasses, I might not even recognize her. She seemed an average person to me, certainly nothing to indicate her present intentions, though in retrospect one thinks, well, she does look rather angular—hard, even—and she does have a certain masculine swagger, and so on. But she never struck me as a woman who would contemplate changing her sex. I know that sounds silly, Di, but some people give the impression that they're capable of major transformations. Susan did not. It'll be interesting to see if/how she/he changes her/his personality.

Stephanie is quite beside herself. Steph knows Susan a little better than I do; for all I know, she may have been her lover. She cannot bring herself to imagine why any woman would change her sex. I think she's past the livid stage and is now preparing for some serious rationalizations. I also think she's having a little trouble with the political implications of all this.

"She's just a dumb one, that's all," said Stephanie over a hurried breakfast. "She doesn't understand what she's doing. She's crazy."

"Steph, she's still your friend."

"My friend? My friend would have told me about this long ago, when I could have talked her out of it. Not now, when she's already been taking hormones, she's dressing in men's clothes, she walks and talks like a man, she probably tries to pee standing up. She got a tattoo; that's what Pam said."

"What is wrong with a tattoo?"

Stephanie glared at me. "It's an anchor. It's a fucking anchor. On her arm."

"Oh."

"Oh, Carolyn, she's losing all her soft skin. Shit! She's just crazy."

"Well, Stephanie," I said, sipping a new tea, which turned out much too weak, "it's not as if it doesn't happen."

"It doesn't happen to someone I knew—know—knew."

"Well, this time it did. Would you like me to make you a sandwich for later while you're pouring down your caffeine? I'm not going to drink this tea, anyway."

"I'll get something at the site."

"Steph, she, or he, he's probably always felt like a man; he was probably born that way. It's acting as a woman that's the pretend part, don't you think? Steph? Can't you feel good that sh...that he's finally at peace? Don't you think your friend will be happier this way?"

"As a man? Carolyn, she won't be either man *or* woman. They won't give her a penis; they don't make them good enough yet. She'll be halfway. And even if they do give her one, it won't be for a long time. You think she'll be happy looking like a guy until she takes her clothes off?"

"I don't know," I said honestly. I've known three transgender people, none of them well, and all of them man-to-woman. Each had a distinct character, but all of them were absolutely convinced that they were born women and that the only thing inconsistent with that was their physical gear. We sat in silence for a moment or two, but I was curious about the politics.

"Does she still express the same views about feminism and the rest?"

"Who knows?" Steph was putting on her coat to leave. "How can you believe anything she says now, anyway? It's not going to make any difference in another year. You'll see changes."

"What kinds of changes?"

"Just changes." She kissed me on the cheek. "She'll forget all about being a woman, Carolyn, because she's trying to forget now."

"Hm."

All kinds of things were going on for me during the spring and summer of 1977. Philip was becoming increasingly hostile toward me and my bisexuality. Shelly had tossed me back for a different kind of fish, and I had to take a long look at that relationship as well. I eventually decided that it had been the right thing at the right time.

But I also knew that Shelly was no aberration. I enjoyed her as Shelly, but I enjoyed her as a woman, too. I loved the softness, the smoothness, the roundness of the female body and, not incidentally, took a greater appreciation of my own body. I joined a lesbian/bisexual group, did some volunteer work with sexual-minority agencies in the Seattle area—hence my exposure to transgender people—and began to identify with gay women. The question that Philip asked me the night I had first made love to Shelly was being answered. I'd dealt with most of my anxieties intellectually and had either resolved them or repressed them beyond reach. I was feeling good about myself, and when I did think about Philip, I tended to view him as an obstacle to my growth, rather than a support. He was in turn indifferent, confrontational, and patronizing.

I'm walking along a country lane, a poor and inexperienced young maiden, when I hear a clattering of hooves, approaching from around a curve in the road. A horse gallops toward me, a gigantic white horse, at least four times my height, mane and tail rippling in the wind, sleek and powerful body, precise in its gait, prideful in its awesome visage. The rider of this horse, clad in a white tuxedo and high-topped shoes, pulls on the reins, and the majestic beast whinnies to a halt before me.

I shield my eyes from this daunting figure, the rider possessing as much majesty as the horse.

"Young woman," comes an authoritative voice, "remove thy arm and unblock thy vision. I have wisdom for you."

"O Great Sage," I say, complying, "anoint this undeserving soul with the oil of thy words."

"Are you calling me unctuous, maiden?"

"No, Your Sageness, only fluid."

"Very well. My wisdom is this: persecution leads to pride."

"O Your Profundity, that is indeed a most wise and telling statement. But kindly elucidate for such an ignorant mind."

"Very well, young seeker of knowledge. Those who find themselves persecuted by society, for whatever reason, begin ere long to take pride in that persecution, derive identity from it, yea, and even gain strength by it."

"But Your Omniscience, does not persecution lead to strength because the persecuted must organize out of fear and so gain psychological and physical solidarity? Somewhere in my humble meanderings I have heard such a counter-theory propounded."

"It is only what people would like to be, not what is. A person who is exceedingly mediocre in every respect save for the one quality that elicits the persecution, or who has inchoate insecurities, is likely to favor such attention. 'It is a perverse caring,' thinks the individual. 'People must care about me if they take the trouble to persecute me. I must therefore be truly special.'"

"O Great Font of All that Is True and Deep, I beg you then to explain why not one of my acquaintances of the homosexual affiliation has ever related to me a feeling of pride *at being refused lodgment, and not one of my female fellows has ever boasted to me of being denied pay commensurate with her male peer. Surely this will be an easy problem for such a cerebrant as yourself."*

"The answer, wayward youth, is that people do not often speak of that of which they are unaware or about which they are confused. Your failure to hear such expressions of pride neither diminishes nor denies the veracity of the wisdom I have imparted to you. But do you not yourself feel pride at being an adherent and practitioner of bisexuality?"

"O Great Dweller of the Left Hemisphere, I possess pride at having altered my life in ways that bring me pleasure and self-knowledge."

"But, babe-in-the-woods, I perceive the situation is different than you are admitting. Do you not glow in the contemplation of others' consideration of your practice as being evil, immoral? Does not your life achieve some direction from the struggle against these others and their hostile deeds? Reflect upon how less exciting, how less meaningful, your life would be without this struggle."

"O Silver-Tongued Wizard, I am such a goose. If the struggle were absent, I would probably communicate my desire to my dear parents that they visit me and my lady loves. And then, fool that I am, I would walk down the path with a female friend and feel no discomfort at holding her hand or kissing her on her sweet cheek. I might even stretch the bounds of my idiocy by urging my sisters to work at better vocations for higher recompense and to battle against a system that compels them to take orders from their male colleagues less qualified than they. That is what I would do were there no struggle. What is a Lord of Intellect to do with such a dumb bunny?"

The Lord of Intellect flicks the reins, and the great high horse bucks, neighs, and races off into the distance, spattering mud all over my country dress.

Yes, indifferent, confrontational, and patronizing about covers it. But I had other things on my mind, too: I was getting accepted into the University of Washington, quite a coup for a former model of cuteness. That was when I met Joe Bennett, Stanley Mankiewicz, and a host of other notables from the physics department.

Neal Starkman

I had been comfortable at Seattle U. It's a hard-working, fairly serious school, but it's not the University of Washington. Seattle U had scant research facilities, and certainly none in my specialty. I had attended colloquia and various lectures at the U of W, therefore, in the hope of making some contacts, or even of learning more about what I still planned someday to do, which was continue my work with superfluid helium. There was often a coffee klatch on Thursday afternoons following a seminar, and I began to attend that as well. It was actually quite pleasant; I got to know some of the stars in the field and also received the intellectual stimulation that I'd not been getting from Philip or anyone else.

Word got around that I'd done work on superfluid helium, and that jibed nicely when a Professor Gebel left for a job with Alcoa. Stanley Mankiewicz took a shine to me, I think, because I was "spunky." He warned me that I'd be teaching slop classes until I "earned my wings," but that I could work in the labs from the beginning. I was to be hired under a series of one-year contracts, and I could begin in September.

This took place over a period of about two months, and nothing was very explicit. I had to go through the formal procedure of applying and making a presentation, but everything was predetermined. I'd become a beneficiary of the old-boy network.

I've just about convinced myself that Chuck Patricelli will never threaten me again, but, Di, I still can't shake the Anxiety Demon. I dream about things I can't remember, I forget appointments, and I'm getting a rash on the soles of my feet, which admittedly may be from jumping. So I took my problems to the highest authority around.

Dr. Stan has a robust laugh, and he wears plaid pants to cultivate a reputation for eccentricity.

"Maybe it's the weather, Carolyn. Fall blues."

"It's not the weather. It's not even the blues. It's something inside that's keeping me in limbo, as if I were between places." I stole glimpses at his desk, as messy as his plaid pants—papers, writing implements, books, journals spread to some forgotten study, grade books, appointment books. I trusted his mind was not as cluttered.

"How's your love life?" he asked.

"Not bad."

"Family?"

"I called my mother the other day. They're thinking of coming out this Christmas. I'll have to handle that somehow."

"Because of Stephanie."

"Yes. I guess I've got some decisions to make there."

"But that's not what's bothering you."

"I don't think so. Those decisions are all logistics. I'm not seriously considering telling my parents about Stephanie and me, not until they've enrolled in Subcultures 101. It's a lot more than my parents. It's not as localized as that. It seems—bigger, more inclusive. You know, when you can hear heavy footsteps down the hall coming closer, and you know it's somebody large, but you just have to wait until whoever it is appears? It's like that, and I'm edgy about waiting."

"I presume your academic problems are leveling off?"

"Thanks to that little money nest you found. I may be getting some results soon, but I'm not satisfied with them. I think I may scrap what I've got and think about another approach."

"As long as the article is on time, Carolyn. But, a word to the wise: don't mess with what you have. We're not in a position to pioneer anything in superfluid helium."

I got the message. Safe street.

"You're feeling better about leaving the helium?"

"Oh, I've accepted it. I'm still a little melancholy about it, but I'll get over it."

"Health?"

"Jesus, you're really covering the bases for me."

"Isn't that what you want?"

"Yes, and I appreciate it. No, my health is fine. And I'm not pregnant."

He laughed. "Glad to hear it. And I'm sure Stephanie will be relieved, too."

Now I laughed. I didn't realize until after our conversation how few times I'd laughed about something like that with someone outside my very close circle of friends. The exchange seemed genuine.

There's no doubt that my discomfort over the public declaration I made at the party is a significant part of my overall feeling of displacement. But, you know, Lady Di, it's too easy. It's got to be more than people knowing I'm gay. I might have rushed the timetable on that declaration, but I'm glad it's out. It's not as if I'm ashamed of being a lesbian woman. I love loving women.

Once I spent a solid hour playing with Shelly's genitals. Not sexually, clinically. She decided that I needed to become more familiar with vaginas and vulvae and clitorises in order to become a really good lover. She brought a magazine to bed with her, took off her bottoms, lay on her back, and gave me the lower half of her body.

It was fascinating. It's so much different when you're looking at and touching someone else. I was more compelled the closer I examined, sort of like finger-spelunking. Her whole vagina constantly changed, the entire structure. First, there were folds here, then they were over there. Now there's a bead of liquid, now this whole side glistens. But even anything called a side is a misnomer. Her vagina was bottomless and topless, and everything else changed shape according to how I pressed my fingers against it. There were caverns and labyrinths, dark passages, and surprising angles. Beneath one fleshy fold was her clitoris—alone, so definite, so self-assured! Yet even it hid, protecting itself; it stood out only when it was excited. What a masterwork! The aesthetics are phenomenal: there's a certain symmetry of asymmetries, so much there in so little space, an undeniable beauty of form and function.

Biology was never my forte, though I picked up a smattering in school. During the time I went with Shelly, I must have read five books on female physiology. Women were so marvelous to me that I wanted to see how we worked.

Pretty awful, Di? Well, I do tend to objectify. In any case, I gave little thought to becoming "lesbian" then. I was still with Philip, and I was still attracted to men. I was bisexual. That was the appropriate category.

But it didn't work out so neatly. The more I read about women, talked about women, and, after Shelly, made love with women, the more Philip backed away. I found that it was not difficult to have affairs with women I'd meet in groups or at dinner parties. I went to a few women's bars, recognized that the lesbian community in Seattle was very strong, and established very transient sexual liaisons, "Mt. Everest liaisons": made for the sole reason that they were there.

I didn't have the fears of "becoming lesbian" that many women have. I was finding out more about myself, and that excited the scientist in me. To live in someone's body for so many years, and only now to be discovering major properties and potentials—I was eager to explore. I didn't have to worry about getting pregnant, or being beaten up or raped. I didn't get the impression I was being used as an outlet for frustration or anger. I felt that I was involved warmly with the women who shared themselves with me.

Neal Starkman

Philip, on the other hand, was ready to give up sex. He couldn't enjoy sex, he said, unless I desired him, and he certainly didn't feel that I desired him. So he'd do without. "I'm sure that will be a negligible loss for you," he said. Philip the Man, needing only to be needed.

Our relationship became worse as the communication faltered. He was self-pitying and bitter; I felt guilty, and angry at him for making me feel guilty. Half a year after I broke up with Shelly, Philip quit his job at the old-age home and got a job driving a cab. We went to a counselor.

"What do you mean, you're quitting?"

Mary Ann stood before me in my office. She wasn't shaking her head anymore.

"I've thought about it, Carolyn, and this is right for me." She sat down, and I rolled my chair in front of my desk to get closer to her.

"But, Mary Ann, didn't we discuss this? You said you'd go the year, see what happened."

"I know, Carolyn, but I miss Ray, and he misses me, and we're in love. Why wait? Why be miserable? I can always get back into academics."

"You're already discussed this with Ray?"

She nodded. "It's really for the best, Carolyn. I'm not cut out to be a super physicist like you are. I think Dr. Mankiewicz agrees with me. We had a long talk, and he was very nice, but he said to do what I thought was best."

I wondered how hard Dr. Stan tried to persuade Mary Ann to stay. "He's letting you do this? Walk out on your contract?"

"Carolyn, don't be angry with me or Dr. Mankiewicz. I'm mature enough to make up my own mind, and I know this isn't very feminist or anything, but I do want to raise a family. That's what I want to do."

What can you say, Lady Di? I looked into her eyes and saw Ray. So I put my hand on her shoulder. "Mary Ann, it's like I said before. We can use more women physicists, and I hope someday you decide to reenter the field. Politically, I'm disappointed. But personally—" I tried to smile—"I hope you're very happy with your decision."

"Thanks, Carolyn," she said, and reached over and hugged me. "It means a lot to me to get your blessing."

"Well," I said, "you've got it, though I wish it were Ray's colleague giving *him* the blessing."

She laughed, the crisis apparently over in her mind. "I heard you're getting to finish your research now. Congratulations."

"Yes. As a matter of fact, I've got till the end of the school year to work with my helium. It's quite a load off my mind. I don't know how it happened, but there was apparently some contingen—" I had a dark feeling. "Mary Ann, when did you talk to Dr. Mankiewicz?"

"I don't remember. A few days ago."

"A few days ago. And you told him you'd stay the quarter, but leave before winter?"

"Yes."

I should have known; Dr. Stan was playing us off each other.

"Mary Ann," I said, "it's your salary they're using to help me continue! I can't believe it!" I got up to go to the door.

"Where are you going?"

"To tell our chairman what I think of his contingency fund!"

"Wait, Carolyn." She gave me a sheepish grin. "I suggested they use my money for you." Her face still held that Dick Clark look. I never could appreciate Dick Clark. "It was my idea. Dr. Mankiewicz was against it until I convinced him it made sense."

I came back to my chair, disbelieving. "*You* suggested it?"

"Carolyn, I want you to continue your research. You're a good scientist. I probably won't last here, anyway. It makes sense. By the time they hire someone else, they can take my money and give it to you. I made that a condition of my leaving—under the table, of course." She lowered her eyes. "I wasn't supposed to tell anyone, especially you."

"You fool!" I stood up, my hands on my hips. Mary Ann cowered. "You go back and tell him you're staying on! Do you think I want to continue my research knowing you gave up your job—your damn career!—for it? What do you think I am?"

"Carolyn, I would have quit anyway! I'm doing this for you! What's six months? You said it yourself—the field needs women physicists. I'm not going to be one, but you need the support. I thought you'd be pleased!"

"Pleased? Hell, I'm pleased! I'm outraged. Mary Ann, don't you see? They're using you; you play right into the stereotype. Let them find other money to support me. I don't want yours."

She got up and became taller than me; I lost my physical authority. She had started to cry. "It's too late, Carolyn. I'm sorry you feel this way. I guess I should have been selfish and not given a damn about you. Thanks, Dr. Anderson."

"Mary Ann—" She rushed out the door.

Shit.

I find myself observing my own behavior now more than I used to. Still trying to find answers, Lady Di. But, as Gertrude Stein said, sort of, "What are the questions?" What will I see myself doing that will give me the big insight?

So we went to Debbie and Pam's party, and I forgot to observe myself; it happens. Debbie and Pam live in an old Victorian Capitol Hill house with a view of Lake Washington if you stand out on the porch, which we did, but only for a short time, because Seattle autumns are wet and chilly.

There were some old friends, as well as many people I didn't know: all women, straight and gay, and quite a few attractive ones. Several times Steph and I caught each other ogling someone. I'd usually respond with raised eyebrows and a smirk, she with a subtly obscene gesture, like running two fingers across her tongue.

We're not all that *pairsy* at parties, but we do usually end up sitting next to each other. At this party, though, the seating was such that she took an arm of a couch across from me, in a group of about eight. The evening was winding down, the booze plateaus had been reached, the early leavers had left, and the remainder of the crowd had settled into comfortable physical and emotional cubbyholes.

I'm a talker, Di, and I'd been in the middle of a dozen discussions that night—whether or not black dialects should be taught in schools; the hazards of depilatory creams; the latest movies; the feminist protests at the new Mormon temple; the toxic shock syndrome scare, which was becoming a syndrome itself; elections, all kinds; and of course the impending—or ongoing—sex change of Susan to Stewart. Stephanie and Pam had arrived on the scene just as we started talking about it. Stephanie immediately tried to change the subject, without pretense.

"She's a crazy woman. We should talk about where to put her until she finds her marbles."

"Oh, I don't know if she's crazy," I said. "She must have her reasons."

"I'll tell you who's crazy," said Stephanie, casting a thunderbolt at me. "It's this guy who rides the 7 bus in the afternoon. Has anybody ever seen him? He's always doing this." And she shrugged her shoulders spasmodically while rocking her head back and forth.

Naturally, no one had seen that person, but someone thought she had a teacher in grade school with similar symptoms, and the discussion was off in the direction of people-I-have-known-with-grotesque-disorders. I went to refill my wine glass, thought better of it, and brewed some tea instead. When I returned, I stood behind Stephanie and stroked her neck. One of the women was relating the experience of a college teacher who had no use of her arms and had to write on the blackboard by holding the chalk in her mouth. I never heard the part about how she *picked up* the chalk, though.

I waited till we were in bed before I said, "Why don't you want to talk about Susan's sex change?"

"Carrie," she said, kissing me, "tomorrow, please?" It was late, and she had overdrunk as usual, but I was overcurious as usual.

"Promise?" I said.

"Mm-hm," she promised.

The next morning, I woke her up by licking between her fingers and then started to kiss her arms, shoulders, and neck. She got all set for a big kiss on the mouth, when I said, "It's tomorrow."

"What...What do you mean, it's tomorrow?"

"Tomorrow is when you promised yesterday to tell me why you don't want to talk about Susan's sex change."

"You bitch! Okay, what do you want to know?" she said, sounding somber.

"Why are you so upset about Susan changing her sex? Were you her lover?"

"No." She sighed. "I hate talking about her. It's just stupid, Carolyn. I've known Susan for five years. I liked her—well, I wasn't crazy about her, we were okay friends—but there was something strange about her. Oh, Carrie, there *was*, I would have said that even before I knew about this. That's what I thought. Like she was hiding something. She made me uncomfortable.

"I went to her place once. A few years ago. I don't know, dinner maybe, maybe just a few drinks. It doesn't matter. I don't remember much about it, except that she asked me if I wanted to make love. I mean, she's not that hot stuff, but she was okay, you know? Anyway, I'm sure I would have said no, but I never got the chance. She got all excited and asked me if I'd ever made it with a woman wearing a dildo. I said yes, sure, but I didn't like it too much. Besides, I said, why do you need a dildo?

"She started to cry. It sounds dumb, but she just started crying. I don't even know what I said. I mean, okay, maybe now it makes more sense, but she—it was just a weird scene. I've been in weirder scenes, but I guess I wasn't in the mood for this one. Shit, Carrie, I couldn't stop her crying. I mean, we both had a few beers in us, but not that much that I couldn't tell that she was really strange, so I left. I just left, didn't say good-bye or anything."

"Did you see her after that? You must have; you said that was a few years ago."

"Yeah, I saw her, but never alone. I felt stupid. Probably if she was smart, she felt stupid, too. It's no big deal, Carolyn. I think she's a crazy woman. I told you. I've talked to other women who've known her since then; they'll tell you."

"That she's crazy?"

"Or strange."

"Come on, just because she wanted to use a dildo on you?"

"Just strange in general. I can't explain it."

We lay there for a while. I was thinking about interactions and external factors and experimental manipulations. Steph's hand was cold.

"Steph, again, don't you think Susan/Stewart really believes she's...he's a man? Why else do you think a woman would want to change her sex?"

"Because this male-supremacist society has her convinced she'd be better off as a man. Because she's taught that being a woman means you're weak and dumb and good for nothing except cooking and making babies...and getting fucked. She bought it, Carrie, she bought the snow job so much she figured, shit, I might as well *be* a man. Then I can have a housewife and lots of money and power. I can boss people around.

"Also she's a dyke. Men can't stand dykes. You know why?"

I knew why. The same reason men can't stand the idea of a clitoral orgasm. "Because lesbians—dykes—don't need men."

"That's right. That's exactly right. Lesbians don't need men, and men are afraid of that. So dumb bitch Susan thinks that men are afraid of her and don't like her because there's something wrong with her, not them. So she thinks, well, I'm going to change. Just like that. She thinks she's going to be rough and tough, and smoke cigars and shave, and sweat and smell, and play football, and have that dumb-ass anchor tattoo. She's going to be one of them. She got tired of fighting them, Carrie, and she decided to join them.

"But she'll never be one of them. Men will never accept a former woman. It's not pure enough for them. They'll freeze her out, Carrie. She'll be between woman and man, and she'll hate it."

"Why don't you tell her all that? And then maybe she can tell you about how she feels about all this. Who knows, Steph, maybe you'll change your mind."

"She'd never listen to me. Hormones have probably hairballed her brain. She'd listen to a man now, but no man would tell her. Forget it. Just forget the whole thing. Write her off."

"Maybe you should try."

"Forget it."

"Maybe you should try."

"No."

Stephanie's father's birthday is tomorrow, and I know she's upset about that, too. Stephanie detests her father, always has, but she calls him on his birthday. He lives just north of Seattle, in Lynnwood. Her mother died a few years ago.

Stephanie's father is an old Filipino, about seventy-five. He's also an alcoholic and, according to Stephanie, a wife-beater. Her mother died of a stroke, but Steph has no doubt that her condition was helped along by Mr. Marillo's frequent bouts with the bottle and Mrs. Marillo.

Still she calls him on his birthday. The old man lives, alcoholism and all, and she calls him and asks how he is, did he get the tie/socks/belt she sent him, and so on. The conversation is always brief, as are the other three or four she has with him during the year, but she dreads it for several days before and stews over it for several days afterward, like a bad job interview. She never visits him.

I don't know why she calls him. I think it has something to do with loyalty and guilt and punishment and need for approval, but she never talks about it. I know she was thinking about the call tomorrow, and she was disturbed about Susan/Stewart, so that was that.

So I can extend the lambda line by superheating my helium. That's fine. And when I increase the rotors, the vortices resemble the bloodshot eyes of a wino. I lose all parallelism to the rotation axis, and I don't know why.

I can produce the vortices, and I can describe them once I've produced them, but I don't know why they're there, or why they appear only at certain levels of rotation and not at others, or why they collapse into chaos. Can I actually write this paper without mentioning what I'm really looking for?

Sure I can. The *paper* is the end, not pedestrian descriptions of electromagnetic spectra affecting vortices that most people couldn't care less about, anyway. You go with what you know, not with what you don't know—the first rule of scientific publication. You should have learned that by now, Dr. Anderson.

My father would be totally perplexed by my conflict. A scientific know-nothing if there ever was one, my father. What's the difference, he would say. God causes it to happen. What more do you need to know? What more does anyone need to know? Isn't it enough to be able to describe these vortices? Isn't it enough to be able to make them occur?

No, of course not. It's never enough. You never know as much as you want. I still believe that if I look at those vortices closely enough and long enough, I'll find out what makes them spin.

I sent Mary Ann a semi-apologetic note, but she still ignores me in the halls. I have to talk with Dr. Stan about this sometime.

This morning, Joe Bennett stopped by to tell me he admired me for being an assertive, independent-minded woman.

"Why, thank you, Joe," I said. "I admire you for being an assertive, independent-minded man." I smiled at him; he didn't smile back.

"I mean it, Carolyn. I do."

"I do, too, Joe," I said. "I—"

"God damn it, Carolyn! Can't you be serious with me?"

My office has seen a lot of drama lately.

"I'm sorry," he said, after I didn't respond.

"Is it Marge?" I asked. "Why don't you sit down? I've got a few minutes before an appointment."

He didn't sit down, and in fact walked past me to the window. It was a cloudy day; there couldn't have been much to see.

"It's nothing. I'm just a little high-strung."

"Want to talk?" I swiveled my chair around, but his back was to me. He shook his head and sighed.

"Nothing to talk about, really. It's just a phase; we both know it. She's got to get it out of her system. A fling, she calls it."

"Anyone in particular?"

"A guy in her mechanics class."

"Was he at the party?"

"No. I've never met him."

"Just support her, Joe. You love her?"

"Sure I do. I wouldn't have married her if I didn't love her."

He sounded like my mother. I got up and placed a hand on his shoulder. Good for Marge, I thought.

"Good for you," I said. "Just hang in there."

Neal Starkman

Today, also, a caucus meeting of women from various disciplines around the university. We're sponsoring a "Women in History" week, which will feature a series of lectures about women who have influenced civilization far beyond their renown. It's going to be quite exciting. We're shooting for March and have already lined up speakers and are getting up committees to research movies and artists.

There was a minor scuffle between those in the caucus who wanted to call the program "Women in Herstory" and those who thought that was plain silly. I was—surprise—right in the middle. The caucus is not composed of all feminists, not by a long shot. We have a wide range of intelligent, professional women; some of them, I'm sorry to say, have far to go in terms of their awareness of issues affecting them. Many of them were the ones against the change. On the other side were the Feminists—as opposed to feminists—mostly from sociology, social work, "soft" sciences. Me—gosh, Di, I don't think it's silly at all to revise the language along nonsexist lines. But in this case it seemed a bit much. It's not as if the letters H, I, S have to be separated every place they appear together. We still say "this" and wouldn't think of changing it to "ther." Also, changing "history" to "herstory" would alienate some moderate-to-conservative women who might otherwise attend the lectures.

The problem was, Di, that I didn't want to align myself with the anti-language revisers. Jesus, voting with the oh-so-liberal sociologist is bad enough on most issues; but this time I would have had to toss in my vote with the "suits"—the women from administration, education, and, yes, athletics. To explain myself seemed just too difficult today. So I abstained. The anti-revisers won, and it will be "history," not "herstory." Carolyn Anderson, a strong neutral force in women's rights.

What else today. A post card from my mother. My mother sends me picture post cards from St. Cloud, Minneapolis, and towns Minnesotan. About two a month. I should probably have saved them from the beginning, when we came out here four-and-a-half years ago. Today's post card was typical: a picture of the Metropolitan Zoo and the message, "It's getting pretty cold here. 28° yesterday. Pop bought more oil. Do you need anything? We have money. Love, Mother."

It's hard to write back. But I do, monthly. I tell her what I'm doing, sort of, and I tell her what the weather's like. And I always end up feeling extremely guilty. Because, you know, Di, I never really tell her what's happening to me. I never really tell her how I'm feeling. I don't tell her about Susan/Stewart, I don't tell her about Stephanie except in superficialities, I don't tell her about the lesbian women's group I participate in, I don't tell her about my work because she won't understand it. Jesus, sometimes I find myself hiding the truth about the weather. What's left? Sham. She writes to her daughter Carolyn, and she gets a letter back from some simulacra, a slice of cellophaned, processed American cheese product. I always down two glasses of brandy when I write to her, one before and one after.

And let's see—an unsettling conversation today. I took lunch in the Union, not uncommon because it's cheap and right next to the physics building. It was crowded, and a man sat down at my table and began talking to me. Not a come-on, though really, who knows. His name was Michael, and he taught vocational ed. I wasn't attracted to him, but he seemed all right—quiet for a man, but not meek, either.

Well, we talked about the elections and "Women in History" week. He was supportive and said he always thought Margaret Sanger was given short shrift. I told him that I taught in the physics department, and he said that maybe he'd drop by one day. I didn't encourage him, and he left.

That, Lady Di, was not the unsettling conversation. The unsettling conversation came about four hours later, when I met Marcie for a glass of wine after my afternoon class. I told her I'd been thinking about lesbianism.

"That's not unusual, is it?" she said.

"I mean critically," I said. "Not in the sense of not loving women or not being solidly in support of women's issues, but in regard to men."

Then I told her about the man I met at lunch. "He was nice, Marcie, he seemed nice. I wasn't attracted to him. I don't think that I would have been attracted to him even in my straight days, but, I don't know. Am I shutting myself off? I found myself deliberately not smiling, deliberately not talking with any animation, and not wanting to trust him or encourage him to stop by my office. Maybe I'm missing out on something. Maybe he has something to offer me. I'm not so busy that I can't have lunch with him, for example."

Marcie leaned forward over her glass. "Look, Carolyn, there's just so much time and energy anyone has. If you think you should spend that time with a man, go ahead. But I'd rather work with women, help in the struggle. That guy may seem really nice now, but if you encourage him to see you, what kind of an idea do you think he's going to get? What's he going to expect from you?"

"Just because he expects it doesn't mean he's going to get it. Marcie, even if I were straight, that'd be the case."

"Carolyn, why bother? I mean, why bother? He's going to end up giving you the same old lines, and who needs someone like that? I don't, that's for sure."

I thought about time and energy and people. "I don't mean that I should go out and solicit male friends. I agree with you about the struggle. But I'm not a separatist. I don't believe all men are inherently evil. It just seems that I'm spending more energy avoiding them than by, I don't know, than by just being natural." That didn't sound convincing even to me.

"I'm not a separatist, either," said Marcie. "I sure wouldn't be working where I'm working if I was. It's fine to sit with someone and have lunch with him. Great. But you have to watch yourself. You know that, Carolyn. He's going to think he can take care of you or fuck you or whatever. You know that happens. I don't feel comfortable with it. I'd rather spend my lunches with you or Stephanie or Ann, someone I can talk with, without wondering about what's going on in your mind while you're smiling at me."

Unsettling, Di. Everything seems unsettling to me. The equations muddy, the categories fuzz up, the security fades away. What wretched self-indulgence you are, Di!

One of the last things Philip told me was unsettling, too. It was near the end, after the arguments, after the counseling, certainly after the cessation of sex, after all those things that signal an end to a relationship. There was a period during which we could talk to each other dispassionately, because we knew there was nothing left to be emotional about. Anything we could possibly lose had already been lost.

He told me he chose to be the way he was. Even though he might be miserable and lonely and detached from people, even though he might lose me, he still wouldn't accept an alternative. He said he lived by principle, not circumstance, and that if he was going to hell, he'd jump in, not fall or be pushed.

Then he smiled at me and said, the same with you, Carolyn. You're damned, but you accept no alternative.

Stephanie has called me a stubborn bitch on occasion, but I'm not stubborn the way Philip was. I am flexible; I control my stubbornness. I'll never fall into Philip's mode of thinking. Circumstances do make a difference, Di, and I'll never give in to some abstract individualism in order to uphold a rule while at the same time I'm losing my job or my lover. Certainly not my lover. What's the damn point? As my dentist once said to me after cleaning my gums—a bad joke I never understood until years later—"That's a pyorrheic victory."

When Philip and I first came to Seattle, we took a weekend trip to the Pacific Coast, rented a cabin there. Neither of us had ever seen the Pacific Ocean, and, because we were still making the transition from freedom to unemployment and not as pessimistic as we perhaps should have been, we weren't averse to spending money and having a good time.

Not that there was much to spend money on. We bought food at a nearby grocery, cooked in the cabin, and walked on the beach. It was a wonderful few days. The weather behaved, although the water was far colder than we'd anticipated. There were few visitors—it was not the season for tourists—and the beach was virtually all ours. We couldn't have asked for a more romantic setting. The cabin had a fireplace and kitchen, so we had the best of the primitive and the modern. It was idyllic.

A little patch of sand to the north of our cabin assured us total privacy, even though, technically, it was part of the beach. We'd take a quick swim, run back to the sheltered part of the beach, strip off our suits, and lie on the sand until the sun dried us. We still had our Minnesota blood, and sixty degrees was an oven to us. We were silly in love, and though I was hesitant at first to take my clothes off, it soon became apparent that no one would happen by.

Sunday morning we got up late, cooked some breakfast, and teased each other with little squeezes and kisses. It was our last day, we had to check out that afternoon, and we didn't want it to end. We walked around the kitchen in ways to come in contact with each other and bestow a pat or a kiss on the neck. Our suits were a little damp from the previous evening's swim, so we decided to chance a skinny-dip.

We had a great time and stayed in the water for maybe twenty minutes. The waves weren't high, but we knelt down to keep in the water. I remember my nipples straining to break free of my breasts because it was so cold, and Philip doing his best to help them with his mouth. We held each other in the water and teased each other some more. He was hard, and I was wetter than the water, but we settled for long kisses. Eventually, we ran from the ocean and collapsed on the sand, exhausted.

The sand was delightfully warm. I rolled on to my stomach and rubbed myself into the beach, the sand giving just slightly under me, not irritating at all. I stretched my arms above my head, and I remember Philip kissing my ear. I closed my eyes and probably fantasized about penises.

I don't know if I actually slept or not; it doesn't make any difference. But the first thing I recall was a chill running up my leg. It was a little tickle above the inside of my knee. I sighed and opened my legs a little wider, trying to attain unity with the sand. The tickle didn't recur for at least another minute, but then there it was again. First one leg, then the other— very lightly, not like a kiss, but almost like a fingernail, gently, tenderly, aimlessly.

I lifted up my ass very slightly. The tickling continued, the pressure barely noticeable, but moving steadily upward, one thigh, the other, back to the calf, but then up again. I dropped my ass to the ground, and it got tickled.

I began to rotate my hips a bit, trying to complement the feathery caresses I was receiving. I pictured Philip behind me, never grabbing, never pressing, just the slightest touch at unexpected places and unpredictable times. It was a maddening ecstasy. The tickling intensified in frequency the closer it got to me, but it was always light, always tentative. I extended my legs yet wider and grabbed handfuls of sand. I burned, waiting for that final clasp, that final plunge, that final consummation that never would come.

But *I* came. I moaned and moaned again in one glorious paroxysm of pleasure, and I heard Philip cry out, "What's wrong?" then "Oh, Jesus shit," as if he were coming, too.

I relate this incident for two reasons, Di. One is its cathartic effect. I've not told this to anyone, not even Stephanie, especially not Stephanie, and I swore Philip to silence. I think it was perhaps the most humiliating moment of my life when I heard Philip choking with laughter and saying, "Turn over, turn over," and discovered that I'd been making love for the past five minutes with an ugly, dirty, disgusting sand crab, and enjoying it as well. The damn thing was just crawling around in the sand between my outstretched legs, and its little antennae were doing their lascivious things.

Philip roared for half an hour. I cried for most of that time. Neither of us believed it could actually happen, and if Philip hadn't figured it out before I did, I would have tried my damnedest to convince him it hadn't happened. I was angry, ashamed, embarrassed. It was so damn preposterous. It could have torn me up, I yelled. Philip, still in hysterics, said, no, that couldn't have happened, it was too gentle, and offered to take it home, you know, put it up for a week or two, maybe we could get into a threebie, as he called it. He really laid it on thick, Di, putting his nose in front of the horrid crustacean and asking it if it still respected me. Then he put his arm around me and asked, in mock seriousness, "How was it? Was it good for you? It was good for it." If there had been a cigarette lying around the beach, I know he would have stuck one in the crab's claw. It took me all day to forgive him.

But that's the second reason I tell this, Di. I'm happy now, and I think I'm more myself now than I was then. But for all the rough times with Philip, there were those little islands of fun and joy. It's good for me to realize that. I miss it. And sometimes I miss him, too. Two years since he died, and I still miss him. It's difficult to forget the good times, the little moments, even the exasperating ones, like the post card I got the week after we returned from the ocean. It had a picture of a crab on it and a scrawled message, "Come back. We can work it out."

8. PHILIP

In the spring of 1978, I moved out. We settled our finances, said goodbye, and I walked away.

God, that sounds sterile. So cold. But I was in a trance for a month. All the discussions had been finished, all the questions answered, the emotions ready to be stored in different-shaped memories. And yet, and yet, the intellectual Carolyn would debate the emotional Carolyn constantly those last few weeks with Philip and the first few weeks without him. All the old saws, Di—am I betraying him by leaving, have I given us enough of a chance, am I being truthful? There came a time when I had to say to myself, it's done, it's over, get on with your life.

Philip, predictably, never tried to prevent me from leaving. He agreed that I was making the correct decision. His outer intellect proved sturdy, constructed as it was for just such exigencies.

"So you're really leaving." This at the kitchen table, thinking about what to buy for dinner, but neither of us hungry.

"I think I should."

"Got a place picked out?"

"You know I do; we talked about it."

"I forgot; sorry."

"You have enough money for the rent?"

"For now. I'll move, too, soon. I'll be all right."

"Do you know why I'm leaving, Philip?"

I wearied of discussions, but I was so afraid of not making my reasons clear. Philip too often walked away from arguments. I didn't want to rehash the issues, but I also didn't want him to have the excuse that he didn't understand me.

"Do I know why you're leaving? Well, for one thing, you aren't stimulated by me anymore—sexually, intellectually, emotionally, whatever. I don't attract you; you neither need nor want me. Your lifestyle—lesbianism, feminism, the rest—doesn't complement my lifestyle. And finally, I suppose you've been frustrated with counseling."

"Philip, do you have anybody to talk to? Maybe you can see a counselor by yourself."

"I'll be fine."

"Philip?"

"What?"

"I'm really sorry, Philip."

"Nothing to be sorry about. I want you to be you. It doesn't seem that you can be you with me around. So you should leave. Very simple."

"It's not so simple, and you know it. What about what you want?"

"What about it?"

"I'm afraid that you'll withdraw completely."

"I have withdrawn completely. Haven't you noticed?" He looked up at me, and I felt that my stomach was tied to my throat. He appeared ten years older, face drawn like he was sucking through a straw. He had pockets under his eyes so that he could hide them when he didn't want me to see him cry; and his attire even sloppier than usual—all the marks of someone who didn't care what he looked like anymore.

"Look," he said, "if you're so worried about my welfare, then don't leave. Carolyn, the only damn thing I have left is a deep honest love for you. I will always have that. There's nothing you can do about it. I love you as much right this instant as I did back in Minnesota. And if that means anything at all, it means that I should be willing to let you leave when it's to your benefit to do so. I am willing. And I say good-bye. Nothing's lost; it just stops."

And so it stopped. I left and never saw him again. Three months later he was killed in a taxi crash. The hospital called me because I was still listed on his medical cards. I was with a woman that night, and somehow she helped me through to the next morning.

Philip's parents came out, and I barely recall what they even looked like, much less said or did. We didn't hug, and I think his father was all business. Maybe he blamed me for leaving his son, though I doubt Philip went into any explanations of our relationship. I don't remember much of that time at all, except insanely thinking, this is what grief is. This is sadness, and this is anger, and this is what it is to wonder why God is so fucked up.

There was a passenger in Philip's cab who survived with a broken leg and a lot of bruises. The passenger said that he recalled asking Philip what time it was, and the next thing he knew he was lying in a wreck by a telephone pole. The sirens told him it was serious.

But I know what happened. The month I left, Philip's crazy uncle had sent him a digital wristwatch, the kind you needed two hands to make the time appear; the face of the watch was blank until you pressed a knob; really stupid idea. Philip's own Timex had just stopped after ten years, and so he wore the gift. He took his right hand off the wheel to press the button on the watch for the digital readout and lost control of the cab. Ironic in a *Camusian* way. Pre-masturbation Philip would have been amused.

Strangeness, Lady Di. I just spent a day with David. I think it was a day; it could have been a year or a minute. David has that effect on you, where he sort of sucks you into his timeless world and then puts you back where you came from. Some people enrich you; David drugs you.

Steph had called, said she'd be home late because of extra work. I got hungry, so I made a junk omelette—you chop up broccoli and onion and green pepper and carrot and whatever's lying around the refrigerator, and you mix it into the eggs, which are separated, mixed again, fried, and broiled. Wonderful. Separating the eggs makes it puffy, and broiling it cooks the top part of the omelette and makes it even puffier. Call it Carolyn's Puffed Junk Omelette. And excuse the culinary aside, Lady Di.

The phone rang about three-quarters through the omelette, and the voice was pure nostalgia.

"Hi, it's David."

"David! Where are you?"

He was twenty minutes away at Sea-Tac Airport, he was leaving for Anchorage the next afternoon, and could he crash for a night? Just like David, letting me know he would be in Seattle only after he'd arrived in Seattle.

I drove down to the airport and thought about which Carolyn to reveal. We'd exchanged a few brief, quasi-newsy letters since I'd left Minnesota, and I'd seen him twice during vacations. Our interactions were superficial, ephemeral. He knew Philip had died, and he knew I was living with someone named Stephanie, but I had never discussed my relationship to

Stephanie with him, and the two of them hadn't met when Steph came home with me last Christmas. Would it be appropriate now to tell him I was gay?

David probably would have looked thin were it not for all the clothes he was wearing—boots, overcoat, scarf, sweater, hunter's hat. He looked like a Sherpa. We hugged, but I couldn't feel him.

"I'm going to Bethel for a year," he explained. "It's supposed to be cold there."

"Where's Bethel?" I asked, on the way back to the house.

"I'm not sure," he said. "West of Anchorage, I think. But they're paying me $58,000 for this job in their clinic."

"What about Sally?"

He didn't change expressions. "She quit Planned Parenthood and started a consultant business. She said she wants to be selfish now."

"Meaning?"

I got no response and tried again.

"What does that mean, she wants to be selfish?"

"I don't know."

"How are you, David?"

"Fine, how are you, Carolyn?" Somehow this conversation was either too shallow or too deep for me, and it struck me that with David I never knew which.

"I'm fine," I said, and determined to take charge. "I've been working with superfluid helium, but I'm going to have to end it soon. They're making me switch to something else. Budget cutbacks."

David nodded.

"And I've been involved with the women's caucus at the university."

David nodded.

"That's the Space Needle." I pointed to the left. "It was originally at the airport, but they moved it."

"It looks good here," said David.

It was a challenge to have a discussion with him.

"I'm living with Stephanie," I said. "I don't remember if you met her when I brought her back with me to St. Cloud. I didn't tell you this before, but Stephanie and I are lovers."

David nodded. "That's good, Carolyn. Does that interfere with your helium studies?"

Now I nodded. "David, don't you have any reaction to the fact that I am a lesbian? We've known each other since we were kids."

David frowned, like he'd given the wrong answer on a test and now had a second chance. "Well, I'm a little surprised." Then he nodded, satisfied with the response.

I switched trains. "David, why are you leaving Minnesota?"

He shrugged. "Well, the money's good in Bethel, and I think I'm making it tough for Sally being back there. She's just starting out, and she's keeping herself busy."

"Won't you miss her?"

"Sure I'll miss her. She'll find someone else."

That was how the conversation went till we got home. I fixed him a sandwich, we talked some more—or I talked and David nodded his head—

and I allocated some space for him in the extra room. David said he wanted to take a shower. I gave him towels and then went out to the store three blocks away to buy milk and eggs for breakfast.

I'd forgotten about Stephanie.

8:41 p.m.

DAVID takes off his remaining layers of clothes, piles them in the corner of the bathroom, and enters the shower.

STEPHANIE waits for a traffic light one mile from home. Work has made her anxious because she feels her boss is taking advantage of her, but she can't prove it.

CAROLYN walks to the store, smiling over David's serenity. She remembers the "old days," when they were in high school together.

8:43 p.m.

DAVID lets the hot water splash off his tired body. The sound of the shower comforts him as much as the divestment of all those shirts and sweaters.

STEPHANIE pulls into the driveway; it has been a long, exhausting day, and she needs to relax.

CAROLYN looks at Orion in the sky, wonders how Sally's doing.

8:46 p.m.

DAVID is lost in the shower. He is soothed by the warmth of the steam, the pulsation of the water, the slippery sensuousness of the soap.

STEPHANIE lets herself in the house. She hears the shower and considers, maybe she should join her lover. But, pausing outside the bathroom door, she decides against it. She does not notice David's clothes.

CAROLYN checks her wallet to make sure she has enough money; she finds a dime on the sidewalk in front of the store and picks it up. It must be a good omen, she thinks.

8:55 p.m.

DAVID steps out of the shower, refreshed, invigorated. He towels off and, still nude, brushes his teeth.

STEPHANIE has removed all her clothes except for her panties and has begun to jump in the living room. As she bounces up and down, her lungs take in more air, her muscles loosen up, and she closes her eyes.

CAROLYN ambles back with the groceries, speculating how much David usually eats for breakfast and thinking how odd it will be having breakfast with David and Stephanie. This thought explodes in her mind, and she stops short. She just briefly figures the chances of Stephanie's returning while David is still in the shower. She concludes that the chances are slim, but begins to jog, and then breaks into a furious sprint.

8:59 p.m.

DAVID has dried himself, slips on a new pair of underwear, and opens the bathroom door. He is about to fetch his suitcase for clothes but then hears a strange, rhythmic sound from the living room. He decides to investigate.

STEPHANIE has heard the bathroom door open, smiles, and yells out, "Hope you saved some hot water for me, Cream Butt, or do you want to give me a tongue bath instead?"

CAROLYN has noticed Stephanie's car parked out front and, gasping, stumbles up the front steps, slipping once and almost dropping the eggs. The door is locked, and she fumbles with the key.

9:00 p.m.

DAVID walks into the living room, still clad only in his underwear, and sees a woman, clad only in her panties, jumping up and down, eyes closed, and smiling.

STEPHANIE hears a key turn in the lock, frowns, and jumps 180° around, opening her eyes as Carolyn bursts through the door, panting. Stephanie smiles upon seeing Carolyn, but the smile vanishes abruptly.

CAROLYN almost falls into the living room. In the rear of the living room, she faces semi-nude David, eyes wide open. In the front of the living room, she faces semi-nude Stephanie, still jumping, eyes wide open. Carolyn knows that Stephanie is curious as to who is behind her.

Carolyn knows that it is extremely important for her to make introductions before Stephanie turns around.

"Stephanie," she says, gesturing, "this is my good friend David, from Minnesota. David, this is my lover, Stephanie."

Stephanie, *still* jumping, turns around slowly and nods. "David."

David nods, too, in time with Stephanie's jumps. "Hi."

"Well," says Carolyn, "would anybody like some tea?" Her voice breaks on the "tea."

David's visit was instructive in that it wasn't instructive. Nothing fazed him—nothing, that is, after meeting Steph. I don't know what I expected from him—kinship, maybe, a closeness. But I couldn't get a grasp on who he was. We talked that evening after Stephanie had gone to bed, and I took him to the Space Needle today, which I'm sure he enjoyed. But he just didn't seem emotive about anything, not Seattle or Sally or his new job or my lesbianism. I didn't even ask if he still took drugs. After awhile, I resigned myself to relating to him as if he were a piece of cardboard.

This afternoon I took him to my lab, showed him my equipment, explained a little about the vortices. I even tried to articulate the problems I was dealing with.

"You see those vortices?" I said, pointing to an illustration. "Little whirlpools. They're driving me nuts. I can make them appear and disappear, but I don't know precisely what causes them. I watch them for hours, and I can't figure it out. My whole academic life has centered on what makes those things spin. I'm beginning to hate them."

David stared at the figures and all my lab paraphernalia. He shrugged. "Well, Carolyn, if they didn't spin, you wouldn't see them at all."

"Uh-huh," I said. "Let's go, David." We ate salmon for a late lunch, and I drove him back to the airport. We hugged at the gate, and it felt as if I were hugging his clothes, not him.

So I guess I've lost a friend. I think I might have been pleased even had he tried to lay a sex trip on me; at least that would have shown he cared. Maybe ice-cold Bethel will warm him up. Meanwhile, I feel as if one of my roots has been severed. And if I hoped to get some information about the Carolyn-that-was to help predict the Carolyn-that-will-be, then I was disappointed. The very strange thing about the whole encounter is that he seemed happy.

"How's the diary coming along?" Stephanie is always concerned about me.

"Not too bad. I'm just unsure of where I'm going."

"Want me to help?"

"Help? How?"

"I don't know; how do you feel?"

"Very tense."

"Want to jump?"

"Maybe I'll take a walk."

"Want company?"

"No, I don't think so. Thanks, Steph."

"Carolyn?"

"Yes?"

"Anything you want to talk about with me? David? I'll even talk about Philip, if you really want to. I mean, if you really, really need to."

I smiled. She is a dear one. "Thanks, Steph. And thanks for being so understanding about David, too. I know I've thanked you before and apologized before, but I appreciate your giving me the space to be with him. I'm just feeling wound up, that's all. Really. I'll let you know."

I'm always tense, and sometimes I'm hyperactive and tense. I was never this way before. What is happening to me? I cried last night. I didn't even know what I was frustrated about, and that intensified the frustration. Maybe I need to see a therapist, this time by myself.

"Philip, can you accept Carolyn's bisexuality?"

"Yes."

"Can you accept Carolyn's promiscuity?"

"Promiscuity?"

"Having sexual relationships with several people."

"No, promiscuity means having sexual relationships with several people indiscriminately. Carolyn's not indiscriminate."

"Thanks, Phils."

"I'm sorry. Can you accept Carolyn's having sexual relationships with several people?"

"Yes."

"Do you think he accepts it, Carolyn?"

"I think he accepts it intellectually and philosophically, but not emotionally, even though I'm sure he would like to."

"Tell him."

"Philip, I don't think you emotionally accept my having sex with other women or men."

"Philip?"

"Yes?"

"What do you say to that?"

"What I said before. I accept her non-monogamy. That's not an issue. What is an issue is how we feel about each other. We're becoming different people."

"How are you different from Carolyn, Phil?"

"It's Philip. Carolyn is headed toward lesbianism. It could be socialism or deism or Republicanism. It's still an *ism*. And I can't relate to *isms*. The fact that it happens to be lesbianism obviously exacerbates the situation, because, as we know, lesbians don't normally have sex with men."

"But you don't have sex with Carolyn now, do you?"

"I guess I feel that in spirit she's already lesbian."

"Philip, my being a lesbian woman is no more restrictive than you being a heterosexual man. And I resent your labeling me lesbian, anyway. I don't consider myself lesbian."

"Car', your being lesbian is pretty damn restrictive to our relationship, given we're opposite sexes. And it doesn't matter what you call yourself. It's evident by this time where your preferences lie."

"That's your problem, not mine. You're the one who withdraws after I see another person. I'm still with you."

"Carolyn, I don't want you to be with me if it's not to your benefit. That's inane. If you can grow sexually, then do it. If nothing else, I don't want you to end up resenting me for keeping you away from women, or for remaining bisexual. Anyway, why keep pretending you're not lesbian? You've had four or five lovers since Shelly—all women. I'd say that's statistically significant."

"Well, of course I've been with women. It's new, I'm learning about myself, it's natural for me to spend more time with women."

"It doesn't matter why you're doing it, Car'. The point is, that's where you're going. Fine. You want to be with women? Be with women. But don't expect me to feel wanted while it's happening."

"Carolyn? Do you accept that?"

"Yes."

Counseling was awful. Philip would out-logic both me and the therapist. When the therapist saw through his intellectual tricks and called him on it, then Philip played deaf-mute. It was such a surrealistic scene. I'd almost want him to say something nasty or self-defeating, so I could say, "See? That's how he is. That's what I have to put up with." It's like praying that your car continues to make those horrible noises when you take it to the mechanic.

Oh, shit, Lady Di, I didn't even know what I wanted from those sessions. We told the therapist we wanted to sort out which of our problems were reconcilable, but we only said that because neither of us could articulate what it was we really wanted. There was no sense to it; we learned nothing that we couldn't have learned sitting around the house and saving sixty bucks a week. We eventually discovered that none of our problems were reconcilable.

Headaches. I've got multiple headaches today, in various parts of my poor head. I spent two hours teaching class, two-and-a-half hours making a run in the lab, and an hour talking with Stephanie about dinner tomorrow night, when several women from her crew group are coming over. I call it a crew group because they work together on construction and also meet socially to discuss women's issues and what's going on in the community. I've never met any of them, I know nothing about carpentry, and I haven't been in the mood for small talk. The dinner will be a partial potluck; we're going to prepare dessert and some salad.

Lady Di, I have to confide this to you: I masturbated today, in the lab. I've never done it in the lab before, and I did it spontaneously, but I'm not certain why. It wasn't dangerous or thrilling or anything like that. I kept my pants on, and I would've heard anyone entering the room before they'd see me. It was out of frustration, I think. It's about the fifth time in the past few weeks I've masturbated to try to relieve tension. I say try, because, while it does relieve some tension temporarily, the pressure comes back soon thereafter, plus I feel angry at myself for avoiding an issue, whatever the issue is.

When I was a child, I'd always run to my mother if I was feeling bad. She never really did or said anything to make me feel better, but she was always there. Steady was my mother, and still is, probably too steady. She's always there for my father, too, unwavering in her selfless loyalty. Makes you want to throw up.

I couldn't go to my mother now. It would be like trying to explain modern society to a Martian, or recapping the past twenty years to someone who's been in a coma. Where could I begin?

Well, Mother, first recognize that these are my values: political, sexual, and the rest. Given those values, you can readily see why I behave in the following manner. Now then, here are five thousand things that have occurred since I became an adult, the relevant events in my life. You've got that so far? All right now, Mother, this is my situation at the current time, plus short biographies of the people who play important parts in my life. Oh, I almost forgot, you'll need these brief explanations of several subcultures you're probably unfamiliar with. Now here's the genesis of my feelings about...

Hopeless. My mother will not solve my headaches. But maybe the headaches are a sign that I'm approaching a resolution. Optimistic Carolyn.

"Philip, do you love Carolyn?"

"Yes. Very much."

"How do you express that love to her?"

"By letting her be herself, sticking with her when she's down—"

"Let's return to those you mentioned in a little bit. What about physically? How do you express your love to her physically?"

"We've been through this. It's futile. I can't compete with a woman. If Carolyn gets off with women as a class and not with men as a class, short of a sex change, there's not a hell of a lot I can do about it."

"Carolyn, how do you feel when Philip suggests you don't enjoy sex with him?"

"I feel he hasn't given it a chance. He's pulled away. You *did*, Philip. I didn't lose interest; you just stopped."

"And why do you think I stopped? Why would I stop? I love you. I love your body. What possible gain is there for me to stop having sex with you?"

"Maybe you want me to feel bad about my other lovers. Maybe you want to punish me by sending me on a guilt trip."

"I'm causing the possible dissolution of our relationship just to make you feel guilty?"

"Philip, I don't know. I don't know why you do what you do anymore. I can't tell. All I know is, we used to be affectionate with each other, and one day last month you told me you didn't think it was a good idea if we made love anymore. I don't want a relationship like that. What's the point?"

"Philip, what if Carolyn refused to consider a relationship with you unless—"

"Wait a minute. I want to clear up something first. Car', just tell me straight and simple: the last few times we had sex, did you enjoy it?"

"I can't even remember when that was."

"Take a wild guess. In general, did you enjoy it?"

"Well, you were withdrawing even then. You weren't very affectionate, passionate. No, I didn't enjoy it."

"Or me. You didn't enjoy me."

"It's not a matter of enjoying you or not enjoying you. You're not a slice of pie. I always like it when you give me affection, but you can't isolate—"

"Just tell me: Do you like making love with me?"

"Yes, of course! Yes! No! I don't know, oh, Philip, I don't know. I tried, I really tried. I tried."

There was one brief period I thought we might make it, one hiatus from the despondence and the bitterness. It was about half a year after we'd arrived in Seattle, and I'd begun to realize that the rigors of unemployment were sealing in Philip's previous negativity like plastic laminated onto a wound. I'd been teaching at Seattle University, and Philip had been searching for jobs and honing his surliness.

I came home one day in the late afternoon to find him sitting on the couch, his face as vacant as the TV screen in front of him. Oh, no, I thought, what now? I decided to play it casual.

"Hi." Kiss on the cheek. "What's up?"

He didn't say anything for a moment, and then, "I made a big mistake today."

"What is it, Philip?" I sat down next to him on the couch and put my hand on his shoulder.

"Well, I found myself with a few hours of blank time. You know, I was waiting for that interview call. So I didn't feel like doing anything much. It was this morning it happened."

"*What* happened?"

"I put on the TV."

"And?"

"And, I watched it for three hours. Straight. I'd never really been cognizant of what was on. I mean, I'd read about it, sure, and I've even made jokes about it, but until today, I never really, really knew." He was holding his knees with his hands, and nodding. I tried to flippantize the conversation.

"Well, it was pretty bad, I take it. Guess that's the way it is sometimes."

"Car'," he said, shaking his head and slapping his knees rhythmically with the cadence of his speech, "what makes people act that way? I mean, what does it? Genes, environment? The morbidity is utterly phenomenal. Have you ever watched a quiz show?"

"Oh, maybe as a child—"

"It's incredible, simply incredible. This is what I majored in social psychology for. Now I understand. But never in my most horrible, fantastic nightmares could I have imagined human beings acting in such a way. It...it was unreal, absolutely unreal."

He wasn't looking at me, but staring at the screen again, becoming more agitated, playing drums on his kneecaps. I started to look at the screen, too, as if the shows were still on, inside the set.

"Where have I been," Philip continued, "not to notice this? This has been going on for years and years, and I have been oblivious to it. The sheer imbecility of those people; the smarmy, pathetic zeal of the hosts, their total lack of dignity, their conscious disregard of any remotely positive human quality—"

"Philip, take it easy."

"Take it easy?" He got up, walked to the window, and turned to face me, gesticulating out the window at the world.

"Carolyn, millions of people out there watch those shows. Millions of people stamp their feet and shriek and identify with the studio audience. Those shows couldn't last unless all those viewers around the country tuned in. They yearn, Carolyn, for the opportunity to get up there with the emcee and his moronic cash lady, or whatever she's called, and try to win big bucks by acting like fools, *aggressively* acting like fools! Car', it's entirely conceivable that thousands of housewives close their eyes each night with their husbands pumping hot stuff into them and fantasize about pressing buzzers and ringing bells and hugging that sleazeball emcee! That's conceivable, Car', I know it is. Can you imagine what kind of person the emcee must be? What it must take biologically for those behaviors to occur? In public? What chaos must reign in that man's mind?"

Philip put his hand to his brow, as if that latest thought was too astonishing to comprehend. I took the opportunity to get him sitting down again, but he bounced up, fending off my efforts.

"And the questions they ask! My God, do you have any idea of the intellectual level we're talking about here? I mean, I'm not exaggerating,

Neal Starkman

Car'. A twenty-five-year-old white man, okay? Not disadvantaged now. We're talking privileged, young, white, male, a manager of a retail store. He was twenty-five; he did not know who was vice president under Eisenhower. He hadn't a clue! Not a clue!

"Okay, okay, he's too young, you say, and maybe history isn't all that important. Okay, a woman. A woman on the very same show was stumped—she blew fifteen hundred dollars—because she could not identify which of three vegetables grows beneath the ground! I mean, Carolyn, we're talking about raw intelligence, the general gunk your brain's made of. You can live and die in a big-city slum, hundreds of miles from a farm, and just *reason* that cheese is not a vegetable, and that if it was it would never make it out of the ground in cellophaned wheels. Christ—"

"Philip, settle down."

"Oh, Carolyn, don't you see? They're not atypical, we are. They're the ones whose programs are on TV. They're the ones who go out and buy the products with scents of pine and lemon in them. People like them all over the country tune in every single goddam day and match wits against someone who thinks cheddar is farmed like cattle."

I knew I had to calm him down before he got into the soaps. So I sat him on the couch for the second time, took his hands in mine, and tried to pinion his eyeballs with a hard stare.

"Philip, listen to me. You're taking this too seriously. Listen. The world is a big place, Philip. There are all kinds of people in it—good and bad, intelligent and stupid, sophisticated and crude. And everything in between. You have to face the facts—the world isn't the way you'd like it to be. It never was. You can't change that, so why don't you try to live with it? Philip, there are people out there who see it your way, too."

Carolyn the Cliché-Monger. But it worked, Lady Di, at least for a few weeks. He mulled the rest of the day but was more pensive than despondent. And the next day, and for the next few weeks, he was different, alive again. He smiled, he touched me a lot more often, he even made little jokes. He cut out letters from a magazine and taped them into a crude note, which he sent to the president of Seattle Pacific College. The note read, "We have your magazine. Renounce Christ or you'll never see it again." I thought, if only he could get a job now. But he lost out on a position he was hoping for, blaming it on affirmative action. And the very next day, I got my massage from Shelly.

"Philip, why don't you tell Carolyn about how you felt when she told you she'd made love to Shelly?"

"I wasn't particularly surprised, I don't know why. I sensed that something important was happening and so decided to assimilate before responding."

"Didn't you have a gut reaction?"

"Oh, maybe I felt a little hurt, but only for a second or two. I suppose for an instant I didn't feel special anymore. But then I thought: wait a minute, why should you feel bad if Carolyn is feeling good? So then I felt better, because I knew that she was happy doing what she was doing."

"God, Philip, I can just picture you thinking like that. So logical."

"Do you resent Philip's being logical?"

"If he's thinking, it doesn't seem like an honest reaction; he's not letting go, not being open with me."

"I was being open. That's how I felt. That's how I feel now. I want you to do what's best for you, what makes you happy."

"What about you? You can stand outside the situation and say it's logical to feel this way, so that's how I'll feel? You're able to be so detached that you can put aside your emotions?"

"Would you prefer I flew into a jealous rage?"

Neal Starkman

"Carolyn, do you feel that Philip is controlling himself too much?"

"Yes. It's just like the alienation, Philip. You always feel alienated. Well, you make yourself feel alienated. You control it just like you control your emotions. You've always controlled it."

"Carolyn, I have a choice of living in a world of alienation or a world of fantasy. I've chosen the former because of my high regard for honesty. It's not a matter of controlling my emotions or even my alienation. I don't consciously go about holding things in. It's merely a matter of doing the best I can with reality."

One hell of a day, Lady Di, and I feel like my superfluid helium, internally spinning at unpredictable angles from indeterminate causes. In fact, I spent a good part of the afternoon in the lab, adjusting a few calculations, checking rotors and meters, varying spin times and temperature gradients, and pondering the politics of telling Mankiewicz that I'd like to forgo the easy publication for the time being, thank you, to pursue a long shot about magnetizing the field around the whirling helium.

I got lost in the lab. I can see why the theoretical physicists like Dorothy Wu appear to be off-center. Their labs are in their heads, always with them. Carolyn-in-the-middle again. I can attach myself to the laboratory for a little while, and I enjoy the mental masturbation of playing with theories and building on principles and expanding previous work by other mental masturbators. So somewhere, somehow, I must be getting pleasure from this colossal self-examination. But soon I'd need to find out what was happening outside. I'd need to hold Stephanie, to roast chestnuts with Darrel, to attend a caucus meeting. I need that people contact, Lady Di. I guess that's why I'm in condensed-matter physics and not high-energy physics (it leaves me more time to be a social bug).

That's what Philip called me, a social bug. He also described me as a walking reinforcement grabber, because people were always coming on to me for one reason or another. Philip had a rough time understanding how comfortable I am with people.

"Do you really enjoy your parties?" he once asked me as I primped for an evening with some friends.

"Do you really enjoy staying home and reading Dostoyevsky?"

"I know, let's compromise. You stay home and we fuck."

"How about compromising by waiting for me to come home, and then we fuck?"

"You come home too late."

"Take a nap, and you'll be all rested up when I return."

"You might not return. You're so damn friendly, you'll probably go home with some fetching nymphet."

"Oh, Philip, I'm sure I'll be home."

"Promise?"

"No."

I liked the come-ons, Di, what can I say? I've never been so superattractive that I've had to fight people off, and I felt that I was reaping the compensation for all those lonely high-school nights, when boys would be afraid to call me up and ask me out lest I use a word they couldn't understand. So I made the most of it.

Yesterday afternoon, though, I was no social bug. I sat and watched my spinning helium and for once put Philip's dervishes out of my mind and thought only about how I could get the patterns I needed. You have a substance, you rotate it, you bring it down below its lambda point so that it separates into two substances with different viscosities, you stop the rotation—nothing new so far. I'd kept the helium going for maybe two hours and was considering how time factored into the normal helium/superfluid helium ratio, when I remembered that Stephanie's group was coming over and I had to get back. Luckily, I was only twenty minutes from a break; I wondered if Marie Curie had to be on hand for cooking and hostessing.

I packed up my notes—I've been working as much at home lately as in the lab—and felt for the first time that maybe, just maybe, I could crack the secret of the vortices. I even visualized the title of my paper: "What Makes Helium Spin?"

I made it home by 5:15 and found Stephanie in the kitchen. She was talking to me while shredding lettuce, as if I'd arrived three minutes earlier.

"…I'm going to wait until the meeting. You'll hear it then. Those bastards. This is going to be big. Got a lot of work ahead of us, girl, lot of work."

The lettuce was being shredded not only in the salad bowl, but also on the counter, the walls, and the floor. When Steph is upset, she mumbles and gets hyperactive. I took off my coat, put some groceries in the refrigerator, and hugged her from behind, till she put down the massacred head and held my hands against her.

"Thanks, lover."

"Want to tell me about it?"

"No; hold me, though, for another minute. There's a dip and a salad to make."

"I'll make it, Steph. What time does everybody get here?"

"Six. And I think we're low on coffee. And I forgot to buy ice cream."

"Anything else?"

"The cake's in the oven. But I ran out of cinnamon. Had to use, what is it, cardamom. It had 'mom' in it, so I figured it should be okay. Do you still love me?"

I kissed her, put my coat back on, and shook my head at her. "Passionately. Ice cream and coffee. What kind of ice cream?"

"Black walnut."

"And if not that?"

"Oh, they'll have black walnut. See you later. Carolyn?"

"Yes, my chef?"

"Thanks, sweetie."

I picked up coffee and black cherry ice cream, figuring that it had a "black" in it, anyway. I hoped on the way back that I wasn't being too clever because I didn't know what kind of cake Steph had made. In all honesty, Di, I was trying to fill my mind with minutiae so I wouldn't think so severely about what was troubling my Stephanie.

When I returned, one of the women had arrived. She was a tall blonde woman with sharp features and sunken eyes; she was introduced to me as Barbara. Within the next hour, the rest had assembled—Claudia, Betty, Janet, and a woman everyone called "Junior."

We ate an eclectic meal—salad, Barbara's homemade raisin bread, Claudia's hot string-bean-and-almond loaf, Betty's fresh calamari, Janet's doctored canned pea soup, and Junior's chenin blanc. They all either worked with Steph or had worked recently with her, except for Betty, who was Claudia's lover.

My mind was on Stephanie and helium, in that order, but the conversation during dinner was pleasant enough to keep me attending to our guests. Apparently, everyone knew each other well enough to toss out innocent jibes; each seemed to know the other's tolerance. Steph was preoccupied, and I helped with serving and telling people where the kitchen utensils and bathroom were. I mostly kept quiet and ate, while everyone else exchanged mundanities. We all sat on the floor, and indeed the atmosphere was so relaxed that I didn't have to put on the radio for background music, my original plan.

Janet, a rough-looking woman, lean, confident, fortyish, had a ready smile and used it on me.

"Carolyn, I'm glad to finally meet you. Stephanie keeps telling us about this physicist she lives with, but we thought she was making it up."

"I'm real," I said, returning the smile a few foot-candles lower.

"I can see that," said Janet, freezing my smile.

"Easy, Jan," said Barbara, "you're not cruising tonight," and everyone laughed, including Janet, though she still kept her eyes on me.

"Sounds like you have a reputation," I said.

"Who, me?"

"You should see her in action, Carrie," said Steph, admiringly. "She can charm your pants off at fifty paces."

"Look who's talking!" said Janet. "Old Marillo here used to talk her way into more Calvin Kleins than Brooke Shields!"

Steph got embarrassed at that, since that's pretty much how she met me, and Janet noticed Steph's embarrassment and contracted it for herself. The chain reaction went around the room, until Barbara asked me what I did as a physicist.

"Well, I teach," I said, "and I do some research. I could describe the research, but it's really not very interesting." That was a mistake; it begged for someone to follow up on it.

"I want to hear," said Claudia. "I've never met a physicist before, not a woman one, anyway."

"Well," I started slowly, "I work with superfluid helium. I cool it down to pretty close to absolute zero, and then I, uh, I do different things with it. I rotate it, I used to send it through templates, uh, filters, I vary the temperature, I send currents through it."

"What for?" asked Janet, and laughed. I felt like a display, and Stephanie didn't help by beaming at me like I was her new Christmas toy.

"Well, superfluid helium behaves in ways that are interesting to scientists." I didn't want to sound condescending, but I was also aware that no one could possibly be enthusiastic about what I did with superfluid helium. "No other element, for example, retains its liquidity down to absolute zero."

"What about antifreeze?" asked Junior.

"Well, antifreeze would solidify way before it got to absolute zero."

"That's not regular zero, right, Carolyn?" prompted my lover.

"Uh, right. It's zero on the Kelvin scale, which is 273 degrees below the Celsius scale. So, I'm talking about, oh, 450 degrees below zero Fahrenheit. Pretty cold." By this time in my life, I called this my absolute-zero speech.

"Four hundred and fifty below zero?" asked Junior, wide-eyed.

"That's right," said Stephanie, arm on my shoulder.

"It's really just a matter of having the right equipment," I said. "Pumps and all."

"Tell them about the two heliums," said Stephanie.

"Oh, Steph, I don't think—"

"No, go on. Didn't you tell me once that there were two of them, or something?"

No one else encouraged me to talk, but I didn't want to upset Stephanie more than she already was.

"Well, the helium separates into normal helium and superfluid helium—we call that Helium II—when it gets to a certain temperature. The temperature is called the lambda point. Actually, there are more than two heliums. The superfluid helium does different things than the normal helium does. For example, its viscosity is zero. I've been rotating the helium in a cylinder to determine the levels at which quantized vortices appear and disappear, and also to determine why certain temperature gradients affect the angular momentum of the vortices. It may be that the ratio of superfluid to normal helium has something to do with the way the vortices are formed, because the vortices appear only at certain predictable temperature levels and not at others, and apparently disassemble at a threshold rotation frequency. It's possible that by inducing an electromagnetic field around the rotors, I might be able to, uh, well, that's getting too complicated."

"And she works with computers, too," said Stephanie.

"Really," said Claudia, "those things always confused me, except the kind, you know, you play with in stores, like with those new toys."

"Tell them about the computer," urged Steph.

"No, I really don't want to," I said.

"Hey, my friends don't know you; we all talk about what we do."

I was feeling awkward, eggheadish, the mirror image of Stephanie's Karen Black. "But you all do fairly similar things. What I do is another world. I can't explain it so that laypeople can relate to it."

Barbara caught on. "I could go for some coffee," she said, and that gave me an excuse to take up dishes and make coffee and tea. Steph followed me into the kitchen, and I surprised her by asking her not to showcase me anymore.

"What do you mean, showcase? I just want my friends to get to know my lover."

"That's fine, Stephanie," I whispered, "but I don't want to talk shop. It's boring."

"You're afraid my friends aren't smart enough to understand," she said, helping me with the coffee.

"It's not that. I do very technical work. People outside the field, smart or not so smart, find it hard to understand. Even physicists can't always understand other fields within physics. It's, it's like another language. It's no reflection on your friends, or anybody."

But Stephanie was not in a buying mood. "You know, just because we work with our hands doesn't mean we don't use our heads."

"Stephanie," I said, but she was already out of the room and I was developing a headache that I suspected I would be allaying with massive doses of alcohol.

When the coffee and tea was ready, I brought it out. Stephanie had served everyone her cardamom walnut cake—the black cherry ice cream had been a mistake, no one wanted any—and had already begun the serious discussion without me. I sat between Junior and Claudia, nursing my hurts.

"…all the facts, it'll be in the papers tomorrow. But she's in trouble, and we've got to help."

"Why would they even arrest her?" said Janet. "Who's the source on this, Stephanie?"

"I told you," said Stephanie, "she works downtown in the police department, but they'd fire her in a second if they knew she leaked. Just the excuse they'd need. Listen, this woman thinks that there's going to be some heavy doings on this. You just know that they want to pin this on Georgia to damage her credibility to the community. They don't have enough to convict her, but they can make it so she'll be out of commission for a year."

"But being arrested won't damage her credibility," said Barbara, whom I was beginning to like. "In the community I know, it would strengthen her credibility."

"Credibility or not, you can't do much behind bars," said Janet.

"That's true," said Junior.

"Well, what do we do?" asked Claudia.

"March," suggested Janet.

"Wait a minute," and we turned to Betty, who hadn't talked much the whole evening. Betty didn't look like a tradeswoman at all, and in fact I still don't know what she does for a living. She was not only frailer than the rest of us, but also paler, like she didn't spend time outside. If anything, she could have been a physicist. "I don't understand," she said. "Georgia Poseta is a Third World woman, isn't she? This is going to take some coordination. We should get a lot of groups involved in this."

"That's why we have to organize," said Stephanie. "I'm speaking with Holly Christianson of the Women's Center and Sharon Mollabee over at FemGroup tomorrow. Look, I don't represent anyone, and that's probably good politically. I have the contacts and the experience, and I think they know I can put it together."

"We should get Georgia out on bail, first thing," said Janet.

"Why don't we call NOW and get some national publicity?" put in Betty. "Self-defense is a big issue."

"All right, one thing at a time," said Stephanie, and started to take notes on a telephone pad. "Coordinate with Seattle centers. And NOW."

"Don't forget bail," said Claudia.

"And bail…"

"What do *you* think, Carolyn?" Junior was addressing me, but I was lost.

"Um, I don't know. I missed something. Who…what happened?"

"Georgia Poseta shot her landlord. He's still alive, though," snapped my lover, sounding sorry he was still alive. "He let himself in with a master key while she was taking a shower. He went for her, and she shot him. Clear self-defense."

I recalled Stephanie walking—or jumping—in on David. "Did she call the police?"

"Yeah, but she didn't expect them to haul *her* in. We'll get more news tomorrow."

"Maybe we ought to have a rally for her, show her some support," I suggested, which made sense to me at the time.

"Oh, yeah," said Junior. "That way all the groups can get together."

"Well, hold on," said Barbara. "I don't feel entirely comfortable plowing into this. We really don't know the facts yet, do we?"

"I think time's important in this case," said Stephanie. "If we let it go on, it'll be harder to help her."

"But I don't see—"

"Yeah," said Jan, "it's a sign of weakness to—"

"—why we can't wait to investigate it more and then set up a rally, or whatever."

Stephanie continued to take notes in the ensuing silence. "Well," she said, "I don't see why we can't gather as much information as we can while we're planning. We *should* do what Barbara says."

"So," said Jan. "A rally downtown?"

"No, we'd never get a permit," said Stephanie. "It'd have to be in a park."

"Myrtle Edwards," said Betty. "It's close to downtown, and it's long, for marching."

"Volunteer's better," said Claudia. "Bigger, lots of grass."

"Look," said Stephanie, "we have to wait until the meetings tomorrow. Then we can work out bail, shit like that. Besides, we have a lot of groups to get together on this."

"Those assholes," said Janet. "You'd think the poor woman's been through enough."

"Steph?" I had me a cold lover in a cold bed.

"Yeah."

"Steph, I really wasn't looking down on your friends. Really. I just feel uncomfortable talking about my job, that's all. I don't ever feel that anyone else can possibly be interested in it. Plus I feel bad about ending my helium work."

"It's okay."

"It's not okay if you think I'm a snob. I'm not a snob. I'll prove it to you: I'll suck on one of your toes. Would a snob do that?"

That got her at least to turn over.

"Which toe would you like sucked?" I deadpanned.

She tried to stifle a grin. "All of them, five at a time. Your mouth's big enough for the job. And then do my fingers. And my ears. And then I'll decide if you're a snob."

"Well, actually, my making the offer was the sign that I'm not a snob. A snob wouldn't make the offer. Following through with it would be superfluous."

She started to roll back over.

"Now, wait on," I said, grabbing her back, "tell you what I'm going to do, seein' as you're a pretty nice kid, and seein' also as I've got a whole lot of wine in me. I'll kiss those toes, and those fingers, but—"

"And the ears, too. And it's sucking, not kissing."

"All right; Jesus. Picky, picky. I'll do all that, but first you have to tell me who Georgia Poseta is."

"You never heard me talk about Georgia Poseta?"

"Don't remember."

"Georgia Poseta works for USA, the Urban Sisters Association."

"Oh, I know them. Radical lesbian women. Didn't they do something with City Light a few years ago?"

"It was last year—a lawsuit about hiring, and they also hanged the president in effigy. Big ceremony downtown. But they're mostly underground, do a lot of organizing and stuff. Georgia was founder and first director; now she's just a member but still a power. They're not even officially a lesbian organization, but most of the members are gay women. I was part of it a few years ago—in my younger days—but I had a fight with the director after Georgia and left."

"How big is the USA?"

"Hard to say. But they're loud when they want to be. That's what counts. Anyway, Georgia's fought for years in Seattle, lately against the cops for how they've treated rape and battering victims."

"She's got enemies on the police."

"Let's say the force is not with her. The commissioner, Langdon, has publicly stated that she's a nuisance. So now, when she tries to defend herself against an attacker, they're going to get her. A great opportunity."

"Is it her word against his?"

"The landlord's? Yeah. Hawkins is his name, Clifford Hawkins, I think. Still in the hospital. I don't know, all this happened this afternoon. I'll get more details tomorrow."

"It'll probably be in the paper."

"They might try to hush it up."

"Why?"

"Because it doesn't look good if a woman is charged with attempted murder, or manslaughter, or whatever they're going to charge her with, when it's obvious she tried to avoid being raped. I mean, Carrie, how stupid do you think the public is? There she is, dripping wet, nude, and they're making her out to be the aggressor? Shit."

"Where'd she get the gun?"

"I don't know, but it was probably hers. Woman in her position'd be nuts not to carry a gun. Hey. I just got a chill."

"Do you want another blanket?"

"No, it's in my toes."

"Oh, Steph, I'm so sleepy."

"I'll whistle, keep you up."

"That's okay, just give me a nudge down there if I nod off."

Philip didn't have other lovers when he was with me. He steadfastly held to his right to have other lovers, yet he never seemed excited about anyone else. He said he had to go through five steps to become physically intimate with a woman: first, he had to meet her; second, he had to be attracted to her; third, she had to be attracted to him; fourth, he had to be assertive enough to do something about it; and fifth, there couldn't be complications: no husbands, jealous lovers, venereal diseases, and so on. He said that it was hard enough getting past the first step.

I was the opposite. I was uncomfortable about non-monogamy—Mother and Pop's influence there—yet there was Shelly and Gail and Tracy and a few others. Once I committed myself to my sexual smorgasbord, our relationship worsened, and Philip told me it would be a bad idea for him to have other lovers even if he made it through all five steps.

"Why?" I asked one day, as we walked through the Arboretum.

"Because, first of all, I don't want to foist my problems on another woman. Second of all, I think another woman would only complicate our already complicated relationship. Third of all, I love *you*, not anyone else. And fourth—"

"Fourth? You must feel pretty strongly about this."

"Fourth of all, most of the women I meet these days are over sixty-five, and the few young ones around the home are either undesirable or unavailable."

We were serpentining through the Arboretum, the Seattle flora in early summer blooms—magnolias, cherry blossoms, peonies. The air was layered vertically with different fragrances, and it was possible to pretend that you were lost in a forest rather than a city park. Every fifty feet or so, we'd have to make a decision about which path to take. It didn't really matter, because one of the pleasures of the Arboretum is discovering new trails, and they all ended at about the same place, anyway. But soon I realized that I'd been making all the decisions, taking the lead to the left or the right or straight ahead. At the next fork, I purposely held back. Philip hesitated, then asked, "Which way?"

"Up to you," I said, and he turned left.

"There's always quickies," I suggested.

"What's the point?" he said. "I hate small talk and game-playing. I'm not a very good seducer."

"That's what you told me when we first met."

"It's still true."

"How about men?"

"Sorry, not for me."

"How do you know until you try? *I* suck your cock; *I'm* still alive and healthy."

"Car, that you at one time did that is marvelous. It's not my choice."

"I thought you're supposed to be so open and objective. You call it a choice. It's not a choice; you haven't even considered it. How do you know? You might like it. You don't have to suck someone's cock. Let them do it to you. You could get picked up in a gay bar. Look at all the fun you might be missing out on."

He wasn't moved. He walked ahead, hands clasped behind his back, looking not at the trees and ponds and flowers, but at the ground directly in front of him, like a slug-detector.

"Carolyn, I recognize the hypocrisy in all of this. I'm not dense; I see the double standard. But I'm hopelessly biased. It's like spinach."

"Spinach?"

"Yeah, like spinach. I've always hated spinach."

"I never knew that."

He smiled. "Now you know. I don't remember ever tasting it, but I know I hate it. I can tell merely by looking at it that I hate it. Christ, it's stringy and limp and god-awful green and chartreuse. It looks like it's been scraped off the hull of an old warship. If it tastes a hundredth as bad as it looks, I'll die a slow, agonizing death. It's the same thing with men. I'm not homophobic. I don't fear men. I just don't want to have anything to do with them physically. Shit, I don't even like my *own* body; you expect me to cuddle up to another one just like it?"

"A definite hang-up, Philip," I said. "You probably had a traumatic experience with spinach as a child. Maybe your mother forced you to eat some that was spoiled, and you've repressed it."

"I thought I was the psychologist here. I can't win if you play Freud. If I deny it, I'm being defensive. If I accept it, I'm intellectualizing. And if I can't remember it, then obviously I'm using repression as a defense mechanism."

"Would you like me to switch back to being a physicist? I can talk to you about how different forces interact on a solid object."

"No, I know it's a hang-up. It's two hang-ups, for that matter. The first hang-up is my refusal to consider men as sexual partners. And the second hang-up is my refusal to do anything about the first. And I won't. Even if it halves my chances of getting laid."

The control in the relationship was up for grabs, and I took it because I was more able to use it. It became impossible to distinguish Philip's concerns about us from his general despondency. His release wasn't alcohol or other women or work; it was depression. When he really indulged himself, he'd funk out for days. We talked less, and I became less interested in him, which he saw as evidence that I no longer loved him. Seemingly innocuous remarks were fraught with innuendo; casual conversation turned into bitter argument. We second- and third-guessed each other. Shelly and my ensuing lovers were a welcome relief, bright colors in an otherwise dull tapestry of life with Philip. We hurt each other continually, and then I began to act in ways not to hurt.

"Carolyn, what do you want from your relationship with Philip?"

"Oh, God, lately, just some peace would be nice, a surcease from the fighting, some mutual understanding."

"Tell us some specific things Philip could do."

"Okay. He could smile more. He could interpret what I say more positively, so I don't have to constantly prove that I'm not out to hurt him."

"How does that sound to you, Philip?"

"I don't think she's out to hurt me. I think she discounts me. She's cast me into the same mold as all men. When I try to defend myself, she gets upset. It's very difficult to respond positively when all you hear is arguments from a narrow perspective, and your own arguments are either not accepted or put down unequivocally. I don't feel like smiling when I know I'm not respected."

"Philip, I respect you for who you are and what you are. But part of what you are is a man. You can't do anything about that. I look at you as a man. As a man, you do certain things, act certain ways; it is and always will be your history."

"Philip, I get the feeling you resent Carolyn labeling you as a man, or as a heterosexual, or as anything."

"Of course I do. I don't deny that I'm male."

"But you deny that you behave in certain ways because you're male?"

"What's the difference? What difference does any of this make? We can't go to a movie unless it's directed by a woman or it's about a woman. We can't watch a TV show without her pointing out every victimization of a woman. We can't have a discussion without her bringing up something about sexual minorities or women. Carolyn, I'm tired of it! Why are we even here talking about this? Either you know me or you don't. I have to believe that if you knew me, we wouldn't have the arguments we've been having."

"Maybe I don't know you."

"Terrific. That's just terrific."

"You changed, Philip. You used to love life. That sounds trite, but it's true. You used to have fun—with me, with others, but especially with yourself. Now what are you about? You gripe about the world and how alienated you feel, you're defensive about being a man, you're depressed half the time and angry the rest. How can I live with someone like that?"

"I suppose it depends on your tolerance. It used to depend on your love."

"Philip, what do you want me to do? Tell me."

"What do I want you to do? Respect me as me. Listen to what I say, but be yourself. I don't want you to do anything you wouldn't do normally. That's not me. I'm not your average controlling male. Carolyn, there's nothing more I can tell you. You know how I feel about groups, about the danger of losing one's identity to a group, and you know that the more you talk about women and bisexuals, the more estranged I become, not because I'm prejudiced against bisexual women, but because I'm prejudiced about dervishes. Forget that, you don't understand, but, God in heaven, why would I be prejudiced against bisexuals? It could be any group. And I don't relate to that. If you know me at all, you know I don't relate to that. And if you know me at all, you also know that it's pretty damn difficult for me to wait for you to decide whether or not to take the person I love most in this world out of my life."

"Oh, Philip. Jesus, Philip."

Oh, yes, Lady Di, the sessions with the counselor were just delightful. Well, it worked, in one sense. It became apparent after three months of weekly sessions that the breach was irreparable.

It is Saturday, 9:30 in the morning, and I write to you in bed, Lady Di, while Stephanie is on the phone playing coordinator.

I read that and it sounds sarcastic. Why am I negative?

The past few days have flurried by. I visited Dr. Stan and tried to learn what had happened with Mary Ann. He was hanging a picture of Mt. Rainier when I came in and told him that I felt sick about taking Mary Ann's money and that I wished he'd told me.

"I took that picture myself, Carolyn. Like it?" He stood across the room to admire it.

"Yes."

"Carolyn, it was all Mary Ann's doing. It's true that I'm juggling to get from personnel to supplies, but that's because I respect your work. And I know you know enough not to mention this beyond the office. Carolyn, Mary Ann would have quit irrespective of your or my actions. I can't believe I got that with an Instamatic. Must all be in the eye. What do you think?"

"You're making light of this! A woman's career is ruined—"

"By her own hand, Carolyn. What do you want me to do? Rehire her? I can't." He sighed himself into his chair. "I appreciate the politics of hiring women in nontraditional disciplines, and I will try to exert influence to hire another woman to take Mary Ann's place, though I can't guarantee anything. But that's truly all I can do. All I need from you is that article, and that will justify any questionable maneuvering I've done."

I knew he was right. I wished I could have prevented Mary Ann from quitting, but maybe I was powerless to do that.

"Carolyn."

Dr. Stan looked at me intently. "Something else, but it may be nothing. Mary Ann came in yesterday and wanted to know if it was true about your, uh, sexual orientation. I told her she'd have to talk with you about it. But she appeared angry."

"Oh, God." What next, Di?

"Carolyn—" as I was leaving—"don't leave your notes in the lab at night. Just to be safe."

Yesterday I was invited to a dinner party by one of the intro physics teachers. I was so surprised at the invitation, I gushed out my gratitude, only to learn that essentially everyone in the department is invited. Oh, well. One gets used to living with embarrassment.

I should have known. I'm rather an odd breed here. The physics teachers are well apart from the researchers. The researchers live physics, the teachers live students and test scores. The teachers are the underlings of the department, even lower than research assistants. "They're mechanics," said one of our nuclear boys at a departmental meeting. "They don't have to think as much." Old Carolyn, therefore, is a half-mechanic, suspected by both groups.

So I've taught my classes and I've run some printouts past my weary eyes, and I've tried to keep out of Stephanie's way. I used to like politics a lot, but for some reason I can't get excited about Georgia Poseta.

One thing, I've been calmer lately. I haven't been sleeping well, but during the day I've mellowed out. No headaches, except one really bad one last night. There's not much left to write about Philip; maybe I needed to expunge him from whatever level of consciousness I tap to write to you, Di.

I should see Darrel sometime. I haven't spoken with him since we roasted chestnuts. He's so sweet; I enjoy him. He's one of the few gay men I know who's in a fairly stable sexual relationship. But Darrel is so easy to be with, it's hard to imagine him fighting with a lover, though I'm sure it happens.

Now my parents could never accept that. How many parents, after all, would choose for their child a stable gay relationship over an unstable, even destructive heterosexual one? Oh, God, why fret over it? Sooner or later, dear Mother and Father will have to be told. Well, at least they won't complain about Stephanie's being part Filipina or wonder who our kids will resemble.

Christmas vacation is in a few months. Steph and I should definitely go somewhere. I'll be finished with the current runs in the lab, one way or the other. She has a few weeks coming to her. We should go to Mexico or Hawaii, someplace where we can soak up sun and each other. Things have been so busy, we haven't had much chance for really slow lovemaking. Couples need that.

Philip liked that. He had an almost childlike joy with lovemaking. I would lie back in bed, and he'd play his fingers over my body, like he was examining a piece of fine sculpture. He would revere me, Lady Di. He would treat me so gently that *I* began to think I was precious. After a time, though, I came to feel objectified: I didn't want to be a piece of sculpture, I wanted to be Carolyn. Naturally he was miffed when I asked him not to put me on a pedestal. I couldn't make him understand that I wanted him to be tender but not adoring.

There was an evening we were lying in the dark, caressing each other. I remember being impressed with how impressed he was.

"What?"

"I feel good," he said softly. "Making love amazes me."

"Why?"

"Because everything else in the world is give-and-take. You give up something to get something. You don't get something for nothing. All that. But lovemaking—it's a give-and-give. The more pleasure you get, the more I get. There's no loss, absolutely no loss in the process. It doesn't seem like it ought to work."

"You're so pessimistic."

"It just seems that making love should be treated differently, more respectfully. Can you imagine why anyone would disapprove of what we're doing? How many activities can you think of that provide all gain and no loss? Yet for as long as humans have been around, there've been people against making love, violently against making love."

"Hey, don't get down."

"I'm not down. This is me."

And it *was* him. That part of him became overwhelming in the end, that part of him that, in the midst of experiencing tremendous pleasure, could lament the history of sexual oppression.

Maybe I should buy myself a new wardrobe, in case I have to apply for a job somewhere.

Now why did I write *that*, Di? Am I insecure about my work? Do I suspect that my helium equations will never pan out, my students will rate me an unprepared teacher, and Dr. Stan will not renew my contract? Is he only pretending to be on my side when, in fact, at this very moment, he's chairing a meeting of the Committee to Abolish Lesbian Physicists?

Neal Starkman

I have insecurities, to be sure, but as I look over the last few pages here, Lady Di, it strikes me that I'm rambling. And when I ramble, it usually means that I'm avoiding something. What am I avoiding?

Is it Stephanie? Is it the rally she's trying to organize? I don't know why I should avoid it. There's no reason I shouldn't lend all my talents, such as they are, to the effort. I'm able to organize; my job's not in jeopardy for doing it. It should be the most natural thing in the world to help my lover in a cause we both believe in. Why don't I go into the kitchen and say, "Steph, let's get two heads working on this"?

People like me to work with them because I'm a cool one. When I first met Steph, she was involved in a work battle, not unusual. Her construction boss, a really nasty man who has since been replaced with a less nasty man, had turned down an employee's request to bring her child on-site. The woman was a single parent and couldn't afford to send her kid to a day care center. Steph had been ready to picket her own company, a move that no doubt would have cost her her job and probably would not have helped the mother.

So I did a little research into the appropriate municipal laws and also checked into low-cost day care centers. Then I met with the woman. She didn't want any trouble; she only needed someplace to keep her kid while she was working.

I pointed out to Steph that one, there was no legal obligation for her employer to provide day care; two, it was dangerous to keep the child on-site, anyway; and three, the employer was unlikely to cooperate no matter what Steph said or did. We found a woman in the neighborhood—through women's center contacts—who would keep the kid during the day in exchange for a little money and use of the mother's car.

Stephanie was pleased. We always learn from each other—she from my education, I from her sense of purpose. So why am I not helping with this campaign, Lady Di? They're planning a rally at Volunteer Park, they're raising defense money, they're coordinating with different groups. Why am I holding back?

It's true that I'm under some pressure to finish the data analysis, but surely that's not crucial; it never has been before. I do have to make a final decision about whether or not to submit the article for publication in its current state, and I do admit to identifying perhaps a bit too much with solving the mystery of the vortices.

I have a caucus meeting coming up, and tests to grade, and a seminar to attend. My relationship with Mary Ann ended on an awkward note, to say the least. Hell, Lady Di, I can think of a dozen reasons I can't help on this campaign, but they all seem like excuses to me.

What makes matters even sillier is that I know Stephanie expects me to participate. She's getting suspicious already about my lack of enthusiasm but has been too busy to say anything. I don't know exactly what she'll want me to do, but it will probably mean making some phone calls to authorities, maybe planning publicity, strategizing. Whatever it is, it shouldn't be a compromise.

Now why did I write *that*? Why should it be a compromise? Maybe I'm thinking too much, examining things too closely. Maybe I need to step back a bit and then plunge ahead into the rally. I probably should just do whatever it is I should do.

Then again, you can't get too much sleep.

9. CAROLYN

THEY'VE GOT ONE OF OUR SISTERS!

Georgia Poseta, one of Seattle's strongest voices for women's and gay rights, and a Woman of Color, has been arrested for defending herself against an attack by her landlord. The male-supremacist prosecutor's office has charged her with first-degree assault and set an impossible bail of $25,000! Georgia has been hassled by the authorities since she was thrown in jail on October 22—prevented from making phone calls, physically and verbally abused, and denied due process under the law. Because of her outspokenness on behalf of women's and gay rights, it has been decided that she will "be made an example of." Sisters! Help raise money for Georgia's bail and her defense. Don't let the racist and heterosexist legal system beat her! Fight for your rights as women and sexual minorities! Next time, it could be you!

Neal Starkman

RALLY

Volunteer Park, Saturday, November 1, noon. Speakers will include Midge Fielding, Office of Women's Rights, and Maureen Wilson, Capitol Hill Tenants. For more information, call Stephanie Marillo, 426-6325. Georgia needs your money and support!

"Carolyn, I want you to speak at the rally."

"Me? Why me?"

"Because people listen to you. And you've got a hotshot degree. And you can talk in front of a crowd."

"Oh, Steph, I really can't, I—"

"Carrie, just five minutes. Three. Three minutes. You won't be the only speaker. We need you, honey. I want someone who's not aligned with any group, someone who'll be accepted by everyone."

"But I don't know anything about the case. I'd feel ignorant."

"You know as much as anyone. You know that Georgia Poseta is not getting equal treatment because she is a lesbian Filipina feminist and she speaks out for what she believes in. Do you think a straight white male would even have had charges brought against him?"

"Well, I can't quite see the situation."

"Carolyn, I talked with Celia Stuart, Georgia's lawyer. She thinks the whole thing is a farce, but she's going to have to mount a defense. It looks like they want to put her away."

"I thought they just wanted to destroy her credibility."

"She could get five-to-ten years, all for defending herself, Carrie. That's what happens to women when they get too powerful."

"Can I talk to Celia Stuart about the case?"

"Carrie, she's doing all she can just to get the facts straight. I hear they won't even let her in to see Clifford Hawkins. Look, there'll be other people to talk about the case at the rally. All I want you to do is get to the intellectuals in the crowd. A lot of intellectuals have money. We need a lot of money, kid."

"I know, Steph. It's only that—"

"Honey, no one will think you're a bull dyke for speaking, if that's what you're worried about. Most of the speakers won't be. I'd never have gotten everyone together if that was the case. See? I know politics."

"It's not that. I don't care about that."

"Well, what is it?"

"I don't know. For some reason, I don't feel comfortable."

"Carrie, it would help Georgia, and it would help every woman in the future who's in a situation where she has to defend herself."

"And it would mean a lot to you."

"Yeah, it would mean a lot to me."

"Oh, fuck, Steph. This isn't what I had in mind for helping on this thing, but sign me up. Only for a few minutes, though."

"Three."

"Two or three. And I'll keep it general."

"Three. Come on, your speech'll probably be interrupted by applause so much, you'll go ten, anyway."

Neal Starkman

"All right. Three minutes. A general speech about women's rights."

"I knew we could count on you, professor."

And that is how Carolyn came to be scheduled to speak at the big rally this Saturday.

I'm writing this in the lab, Lady Di. I feel as if I'd just run a marathon and was then told I had to run another five miles. I'm feeling alone, too.

Several months after Philip was killed, I attended a physics conference in San Francisco, and I think I felt then like I feel now. I couldn't get through to anyone. All the people there were physicists like me: the prima donnas, espousing their theoretical philosophies, sating their raging libidos; the graduate students, cerebral neurotics stuck in their sycophancy; status-quo managers; tenure researchers; publication seekers; hangers-on to outmoded and ill-used value systems. A wonderful bunch. Most, of course, were men. The women all seemed to be either attached to one or more of the aforementioned or else "young" like Mary Ann or else "old" like Dorothy Wu. Maybe I have higher standards for women.

I met only one interesting person. I was at one of those get-together cocktail parties hosted by a delegation from California and joined a group of either six or seven, depending on whether you counted the woman cuff-linked to one of the men. An older, distinguished man was talking to us about something called "cognitive physics," the gist of which was that all physics is in one's own mind, all phenomenological. I assumed that he was on the faculty of perhaps Berkeley or Stanford, because his erudition was unquestionable; I got lost in the metaphysics after a mesmerizing three hours. Later I found out he sharpened knives for kitchen stores and lived in his car.

Right after the physics conference I decided not to think about anything but work. I rededicated myself to teaching and research, partly to immerse myself in nonthreatening activities and partly to assure myself that, indeed, my job was secure. I had the first- and second-year willies about being a professor. It's a long way from St. Cloud to the faculty room at the

University of Washington's Department of Physics. I experienced perverse fantasies about what might happen if my "true self" were discovered:

"Oh, Dr. Anderson, we've been looking over your contract and have found a minor error, a technical misunderstanding. You see, we originally intended to hire you as a professor's *assistant*, not an assistant professor. We'll make amends immediately. Now, you *will* be getting paid by the hour…"

So I plunged, so to speak, into superfluidity studies, and I'm still floundering. No, that's unnecessarily self-abasing; I'm actually quite proficient at it. I've pushed the helium through templates, given it baths, rotated it, heated it, cooled it, second-sounded it. I was even thinking of magnetizing it someday. All to figure out what causes these vortices to occur at some levels but not at others. I'll figure it out. I have so much damn control in this lab, I'm so manipulative. I may not know what I'll obtain as a result of my manipulations, but here at least I act.

Out there, I've been passive. During the Philip–Stephanie interim, I frequented women's bars, not to be picked up—though that happened often enough—but to talk and be talked to. You know, I'd have a bad day in the lab, and I wouldn't feel like expending any energy, so I'd drop in to the bar and play passive. If I met someone, fine. If I developed a friendship, fine, too. If I acquired a lover, fine, three. And if nothing happened, then I enjoyed my wine and the music. Adiabatic Carolyn—no energy given, no energy received. I was a sponge, sopping up whatever moist socialization was lying around:

"Would you like to dance?"

"Sure, why not?"

Or:

"I think it's really important to know yourself, find out where your points of energy are, and then tap them so that you can be an efficient energy-being."

"That sounds reasonable."

Or:

"I'm going to get you a kerchief, Carolyn. They look really neat. Let's see, for you, a blue one, light blue, to match your eyes, with navy polka-dots."

"Okay."

Or even:

"The most important thing is nuclear energy. We have to stop it before it destroys us. The big businesses are playing craps with our lives to fill their coffers, and we can't let that go on any longer."

"You're right."

How did anyone trust me then? I couldn't even trust myself. I stopped thinking for myself, and other thoughts became pretty attractive in filling the void, especially when all of them were equally meaningless. I had only one driving passion outside my work, and that was women's rights. I made contact with almost all of the community groups at one time or another and got involved with rape, domestic violence, housing, divorce, lesbian child-rearing, single parenting, minority discrimination, chemical dependency, education, and the professions and job training. It felt good, Lady Di; I busied both hemispheres.

I should be working on my speech. It really won't be much different than speeches I've given in the past. Let's see:

"My name is Carolyn Anderson, and I want to stress the importance of giving money to support Georgia Poseta's defense."

Is that fiery enough? Well, maybe I have to build a fire slowly.

"Georgia Poseta has tirelessly stood up and spoken out for women; now she needs you to stand up and speak out for her."

Well, does that make sense? Certainly she needs us to help her. But are we obligated to help her? No, but she wasn't obligated to help us, either. Maybe the question is the extent to which we're helping her. It's true she deserves to be represented. But she is represented. What are we doing, then? Well, we're contributing time, energy, and money. But does that imply something about her innocence or guilt? Better press on, despite dubious logic.

"Georgia has been charged with first-degree assault for the simple reason that she defended herself. She didn't submit to Clifford Hawkins's intentions; she didn't succumb to the pressures of the passive role her society has forced upon her and all women. She resisted. She did what any man would be expected to do, what any man would be castigated for not doing."

"Castigated" may be too much. "Scorned" is better, though Stephanie did say I'm supposed to appeal to the intellectuals. But that's good; I worked in that passive-role stuff.

"Georgia shot her landlord while he was in her apartment. *Her* apartment. She acted outside the bounds of approved conduct for a woman, and now she is being punished for it. We cannot let this happen. Georgia represents all of us. If she goes down, we all go down. How many of us will feel safe, knowing that to defend ourselves means risking imprisonment? Is that the choice we face: being raped and beaten, or being imprisoned?"

Oh, gosh, Carolyn, that's not really the choice we face, is it? It's not been established that Georgia was defending herself. Or is that a given? Jesus, maybe I'm being too literal. This is a rabble-rousing speech, after all, not a thesis.

Which reminds me that I ought to be spending my time preparing my journal article. I can now rotate the helium in three different ways, all within a 1.2° temperature range, and produce the vortices, only at certain levels. But I can also estimate the kinetic energy of the vortex lines. Nothing remarkable, but it will make the article.

Still, it's tempting to scrap that and hook up another apparatus, push the helium through a mixed-torque rotation, and keep the temp at 0.8°. Then I can trap the Helium II while the other spills out. But we're talking about bucking most of the superfluid procedures of the past fifteen years, delaying the article indefinitely, insulting Dr. Stan, and possibly making a jerk of myself. Ah, the temptation of greatness, Di. If only these vortices knew how they affected my life. I'm so close to trading that professional security for finding out what causes the little fuckers.

It's crazy hallucination time. I must have dozed off to Escape City. But I have this recollection of Marie Curie, straight out of a textbook—white lab coat, wisdom-lined face, granny glasses. Only the face wasn't Marie Curie's; it was my father's. And the figure was standing in front of my helium and tut-tutting. "What's wrong?" I asked. "Tell me what's wrong." But the figure just kept gazing at my equipment, head shaking, disapproving.

There's got to be something about the temperature levels, something I'm not seeing, or part of me isn't seeing. I've watched the vortices until I see them in my food, in the pattern of my sweater, in my lover's eyes. Why do they whirl only at certain temperatures?

Oh, maybe I should plot out my speech first. General. I can't keep it general, damn it. I've got to find out more about Georgia. Stephanie said she shot Hawkins in the bathroom, which doesn't make sense, because who keeps a gun in the bathroom? But one newspaper report had her shooting him in the living room. Does it make a difference? No; he still burst in on her. She was still defending herself.

Maybe some pathos:

"I'm asking you today—all of you—to give, just a little. Court expenses are high. We can't lose this because of a lack of money. Give of yourself." Oh, shit, that makes me sound like Jerry Lewis.

I wonder if I should tell them who I am, or will Stephanie do that? Why should they listen to me, anyway? I know about physics; how does that qualify me to speak? If I were a lawyer, perhaps; but I don't know anything about this.

The PhD worked magic in some of the counseling groups I joined. I liked the respect—I earned my doctorate—but the dynamics of the group sometimes got to be a little silly.

Group Member 1: "She's just so cheap, I can't take it anymore! You know what she started doing? Reusing toothpaste! Have any of you ever had a lover so cheap? She brushes her teeth in the morning, spits the toothpaste into a cup, then in the evening she dips her toothbrush into it and uses it again! Is that cheap?"

Group Member 2: "That's gross."

Group Member 1: "It's not as if she doesn't make enough money to live on; she's just insecure. She doesn't buy clothes, she won't go out to eat, she won't take a vacation, she won't put the heat on even if it's freezing, she cuts her own hair. I'm afraid I'll catch her one day wringing out tampons!"

Group Member 2: "Oh, that's really awful."

Carolyn: "On the other hand, she's not harming anyone."

Group Member 1: "That's true; I suppose I could learn to live with her. She has other qualities."

Group Member 2: "People are too materialistic, anyway."

Carolyn-the-Expert-on-Everything. My ego was not so downtrodden that I required blank-check bolstering, so I switched groups a lot.

"THE TRUTH ABOUT MARGE," OR "FOR BENNETT OR WORSE"

I had lunch with Joe Bennett. We grabbed hot dogs and walked around campus eating them. It was pleasant; he never mentions the party, my coming-out party. I could almost convince myself it never happened. Except I do dread the day I pass a bookstore and see *My Dog's Pot*, by Harold Sellers.

Joe's too busy worrying about his wife these days to psychoanalyze his lesbian colleague. We talked a little about my vortices, Joe now suggesting I set up a different analysis to break down the vortex schedules, as long as I "remember the article, Carolyn; that comes first." Then neither of us said anything. I decided I might as well bring up the subject of Marge; that was obviously why he suggested the lunch. Therapist Carolyn.

"She's got a date tonight," he said; he didn't look at me while we walked, but checked around in case someone we knew might be eavesdropping.

"Where are they going?" I asked.

"His place. Dinner."

"Well, Joe, maybe that's all it will be."

"Marge said not to wait up. I'm just glad we don't have kids."

We passed the tennis courts. It was such a beautiful day, I really was having a hard time being serious. Brisk weather reminds me of Minnesota.

"Well, it'll all be over by the morning," I said, hoping that didn't sound too unfeeling. A boy was chasing a girl across the grass, and he slipped and fell on his face. I laughed.

Joe misinterpreted. "It may be funny to you, Carolyn. Your lifestyle is different from mine. Marge and I come from strong traditional backgrounds, where marriage vows mean something, where fidelity means something." He shook his head. "The guy sounds like such a jerk, too. Why couldn't he have at least been a professor? That I could understand, someone intelligent. But some bozo from her mechanics class..."

"She's talked about him?" I asked, trying to get back into the flow of the conversation.

"Talked about him? She derives pleasure from teasing me about him. 'He's so virile.' 'He's so'—what did she say—'animalistic.' Animalistic. Animalistic, my ass. Brawn over brains, Carolyn; it's a sad state of affairs."

Poor Joe. He wasn't an Adonis, but he had nothing to be ashamed of. Marge obviously knew where to hurt him.

"The asshole's even got a damned tattoo," he said. "Can you believe that? A tattoo."

We walked on. No, I thought, it was highly unlikely. I watched an old man feed birds from his lunch. Symbiotic.

"What kind of tattoo, Joe?"

"You wouldn't believe it."

"An anchor?"

We stopped, and Joe looked at me. The wind was blowing his hair off his forehead, revealing worry lines.

"Yeah, an anchor. Is that funny?" I was trying, unsuccessfully, to hold a smile in, which must have given my lips a peculiar curl.

"Is his name Stewart, by any chance?" I asked.

"Yeah," said Joe. "You know this guy? Is he some kind of stud or something? Carolyn, what is so funny? Why are you laughing? Carolyn, stop laughing!"

Neal Starkman

A letter from my father today, in addition to a post card from my mother. The post card was a photograph of a tree somewhere in St. Cloud. On the reverse side was a recapitulation of the triviality of the month. This month's episode related the incident of the "Neighbor Whose TV Blew Up in the Middle of the Night." She always leaves out some important bit of information, though, usually the part that would make the message sensible. Drives me batty.

My father's letters come every three or four months. He wants to know if there's anything I need, follows that up with a little spiritual piety, and spends the rest of the letter talking about the latest moral crisis he's had to endure.

Today's letter was about Estelle Carson, wife of the dentist I used to see as a kid. Dr. Carson died three months ago, and now Estelle is in a bad way. My father tried to comfort her, even got her a job working in a florist's. But apparently Estelle has been badgering my father about why the good Lord saw fit to take Dr. Carson away. "I told her," wrote my father, "that maybe the Lord wanted her to learn more about herself. Ed had done what he could do while he was here—helping children have strong teeth—and now maybe it was her turn to do something, and she should pray to Jesus Christ for guidance. I know you're always interested in what women do, Carrie, so that's why I'm telling you. See, your Pop's become a Women's Libber."

Someone should tell my feminist Pop what a waste of Estelle Carson's life it was to exist in the shadow of her husband all these years, and how pathetic it is that she has to wait till her husband dies before she can do something worthwhile. She's probably never done anything by herself before.

I walked around Green Lake today with Marcie. The weather was what most people think Seattle weather is like all the time: gray, misty, raw. But the walk was fine. Marcie quit her job, but she doesn't seem too concerned about it. Unemployment insurance helps, and now she can start thinking seriously about being a counselor. I can't quite see Marcie as a counselor, though. I think counselors should have to put gauze over their personalities, and I'm not sure Marcie could do that. She's too Procrustean; she'd interpret all women's problems as basically the same. Maybe they are.

Green Lake is nice to walk because you don't have to think about where you're going. It's 2.8 miles around, well under an hour, and you get to see ducks and loons and rude geese and clumsy swans, skaters and joggers and all kinds of people, including some nice bodies. There have been times when I've gotten angry at the bicyclists who use the walking lane, but I can control the anger if I concentrate on something else. Today we talked about the rally and Georgia Poseta, and I barely noticed the bicyclists.

"Do you know about the arguments?" Marcie asked me as we huffed along.

"What arguments?" I'd been avid for any information, but not much could be substantiated outside the newspaper and TV accounts. The landlord, Clifford Hawkins, was shot twice in the stomach at about 4:35 p.m., October 22. Police were summoned to the scene by Georgia Poseta, who claimed to have shot him in self-defense after he let himself into her apartment and attacked her while she was taking a shower. According to Georgia, they struggled, she fled into the living room where she kept her gun, and she threatened to shoot him. He laughed and lunged for her, and she shot him and called the police. Georgia told the police that her landlord had been harassing her for months and once threatened to "show her what a real man was like."

According to Hawkins, still in the hospital, he came to the apartment to make some repairs in the kitchen. He knocked, but no one answered, so he let himself in with his master key. On the way to the kitchen, passing the bathroom, he heard the shower running and started to leave. He must have banged into something, he said, because Georgia then heard him, came out of the bathroom, and started to scream and kick him. She wasn't wearing any clothes. Hawkins claims he stumbled against the wall, and she ran into the living room. When he got up to leave, she screamed at him again and shot him.

Hawkins apparently had some tools with him, though Georgia denies there was anything in the kitchen that required fixing. On Georgia's side, Hawkins had a reputation as being something of a pig, his views of feminism the other side of Phyllis Schlafly.

"They'd argued the day before about something or other," Marcie was saying. "One of the neighbors heard them."

"What were they arguing about?"

Marcie shrugged. "Don't know. Just heard it through the grapevine."

"Isn't there anything coming out that can be verified?" I complained. "Maybe they were arguing about a leaky kitchen faucet. That doesn't help at all."

"Wait for the trial," she said, looking back to smile at a young child bouncing in the backpack of a jogging mother. It dawned on me that we were walking in the opposite direction from everyone else. "I also heard the gun wasn't registered," she continued. "Probably some propaganda from the prosecutor's office."

"I doubt that's relevant, anyway. Marcie, what do you think about all of this?"

I respect Marcie's opinions, because she's thoughtful and intelligent, but I temper them, because I know she's coming from an anti-male philosophical bent that I can't wholly accept. She's a good attitude vane, though; and her thoughts often stimulate mine.

"She had a right to protect herself, Carolyn. That is simply without question. He could have threatened her with anything—a screwdriver, his fists. I'm glad she shot him. There have been too many cases of landlords, lovers, and ex-husbands and -boyfriends barging into women's apartments and women being caught without any recourse. Maybe this will be a test case. I hope so."

"But what if he did come in by accident?"

"Carolyn, do you think it was an accident? Come on."

"No, I suppose not."

And that was true. I suppose that Clifford Hawkins had nasties on his mind, that he did threaten Georgia, that he didn't believe she would shoot him, that he's plotting right now in the hospital bed how to get even with her. And regardless of what I suppose, Georgia deserves the best defense, and there's no reason I shouldn't help raise money for her.

So what's the problem, Di?

Evening quietude. Enwombed in high-back stuffed chair. Thoughtless thinking, my brain a closed circuit.

"What's the problem, sweet?"

Stephanie is gathering materials together like Lois Lane on a hot scoop. She has her coat half on, and a slice of toast is clenched between her teeth. Oddly, she's been jumping less these days, just when you'd think she'd need to most.

"No problem, just thinking."

"Writing your speech?"

"No, I've already got a good idea of what I'm going to say."

"I lined up Jessie Marks from NOW. She's flying in tomorrow and staying with us tomorrow night."

"Good, that'll be a help."

"Writing in your diary?"

"Some."

"Carrie, is something bothering you?"

"Yes. I'm getting headaches again. And I'm anxious. I feel like my head's on a turntable and my extremities in a sauna. My organs move around inside me, and I want to cry for no reason. My period's early, I have occasional trouble hearing, my mouth is dry, causing my lips to chap, and I f-find that I've developed a tendency to s-stutter. I have no appetite, and, strangely enough, I either blink too rapidly or not at all. There's a hideous green spot on my arm, and I always seem to hear my heart pounding. Sometimes, just sometimes, my limbs don't obey my commands. In sum, I feel like my whole body is getting a d & c."

"Poor Carolyn. Listen, I have to run. Meeting on Capitol Hill. See you before eleven. Maybe not. I'll call."

Stephanie is solace. Like Philip, she steadies me, grounds me, maybe even pulls me along in the direction she's going. Maybe I'm a hitchhiker on the road of life, Lady Di, forever drawn and expelled. How does one cope? Philip said he never boycotted anything because everything was bad, and if he was entirely principled, he'd starve. So you have to choose your sellout points. A publication, a job, one hopes not a life.

Bullshit. Stephanie never has these problems. She always knows what to say, what to do, what to think, always has her finger on what's right for her. How the hell does she do that? How do you get to know yourself that well?

She was the most interesting person I'd met in years. So different. Big family, Catholic, Third World—sort of—urban background, avowed lesbian, activist, laborer, nonintellectual, tall, dark, and handsome. She was my antimatter, with fascinating properties and exotic origins.

Even the sex was different. She was so damned confident. It wasn't that she was a gymnast, nothing like that; it wasn't even that she was exuberant like Shelly. She just had so much experience making love, and making love well. She could gauge my mood and offer me something that would complement it exactly, uncannily—fervid, consoling, playful, serene, and more, with mixtures thereof. It was like programming what I wanted before going to bed. Usually it takes months, even years, to arrive at that compatibility. It's a testament to how perceptive she really is about people.

This summer, she and I went out for dinner one evening, very nice place, my choice and treat. We got all dolled up, she in an intensely mauve suit I'd bought her the first Christmas we'd been together, and I in a beige cotton-silk skirt-suit. Boots for me, and a little jewelry, even a little perfume. We knocked each other out getting dressed, fancy half-slips, my hair recently cut, hers recently trimmed, the works. It was difficult to leave the house.

Well, we had just started in on our meal. I remember glancing up from my soup and catching Stephanie smiling to herself.

"What are *you* thinking about? Though I can guess."

Stephanie broadened her smile and shook her head. "Tell you later."

"Oh, come on. Tell me now."

She shook her head again. "Can't."

"Whisper." I leaned forward.

"Okay," she said in a whisper, "but keep looking at me. Don't turn, okay?"

"All right."

"There's a woman, three tables to your left, sitting with a guy. She's wearing a green dress, lot of jewelry. Brown hair, no lipstick, nice body. Maybe thirty-five."

"You know her?"

"Nope." Smiles again.

"Well, what about her?"

Neal Starkman

Stephanie tasted her soup, grimaced, and sighed. "Well, Carrie, if she could have whatever she wanted right now, you'd be spread-eagled right next to that bottle of wine they're drinking."

Naturally, I turned to the table and, sure enough, there was this attractive woman talking to her companion, also pretty nice-looking, and as I watched her she put a fork of something or other in her mouth, turned my way, and gave me a courteous smile, at which point I whipped my head back to Stephanie.

"I told you not to look," she said.

"Oh, come on, she's with somebody. She's straight as a curtain rod."

"Whatever you say, Carrie. You know best." And Steph returned to her soup.

"All she did was smile at me. How can you jump to such a conclusion?"

"You're probably right."

"I mean, you must have some reason for thinking that. Is there some secret lesbian gesture that I haven't been let in on yet?"

Stephanie, mauve and bronze aggressive beauty, put down her spoon and looked at me. "I can smell a woman in heat."

"Oh, Jesus. Let's not be crude in such a fancy place. At least wait until we get in the car."

"This soup is weird."

"I like it. It's watercress. A smile means absolutely nothing."

"Carrie, have it your way, if it'll make you feel more comfortable. I mean, God knows you're a veteran of the gay community; you must be able to pick up on these things by now. I'm sure you're right. It was just a smile, and smiles mean absolutely nothing."

"Absolutely."

But an hour later, when I emerged from the stall of the women's room and Ms. Woman-in-Heat propositioned me on the spot, I amended my theory of the significance of a smile.

"Uh, no, thank you. I'm with someone."

"Are you sure?" I swear, Di, she licked her lips. A souffle of sophistication in the dining room, she had transformed herself into wanton soup. How did she even know I was gay?

"No, thank you. Really. I appreciate it. Really."

"Call me?"

I rushed back to my lover before my new acquaintance could write out her phone number, or cop a feel, or whatever it was she was planning to do.

"I thought only men did that," I said, as I lifted an empty cup of tea to my mouth.

"Welcome to the real world, honey."

Tomorrow is Friday, and tomorrow's tomorrow is Saturday. I feel like taking a walk, Lady Di, but I feel more like writing to you. Let's be methodical about this. Let's set down all the influences that could be the source of my anxiety.

No, that's not sound strategy now. Let me instead watch some TV and think about class tomorrow and hope the weekend passes quickly. I have the distinct feeling that by the end of the rally, or soon thereafter, my anxiety will be gone.

Neal Starkman

My hands are not yet steady, but I need to write this down. An awful thing happened after class this morning, an incident that was so uncalled-for, so unexpected, that I lost control. Di, I totally lost control. Unprecedented.

James Andrews—the student who winked at me some time ago—approached me after class and asked me out. I was packing up my books and papers—everyone else had left the room—and he stood before my desk, grinned, and asked me to dinner.

"Not necessarily tonight, or even this weekend," he added nonchalantly. "I realize you must have other commitments."

I tried to look preoccupied, said thanks, but I never go out with my students; this is true.

"If I wasn't your student, then you would go out with me?" he asked, with an inflection that was not so much boyish as pure cock and strut.

"Well, I don't think so," I said, smiling, being nice. "I think I'm a little old for you."

Some people get the hint; others you have to paste onto their eyeballs.

"I'm sure you're not," he said, moving closer to me, still grinning, eyes steady on me. The desk was still between us, but now his fingers were playing over it. "Why not give it a try?"

"Mr. Andrews—"

"James. Jim."

"Mr. Andrews, I'm very flattered, but I'm living with someone, who is my lover, and we don't go out with other people. But thank you for the invitation."

"You don't like men, do you?"

That was a shock. He hadn't changed his tone; it was as if he had planned to say that all along, which lent an air of manipulation to the conversation that hadn't been there before. I like to think that my sexual orientation doesn't show in class, that I treat my male students the same as my female students, though I'm aware of my position as a role model for the latter. But who knows how people find things out about you. Maybe Joe Bennett scratched it into the wall above a urinal.

"What do you mean by that?" I asked, hoping my eyes looked cold and steady.

"You don't like men. I can tell."

"Just because I don't want to have dinner with you, you infer I don't like men. That's pretty egotistical, if you ask me, Mr. Andrews."

He shrugged. "It's not only that. I expected you to say no."

He grinned again, and I'd had enough. "Mr. Andrews, I'm leaving now. It's been engaging."

"Have you ever been raped?"

"What?" He stood between me and the door, though the door was open and there were plenty of people in the hallway. But I was scared. That fear that seems always to be inside me rushed up and out my throat, stared me in the face, and plummeted back inside. He could overpower me, hurt me, even kill me, I thought. He could even be the Fife rapist. And once I gave it reentry, the fear ransacked my insides. He could have a gun, a knife, force me to lock the door. He could make me do anything to him. He knows where I live, he could follow me home, surprise me in bed, kill Stephanie. Maybe he's already killed Stephanie. He's so much bigger and stronger than me, and he knows he has the power and the control. I started to shake. I felt my body go cold.

"I always thought lesbians were raped in childhood, or at least adolescence," he was saying, "and that's why they're turned off by men.

Neal Starkman

You know, a dirty old uncle, a brutal first love," he chuckled. "You're a pretty good looker, so I know it's not 'cause you can't get any men. Maybe I can help you, know what I mean? Why don't you let me take you out to dinner?" He winked. "My treat."

The words took meaning in my brain, and my irrational thoughts disappeared once I understood what he was telling me. And then the fear, too, disappeared, and it was replaced by an overwhelming, consuming anger. Here we were, two human beings, yet I was made to feel afraid merely by his presence, his attitude. I hated him. I hated him for his presumption, his ego, his swagger, his damned existence in my world. I wanted to kill him. I wanted to kill all the men who make women cower, who cause them to carry the fear around with them like a perpetually unborn child. I wanted him to give me an excuse to kill him. He was no longer a person to me; he was a symbol, a leering symbol of everything I had struggled against. I wanted to make him suffer.

My voice was controlled, but that was the most effort I've ever had to exert control over it. I fancied it was like a laser cutting through diamond, a sharp, incisive, final voice that could kill without hesitation or remorse.

"Mr. Andrews," I said, fixing him to the spot like a pin to a butterfly, "it is none of your damned business what my sexual experiences have been. Nor do I grant you the right to ask me about them, nor even think about them. Furthermore, Mr. Andrews, I know you. I know you very well. You're one of those 'boys' who think you can make women come at the drop of your pants and convert every gay woman into your concubine. It's a fantasy, Mr. Andrews, a fantasy borne out of insecurity and no doubt extreme sexual incompetence. I would like to see you try something with me. I want you to. Right here! Close the door! Close it and come back here and try to kiss me or fondle me! Try to unbutton my blouse!" My voice began to quaver, and I knew I was shouting, but I didn't care. I just didn't care anymore. The control was unimportant.

"You and me, Mr. Andrews! Isn't that what you want? Right here, let's go! Have you ever heard of the term 'emasculating woman'? I'll show you what that means, Mr. Andrews! I'll tear that two-inch prick of yours out from its roots if I have to use tweezers to do it! Come on, Mr. Andrews, what happened? You don't seem so ready anymore! Can't get it up? You cock-heavy asshole bastard! You damned frigging man-bastard! Why don't you go fuck yourself and then overcompensate with some 'girl' who'll fake an orgasm for you! Damn you! Damn you!"

I was shaking so hard by this time that I had to steady myself on the desk, and he was still there, he was still fouling my universe, not smiling anymore, but still so *there*. I didn't know what to do with my anger; the screaming, the words only intensified it. He hadn't disappeared, he hadn't been humiliated enough. I wanted the words to stab him, hurt him, and they hadn't. I felt my throat constrict, my tongue collect saliva from the upper part of my mouth, my lungs fill with air, and then I spat at him. I spat full force directly into his face, and I yelled as I did it. I wished it had been acid. He gasped, his eyes voluminous, the drool half stuck on his cheek and side of his nose where it splatted, dripping off his face to the floor. I grabbed the chair with both hands. He didn't even wipe away the spit but turned and fled from the room.

I must have stood there for several minutes, trembling. So this is what rage is, I thought; and as soon as I thought that, I knew I was back in control, examining my feelings again.

I looked around me. I was in my classroom. Of course. In a classroom in a building in a city. Some faces peered into the room by the door, then removed themselves. I was back in my room. But for a minute I'd been in another world. All I could see was that grinning, swaggering boy, so sure of himself, so damned cocksure of himself, standing there like a six-foot erection, with no conscience, no sensitivity, no moral consideration of anything but the satisfaction of his own patulous ego.

Di, I hadn't suspected I could get so angry. I finally tottered over to the lab, where I am now, and tried to cry. I squeezed perhaps eleven tears out of my blues, and that was it.

Neal Starkman

I've managed to conduct my work with all that hate inside me. Amazing. While my conscious has monitored the gauges and valves and switches, my subconscious was spinning men in the air at such speeds that the centrifugal force tore their limbs from them, or plunging them into liquid nitrogen so that their blood froze upon contact, or pretending, perhaps, that men were never on this earth to begin with.

And then I found the note. It lay by my files, with a happy face on it. I hate happy faces. It was short, and written in red ink.

> *Dear Carolyn,*
>
> *I came over here to break something, to hurt you, because you hurt me. But I chickened out. I'll never forgive you for not telling me about yourself, after I burned your ears about my problems with Ray. I thought we were close enough for you to trust me. But I still want you to have good luck this year, and a good career. You deserve it.*
>
> *Mary Ann*

Ah, yes, Di, nothing like a good dose of guilt to cap off a delightful day.

Tonight, after work, I'll go see Darrel. He relaxes me. Just for an hour, and then I'll head home and meet Jessie Marks and get all motivated for tomorrow. I'll bring all my vortex notes with me and spread them all out on our dining-room table and give myself sixty minutes to see the light. If nothing clicks, then the hell with it. I'll just do enough to get an article published. Maybe it's not my lot in life to discover what makes the vortices do what they do. I can live with that, Di. So they spin; big deal. So it would be nice to know why they spin. Okay. But I've got to take care of myself. Who knows, maybe after a little disciplined observation, some mental somersaults, and help from the Aha Fairy, I'll see it all.

Times like this, it must help to be a believer.

It's well past midnight, and I should be sleeping in my bed instead of writing at my desk, but I'm racing. I could probably jump for an hour tonight. And tomorrow: I have given up pretending it's just a rally. I can't convince myself that it's only getting up and saying a few words about women. Everyone I've spoken to since this broke thinks I'm crazy when I even begin to express my concerns.

Darrel was kind; I knew he would be. He and Steven were preparing dinner when I arrived, and they scurried around the kitchen like little windup toys. Darrel could see I was upset and asked me if I wanted a drink.

"If you have any brandy, Darrel, I'd be eternally grateful."

Ten minutes and a few fiery swallows later, we were all in the living room, me in an exquisitely carved love seat out of a history-book century, Darrel and Steven on a plush burgundy couch I would probably never buy even if I could afford it. They were digging into salads, Steven occasionally asking Darrel in a whisper if he needed more pepper or another napkin or a refill on his wine. The salad looked delicious, but I had no appetite. I must have looked like hell.

"Rough times, Carolyn?"

"Well," I started, wondering where to start, "I think I may have to compromise myself by going for a publication when I should still be doing more research. Then, of course, the research I love is being ended by cutbacks in the department, and I have to do different work next year. I've been writing a journal the past few weeks, and I'm caught up in some sort of ridiculous identity crisis. I came out to someone from my childhood recently, a man friend, and he reacted with about as much excitement as if I'd told him I'd bleached my hair. Then I insulted another friend, a woman colleague, by *not* coming out to her, even though I led her to believe we were close with each other. This morning, a student accused me of being a lesbian, which of course I am, and I responded with a series of internally physiological reactions that culminated in a blistering harangue and in my actually spitting in his face."

"God," said Steven, one of the few words I'd heard him say, ever. He looked to Darrel for a reflex-check. Darrel's eyebrows were raised, but I knew he'd be supportive. It's impossible to imagine Darrel being other than supportive, tender, ingenuously caring. I can understand why Steven attaches himself to him like a mushroom to a log.

"And—" I finished with the real problem—"I'm scheduled to speak at the rally tomorrow, and I'm not sure what I should say, or even if I ought to speak at all."

"Why not, Carolyn?"

"Why not? I wish I knew. I don't know. I've been bothered for a month by headaches, anxiety, insomnia, depression, you name it. And it's all coming down to this. I know it, I feel it. Tomorrow's speech, what I say, is going to be the end of it. This...this talk I'm supposed to give, three minutes' worth, is very important. It seems to tie in with everything I've been feeling lately. Or everything I've almost been feeling. It's—It's like I can't quite get it. It's there—something—but I don't know what it is. It's probably something very trite and obvious."

"Maybe," tried Darrel, "this speech is your public declaration. The world will finally know who Carolyn Anderson is. There's no more doubt. You are Carolyn Lesbian, sexual minority! No turning back! Out of the closet! Hooray for Carolyn!"

Darrel looked so hopeful, I wished it were that easy, Di. But that wasn't it at all.

"No, no, I'm not nervous about coming out or anything. My God, Darrel, I've spoken about women and about sexual minorities in front of groups before. And last week I even came out to my colleagues in the department. No, it's not that. It might have something to do with it tangentially, but it's more than that. For some reason, I've been afraid to speak. Reluctant. I don't know why."

"You're not nervous?"

"No. I'm just...I'm not sure it's right."

"What's not right, Carolyn?"

"Speaking on behalf of Georgia Poseta, I guess."

Darrel put down his glass, and Steven got up to refill it. "Girl, you are crazy. Next to Georgia Poseta, Joan of Arc was a slut. You have to support her. Have you heard the way she's been treated in jail?"

"Oh, Darrel, what if that landlord—Hawkins—what if Hawkins is telling the truth? We don't know he's lying. What if he came in by accident, like he said, and Georgia got as mad as I was this morning and blew a hole in his stomach—two holes—without any provocation at all?"

"Carolyn."

"Oh, God, Darrel, I don't even know what I'm saying anymore. It's like I'm trying to find an out, trying to make excuses so I don't have to speak. Maybe I *am* scared."

He came over and sat beside me, started to knead my shoulders.

"You're tight."

"You should feel my brain."

"Why don't you stay with us this evening? We're getting dressed up to go trick-or-treating in a little while."

"Trick-or-treating? My God, I completely forgot it was Halloween."

"Do you want to see my costume? No, never mind, I can't show you, but it'll be great."

Neal Starkman

"What are you two going as?" I asked.

"Oh, show her," said Steven, looking lonely but attentive on the couch and beginning to giggle.

Darrel sighed dramatically, and Steven put down his salad and rushed out of the room. When he returned, he held out a large tan body suit with three legs, the middle one wider than the others. I couldn't tell what the stocking was made of, but it was obvious that two people were meant to wear it. Distinguishing the garment was a series of Asian characters seemingly tie-dyed into it, all the way down the fronts of the legs, one line on each of the outer legs and two down the middle.

"I made that myself," said Darrel. "Steven did the characters. They're authentic Mandarin."

"It's very, uh, striking," I said.

"Can you guess what it is?"

"I'm lost," I confessed.

Darrel smiled proudly, while Steven continued to display it for me.

"We're going as chopsticks."

At the door, Darrel gave me a hug. "Carolyn, it will all be over tomorrow. You'll be glad you spoke. You'll be glad you had the chance to help Georgia."

"Do you know her?"

"No, but I heard her speak a few times. Carolyn, gay people have to stick together."

"Oh, I know that, Darrel. That's what makes this so hard."

"Have you talked to Stephanie?"

"About my speech? Not really; she's been so busy. The only time we have together is at night, and then she's been really tired."

"She's working hard for this rally."

"I know, and I can't let her down, either."

"You won't."

"Tell me it'll be all right, Darrel."

"It'll be all right."

"You'll do good tomorrow," said Steven, from inside the house.

"I hope so, Steven. If not, can I live with you guys?"

Nervous laughter. Stupid joke.

Home was the proverbial hive; only the cigarette smoke would have killed off the bees. Everyone seemed like they knew what they were doing—very directed, very animated. I felt as if I could walk around naked and no one would notice. Stephanie was on the phone, Debbie and Pam were sitting at a table with two women I didn't know, and about six other women, some of whom I recognized, were standing in the living room, talking about sentencing procedures and security. A sloppy pile of M&M's packages lay near the door. The rooms were graveyards of pizza, beer, wine, cigarettes, and coffee. And paper, sheets of yellow and white paper—whole, torn, crumpled—with handwriting, diagrams, printing. So much paper. Too much paper. Paper that looked just like my notes. Paper that someone wouldn't think twice about throwing away.

Jessie Marks was a tall, spare woman with clear, deep-set eyes, long hazel hair that needed a perm, and a clipped and determined gait. She wore a suit and looked professional and tight. She carried herself well—appeared as if she considered herself attractive—and I sensed she had the compulsivity and personal force to manage people as well as programs. She noticed me and strode over, extending her hand. Her speech was as clipped as her walk.

"Jessie Marks. You must be Carolyn. Glad to meet you. Stephanie described you. This is an important rally tomorrow, Carolyn."

"Yes, I know," I said.

"What will you be saying in your speech? Stephanie mentioned you might talk about women's right to privacy."

"Yes, I might. I thought I would keep it general, maybe something about how women need to have more confidence in themselves."

"That's very important. I can see the tie-in with self-defense, too. More confidence, more belief in one's own abilities to defend oneself. Good, I like that. I understand you're a physicist."

"Yes."

"That's wonderful. I always had trouble with science. Except for political science. I wanted to take credits in the natural sciences, though—you know, biology, chemistry—because it was so nontraditional for a woman. My mother had an intuitive grasp of chemistry. She could have been a great scientist, had the opportunities only been there for her."

She spoke as I speak when I'm manic. Indeed, the thought that she was speaking normally depressed me; if she ever got nervous, I wouldn't be able to maintain my end of the conversation.

"What did you end up with, Jessie, uh, what kind of degree, I mean."

"I have an MFH—that's a master's in feminist history—from Penn. I wrote my thesis on the comparison between the dissatisfaction feminists felt with the labor movements of the 1840s and the dissatisfaction feminists felt with the, quote, revolutionary movements of the 1960s, unquote. In both cases, women were disenfranchised out of movements that hypocritically maintained they were fighting for freedoms for working people, and in both cases the women decided to strike out on their own. Fascinating dynamics."

"It sounds—"

Steph got off the phone then and came over to kiss me on the cheek. "I see you two have met. Carolyn been telling you about her helium? Ann," she yelled across the room, "talk to KVI in the morning, will you, honey? The guy's name is Craig Winchell; he'll be in at nine."

"Got it."

"Thanks." Back to us. "I'll be glad when tomorrow's over."

"You're doing an excellent job, Stephanie," said Jessie Marks. "I want to go over some publicity stratagems, however. I mentioned before the importance of expanding the focus to prevent the rally from being viewed as predominantly a lesbian affair. We want to make sure that all women see the issues, that they see how important they are to all women."

"Right. Uh, give me five minutes, okay?" Stephanie held up a hand.

Jessie looked at both of us. She did not smile. "Got all night," she said, and walked into the living room.

"How you doin', kid?" Steph asked, putting her hands on my shoulders.

"I don't know, Steph. I had a bad day today. This morning I spat at a student. On a student, actually."

"What?" Stephanie had been racing, and now she hit a speed bump. "You spit on a *student?*"

Now a few others heard, and the room became quiet, except for one of the women on the phone, checking out equipment or something. Jessie Marks came back, too.

"A guy," I said. "It wasn't anything. I just overreacted." Now I wanted to minimize it, Di. It didn't seem as significant as it had been that morning, or even when I was at Darrel's.

"I've been tense, he said some wrong words, and I blew up."

"You *spit* at him?" Stephanie repeated. "You?"

"We should call you Carolyn St. Helens from now on," yelled Pam from across the room, and everybody laughed.

"What did he say to you?" asked someone, as Steph put her arm around me.

"Oh, I'm not sure I want to talk about it. I was upset earlier, but I think I'd just as soon forget it now." I must have given such a pitiful look that everyone concluded I'd had enough headaches for one day. Or they figured they'd hear about it later. Or they were too concerned with the rally to listen to my melodrama. In any case, they turned away, some shaking their heads, one muttering, "Bastards."

Stephanie led me to a corner of the room.

"I can't believe you spit at him. I've never seen you that excited. Are you okay?"

"I'm fine."

"Hungry?" she asked.

"I'll grab something in a little while. Stephanie, I'm really in a state. I don't know if I can go on tomorrow."

Stephanie was genuinely trying to attend to me, I know that, Di, but even I could see the shards of conversation hurtling through the air, and I know she wanted to get back into the living room and intercept some of them. Her eyes couldn't focus on me.

"Carrie, you'll get over this by morning. Why don't you rest up. Take some—"

"I'm not tired. I'm...I don't know, Steph, maybe I need more convincing."

"Convincing? Of what? Oh, Carrie, look, are we in the same world? All the shit that's come down the last week, and you're not convinced that Georgia Poseta shot that scumface in self-defense? Carolyn, why are you getting so sticky all of a sudden? It's clear, clear, clear. It's a big issue. Women need to be able to protect themselves and not be thrown into prison for it. Why am I *telling* you this? You know all about it. And I know Georgia Poseta. She wouldn't use a gun unless she absolutely had to."

"Steph, *I* might have used a gun today if I'd had one." I was conscious of my voice; I think it was getting shriller.

"Carolyn Anderson, listen to me—" and Stephanie was paying full attention to me now—"Georgia Poseta needs you tomorrow. I need you. The community needs you. God damn, girl, open your eyes. She was taking a damn shower. The man let himself into her apartment. She's standing there, no clothes, no protection, no nothing, Carrie. Do you think Hawkins stayed there because he wanted to talk about a leaky faucet? Use your head. She was damned lucky she had a gun. If she didn't, Georgia might be the one in the hospital, not Hawkins."

Jessie Marks came over. "Trouble?"

"I'm just not feeling well, that's all," I said.

"From this morning?"

"From this month," said Steph, and turned to our guest. "Let's go over the layout of the park," she said, and they walked away.

I made myself a cheese sandwich and brewed a cup of tea. I laid out my notes on a corner of the table no one was using and tried to fancy helium vortices like the pirouetting elephants in *Fantasia*, but the activity—the phone ringing, the door bringing people in and letting them out, the cacophony of voices—disturbed me. I felt as if I were a visitor in my own home and things were going on without my control. It was the sensation of walking through a hurricane unscathed, and once more I thought of observing a play from the vantage point of the stage, but not being an active character, more a sentient prop.

At 10:00, some women came in with a Baskin-Robbins ice cream cake, and the group devoured it. This signaled an end to the planning, and people got their coats on and hugged and kissed everyone else good-bye, gathered up materials and papers (papers!), then left. Suddenly there were just Jessie Marks, Stephanie, and me, and it was very quiet.

"This place is a mess," I said, surveying the floor, the furniture, and even the walls.

"Let's clean tomorrow night," said Steph. "We need to get some sleep tonight."

"Breakfast on me tomorrow," said Jessie. "You pick the restaurant. It'll be a tough day. We'll probably have counter-demonstrators. People don't like women to be making speeches. The truth is hard to take."

It was then I passed by the table. "My notes. Where are my notes?" I asked, calmly at first.

"What notes?" asked Jessie, as I started to scrabble through the papers on the table.

"My notes! My vortex notes! All my work!" I yelled, tossing paper left and right.

"Take it easy, Carrie; we'll find them," said Steph. "What do they look like?"

"What do they look like? They look like notes!" I said, on my hands and knees, wading through the field of paper. "Just white lined sheets of paper with figures and words on them! Five sheets of paper! Notes, just notes! I was planning to go over them one more time! Just one more time! Half an hour, that's all! Damn! Damn! They were the notes for the article, not the old one, not the regular one, the new one, the one that was going to be the solution! They were going to solve it, the key! It was the key to those damned vortices! The descriptions! All the information is in those notes!"

I think Stephanie thought I was going to come apart at the seams, because every few minutes for the next forty minutes she would lay a hand on my shoulder and say, "Just relax, baby."

We tore the house apart, including the garbage. Jessie helped, though I'm certain she was beginning to have some doubts about my sanity. I called up Pam, and Ann, and a few others. It was useless.

"Look," said Stephanie, when we'd pawed through everything for the third time, "somebody probably took them by mistake. We'll find them later. They can't just disappear."

I was sitting on the turtle in a trance. Jessie stifled a yawn.

"It's okay," I said softly. I knew someone threw them out where I'd never find them again. I knew my time had run out. "It's okay," I repeated, as I got up and hugged Stephanie. "Thank you both for helping. It was not meant for me to know. Let's call it a night."

We set up Jessie in the guest room and went to bed, but I couldn't sleep. I thought of James Andrews—he of the spat-upon face—and of Darrel and Steven, Jessie, and Stephanie. I hadn't seen Marcie tonight, and I wondered if she knew Jessie Marks was coming and had something against NOW, not generally esteemed by radical feminists or lesbians. I thought of my whirling vortices, laughing, their secret safe for who knows how many more years. I thought of David and how calmly he would react to this. He'd shrug and say, "Well, I guess you'll just have to submit the original article." I thought of the rally and what I would say.

"Tell me a story," I asked Stephanie. She was quiet, no doubt thinking of the rally and all her responsibilities. "If you're not too sleepy."

"What kind of story?"

"Something that will make me happy." The bed was warm, and I was glad Stephanie was next to me. I felt terribly alone, nonetheless, alone and unaccountably sad. I should be supporting her now, I thought. She's the one who's worked hard all week. She's the one who's given of herself. I haven't done shit.

"Did I ever tell you the time I found out I was Filipina?"

I put my head on her stomach; it was tight and smooth, and I thought I could hear her heart beat. I rested my hand on her leg and smoothed her hair. "No."

"I was a little girl, maybe seven or eight. All the kids in school were outside playing. I was probably on the swings. Liked the swings when I was a kid. Liked to be higher than everyone, see them below me. Oh, not like, you know, to be God or anything, but I just liked it up high. And I liked to come down in a rush, too. Still do.

"Anyway, I was on the swings during recess. And there were some kids nearby, playing in the dirt. And I wasn't paying much attention to 'em; you know, they were laughing and shit like that. And one of them was saying, look at you, you're all dirty, to one of the kids; look at you, you're all dirty. And this kid—I remember this real well—this little boy, he must have seen me on the swings, he said to them, he said, I may be dirty now, but I'll never be as dirty as Stephanie. And they all laughed.

"I didn't know what was going on, what he meant by that at first, but then I looked down at my arms and legs, well, you know, when you're swinging, you don't even have to look down at your legs, they're right in front of you. And I understood what he meant, what they all meant. I *was* dirty. My skin looked like there was dirt all over it. Dirt that would never come off. And that's when I realized I was Filipina."

I didn't say anything for a few moments; then, "That's supposed to make me happy?"

"Yeah, don't you think it's important when people find out who they are?"

"But it must have been so painful! Such a little girl—"

"It was pretty bad then, I guess. But it's okay now. I'm glad that boy said that. I really am. Want to know how I found out I was a dyke?"

"Not tonight. I can't take much more happiness tonight."

"Good night, Carrie. I love you. And I'm sorry about your notes."

"'Night, Steph. Me, too."

But I sneaked away, Di, to write to you. I won't have another chance to write to you before the rally. The next time I write, it will all be over, everything—the rally, the speeches, the headaches, the indecision. I know it will.

You know, Di, it's not supposed to be like this. I'm thirty-one goddam years old, and I don't know what's going on. Am I the only one like this? Who else do I know that splits their head open trying to decide if they're this or that? It's intellectual masturbation.

Masturbation. That's what I'll do when this is finished. I'll wait until the last speech has been spoken, the last cheer cheered, the final hurrahs filtered into the air of Volunteer Park. No, I won't even wait that long. I'll wander off right after *my* speech, wander off into the art museum, head straight for the women's room, and masturbate myself into oblivion.

Carolyn the Escapist.

Carolyn the Activist.

Carolyn the Scientist.

Carolyn the Feminist.

Carolyn the Lesbian.

Neal Starkman

Carolyn the Dope.

I spill these words out, Di, and I read them and reread them and I yearn to see a pattern, some clues, anything that makes sense. I fear my last chance was on those vortex notes, what makes the vortices whirl, what makes me tick.

But let's be methodical about this. I really don't have much choice about tomorrow. I can review the case, I can talk about the right to privacy, I can discuss my general views of feminism. Shit, Carolyn, if you're exceptional enough to be a professor of physics, then you should be exceptional enough to suffer crises like this, even if you're too old to be suffering an adolescent crisis and too young to be suffering a midlife crisis. It all works out. Better to be miserable and awake than at peace and asleep.

Oh, Mom, where are you when I need you? You would know what to say: you would say nothing and everything. And I'd still be miserable, probably more miserable. Lady Di, the night I relinquished my virginity was like this. I had the feeling of moment. Something significant was about to happen, something I'd look back on with veneration. And that night I wrote some words down on a sheet of paper long since destroyed.

I was in my boyfriend's bedroom. We had just tacitly agreed to swap my hymen for our pleasure—it seemed like a fair trade on the face of it—when I excused myself to go to the bathroom. And in the bathroom, I took a notepad out of my purse—I was prepared—and put the pad out in front of me, and I wrote down, "These are Carolyn Anderson's last words as a virgin." That was all I wrote. I don't know, maybe I felt that afterward my penmanship would be different, more sophisticated or something. In any case, I forgot to make the comparison until weeks later, and by then I realized how asinine I'd been.

But that's how I feel tonight, Lady Di. I feel that once again, these are Carolyn Anderson's last words as a virgin.

Dervishes

It was a beautiful day for a rally. Still is, I suppose, but I can't see the day from in here. The lab is shielded from the tumult of the world. There's a definite serenity in here, as I sit among the inanimate objects of my profession. My own little womb, a womb of my own.

It was simple, Di, as I thought. But of course I also thought it would be complicated, and sometimes I thought it would be both simple and complicated. But it was simple, and funny, and sad. And I think I'm okay now. I think it's all going to be okay.

There was little time in the morning for talk. I woke up to Steph's gentle kiss on my cheek, though I probably could have slept through a rally in our bedroom. Steph and Jessie Marks had both showered already. I shook the dream dust from my dendrites while Stephanie paced the house and bounced contingencies off us—frenetic engineering. We drove to breakfast; I had to tell my lover her shirt was unbuttoned twice.

Jessie talked sparkles, and it was obvious that she was accustomed to this kind of thing. I was still hazy from lack of sleep—it's my fault, Di, not yours—but the tea in the restaurant picked me up. I felt strangely clearheaded, as if my mind had vacuumed itself during the night in preparation for some serious thinking. The helium weighed on me, but the assurance of an easy article was a convenient rationalization. I even thought briefly of old Mrs. Nardquist. Perhaps I should have called her, brought her with us to the rally. Her and her lover.

Jessie wore another suit, which I thought a bit out of place for a rally, but maybe that's what women wear at rallies in the East and she hadn't adapted. Stephanie and I didn't dress special, unless you count the "Free Georgia" buttons as special; it was cool out, and our jackets would have covered anything else, anyway.

"Blue sky. Good omen," staccatoed Jessie as we looked out the window of the pancake house.

"I bet we get a thousand," said Stephanie.

"You'll get a thousand," assured Jessie. Then, boosted by her own prognostication, she really went out on a limb. "You'll get three thousand."

"You think so?" said Stephanie. "I hope so. God, I hope Ann remembered to call KVI. Oh, shit, and Maureen said she might need a ride. I've got to call." And she bounced up and away from the table.

"Steph's a mess," I said to make conversation.

"My man-friend is like that," replied our guest. "He's always agitated before an important event. Still, he does a competent job. So does Stephanie. If all women devoted a tenth as much energy to the struggle as she has, we'd all be in better shape."

"I belong to a women's caucus at the university," I said, then immediately realized how defensive that sounded. Too late, I thought, and continued. "It's necessary to make matriculating women aware of the services available to them on campus. Plus there's a lot of internal procedures that need reform."

"That's important work, Carolyn. You must devote a lot of energy to it." Jessie smiled, making me feel like a ninny. Is that what I've come to, I thought, begging for compliments from a professional feminist who thinks everything is "important"? The small-time Seattle activist sitting up for a bone from Ms. NOW. What a picture. I switched the conversation to security.

"You don't think there'll be any trouble, do you?"

"You never know," said Jessie sagely. "There are people who don't like women to step out of their role. It scares them. That's the reason I wanted to stress that this is a struggle for all women, not only lesbian women. That was the understanding we had before the main organization sent me out. The last thing we want at this point is to disenfranchise anybody."

It struck me that Ms. Marks was being rather defensive herself about the gay issue. Was that her thing or NOW's?

Stephanie came back to the table, but her mind was already in Volunteer Park.

"I'm ready," she announced.

"Plenty of time," I said. "It's only ten-fifteen."

"Yeah, but I've got a million things to check. And we're supposed to pick up Maureen Wilson, and I told her we're on the way." Stephanie had her coat on, and it was evident she was leading the parade.

Maureen Wilson, vice-chair of Capitol Hill Tenants, was a fat, feisty woman who wore her curly hair too short for her shape. I decided I liked her when I noticed her give a quarter-frown at first sight of Jessie's suit. She carried a clipboard and pad with her. One of her tennis shoes had a hole in it. A green sock poked through the hole. Wonderful.

Maureen lived only a mile from the park; we drove in and Stephanie parked, then jumped out to do her million things: check security with the male uniforms who met us at the car; walk out to the stage to set up microphones; meet with the dozen or so women already there. Maureen, Jessie, and I held ourselves in limbo.

The area for the rally was a large green expanse, maybe seventy-five yards by fifty. At the head of the expanse was a slightly raised stage of concrete, with walls behind and on the sides about six feet high. At the foot of the expanse was the parking strip leading to the Seattle Art Museum, maybe another seventy-five yards away. To your right as you faced the stage were evergreens, thick and secretive, and to your left was a fenced-in reservoir. The air was cool, the sky clear, the wind calm.

The museum had opened at ten, and people lazily walked there and back, but you could tell our crowd from the museum-goers. Even as I watched, our people began to gather in groups of two, three, four, more driving in, walking in, recognizing and hugging each other, hiking up to the stage to offer assistance, or just lolling about. As my excitement grew, I mentioned as such to the woman at my side, who I'd thought was Maureen but turned out to be Jessie.

"I still get excited," she said. "History in the making, Carolyn. Years from now we'll look back on this. Be proud. Just like Seneca Falls, in 1848. This is where it happens. All over the country, women are gathering in rallies like this. This is where it means something."

I walked over to where Stephanie was talking with Maureen and a few other people. She was directing them. I was proud of her, almost possessively proud. My lover was doing all this. I whispered in her ear, "Can I see you for a second?" A minute later she turned to me, not distracted, but with a light in her eyes that said, "Baby, am I having fun!"

I led her behind the wall of the stage and gave her a big, long hug. "Stephanie," I said, still holding her, "I love you. No matter what happens today, I really love you."

We looked at each other, and she appeared mildly surprised. "Thanks, honey," she said, pecked me on the mouth, and went back to work. When she left, I put a hand to my eyes and discovered they were wet.

I tried to do something to become part of the group that was part of the rally that was part of the struggle. But there was really nothing to do; Stephanie had organized well. I searched for people who would have important things to say to other people.

In the course of an hour, I saw most of our friends, Marcie and Deb and Pam among them. I looked in vain for Susan/Stewart, having extracted a promise from Marcie to point her/him out to me. I didn't expect to see anyone from physics, though I hoped my caucus was well represented. I bumped into Junior and asked her if she'd seen Barbara, but she hadn't.

Darrel and Steven came in the midst of a fifteen-man contingent that later swelled to over fifty. They held aloft a banner proclaiming, "Gay Men for Gay Rights." And all around I began to notice the other groups, some with banners, some with signs, some well-dressed, some outrageously dressed—lesbian women, militant women, radical feminists, separatists, gay men, male bisexuals, female bisexuals, Capitol Hill tenants, other tenants, socialists, communists, straight men, straight women, Filipinas, other women and men of color, the transgendered, s-m's, b & d's, intellectuals, addicts of many types, students, curiosity-seekers—a veritable potpourri, I'm sure, of the oppressed and repressed. The publicity had been comprehensive. And it was a nice day.

At about eleven-thirty, some of the groups started chanting; the chants would be picked up by another group, then another, as the crowd began to assemble. "Women's rights now" was one chant. "We're gay and we're proud and we'll say it out loud" was another. People were revving themselves up, acting as mutual catalysts, constructing a crescendo.

I wandered through and between the various groups, trying simultaneously to assimilate the feeling of the crowd and to localize a feeling that this was not new to me. There was something about this whole scene that I knew I'd encountered before. It wasn't a typical déjà vu; perhaps it was a déjà vu once removed. I didn't think I'd been through a rally like this before, certainly not this big; but this rally reminded me of something I'd previously experienced.

The feeling wasn't yet nagging, and I tried to push it away by getting involved in bits of conversations of the sundry enclaves of people in the crowd: discussions of clothes, of work-related incidents, of movies, of restaurants. I heard one discussion about someone's disinclination to spend Thanksgiving with the folks and another exchange about the primaries and how fortunate we were to be rid of Governor Dixy Lee Ray. There was talk of the Fife rapist and why no one seemed to be doing anything about it, but that if someone were raping men, he'd be caught within twenty-four hours. There were Halloween anecdotes and jokes, of course; some were speculating on whether and when St. Helens would blow again; some were relating toxic-shock syndrome stories.

No one was talking about Georgia Poseta.

Twenty yards away, Stephanie was being interviewed by a TV reporter. Maureen caught my eye and trundled over.

"Have you seen my group?" she asked.

"Capitol Hill Tenants?" I said. "I think I have. They're—" I pointed vaguely—"over there somewhere."

"Good," she said, and made no move to join them. "We need a strong showing. This is an issue we've needed to speak out on for a long time."

I took a stab. "Privacy?"

"Tenant privacy. Tenants have as much right to privacy as homeowners. But we took a poll last year that showed that most people think it's perfectly all right for landlords to have master keys. That's what we've got to change, that attitude that a landlord can do whatever he wants. That's what this is all about. It's too bad someone had to get shot to get the issue into the public eye."

I talked with Maureen for a while longer, but I don't remember precisely what we said, though the subject of our conversation continued to be tenant rights and plights.

My feeling returned with a vengeance. It grew with the size and the intensity of the crowd. I stood there, near the stage, attempting to summon up thinking energy, for now the feeling was too persistent. I had to think it out. Soon I would also have to review my speech.

"Carolyn!" It was Ann. "Carolyn, here's the schedule. Stephanie, Jessie, then Midge Fielding, then Maureen, then Carl Praling from Dorian, then Reynaldo Garcia from the Filipino liberty organization—it's a foreign name, I can't pronounce it. Okay, then there's Sid Feinstein from WCLU, then you. You follow, uh..." She tried to locate Sid Feinstein, but the crowd was too thick.

"I'll hear the announcement," I said. "Don't worry."

Dervishes

"Okay. Good luck, Carolyn. Remember: speak slowly; there's a feedback echo. And don't let the cameras bother you." She let out an excited smile, pinched my arm, and disappeared again into the crowd. More media had shown up: mini-cams, reporters with notebooks, the numbers 7 and 11 and 4 and 5 identifying their allegiances.

The chants began to dominate; there were smiles and laughter everywhere, but also faces of concern and confusion. Many people were standing up, the ground cold, but some groups had brought lunches, and they had set out blankets for themselves. Many people were clapping their hands rhythmically, others were singing. I stood in front of the stage and gazed out at the hundreds and hundreds of people on the lawn; it was as if a large, rough quilt had been laid over a green bed sheet. Soon, I thought, they would cease to be a crowd of small groups; they would congeal into one great single-purposed group, if the speeches were successful.

I hadn't considered my speech since the night before. I was past worrying about it. Why was that, I thought. Perhaps I just didn't care about it; perhaps I would trust my own spontaneity.

The screech of a microphone clearing its electrical throat signaled that the rally was going to begin in earnest, and the crowd cheered. And that almost drowned out the "Testing, testing, one, two, three" of the woman who was in charge of the equipment. I looked around and saw police officers near the stage, mostly men.

But now Stephanie was standing by the microphone, shielding it with her hand while she talked to someone behind her, paper in her other hand, probably her speech. There were chairs set up on the stage, and people sat in them, and I wondered if I was supposed to be up there, too. Some chairs were empty.

I decided to walk to the other end of the green to see how the people on stage appeared from far away. So I had my back to Stephanie when she started to speak.

Neal Starkman

"Sisters!" There was loud applause and cheers at that, and for the first time I considered whether Stephanie had ever spoken before a group like this. Funny, I'd not even thought to ask.

"Sisters and all our friends from the Seattle communities. My name is Stephanie Marillo." More applause for my popular lover. "I'm not going to say much. I'll let the speakers behind me do that." So I *was* supposed to be up there.

"We're here today to support one of our own, Georgia Poseta." More cheers. I passed two women and a cute little girl not more than a year old, wrapped in a red jumpsuit, blonde curls peeking out of the hood. The women were clapping the little girl's mittened hands together, and she was laughing. I walked more slowly toward the rear.

"For you people who've been on the moon the past week, let me fill you in on what happened to Georgia Poseta, something that could happen to any of us. Ten days ago, Wednesday afternoon, Georgia was taking a shower in her apartment on Capitol Hill when she thought she heard a noise. She shut off the shower, grabbed a towel to cover herself, and went to investigate. She found her landlord in her apartment. He'd let himself in with his own key and was now standing there, grinning like an ape, while Georgia was completely defenseless. Georgia demanded that he leave, and he refused. There was a scuffle, and Georgia rushed to her desk, where she kept a gun she hoped she'd never have to use. She reached into the desk drawer, pointed the gun at her landlord, and again told him to leave. He threatened her, and she shot him in the stomach. Maybe she should have aimed lower."

Laughter at this. The groups began to look similar, as if their act of attending to a common stimulus gave them the same appearance, tanners on a beach of sound. I was seeing them but starting to think of another place, another time, and I felt the muscles in my throat tighten and my legs experience a sudden chill.

"When she called the police, Georgia expected them to take her landlord to the hospital and then to jail. Instead, they took *her* to jail, where they charged her with deadly assault." Boos at that, smiling boos. "She remains in jail today, with an unheard-of $25,000 bail. That is one of the reasons we are here today, to help raise money to get Georgia Poseta out of jail. Because, my sisters, this is what happens to women today who try to defend themselves."

More cheers. Cheers that were, after all, merely vibrations in the air striking one's eardrums, bounding around in the ear, making little hair cells twitch and turn. Maybe there are quantized vortices in the ear, too.

I continued walking to the rear, the crowd thinning out. Here was a middle-aged woman with long gray hair in a tweed suit and sunglasses, inspecting the rally from a distance; here was an overweight bearded man in a motorcycle jacket, inspecting the women from a distance; here were a Japanese man and woman, not certain if they wanted to join the rally or observe it. I was far from the stage, but I could still hear Stephanie, my lover, quite clearly. Quite clearly.

"The first speaker you'll be hearing today is Jessie Marks, from the National Organization for Women." Scattered hisses? "NOW thinks this case is very important, so important they sent Jessie out here with a little check she'll tell us about."

The crowd was getting used to the cadence of applause now. Like the waves, every seventh break seemed greater than the six preceding it.

"This is a time for fighting back," Stephanie was saying. "Every gay woman in this audience owes something to Georgia Poseta. She has defended us against the city, the police, the courts, and the state legislature. It's time for us to defend Georgia, and one of the ways we can help her is by raising money for her defense. We'll be going around the crowd, so give whatever you can. This money is for Georgia, but, more important, it's to let the heterosexist society know that we're not going to lie on our backs and be raped by businesses, by the injustice system, by men who don't want to give up their castles, by landlords who don't respect privacy or women. It's time for women to fight back! And if that scares the powers-that-be, well, then we know we must be doing something right! Sisters, I'm going to

Neal Starkman

introduce Jessie Marks now and let her speak, but remember, this is *your* fight, *your* struggle! Fight back! Fight back!"

And now I turned around to see tiny Stephanie in the distance, arm raised, fist clenched, as virtually as one the crowd came to its feet, obscuring her, yelling, "Fight back! Fight back! Fight back!" and cheering and clapping hands and whistling with two fingers in your mouth like I could never do, and I thought of the time Philip made me mad by putting two fingers in my vagina and jokingly telling me to whistle, and it was disrespectful and he didn't know any better.

And I saw the crowd in slow motion, I heard the cheers, I could feel the groups coalesce into one force, paying obeisance to the stage, to Stephanie, to the struggle. I could no longer see the stage through the hundreds of women and men of all kinds and the same kind, like me yet definitely unlike me, and I know that by the time Jessie Marks came to the microphone and Stephanie my lover sat down, and the crowd resettled onto blankets or just the cold park floor, everything had shifted into place, like the solution to a Rubik's Cube, the final patterns emerging after so much chaos for so long, the patterns I knew were there if only I looked hard enough for them. Everything came together, the diverse and the comical and the sad and the once meaningful and the once meaningless. Why the pressure I've been experiencing culminated right at that point, why I've felt ambivalent about my helium article, why I blew up at James Andrews, why I came out at the Bennetts' party, why Stephanie was so upset over Susan's sex change, why conservative Mrs. Nardquist was able to declare her desire for another woman but would never attend a rally like this, why I feel uncomfortable around Mary Ann and Joe Bennett and Marcie, why I challenged Chuck Patricelli on my dissertation, why it's my father and not my mother I should be trying to influence, why I have to be wary of both Philip's dervish and David's equanimity, and why this rally here in the park was both the same as and different from the speeches of the masturbation campaign.

All these things and more, Di, crashed into each other inside my head, and the noise was so loud I didn't even hear Jessie Marks' speech, or the crowd's response, or Stephanie's introduction of Midge Fielding. I was listening instead to my own noises, sounds of men and women telling me what to do. And there was another sound, a little one, sometimes strong, saying, "No, I won't do that." "No, I don't think that's right for me." "No, you're wrong about that." And it was my voice, the voice of Carolyn Anderson, not socialist or feminist or bisexual or lesbian or physicist or even woman, but Carolyn Anderson, who is all those things and more, but who speaks above all for Carolyn Anderson. And I realized I was walking back to the stage, and I was very calm.

Maureen was talking and I couldn't hear her, but I caught Stephanie's eye and motioned her off the stage. She was still excited; I could tell by the way she moved. I walked to the back of the amphitheater, where we had hugged earlier, and waited there for her.

"Why aren't you sitting with us?" she asked.

"No one told me," I said, looking into her.

"Well, come on—" she took my hand—"you should be up there. Hey, how'd you like my speech?"

"Steph, I'm not speaking. I can't."

"What?" Steph's eyes darted toward the sound of Maureen and back again. She knew she had to introduce the next speaker in a few minutes.

"I can't speak," I repeated, feeling like shit and like pearls at the same time.

"Honey, there's nothing to be nervous about. If I can do it, listen, once you get up there—"

"Stephanie." I put my arms on her shoulders and wished my voice were deeper. "I'm not afraid to go on stage. I can't speak because it's not right for me. I'm not convinced she's innocent, and I'm not convinced I should act as if she *were*."

Stephanie looked at me, then stepped back as if I had slapped her; I returned my hands to my sides. "Look," she said, "Georgia Poseta would stick up for you if you shot your landlord. We need you, Carolyn. We need you in the struggle. You're a smart lady, and you should use some of those smarts for us. Carolyn, we have to stay together."

"I know we do, Steph. I know. But not this time. Not this place. Not for me."

"Why not this time or this place?"

"Because I...I don't want to defend someone when I don't know the facts. Raising money for her defense is fine; she deserves that, I agree. But I can't equate all this talk about rights and self-defense and the struggle with her shooting her landlord. I think it's just as likely that she got so enraged he happened to stumble into her apartment that she blasted him without provocation."

"Oh, use your brains, girl! She was stark naked—"

"She was taking a shower. Maybe he knocked and she didn't hear him because she was taking a shower. Stephanie, that's possible. But no one cares, Stephanie. No one knows and no one cares. I've been listening to this crowd, before the speeches. No one knows what's going on. They're all talking about movies, about Halloween. They're here to have fun, or vent anger, or assuage guilt. They're not thinking!"

"They're giving money."

"Stephanie, aren't you listening to me? Nobody is thinking out there! Can't you appreciate how important that is to me? My whole life is thinking, satisfying my curiosity, examining! And none of the speakers are dealing with substantive—"

"Carolyn"—and there was loud cheering; another speaker had been introduced, without Steph—"I want the money, and I want the numbers. That's how things happen. Money and numbers. That's why we organize, just like every other minority group. Only we're not a minority today. Today we're everybody. And that feels good. For a change, we're in the majority, and people listen to us. I'm not taking shit from any man, Carrie—landlord, judge, or cop. And that goes for dead ex-lovers, too."

That was a jolt from nowhere. "What does *that* mean?"

Stephanie fingered me in the chest. "All this is Philip, isn't it? This is what Philip would have said. 'Be an individual.' The typical anti-feminist cop-out: 'I want to be an individual.' Well, there are some things it takes more than individuals to do, Carrie, and you better realize that. Individuals can't make movements, and individuals can't change things. That's just what men would like us to be, individuals; we can't touch them then. The only time we threaten them is when we get together like this."

"You're right. I agree. And next time maybe I'll march or ring doorbells or make signs or speak at a rally. But not this time. This time I can't do it. And it's not Philip. It's me. Agreeing with a man doesn't make you wrong."

She gave up then. She crinkled the corner of her mouth and gave up.

"I've got to go."

"Stephanie, listen, I didn't know until a few minutes ago. I told you as soon as I could."

But she was closed now, her mind back on the rally, off me. "Sure."

"Steph, can we talk about it tonight?"

"Carrie...yeah, we'll talk. But it won't change today. You really let me down. You let all of us down. One minute you're with us, the next minute you're not."

"I guess time isn't the factor that determines whether or not I'm with you."

"See you later."

And that was that. I let my lover down instead of myself. The rally ended without me, but I began without the rally. You and me, Di.

I walked away from the rally toward the bus line, away from the movement, away from Stephanie's numbers, away from the individuals who suddenly had become a powerful, visible majority. And I thought about that for a second, and it reminded me of something David said in the lab, something at the time I considered really vacuous. He was talking about the vortices, the vortices that appear only at certain temperature levels and under certain conditions. I had just gotten through describing them to him, and he said, "If they didn't spin, you wouldn't see them at all." If they didn't spin, you wouldn't see them at all. You wouldn't see them.

I stopped and knelt down and began to cry, right in the middle of the sidewalk. I put my hands to my face and cried and cried, because, Lady Di, at that moment I realized that I'd been looking at the helium the wrong way. The whole time, I'd been looking at the conditions under which the vortices appeared.

I took a bus to the lab, my mind streaking toward conclusions, my eyes ablaze with finger-wiped tears. I rushed into the lab and lunged for a pad and paper. You see the vortices only at certain temperatures, but the potential for the vortices is always there. The natural state is for them to appear, given the enabling stimuli. Thus, the question is not, "What makes helium spin?" as I would have titled my article, but rather, "What makes helium *not* spin?"

It was an effort to resist speaking at the rally. It was an effort to find my voice. People whirl, given the enabling stimuli; it's not difficult to see why. We should be asking why they *don't* whirl.

So many influences: my parents, my teachers, my colleagues, my friends, my lovers. So many of them caught up in their own whirls: my parents with their religion, my teachers with their power, my colleagues with their prestige, my friends with all those whirls and more: popularity, political views, ethnic biases, sports. And my lovers: Stephanie with her feminism and lesbianism; Philip, ironically enough, with his dervishism.

It's easy to see what makes people whirl. They want to be liked and loved and respected in this often difficult world. And they attain security and comfort by disappearing into a cyclone of "I-don't-have-to-think-too-hard-about-this-because-others-have-already-done-so." But how does one break away from that? How can *I* break away from it? I want to behave in ways not because of some prescription but because I, Carolyn Anderson, willfully chose to behave that way.

And I need to do something similar here in the lab. I need to look at the helium *between* those temperatures at which the vortices appear. I need to look at the helium when it's *not* spinning—to try to identify the factors that prevent the helium from taking a whirl in the test tube. I wrote feverishly for an hour, and now I feel like rewarding myself.

Is this it, then? Am I doomed like Philip to never fit, to carom off all the whirling dervishes of the world, to find myself only to lose everyone else? Well, Di, let's hope not. We deserve better. We deserve to be loved by Stephanie, respected by Dr. Stan, understood by the folks, and admired by all our friends. And we deserve good sex, too. Very good sex, even if, sometimes, it's just you and me, Di. It seems like a truly fitting way to end this afternoon.

I just wish it were more comfortable, you know?

About the Author

Neal Starkman has been a writer all his life, developing works for a wide range of audiences. He has written on subjects ranging from a study of why people don't complain to innovative health education. He is dedicated to making complex issues clear and attempting to improve the human condition.

Neal resides in Seattle, Washington, with his wife and son. He enjoys driving his Prius and occasionally going off his low-carb diet.

CREDITS

This book is a work of art produced by Shannon & Elm,
an imprint of The Zharmae Publishing Press.

EDITOR
Shannon St. Hilaire

COVER ARTIST
Tomasz Wieja

COPY EDITOR
Cynthia Scott

COVER DESIGNER
Roberta Hall

PROOFREADER
Kimiko Hammari

TYPESETTER
Shaughnessey Marshall

REVIEWER
Andrew Call

MANAGING EDITOR
Tomiko Breland

PUBLISHER
Travis Robert Grundy

The Zharmae Publishing Press

Spokane | January 2014

Made in the USA
Charleston, SC
01 November 2014